PARADISE NEWS

Also by David Lodge

PARADISE NEWS

A Novel

David Lodge

VIKING

VIKING
Published by the Penguin Group
Viking Penguin, a division of Penguin Books USA Inc.,
375 Hudson Street, New York, New York 10014, U.S.A.
Penguin Books Ltd, 27 Wrights Lane, London W8 5TZ, England
Penguin Books Australia Ltd, Ringwood, Victoria, Australia
Penguin Books Canada Ltd, 10 Alcorn Avenue, Suite 300,
Toronto, Ontario, Canada M4V 3B2
Penguin Books (N.Z.) Ltd, 182–190 Wairau Road,
Auckland 10, New Zealand

Penguin Books Ltd, Registered Offices:
Harmondsworth, Middlesex, England

First American Edition
Published in 1992 by Viking Penguin,
a division of Penguin Books USA Inc.

1   3   5   7   9   10   8   6   4   2

Grateful acknowledgment is made for permission to reprint
excerpts from the following copyrighted works:

"This Be The Verse" from *High Windows* by Philip Larkin. Copyright © 1974 by
Philip Larkin. Reprinted by permission of Farrar, Straus & Giroux, Inc.
"Big Yellow Taxi" by Joni Mitchell. © 1970 Siquomb Publishing Corp. All rights
reserved. Used by permission.

AUTHOR'S NOTE
Many people have generously helped me
with factual information relevant to the
background of this novel.
I am especially grateful to:
Nell Altizer, Ruell Denney, Dennis Egan,
Celia and Maxwell Fry, Tony Langrick,
Paul Levick, Victoria Nelson,
Norman Rowland, and Marion Vaught.

D.L.

LIBRARY OF CONGRESS CATALOGING IN PUBLICATION DATA
Lodge, David, 1935–
Paradise news : a novel / David Lodge.
p.   cm.
ISBN 0–670–84228–1
I. Title.
PR6062.O36P37   1992
823'.914—dc20   91–32128

Printed in the United States of America

For Mike Shaw

"The earthly paradise! Don't you want to go
to it? Why of course!"

> Harry Whitney:
> *The Hawaiian Guide Book* (1875)

PART ONE

Nightly descending through the baroque cloud
That decorates these hills, riding on air,
Thousands arrive by dream at their desire.

William Meredith:
"*An Account of a Visit to Hawaii*"

I

"What do they see in it, eh? What do they see in it?"

Leslie Pearson, Senior Representative (Airport Reception) of Travelwise Tours plc, surveys the passengers swarming in the Departures Concourse of Heathrow's Terminal Four with an expression of mingled pity and contempt. It is mid-morning in the high summer season and, adding to the normal congestion, there is a security alert in operation, because of a recent plane crash thought to have been caused by sabotage. (Three different terrorist organizations have claimed responsibility, which means that at least two of them are trying to obtain a reputation for indiscriminate murder without exerting themselves. That's the modern world for you: the more Leslie Pearson sees of it, the less he understands or likes it.) Passengers are being closely questioned at the check-in desks about the provenance of their luggage, this morning, and their persons and handbaggage scrutinized with more than usual zeal by the security staff. Long, slow-moving lines stretch from the check-in desks nearly to the opposite wall of the concourse, crosshatched by two longer lines converging upon the narrow gate that leads to Passport Control, the Security gates, and the Departures Lounge. The queueing passengers shift their weight from one foot to another, or lean on the handles of their heaped baggage trolleys, or squat on their suitcases. Their expressions are variously anxious, impatient, bored, stoical – but not yet weary. They are still relatively fresh: their bright casual clothes are clean and pressed, their cheeks smooth from the recent application of razor or make-up, their hair groomed and glossy. But if an additional cause of serious delay should occur – a work-to-rule by air traffic controllers, say, or a go-slow by baggage handlers – then, as Leslie Pearson knows from experience, it wouldn't be long before the veneer of civilization began to show cracks. He has seen this concourse, and the Departures Lounge beyond, choked with delayed passengers sleeping under the fluorescent lights in their soiled, crumpled clothes, sprawled promiscuously all over the furniture and the floor, mouths agape and limbs askew, like the victims of a massacre or a neutron bomb, while the airport cleaners picked their way through the prone bodies like scavengers on a battlefield. Things aren't nearly as bad as that today, but they are bad enough.

"What do they see in it?" he says again. "What are they *after*?"

"The free esses, innit?" says Trevor Connolly. He is a recent recruit to Travelwise, temporarily attached to Leslie to learn the ropes: how to recognize and greet the firm's clients, inspect their travel documents to check that they've come on the right day (you'd be surprised) and that their passports are in order, with visas as required, then direct them to the appropriate check-in desk and give them a hand with their luggage if they need it, and answer their questions if they've got any. "Sun, sand and sex," Trevor elaborates with a smirk.

Leslie snorts dismissively. "You don't have to go long-haul to get *them*," he says. "You can get *them* in Majorca. You can get 'em in Bournemouth, come to that, this year – beautiful summer we're having. Not that you'd know it, stuck in this hole." He glowers up at the low, steel-grey ceiling, where all the building's ducts and conduits are exposed in what is supposed to be an ultra-modern style, but which makes Leslie feel as if he is working in a hotel basement or the engine-room of a battleship. "I mean, take this little lot" – he glances at the list of the day's passengers on his clipboard – "Where are they going? Honolulu. *Honolulu!* I ask you – it must take 'em all day to get there."

"Eighteen and a half hours," says Trevor. "Including change of planes at Los Angeles."

"Eighteen and a half hours cooped up in one of those oversized sardine cans? Must be mad. They're all mad, if you ask me," Leslie says, sweeping his gaze like a lighthouse beam across the

4

crowded concourse, a tall, straightbacked, rather military figure (he is in fact a retired policeman). "Look at 'em! Like lemmings. Lemmings." He smacks his lips on the word, though in truth he isn't entirely sure what a lemming is. Some kind of small animal, isn't it, that moves in a mindless pack and throws itself into the sea?

"It's the novelty, innit," says Trevor. "I mean, Majorca, who'd go to Majorca anymore? It's dead common, Blackpool by the Med. Same with Florida, even the Caribbean. You got to keep going further and further to get away from the Joneses."

"Here come two of ours," says Leslie. He has picked out the purple and gold Travelwise labels on the luggage of a young couple who have just come through the automatic sliding doors and are looking hesitantly about them. "Honeymooners, I bet." Something about the top-to-toe newness of their clothes, and the pristine state of their matching luggage, tells him they are newly-weds, though the space visible between them, the wife standing ahead and to one side of her husband, who is pushing a luggage trolley, suggests that the marriage has got off to a slightly dodgy start. They probably got married yesterday, passed the night in a hot and noisy London hotel room, and now they're going to spend the first full day of their married life shot halfway round the world strapped into a pair of cramped dentist's chairs. They'd have done a lot better going to Bournemouth.

Leslie steps forward with a smile, introduces himself to the couple, and inspects their tickets and passports. "Hawaii – an inspired choice for a honeymoon, if I may say so, sir."

The young man grins sheepishly, but his wife looks displeased. "Is it so obvious?" she says. She has straight fair hair held back from her forehead by a tortoiseshell comb, and clear, ice-blue eyes.

"Well, I couldn't help noticing that you're Mrs Harvey on my list, madam, but Miss Lake in your passport."

"Very observant," she says drily.

"Will it matter?" says the young man anxiously. "About the passport, I mean."

"Not a bit, sir. Nothing to worry about. Check your bags at desk twenty-one. You may have a bit of a wait, I'm afraid."

5

"Don't you do that for us?" says Mrs Harvey.

"Passengers are required to identify their luggage in person, madam. Security regulations. My colleague Mr Connolly will be glad to assist you with your bags."

"We can push our own trolley, thanks," says Mrs Harvey, meaning evidently that her husband can, for she sets off in the direction of desk twenty-one without even a glance at him.

"Phew," says Trevor, when the couple are out of earshot. "Glad I'm not in his jockstrap. What a ballbreaker."

"Love's young dream," says Leslie, "ain't what it used to be. It comes of all this living together before you get married. Takes all the romance out of it."

This is a pointed comment, aimed at Trevor, who however pretends to misunderstand. "Right," he says. "That's what I tell Michelle: marriage is fatal to romance."

Ignoring his impudent grin, Leslie ticks off the names of Mr and Mrs Harvey on the passenger list. "Keep your eyes peeled for a customer on his own, name of Sheldrake. See the star against his name?"

"Yeah, what's it mean?"

"It means he's on a freebie. Usually it means a journalist. Travel writer."

"I wouldn't mind that for a job."

"First you've got to be able to write, Trevor. First you've got to be able to *spell*."

"Don't need to, nowadays, do you? Computers do it all for you."

"Anyway, be on your toes when he turns up. Make a good impression, otherwise he might write something nasty about you."

"Like what?"

"Like, '*I was greeted at the airport by a scruffy-looking courier with dandruff all over his uniform and a collar-button missing.*' "

"That's Michelle's fault," says Trevor, looking slightly rattled. "She promised to sew it on for me."

"Appearance is very important in this job, Trevor," says Leslie. "The customers are confused, anxious, when they arrive here. Your turn-out should inspire trust. We're like guardian angels, wafting them over to the other side."

"Get off it," says Trevor. But he tightens the knot of his tie and slaps at the shoulders and lapels of his jacket.

Their next clients are a middle-aged couple from Croydon. The wife, her roly-poly figure stuffed into matching electric blue stretch-pants and jumper, looks flustered and anxious. "He has a heart," she says, thumbing sideways at her husband, who shakes his head and grins reassuringly at Leslie. "He can't be expected to queue like this."

The man certainly doesn't look particularly healthy: he has a flushed, mottled face with a red drinker's nose screwed into the middle like a light-bulb, and his white-shirted stomach droops doughily over his belt buckle.

"I could try and get you a wheelchair, if you like, sir," says Leslie.

"No, no, don't be daft, Lilian," says the man. "Take no notice of her. I'm fine."

"He shouldn't really be travelling all this way," says Lilian, "but we didn't want to disappoint Terry – that's our son. He booked the holiday for us. Paid for everything. He's coming from Sydney to Hawaii to meet us."

"Very nice," says Leslie, as he checks their documents.

"He's done ever so well out there. He's a fashion photographer, has his own studio. He phoned us up one day, six o'clock in the morning it was, well, they have a different time down under, don't they? He said: 'I want to give you and Dad a holiday to remember. Just get yourselves to Heathrow and I'll take care of the rest.' "

"It's very pleasing to hear of a young man who appreciates his parents," says Leslie. "Especially these days. Trevor: take Mr and Mrs Brooks to desk sixteen, explain that Mr Brooks has a medical condition. That's Business Class," he adds for their benefit. "A shorter queue."

"Will we have to pay extra?" says Mr Brooks anxiously.

"No, no, same seats, but we have an arrangement with the airline for checking in handicapped passengers through Business Class."

"Handicapped – I'm not handicapped. You see what you've done, Lilian?"

"Shut up, Sidney, you don't know when you're well off. Thanks very much," says Mrs Brooks to Leslie.

Trevor leads them away with some reluctance, for two youngish women in pastel-coloured jogging suits are hovering in the background, clasping the purple and gold plastic document wallets referred to in the company's brochure as their Travelpaks. Neither of them is outstandingly good-looking, nor in the first bloom of youth, but they are the kind of customers Trevor enjoys flirting with, or, in his own idiom, considers good for a giggle.

"Your first trip to Hawaii, ladies?" Leslie enquires.

"Oh yes, the first time. We've never been further than Florida before, have we, Dee?" says the one in the pink and powder-blue tracksuit. She has a broad, chubby face with big round eyes and a halo of fine light curls like baby's hair.

"How long is the flight?" says Dee, whose tracksuit is mauve and green, and whose features are sharper and less trusting.

"It's better not to know," says Leslie, a witticism that convulses pink-and-blue with merriment.

"Oh, go on, tell," she says.

"You'll be in Honolulu by eight o'clock this evening."

"But that's not allowing for the time change," says Dee.

"She teaches Science," her companion volunteers, as if to explain the acuteness of this observation.

"Ah. Then you've got to add on eleven hours," says Leslie.

"Oh, God!"

"Never mind, Dee, it'll be worth it when we get there." The girl in pink and blue appeals to Leslie: "They say it's like Paradise, don't they?"

"Absolutely," says Leslie. "And allow me to congratulate you, ladies, on your choice of attire for the journey. Both practical and becoming, if I may say so."

Pink-and-blue blushes and giggles, and even Dee smiles a queenly smile of pleasure. They go off to join the long line in front of desk twenty-one. Trevor comes back just too late to offer to help with their luggage, of which they had rather a lot.

"What happened to the birds, then?" he says.

"I dealt with them, Trevor," says Leslie. "I guided them on their way with my inimitable old-world courtesy."

"Garn!" says Trevor.

The morning wears on. The queues lengthen. The atmosphere under the steel-grey pipes and girders becomes stuffier and more charged with frustration and anxiety, as passengers shuffling forward in the long, slow-moving line waiting to go through Passport Control check their watches and wonder whether they will miss their flights. Passenger R. J. Sheldrake, wearing a beige safari suit, and towing a practical hard-shell suitcase with built-in wheels, presents his complimentary ticket, and comments gloomily on the queues. He has a large, domed head, going prematurely bald, and a big, bulging jaw, the rest of his features looking rather squeezed between these two protuberances.

"Don't worry, sir," says Leslie, with a conspiratorial wink. "Just come with me and I'll get you checked in through Business Class."

"No, no, I've got to be treated like everyone else," says Dr Sheldrake (for such is his title according to the ticket). "It's all part of the fieldwork," he adds enigmatically. Declining Trevor's assistance, he disappears, with his wheeled suitcase, into the throng.

"Was that the journalist?" Trevor enquires.

"I don't know," Leslie replies. "It said he was a doctor on his ticket."

"He had worse dandruff than me," says Trevor. "And 'ardly any 'air."

"Don't look now," says Leslie, "but you're being filmed." A burly man with luxuriant sideburns, wearing a two-tone blouson and keenly pressed trousers, is aiming a hand-held video camera at them from about ten yards' range. A woman wearing a yellow cotton frock with a pattern of red beach umbrellas, and a great deal of costume jewellery, loiters beside him, looking absently around her, in the attitude of a dog-owner whose pet has stopped to lift its leg against a tree.

"Bloomin' cheek," says Trevor.

"Hush," says Leslie. "It's another one of ours."

Mr and Mrs Everthorpe have just arrived on a feeder flight from East Midlands. "Don't mind being in our home movie, do you?" says Mr Everthorpe, as he comes up. "I spotted the uniform soon as we came through the door."

"Not at all, sir," says Leslie. "May I see your tickets?"

"Hawaii here we come, eh? Can't wait to get those hula-hula girls in my viewfinder."

"Not if I have anything to do with it," says Mrs Everthorpe, slapping her husband on one of his thick wrists. "I thought this was supposed to be our second honeymoon?"

"You'll have to put on a grass skirt yourself, then, love," says Mr Everthorpe with a wink at Leslie and Trevor. "Tickle me fancy."

Mrs Everthorpe slaps him again, and Trevor leers sympathetically – it is his kind of humour.

The Best family don't seem to run to any kind of humour. Mr Best is greatly exercised about the discount vouchers for various diversions included in his Travelpak – the Paradise Cove Luau, the Pacific Whaling Museum, the Waimea Falls Park, etc. etc. It seems that there are only three sets of these vouchers in his wallet, and there are four Bests. They stand shoulder to shoulder in front of Leslie – father, mother, son and daughter, in perfectly graduated order of height, pale-eyed, sandy-haired, thin-lipped, while he tries to reassure them that the mistake will be rectified by the Travelwise rep in Honolulu.

"Why can't you give them to us now?" says Mr Best.

Leslie explains that they don't keep the vouchers in their office at Heathrow.

"It's not good enough," says Mr Best, who is tall and bony and has a narrow ginger moustache.

"You should complain, Harold," says Mrs Best.

"I *am* complaining," says Mr Best. "That's what I'm doing. What d'you think I'm doing?"

"I mean, write."

"Oh, I'll *write*," says Mr Best darkly, buttoning up his navy-blue blazer. "Don't worry about that. I'll write." He marches off, followed by his family in Indian file.

"He's a solicitor, you know!" Mrs Best throws this final dart over her shoulder.

"Another satisfied customer," says Trevor.

"Some customers are never satisfied," says Leslie. "I know the type. Tell 'em a mile off."

But Leslie doesn't recognize the type their next clients belong to. They don't look like holidaymakers at all. Father and son they appear to be, for they both have the same name, Walsh. The older man, with a lined, narrow, beaky face, and a shock of white hair like a cockatoo's crest, looks at least seventy, and the younger one is probably in his mid-forties, though it's hard to tell because of his beard, an untidy, piebald affair. They are both wearing dark and rather heavy clothes of unfashionable cut. The younger man has made one concession to the nature of their journey and destination: he wears an open-necked shirt with the collar neatly turned down outside his jacket lapels – a style Leslie hasn't seen at large since the 1950s. The old man is wearing a brown striped worsted suit, with collar and tie. He sighs frequently to himself, looking round about him at the heaving, shuffling crowds with anxious watery eyes.

"As you can see, there's a bit of a bottleneck at Passport Control," says Leslie, as he checks their documents. "But don't worry – we'll make sure you don't miss your flight."

"Wouldn't worry me if we did miss it," says the old man.

"My father hasn't flown before," says the younger man. "He's a little nervous."

"Very understandable," says Leslie. "But you'll enjoy it, Mr Walsh, once you're airborne – won't he, Trevor?"

"Eh? Oh, yeah," says Trevor. "You don't know you're flying in them jumbos. Like being in a train, it is."

The old man sniffs sceptically. His son stows the Travelpak away carefully in the inside pocket of his tweed jacket and positions himself like a beast of burden between their two suitcases. "You take my briefcase, Daddy," he says.

"Trevor – give Mr Walsh a hand with the luggage," says Leslie.

11

"That's very kind of you," says the younger man. "I couldn't find a spare trolley."

Trevor, eyeing the two cheap, scuffed and scarred suitcases with disfavour, obeys Leslie with ill grace. He returns a few minutes later, saying, "Queer couple to be going to Hawaii, aren't they?"

"I hope you'll take *your* old Dad on holiday with you when you can afford it, Trevor."

"You must be joking," says Trevor. "I wouldn't take 'im to the end of the road, not unless I could lose 'im there."

"Do you know what a theologian is, Trevor?"

"I dunno, somethink to do with religion, innit? Why?"

"That's what he is, the son, a theologian. It said so in his passport."

Later – some forty minutes later – the old man and his son were the centre of a commotion at the security barrier between Passport Control and the Departures Lounge. When the old man stepped through the metal-detecting door-frame, something on his person made the apparatus beep. He was asked to surrender his keys, and to pass through the door-frame again. Again the alarm was triggered. At the security man's request, he emptied his pockets and took off his wristwatch – to no avail. The official frisked him with rapid, practised movements, running his hands over the old man's torso, under his armpits and up and down the insides of his legs. The old man, his arms extended like a scarecrow's, flinched and trembled under this examination. He glared accusingly at his son, who shrugged his shoulders help-lessly. Passengers waiting in the same line, who had already sent their handbaggage through the X-ray machines, and were aware that it would be piling up in a log-jam somewhere on the other side of the barrier, stirred restively and pulled faces at each other in a mime of impatience.

"You haven't got a metal plate in your head, sir, by any chance?" said the security man.

"No, I have not," said the old man testily. "What d'you take me for, a robot?" He pronounced this word, in a perceptibly Irish accent, as "row-boat".

"We did have a gentleman, once, had one. Took us all morning to figure it out. He'd been blown up by a mine in the War. His legs were full of shrapnel, too. You haven't got anything like that, then?" he concluded wistfully.

"I said 'No,' didn't I?"

"If you would just take off your braces, sir, and just have another try."

Again the electronic beep sounded. The security man sighed. "I'm sorry, sir, but I must ask you to remove the rest of your clothing."

"Oh no you won't!" said the old man, clutching the tops of his trousers.

"Not here, sir. If you would just come this way –"

"Daddy! Your holy medal!" exclaimed the younger man suddenly. He loosened his father's tie, undid the collar button of his shirt, and fished out a pewter-coloured medal dangling from a fine-mesh stainless-steel chain.

"That's the culprit," said the security man cheerfully.

"That's Our Lady of Lourdes, I'll have you know," said the old man.

"Yes, well, if you wouldn't mind taking her off a minute, and passing through the gate again –"

"I've never taken this from off my neck since the day my dear wife gave it to me, God rest her soul. She brought it back from a pilgrimage in 1953."

"If you don't take it off, you don't fly," said the security man, now losing patience.

"That's fine by me," said the old man.

"Come on, Daddy," coaxed his son, and gently lifted the medal and chain over the old man's white head. He poured the shining metal skein into his palm and handed it to the official. The old man seemed suddenly to lose the will to resist. His shoulders slumped, and he passed meekly enough through the door-frame, this time without triggering the alarm.

In the crowded Departures Lounge, Bernard Walsh helped his father replace the holy medal round his neck, steering the chain over the old man's ears, big, red, fleshy protuberances, with coarse white hairs sprouting from their recesses. He slid the medal under his father's yellowish undervest, fastened the collar button of the shirt, and straightened the tie. He felt a sudden lurch of memory: himself, aged eleven, setting off for his first day at St Augustine's Grammar School, his father gravely inspecting his new uniform, and tightening the knot of his school tie, a gaudy maroon and gold, not unlike the livery of Travelwise Tours.

Their flight was not yet being called, so he bought two plastic beakers of coffee from a snack bar, settled down on a row of seats facing a monitor screen, and distributed the newspapers he had bought on the way from central London: a *Guardian* for himself and the *Mail* for his father. But while he was absorbed in an article about Nicaragua, his father must have slipped away. When Bernard looked up from the page, the seat next to his own was vacant, and Mr Walsh was nowhere to be seen. Bernard felt panic hollow his stomach. He scanned the Departures Lounge (and somehow found time to reflect on what a ludicrously inappropriate term it was, "lounge", for this vast, congested hall, with its restless movement of bodies, its hum of conversation, its stale air and dazzle of glass) without catching sight of his father. To see better, he stood on the seat of his chair, under the gaze of eight pale, disapproving eyes belonging to a sandy-haired family sitting opposite with their flightbags at their feet. On the monitor screen the message, "BOARDING GATE 29" began to blink against the number of the flight to Los Angeles.

"There we are," said the head of the sandy-haired family, a tall, thin man, dressed in a neat blazer with chrome buttons. "Gate twenty-nine. On your feet." His wife and children obeyed him in a single movement.

A low moan of despair escaped Bernard's lips. "Excuse me," he said to the sandy-haired family – who, he now noticed, had purple and gold Travelwise labels on their handluggage – "did you happen to see where my father – the elderly man sitting there – where he went?"

"He went that way," said the younger child, a heavily-freckled

14

girl who looked about twelve years old. She pointed in the direction of the Duty-Free Shop.

"Thankyou," said Bernard.

Bernard found his father inspecting the various brands of whiskey in the Duty-Free, standing before the shelves with his hands clasped behind his back and his head inclined forward to read the labels, like a man in a museum.

"Thank God I've found you," he said. "Don't go wandering off on your own like that again."

"A litre of Jameson's for eight pounds," said the old man. "That's a bargain."

"You don't want to drag a bottle of whiskey halfway round the world," said Bernard. "Anyway, there isn't time. Our flight's been called."

"Will it be as cheap in Hawaii?"

"Yes. No. I don't know," said Bernard. He ended up buying him a bottle of Jameson's, and a carton of cigarettes, as one might buy a child sweets to keep him quiet. He regretted it almost at once, for the boxed bottle in its plastic bag was heavy and awkward to carry, in addition to his briefcase and raincoat, along corridors broad as boulevards that seemed to stretch to infinity.

"Are we having to walk all the way to Hawaii?" his father grumbled.

There were moving walkways in places, like flattened escalators, but not all of them were working. It took them a good quarter of an hour to reach Gate 29, and then there was another crisis. When the uniformed girl at the desk asked to see their boarding cards, Mr Walsh was unable to produce his.

"I think I left it back at the off-licence," he said.

"Oh my God," said Bernard. "It will take us half an hour to get there and back again." He turned to the ground hostess: "Can't you issue him with another one?"

"Not very easily," she said. "Are you sure you haven't got it, sir? Is it inside your passport, perhaps?"

But Mr Walsh had left his passport at the Duty-Free too.

15

"You're doing this on purpose," said Bernard, feeling himself going pink with anger.

"No I'm not," said Mr Walsh sulkily.

"Where did you leave them – by the Jameson's?"

"Somewhere round there. I'd have to go back."

"Is there time?" Bernard asked the girl.

"I'll get you a buggy," she said, reaching for a cordless phone.

The buggy was an open electric car apparently intended for the use of infirm or handicapped passengers. They bowled back along the interminable walkways, the driver honking at intervals to clear their path through droves of oncoming pedestrians. Bernard had a queasy feeling that their journey had gone into reverse, not just temporarily but permanently – that they would spend hours searching vainly for the missing documents, while their plane departed, leaving them with their useless, non-transferable tickets, and no option but to take the Tube back to London. Perhaps Mr Walsh had the same intuition – it would explain why he looked suddenly cheerful, grinning and waving at the passengers footslogging their way towards the gates, like a child on a fairground ride. One of these passengers, a burly, side-whiskered man toting a video camera, stopped to film them, swivelling on his heel as they passed.

They found the boarding pass, slipped inside the passport, where Mr Walsh had left them, on a shelf between the Scotch and Irish whiskies.

"Why in God's name did you put them there?" Bernard demanded.

"I was looking for me money," said Mr Walsh. "I was searching for me purse. That fuss at the machine back there, over the holy medal, got me all moithered. Everything was in the wrong pocket."

Bernard grunted. The explanation was plausible; but if losing the documents hadn't been a conscious gambit to avoid boarding the plane, it had certainly been an unconscious one. He grasped his father's arm and marched him back to the buggy like a prisoner. The driver, who was listening to crackling instructions from a walkie-talkie, greeted them cheerfully.

16

"Everything OK? Hold on tight, then. I've got to pick up one or two passengers on the way."

They picked up a gigantic black lady, dressed in a striped cotton frock as big as a marquee, who wheezed and chuckled as she clambered aboard and spread her enormous hips over the back seat beside Mr Walsh, forcing Bernard to perch precariously on the handrail at the side, and a man with an amputated leg who sat next to the driver with his crutch levelled over the front of the buggy like a lance. This carnivalesque spectacle excited much attention and amusement among the footpassengers they passed, some of whom playfully thumbed for a lift.

Bernard looked at his watch, which indicated five minutes to spare before their plane was due to leave. "I think we'll just make it."

He needn't have worried: there was a thirty-minute delay on the flight, and the passengers hadn't even started boarding. Some of them looked accusingly at Bernard and his father as if suspecting them of being responsible. The waiting area was crowded – it seemed impossible so many people could get into the same aeroplane. As they looked for somewhere to sit down, they passed the sandy-haired family of four, sitting in a row, with their flightbags on their knees. "Found him," said Bernard to the freckled girl, with a nod in the direction of his father, and received a tight little smile in acknowledgment.

They discovered a couple of empty seats at the far end of the room and sat down.

"I want to go to the lav," said Mr Walsh.

"No," said Bernard brutally.

"It's that coffee. Coffee always goes straight through me."

"You can wait till we get on the plane," said Bernard. But he had second thoughts: who knew how long it might be before they were airborne? "Oh, all right, then," he said wearily, getting to his feet.

"You don't have to come with me."

"I'm not letting you out of my sight again."

As they were standing side by side at the urinal, his father said, "Did you see the size of that black woman's bum? Begob, I thought I was going to be crushed to death."

17

Bernard wondered whether to make this the occasion for a little homily on respect for ethnic minorities, but decided to let it pass. It was fortunate that the word "black", which Mr Walsh had always employed as a term of disparagement, had become accepted usage in society at large. Though whether Polynesians liked to be called black, he had no idea. Probably not.

When they returned to the waiting area beside Gate 29, their seats had been taken, but a young woman in a pink and blue track suit, observing their plight, took her bag off the seat beside her and offered it to Mr Walsh. Bernard perched on the edge of a low plastic table.

"Which hotel are you going to, then?" said the young woman.

"I beg your pardon?" said Bernard.

"You're with Travelwise, aren't you? Like us." She pointed to the purple and gold baggage label the courier had attached to his briefcase. "We're going to the Waikiki Coconut Grove," she said. He became aware that there was another young woman, similarly attired in mauve and green, sitting beside her.

"Oh yes, that's right. I'm not sure what hotel."

"Not sure?" The girl looked perplexed.

"I did know, but I've forgotten. We arranged this trip at rather short notice."

"Oh, I see," said the girl. "Last-minute bargain. You don't get much choice, then, do you? But you save a lot. We did that one year in Crete, didn't we, Dee?"

"Don't remind me," said Dee. "Those toilets."

"I'm sure you needn't worry about the toilets in Hawaii," said the girl in pink and blue, with a reassuring smile. "Americans are very particular about things like that, aren't they?"

"I didn't know we were going to a hotel," said Mr Walsh querulously. "I thought we were staying at Ursula's place."

"We probably will be, Daddy," said Bernard. "I won't know till we get there." He was silent for a few moments, but felt the pressure of the two women's intense curiosity. "We're visiting my father's sister," he explained. "She lives in Honolulu. We probably won't need the hotel room, but, absurdly enough, it was the cheapest way to travel – to take this package."

18

"What a place to live! Honolulu! It must be like being on holiday all year round," said the young woman. She turned to Mr Walsh. "Is it a long time since you saw your sister?"

"It is that," Mr Walsh said.

"You must be looking forward to it."

"I can't say I'm straining at the leash," he said dourly. "It's her who wants to see me. Or so I'm told." He shot a hostile glance at Bernard from under his bushy eyebrows.

"My aunt is not well, I'm afraid," said Bernard.

"Oh, dear!"

"She's dying," said Mr Walsh grimly.

The young women were silenced. They dropped their eyes, and seemed to shrink and cringe inside their gay athletic attire. Bernard felt embarrassed and almost guilty, as if he and his father had committed some error of taste, or broken a taboo. There was, after all, something incongruous, even indecent, about using a package holiday to visit a dying relative.

2

The summons had come a week ago, in the early hours of Friday morning, at about five o'clock. Bernard didn't have a private phone in his room at the College, because he couldn't afford it, so the caretaker on night duty had taken the call and, construing it as urgent, had woken him up and led him downstairs to the student phone in the lobby. He stood there in his pyjamas and dressing-gown, bare feet chilled by the tiled floor (he had been too fuddled to find his slippers), his head encased in a sound-absorbent cowl covered with a palimpsest of scribbled phone numbers, and heard a hoarse, worn, woman's voice, an American drawl with a stratum of London Irish underneath.

"Hi, this is Ursula."

"Who?"

"Your aunt Ursula."

"Good Lord!"

"Remember me? The black sheep of the family. Or should I say, you?"

"Me?"

"No, not you. Ee-doubleyou-ee. Ewe."

"Oh, yes, I see. But I'm also considered a bit of a black sheep nowadays."

"Yeah, I heard about that . . . Listen, what time is it in England?"

"About five in the morning."

"In the *morning*! God, I'm sorry, I did my arithmetic all wrong. Did I waken you?"

"It doesn't matter. Where are you?"

"In Honolulu. In the Geyser Hospital."

"Are you ill, then?"

"Am I ill? That's an understatement, Bernard. They cut me open, took one look and sewed me up again."

"Oh, dear, I'm sorry." How feeble and inadequate his words sounded. "That's terrible," he said. "Is there nothing they can –"

"Zilch. I've had this pain for some time, I thought it was backache, I've always had a back problem, but it wasn't. It's cancer."

"Oh dear," he said again.

"Malignant melanoma, to be precise. It starts as a kind of mole. I didn't think anything of it. As you get old, you develop all kinds of blemishes. When I finally had it checked out they operated the same day, but it was too late. I've developed secondaries."

As he listened, Bernard was trying to work out how old Ursula would be. The last time he had seen her, she had been a young woman – his glamorous, obscurely disgraced American aunt, with a wedding-ring but no husband, who had visited his parents some time in the early fifties, when he himself was a schoolboy, bringing boxes of American candies with her under the impression that sweets were still rationed in England (not that they weren't very welcome in that pinched and frugal household). He had a memory-picture of her in the back garden at home: in a full-skirted, puff-sleeved dress of red polka-dots on a white ground, with glistening bright red nails and lips, and bouncy, shoulder-length blonde hair which his mother had darkly declared to be "dyed". She must be about seventy now, he decided.

Ursula's train of thought seemed to have taken the same direction. "It's strange talking to you, Bernard. Would you believe, the last time I saw you, you were still in short pants?"

"Yes," said Bernard, "it is strange. Why did you never come back?"

"It's a long story. And a helluva long trip, but that wasn't the reason. How's your father?"

"He's fine, as far as I know. I don't see him very often, to tell you the truth. Relations between us are rather strained."

"We're a great family for that. If you ever write the family history, that's what you can call it: *Strained Relations*."

21

Bernard laughed, feeling a surge of admiration and affection for this brave old girl, jesting in the shadow of death.

"You *are* a writer, aren't you?" she said.

"Just a few boring articles in theological journals. Not a real writer."

"Look, tell Jack how I am, will you, Bernard?"

"Of course."

"I didn't trust myself to call him. I didn't know if I could handle it."

"He'll be very upset."

"Will he?" She sounded wistful.

"Of course . . . Is there really no treatment?"

"They offered me chemotherapy, but when I asked my oncologist what the chances of a cure were he said, no cure, a remission, maybe a few months. I said no thanks, I'd rather die with my own hair on."

"You're very brave," said Bernard, selfishly aware of his own trivial discomfort, rubbing each of his icy feet in turn against the calf of the other leg.

"No I'm not, Bernard. I'm scared to death. To death, ha! You find yourself making these sick jokes all the time without meaning to. Tell Jack I want to see him."

"What?" said Bernard, not sure he had heard correctly.

"I want to see my brother before I die."

"Well, I don't know . . ." he said. He did know: his father wouldn't contemplate such a journey for a moment.

"I could help him with the fare."

"It's not just the expense. Daddy's getting on. And he's never been one for travelling. He's never even been up in an aeroplane."

"God, really?"

"I don't think he's up to flying halfway round the world. Is there no chance of your coming over here to . . . to . . ." He didn't want to say, to die, though that was what he meant. "To convalesce?" he concluded lamely.

"Are you kidding? I can't even go home to my apartment. Yesterday I fell over trying to get to the bathroom on my own. Fractured my arm."

22

Bernard did his best to communicate his dismay and commiseration.

"It was nothing much. I'm so full of painkillers it didn't even hurt. But I'm pretty weak. They're talking about putting me into a nursing home. I need to sort out the apartment, all my things . . ." Her voice faded, either because of the telephone connection or her weakness.

"Haven't you got some friends who can help you?"

"Oh, sure, I've got friends, mostly old ladies like me. They're not a lot of use. They're scared to look at me when they come to the hospital. They spend all the time arranging my flowers. Anyway, it's not the same as family."

"No, it's not."

"Tell Jack I've gone back to the Church. And I don't mean just this week. It's some years now."

"All right, I will."

"He should be pleased about that. It might persuade him to come out here."

"Aunt Ursula," said Bernard. "I'll come, if you like."

"You'll come to Honolulu? Really? When?"

"As soon as I can arrange it. Next week, perhaps."

There was a silence on the line, and when Ursula spoke again her voice sounded throatier than ever. "That's very generous of you, Bernard. To drop all your plans at a moment's notice –"

"I don't have any plans," he said. "It's the long vac. I've nothing to do until late September."

"Aren't you going someplace, for a vacation?"

"No," said Bernard. "I can't afford it."

"I'll pay your air fare," said Ursula.

"I'm afraid you'll have to, Aunt Ursula. My job is only part-time, and I haven't got any savings."

"Shop around, see if you can get one of those charter deals."

This advice, though sensible, surprised Bernard slightly. There had always been a tradition in the family that Ursula was well-off, untroubled by the petty economies that confined their own lives. It was part of her legend – the GI bride who had spurned family ties and religious allegiance to pursue a life of materialistic self-indulgence in America. But people often became parsimonious in old age.

"I'll do my best," he promised. "I'm not very experienced in these matters."

"You can stay in my apartment. That'll save money. Maybe you'll enjoy it, huh?" she said. "I live right in the middle of Waikiki."

"I'm not very good at enjoying myself," said Bernard. "I'm coming out to see you, Ursula, to do what I can to help."

"Well, I really appreciate that, Bernard. I'd like to have seen Jack, but you're the next best thing."

Bernard found a scrap of paper in his dressing-gown pocket and wrote down the phone number of the hospital with a pencil stub that dangled on a string above the telephone. He promised to ring Ursula again when he had made his travel arrangements. "By the way," he said, "how did you know my phone number?"

"I got it from Information," she said. "I knew the name of the college, from your sister Teresa."

Another surprise. "I didn't know you were in touch with Tess."

"We exchange Christmas cards. She usually scribbles a bit of family news on the back."

"Does she know you're ill?"

"I called her first, to tell you the truth. But there was no answer."

"They're probably away on holiday."

"Well, I'm glad I reached you instead, Bernard," said Ursula. "I guess it was providential. I don't think Teresa would have dropped everything to come out here."

"No," said Bernard. "She has her hands full."

Bernard went back to bed, but not to sleep. His mind was too busy with questions, memories and speculations about Ursula, and the journey to which he had impulsively committed himself. Its occasion was a melancholy one, and he was far from certain what comfort or practical assistance he could bring to his aunt. Nevertheless he felt a kind of excitement, even exhilaration,

24

stirring the normally sluggish stream of his consciousness. To fly halfway round the world at a few days' notice was an adventure, whatever the occasion; it would be "a change", as people said – indeed, it would be hard to think of a more dramatic alteration of the dull rhythm of his present existence. And then – Hawaii! Honolulu! Waikiki! The syllables resonated in his head with associations of glamorous and exotic pleasures. He thought of palm trees and white sands and curling surf and dusky smiling maidens in grass skirts. And with that last image there came unbidden into his mind a memory-picture of Daphne, when he first saw her huge, unfettered, naked breasts, in the bedroom of the rooming-house in Henfield Cross, great white zeppelins of flesh, tipped with dark circles like targets, that swung heavily as she turned smiling to face him. It was a spectacle for which forty years of celibacy had left him quite unprepared, and he had flinched and looked away – the first of many failures in their brief relationship. When he looked back, she had covered herself, and her smile had vanished.

He had made a resolution not to think of Daphne any more, but the mind was a capricious and undisciplined creature. You couldn't always keep it on a lead, and it was for ever dashing off into the undergrowth of the past, digging up some decayed bone of memory, and bringing it back, with tail wagging, to lay it at your feet. As dawn outlined the oblong of curtained window in his room, he struggled to efface the image of Daphne's pendulous breasts, swinging to and fro like bells tolling the doom of their relationship, by focusing on his forthcoming journey.

He switched on his bedside lamp and fetched an atlas from the bookcase, where it rested horizontally above his collection of poetry. The Pacific Ocean covered two pages, an expanse of blue so vast that even Australia looked no more than a large island in the south-west corner. The Hawaiian islands were tiny dots clustered together near the seam between the pages: Kauai, Molokai, Oahu (with the name of Honolulu flying from it like a banner), Maui, and Hawaii – the only one big enough to allow a spot of green colouring. The blue of the ocean was traversed by wavering dotted lines that traced the routes of the early explorers.

Drake seemed to have just missed the Hawaiian archipelago when he sailed round the world in 1578–80, but Captain Cook's voyage of 1776 had passed right through it. Indeed, a legend in minute typeface stated, *"Capt. Cook killed in Hawaii, 14 Feb. 1779,"* which was news to Bernard. Staring at the great blue bowl of the Pacific, held in the green, curving arms of Asia and the Americas, he realized that he knew very little at all about the history and geography of this side of the globe. His education, his work, his whole life and outlook, had been imprinted with the shape of a much smaller and more populous sea, the Mediterranean. How far had the early growth of Christianity depended on the assumption of believers that they lived at the "centre of the world"? Discuss, he appended wryly to his thought, conscious of slipping into examiner's idiom. But why not? It would get the Asians and the Africans on the Diploma course going. He wrote a draft question in the notebook he kept to hand for jotting down such ideas. On another page he wrote down a list of things to be done:

> *Travel Agent: flights, fares*
> *Bank (travellers cheques)*
> *Passport valid? Visa reqd?*
> *Daddy.*

After breakfast, which he took in the nearly empty refectory (a group of Nigerian Pentecostalists chattered animatedly over their teacups in the sunniest corner of the room, while at the other end a lugubrious Lutheran from Weimar spooned yoghourt into a hole in his beard and read the latest issue of *Theologicum*), Bernard took a bus to the local shopping centre and went into the first travel agency he came to. The windows and walls of the shop were plastered with brightly coloured posters depicting tanned young people in skimpy bathing costumes and paroxysms of pleasure, fondling each other on beaches or jumping up and down in the sea or clinging to gaudily rigged sailboards. There was a blackboard on the counter with holidays listed like items on a restaurant menu: *"Palma 14 days £242. Benidorm 7 days £175. Corfu 14 days £298."* While he waited to be served, Bernard glanced through a heap of brochures. They seemed extraordinarily repetitive: page after page of bays, beaches, couples, windsurfers, high-rise hotels and swimming-pools. Majorca looked the same as Corfu and Crete looked the same as Tunisia. It made the Mediterranean seem the centre of the world in a way the early Christians could not have foreseen. Like so much else, the popular concept of "holiday" seemed to have mutated in his lifetime. The word still for him evoked plastic macs and wet shingle and cold grey rollers at Hastings where they used to go year after year when he was a child, and Mrs Humphreys' limp Spam salads in the dark and slightly mildewed back dining-room of the boarding house just behind the seafront. Later, a holiday for himself might mean deputizing for some rural p.p. in the summer vacation, or attending a conference in Rome, or accompanying a pilgrimage to the Holy Land – something improving, improvised, or subsidized. This idea of ordering a fortnight's standardized bliss from a printed catalogue was strange to him, though he could see the convenience of it, and the prices seemed very reasonable.

"Next," said a young man behind the counter whose suit seemed much too big for him, since its shoulders had slipped down to somewhere near his elbows. Bernard sat up on a high seat like a bar stool.

"I want to go to Hawaii," he said. "Honolulu. As soon as possible." The request sounded so out of character to his own ears that he had to stifle a giggle.

The young man, perhaps jaded by requests for Benidorm and Corfu, glanced at him with a flicker of interest and reached under the counter for a brochure.

"Not for a holiday," Bernard said quickly. "It's family business. I just want a cheap flight."

"How long d'you want to stay?"

"I don't really know," said Bernard, who had not given any thought to this question. "I suppose two or three weeks."

The young man tapped on his computer keyboard with badly bitten fingers. The standard economy air fare proved to be frighteningly expensive, and there were no Apex fares available for the next two weeks. "I might be able to get you a package for about the same price as the Apex," said the young man. "Last-minute cancellation or something. Travelwise do one, but their computer's down at the moment. Leave it with me."

He walked back to the College. It was a fine day, but the walk was not particularly pleasant because of the heavy traffic on the main road, mainly lorries going to and from the huge car factory sprawled on the outskirts of the city a few miles away. Double-decker transporters, loaded with so many cars that they looked like mobile motorway pile-ups, ground up the hill in low gear, hissing with their air-brakes and stirring the gritty dust in the gutters with their exhaust smoke. Bernard thought of damp sea breezes and the whisper of surf with pleasurable anticipation.

Fortunately, St John's College was set well back from the main road, in its own grounds. It was one of a cluster of theological colleges that had been founded in the late nineteenth century, or early in the twentieth, to train Free Church ministers. The colleges had adjusted to the decline in their constituency and to the more ecumenical spirit of modern times by opening their doors to all denominations, indeed all faiths, and to laypeople as well as to clerics. There were courses in comparative religion and inter-faith relations, and centres for the study of Judaism, Islam and Hinduism, as well as courses on every aspect of Christianity. The students included inner-city social workers, foreign missionaries, native clerics from the Third World, old-age pensioners and unemployed graduates from the local community. In fact almost anybody could study almost anything that could be brought under the umbrella of religion at one or other of the colleges: there were degrees or diplomas in pastoral studies, biblical studies, liturgical studies, missionary studies and theological studies. There were courses in existentialism, phenomenology and faith, situational ethics, the theory and practice of charism, early Christian heresies, feminist theology, black theology, negative theology, hermeneutics, homiletics, church management, ecclesiastical architecture, sacred dance, and many other things. It sometimes seemed to Bernard that the South Rummidge Colleges, as they were collectively known, constituted

28

a kind of religious supermarket, and had both the advantages and the drawbacks of such outlets. It was wonderfully accommodating, had space enough to display all the wares for which there was a demand, and carried a wide variety of brands. On its shelves you could find everything you needed, conveniently stored and attractively packaged. But the very ease of the shopping process brought with it the risk of a certain satiety, a certain boredom. If there was so much choice, perhaps nothing mattered very much. Still, he was not disposed to complain. There weren't many jobs for sceptical theologians, and St John's College had given him one. It was only part-time, admittedly, but he had hopes that it might eventually become full-time, and meanwhile they allowed him to live in one of the student rooms in the College, which saved him a lot of trouble and expense.

He returned to his room and made the narrow, iron-framed bed, which he had left untidily rumpled in his eagerness to get out to the travel agency. He sat at his desk and took out his notes on a book about process theology he was reviewing for *Eschatological Review*. The God of process theology, he read, is the cosmic lover. *"His transcendence is in His sheer faithfulness to Himself in love, in His inexhaustibility as lover, and in His capacity for endless adaptation to circumstances in which His love may be active."* Really? Who says? The theologian says. And who cares, apart from other theologians? Not the people choosing their holidays from the travel agent's brochures. Not the drivers of the car transporters. It often seemed to Bernard that the discourse of much modern radical theology was just as implausible and unfounded as the orthodoxy it had displaced, but nobody had noticed because nobody read it except those with a professional stake in its continuation.

Somebody knocked on his door and called out that there was a long-distance call for him on the students' telephone. It was Ursula.

"Is this a better time?" she said.

"Yes, it's fine. Eleven o'clock in the morning."

"I've been thinking, maybe Jack would come if you brought him with you."

"Well, I don't know," said Bernard doubtfully. "I'm not sure it would make any difference."

"Give it a try. I really want to see him."

"What about the extra expense?"

"I'll pay. What the hell, what do I need savings for?"

"Well, I'll try and persuade him," said Bernard. He spoke sincerely, but with a somewhat heavy heart. If he should succeed, the trip to Hawaii would take on a different, less alluring complexion. "I don't hold out any great hopes," he added.

Almost as soon as he had put the receiver back in its cradle, the phone rang again. It was the zoot-suited young man in the travel agency. He had found a fourteen-day package holiday in Waikiki with Travelwise Tours, at a bargain price, leaving the following Thursday, scheduled flight from Heathrow via Los Angeles. "It's seven hundred and twenty-nine pounds, based on two people sharing one room. There's a supplement for single occupancy, though, ten pounds a day."

"Do you mean I could get two tickets at that price?" Bernard enquired.

"Well, it is a pair, as a matter of fact. A late cancellation. But I thought you were travelling on your own."

"I was. But it's possible that I may have a companion."

"Oh yes?" said the young man, with a kind of aural wink in his voice.

"My father," Bernard felt absurdly anxious to explain.

The young man said he would put the tickets on hold over the weekend and that Bernard would have to confirm on the following Monday.

He made two attempts to phone his father in the course of the morning without getting an answer. After lunch he tried again without success, then on an impulse dialled Tess's number. She answered immediately.

"Oh, it's you," she said frigidly. The last time they had spoken was three years ago, at the family gathering after his mother's funeral. Tess had blamed him for bringing on the fatal relapse. He had put down his untasted glass of sherry and walked out of the house. Strained relations.

He told her about Ursula's illness, and his offer to visit her in Honolulu.

"Very noble of you," she said drily. "Are you hoping for a legacy?"

"It never crossed my mind," he said. "Anyway, I don't think Ursula's particularly well-off."

"I thought her ex-husband was paying her oodles of alimony."

"I don't know about that. I don't know anything about her private life, actually. I was hoping you'd fill me in."

"Not now, if you don't mind. We've just got back from Cornwall. Terrible journey. We left at the crack of dawn to avoid the traffic, but it didn't make any difference."

"Nice holiday?"

"There's a drought down there, we had to fetch our water from a standpipe. If I'm going to keep house, I'd rather do it at home with running water."

"You should get Frank to take you to a hotel."

"Have you got any idea how much it costs to take a family of seven to a hotel?"

Not having any idea, Bernard was silent.

"Quite apart from the problem of Patrick," Tess added. Patrick was her retarded son, brain-damaged at birth. He was an amiable, friendly lad, but he dribbled and slurred his speech and was apt to sweep dishes off the table by accident. Bernard bit back an impulse to suggest that Patrick might be separately accommodated for a week or two. Tess was admirably devoted to Patrick's welfare, but she also used him as a stick with which to beat the rest of the world.

"Look," said Bernard, "is Daddy at home? I've been trying to phone him all day."

"It's the anniversary of their wedding today," said Tess. "He would've had a mass said for Mummy this morning and then gone up to the cemetery."

"Oh," said Bernard, slightly shamed that he had forgotten the significance of the date. "But he should be back by now, shouldn't he? I just tried ringing him."

"He's watching *Neighbours*. He always watches *Neighbours* after lunch, and he won't answer the phone while it's on."

31

"Is that a television programme?"

"Bernard, you must be the only person in the entire country who doesn't know what *Neighbours* is. I'll tell Daddy about Ursula, if you like. I'll probably pop over there this evening."

"No, I think I'd better do it. I was thinking of going down tomorrow to see him, as a matter of fact."

"Whatever for?"

"To discuss Ursula."

"What is there to discuss? It'll only upset him, stirring up the past."

"Ursula wants me to take him to Honolulu."

"*What?*"

While he listened patiently to a stream of expostulation from Tess, to the effect that their father would not dream of it, that she herself would not permit it, that the journey and the heat would be too much for him, that Ursula was being unreasonable, etc. etc., Bernard felt a gentle tug on his sleeve and turned to find a Filipino nun at the head of a small line of people waiting to use the phone. "Sorry, Tess, I can't talk any more now," he said. "This is a pay phone and people are waiting."

"What are you, Bernard, forty-four, and you haven't even got a phone of your own," said Tess contemptuously. "What a mess you've made of your life."

Bernard didn't dispute the general point, though the lack of a private phone was the least of his regrets.

"Tell Daddy to expect me tomorrow afternoon," he said, and rang off.

Bernard took the coach from Rummidge to London the next day. The journey was scheduled to take two and a quarter hours, but the motorway was choked with traffic, cars laden with holiday luggage, some towing caravans and boats, mixed up incongruously with cars and buses packed with football fans, striped scarves fluttering like streamers from their windows, on their way (he was informed by the man sitting next to him) to Wembley for the Charity Shield game, the first of the season. So they were late arriving in central London.

The capital was seething with humanity. Victoria was chaotic – foreign tourists frowning over streetmaps, young hikers shouldering massive backpacks, families on their way to the seaside, weekenders on their way to the country, rowdy football fans – all jostling and pushing and banging into each other. The air was full of shouts, oaths, snatches of football songs, and fragments of French, German, Spanish, Arabic. There were long looping queues for taxis, and for tickets in the Underground. Bernard had never been so struck by the restless mass mobility of the modern world, or felt so harassed and buffeted by it. If there were by any chance a Supreme Being, it would be pleasing to imagine Him suddenly clapping His hands like the exasperated teacher of an unruly class, and saying, in the chastened silence, *"Will you all stop talking and go quietly back to your places."*

Getting to the family home in South London was a tedious business at the best of times. You had to take a scruffy electric train, with an interior decor of ripped seats and felt-tip graffiti, from London Bridge to Brickley, then either walk for nearly a mile or wait for a bus to the bottom of Haredale Road, then toil up the hill to number 12, nearly at the top. Bernard felt a wave of emotion wash over him, with an effect more like nausea than nostalgia, as he turned the corner and commenced his climb. How many times he had bowed his shoulders, weighed down with a satchel full of schoolbooks, against this incline. The uniform terraced houses still stretched up the hill in two staggered rows, each with its railinged area and flight of stone steps up to the front door. And yet there was a subtle difference from the street he remembered from childhood: a variety of detail, a proud display of ownership, in blinds, shutters, porches, aluminium window-frames, hanging flower-baskets. And of course, another change: the road was lined with cars on both sides, parked bumper to bumper. It seemed that even Brickley had shared in the property boom of the nineteen-eighties, though the profusion of "For Sale" boards showed that the bubble had burst here, as everywhere else.

Number 12 looked noticeably shabbier than its neighbours, the paint cracking and peeling on the sash window-frames. There was a shiny new Volkswagen Golf parked outside, whose owner was no doubt pleased that Mr Walsh didn't own a vehicle. Bernard mounted the steps, panting slightly from his climb, and pressed the doorbell. The stippled and tinted shape of his father's face swam up behind the stained glass in the front door as the old man peered through it to identify him. Then he opened the door. "Oh, it's you," he said, unsmilingly. "Come in."

"I'm surprised you can still manage that climb," said Bernard, following his father down the dark hall to the back kitchen. A faint odour of meat and cabbage hung on the air.

"I don't go out much," said his father. "I have a home help does my shopping, and I get my dinner from Meals on Wheels. They bring me two dinners on a Friday and I have one of them warmed up on Saturday. Have you eaten?"

He seemed relieved when Bernard replied that he had. "But I wouldn't say no to a cup of tea," said Bernard. His father nodded and went to the sink to fill the kettle. Bernard took a turn around the little room. It had always been the main focus of the house, and now it looked as if his father spent most of his time in it. It had the look of an overcrowded nest: the television was in here, and his father's favourite armchair, and souvenirs that used to be in the front sitting-room.

"The house is a bit big for you now, isn't it?" he said.

"Don't *you* start on me, for the love of God. Tess is always nagging me to sell up and move into a flat."

"Well, it's not a bad idea."

"You can't sell anything round here at the moment. Didn't you see the For Sale signs on your way up?"

"Surely you'd get enough to buy a little flat?"

"I'm not going to give it away," said Mr Walsh.

Bernard, sensing that he was touching a sore topic, did not pursue it. He inspected the family shrine on the dresser. Grouped around a faded studio portrait of his mother in her youth were photographs of his brother and sisters and their families: Tess and Frank and their five children, Brendan, his wife Frances and their three, Dympna, her husband Laurie and their two adopted boys. Some of these people appeared more than once, in prams, in school groups, in wedding dresses, and graduation robes. There were no pictures of Bernard in this gallery. Pinned to the sides of the dresser with drawing-pins were handwritten lists and memos: *pay electricity; get laundry ready for Mrs P; mass for M. Friday; stamps; milk bottles; Neighbours 1.30.*

"You like *Neighbours*, do you?" he remarked, thinking this would be a safer topic; but his father seemed displeased at having his television viewing habits exposed. "It's a lot of codswallop," he said testily. "But it makes me sit down and digest my dinner." He poured boiling water into the teapot and stirred it. "So what brings you here after all this time?" he said.

"It's been a long time, Daddy, because I had the impression you didn't want to see me." Daddy. The term had excited some ridicule when he was a boy, for the other kids in the street called their fathers "Dad." But it was the Irish way. Mr Walsh, his back turned to Bernard, said nothing. "Didn't Tess tell you why I've come?"

"She said something about Ursula."

"Ursula's seriously ill, Daddy."

"It happens to us all," said his father, so calmly that Bernard was sure Tess had told him the whole story.

"She wants to see you."

"Ha!" His father uttered a brief, mirthless laugh. He brought the teapot to the table and set it down.

"I've offered to go out there, but it's you she really wants to see."

"Why me?"

"You're her closest relative, aren't you?"

"What if I am?'

"She's dying, Daddy, all alone, on the other side of the world. She wants to see her family. It's only natural."

"She should have thought of that when she settled in that place, whadyoucallit, Hawaiee." He twanged the final vowel derisively, like a banjo string.

"Why *did* she settle there?"

His father shrugged. "Don't ask me. I haven't had any contact with Ursula for donkey's years. She went there for a holiday, I believe, liked the climate and decided to stay. She could please herself where she lived, she had no ties. That was always Ursula's trouble, she always pleased herself. Now she's paying for it."

"She told me to tell you that she's gone back to the Church."

Mr Walsh digested this information in silence for a moment. "I'm glad to hear it," he said drily.

"Why did she leave the Church in the first place?"

"She married a divorced man."

"Oh, that was it! You and Mummy were always so secretive about Aunt Ursula. I never did quite know what it was all about."

"No reason why you should. You were only a child in 1946."

"I remember when she came back to England, that would have been about 1952."

"Yes, just after her husband had run off."

"He left her so soon?"

"It was a doomed marriage from the start. We all told her so, but she wouldn't listen."

Gradually, prompted and coaxed by Bernard, Mr Walsh sketched in Ursula's history. She was the youngest of five siblings, and the only girl. The family – the Walshes – had emigrated from Ireland to England in the mid nineteen-thirties, when she would have been about thirteen. At the outbreak of World War Two she was living at home, working as a shorthand typist in the City. She had wanted to join one of the women's services, but her parents had dissuaded her, partly because they feared for her morals, partly because all their sons had been called up, and they didn't want to be totally deserted. When their eldest son, Sean, was killed, torpedoed in a troopship (he had an honoured place in the family shrine, a full-length snapshot of a lance-corporal in battledress, standing at ease and laughing at the camera) they held on to her more tightly than ever. So she continued to live at home throughout the War, through the Blitz and the various waves of V-weapons, working in a Government Department in Whitehall, until in 1944 she met an American airman, a staff sergeant in communications, posted to England prior to D-Day, and fell in love with him. Bernard had seen enough old newsreels to contextualize this narrative: the blacked-out London streets, the huge floor of the *palais-de-dance* with its revolving couples of crop-haired men in uniform and long-haired girls in short, square-shouldered frocks, the climate of danger and excitement and uncertainty, the sirens, searchlights, telegrams and banner headlines. His name was Rick Riddell. "Rick, what kind of a name is that," his father commented. "It should have been a warning to her." Rick turned out to have a wife back in the USA. There was a huge family row. Rick was posted to France and Germany for the closing stages of the war in Europe. When he was demobilized he divorced his wife, who had been playing fast and loose while he was abroad, and wrote to Ursula from America asking her to marry him. "She went like a shot," said Mr Walsh bitterly. "Never mind that it broke her parents' hearts, that were already broken by Sean's death. Never mind that she was abandoning them in their old age."

"But," Bernard interjected, "weren't you and Uncle Patrick and Uncle Michael back from the war by then?" This was a slightly flattering reference to Mr Walsh's war service: he had had a low medical rating and spent most of these years as a member of a barrage-balloon unit in South London.

"We had our own families to look after," said Mr Walsh, getting to his feet to fetch the kettle, which he had set to boil again. "And times were hard. There wasn't much money about. What Ursula brought home every week made all the difference to the old folk. But it wasn't just the money. They needed her to help them get over the death of Sean. They idolized him, you see. Their first-born." Mr Walsh recharged the teapot with hot water, then, with the empty kettle in his hand, went over to the dresser and peered at the photograph of the laughing lance-corporal. "His body was never recovered," he said. "It made it difficult for all of us to believe he was really dead."

"Surely she was bound to get married eventually?"

"We never thought of Ursula as the marrying type. She always enjoyed a dance, or party, but she never had a steady boyfriend. She would always give them the brush-off if they started getting serious. A bit of a flirt, she was, to tell you the truth. That was why it was such a shock when she threw herself at that Yank. Anyway, off she went on the first passage she could get, the *Mauretania* I think it was, to 'Noo Jersey', to marry Rick. At first everything in the garden was lovely. We had letters and postcards going into kinks about America, the honeymoon in Florida, the size of their house, the size of their car, the size of the refrigerator and every blessed item of booze and grub there was in it. You can imagine how that cheered us up, with the rationing like it was just after the War."

"She used to send us food parcels, though," said Bernard. "I remember." He had a sudden memory-picture of a jar of peanut butter, a substance he had never seen or heard of before, on the kitchen table, and his mother saying curtly, when he asked where it had come from, "Your aunt Ursula, where else?" The jar had borne a label depicting a smiling, anthropomorphized peanut, with a balloon coming out of its mouth, saying *"Dee-lish-us!"* He'd had his head smacked for dipping his finger into the jar for an experimental taste of the queer, cloying paste, hesitating between sweet and savoury.

"It was the least she could do," said Mr Walsh. "Anyway, the letters got further and further apart. Rick got a new job in California, he was doing well, working in the aircraft industry, and they moved out there. Then one day we got a letter saying she was coming back to England for a holiday, on her own."

"I remember that visit," said Bernard. "She had a white dress with red spots."

"Mother of God, she had a dress for every day of the week, and enough spots on 'em to drive you crosseyed," said Mr Walsh. "But she had no husband. She had to admit that Rick had left her, months ago, run off with another woman. She couldn't say we hadn't warned her. Fortunately there were no children."

"Was she thinking of returning to England?"

"It may have been in the back of her mind. But she didn't like it here. Kept complaining of the cold, and the dirt. So she went back to California. Divorced Rick and got a handsome settlement, so we understood. She got some kind of job, secretary to a dentist, or something. Then she worked in a law firm. She was always changing jobs, moving from place to place. We lost track of her."

"She never re-married?"

"No. Once bitten, twice shy."

"And never came back?"

"No. Not even when our father was dying. She claimed that she never got the letter till months afterwards. There was more bad feeling about that. Well, it was her own fault that we sent it to an old address."

They drank their tea in silence for a moment.

"I think you ought to come to Hawaii with me, Daddy," said Bernard at length.

"It's too far. How far is it?"

"It's a long way," Bernard admitted. "But by air it takes less than a day."

"I've never been up in an aeroplane in my life," said Mr Walsh, "and I don't intend to start now."

"There's nothing to it. Everybody flies nowadays – old people, babies. It's the safest form of travel, statistically."

"I'm not in fear of it," said Mr Walsh with dignity. "I just don't fancy it."

"Ursula has offered to pay our fares."

"How much?"

"Well, I've been offered a special cheap fare of seven hundred and twenty-nine pounds."

"God in Heaven! Each?"

Bernard nodded. He could tell that his father was impressed, in spite of his next remark.

"I suppose she thinks that makes it all right. Stays away from her family for nearly forty years, and thinks that she only has to crook her little finger and we'll all come running, as long as she pays the fare. The almighty dollar."

"If you don't come, you may regret it later."

"Why should I regret it?"

"I mean, if she dies – when she dies, you may be sorry that you didn't go to see her when she asked."

"She has no right to ask," his father mumbled uneasily.

"It's not fair on me. I'm an old man. It's all right for you. You go."

"I hardly know her. It's you she wants to see." He added, injudiciously, "It's one of the corporal works of mercy: to visit the sick."

"Don't you presume to lecture me about my religious duties," the old man lashed back, two red spots colouring his high cheekbones. "You of all people."

Bernard thought he had dished whatever chance he might have had of persuading his father, especially as Tess turned up a few minutes later, having driven over from her leafier suburb on the Kent border with the ill-concealed motive of monitoring the discussion. Tess, living nearest to Mr Walsh of all his children (Brendan was Assistant Registrar at a northern university, and Dympna's husband was a vet in East Anglia) inevitably had most to do with him, a responsibility she shouldered with a certain amount of self-righteous grumbling to her siblings, and mild bullying of her father. As soon as she entered the house, she began to pick up items of clothing that she declared needed washing, ran her finger over the ledges to complain of the dusting standards of the home help, and sniffed the contents of the refrigerator, tossing whatever failed this test summarily into the rubbish bin. She moved heavily about the kitchen, making the china on the shelves tremble, a big woman, with broad, child-bearing hips, and her father's beaky nose and mass of thick woolly hair, black with flecks of silver in it.

"So what d'you think of this idea of going to see Ursula?" she said to her father, much to the surprise of Bernard, who had been expecting a scornful dismissal of the proposal. Mr Walsh, sulking at the decimation of his food stocks, looked surprised too.

"You're not thinking I should go, are you?"

"I'd go myself," said Tess, "if I could just drop everything like Bernard. I wouldn't mind a trip to Hawaii, all expenses paid."

"It's not going to be exactly fun, you know," said Bernard. "Ursula's dying."

"So she says. How d'you know she's not just panicking? Did you speak to her doctor?"

"Not personally. But she told me he's only given her months to live, even with chemotherapy, and she's refused that."

"Why?" said Mr Walsh.

"She said she wanted to die with her own hair on."

Mr Walsh produced a faint, wintry smile. "That sounds like Ursula," he said.

"Perhaps you should go, Daddy, if you can face the journey," said Tess, putting her hand on his shoulder. "After all, you are her closest surviving relative. She may want you there to . . . settle her affairs."

Mr Walsh became thoughtful. Bernard instantly decoded the message that had passed between them. If Ursula was dying, she would have money to leave, perhaps a lot of money. She had no husband or children. Her brother Jack was her closest surviving relative. If he inherited her wealth, it would in due course be distributed to his children, and their children, as he saw fit, according to their deserts, which would include such factors as filial devotion, respectability, and the burden of handicapped offspring. If Bernard went to Hawaii on his own, there was a risk that his grateful aunt would leave all her money to him, the black sheep.

"Well, perhaps I should go," said Mr Walsh, with a sigh. "After all, she is my sister, poor soul."

"Good," said Bernard, pleased for Ursula's sake at this decision, even if its motives were selfish and its practical consequences for himself discouraging. "I'll confirm the tickets, then. We leave next Thursday."

"Next Thursday!" Tess exclaimed. "How can Daddy possibly be ready to leave by next Thurday? He doesn't even have a passport. And what about visas?"

"I'll queue up for a passport at Petty France," said Bernard. "And you don't need a visa for a short visit to America these days." The young man at the travel agency had advised him of this.

"I'd better make a list," said Mr Walsh. He wrote on a piece of paper "*Make list*," and sellotaped it to the side of the dresser.

"Well, I hope you're satisfied," said Tess to Bernard, as if she

41

had finally yielded to his prolonged arm-twisting. "I hold you entirely responsible for Daddy's welfare."

3

"Sure this is the only way to travel, if I'd known it was this easy I'd have done it long ago, sittin' here like Lord Luck, waited on hand and foot, nice young gels bringin' you your dinner on a tray, and free booze to go with it – more than you get with Meals on Wheels, I can tell you. Oh, darlin', next time you're passin', could I trouble you for another of these dinky little bottles?"

"Just one moment, sir!"

"You've had enough already, Daddy."

"Go 'way, I can hold me liquor as well as any man. I could drink you under the table any day of the week."

"You'll feel bad later. Alcohol dehydrates you."

"Dehydrates my arse. Oh, excuse my French, my love, it was a slip of the tongue. A momentary lapse into the vernacular, it won't happen again. Only this fella exasperates me, treatin' me like a child. What's this your name is, my dear? Ginny? Oh, *Jeannie*! That's a lovely name. '*I dream of Jeannie with the light brown hair . . .*' "

The old man warbles the line in a cracked tenor voice, and then begins to cough – a long, lung-racking cough that seems to be drawn up from some deep artesian well of phlegm.

"It's all right my dear, I'm fine," he gasps at last. "Don't you worry about me. Just a frog in me throat. All I need to settle it is a fag or two. You may laugh, but I'm tellin' you, it never fails. A hair of the dog. Here, have one of these."

"Daddy, I told you, this is a no-smoking area."

"Oh, I forgot. Trust your man to get us a no-smoking seat. Only thinks of himself. Like Ursula, that's my sister. We're on our way to visit her in Honolulu. She's ill, very ill. You know what I mean? *Cancer!*"

The old man pronounces the word in a hissing whisper that carries, like everything else he has been saying for the last hour, past the unfortunate Jeannie and her boyfriend, to Roger Sheldrake, sitting one seat in from the starboard aisle in this central row of six in the tourist cabin of the jumbo jet. Roger Sheldrake frowns, trying to concentrate on his reading matter, a file of statistical tables supplied to him by the Hawaiian Visitors' Bureau, which he is obliged to hold awkwardly in the air above the remains of his lunch, or dinner, or whatever it is, at this now indeterminate time, somewhere above the North Atlantic.

"If you don't want that bit of cheese, Jeannie, my dear, I'll relieve you of the responsibility. Oh, and look, you left some butter too." The old man begins to scavenge for packets of cellophane-wrapped cheese and biscuits and miniature tubs of butter among the debris on his neighbour's tray, stuffing them into his jacket pockets.

"Daddy, for God's sake, what d'you think you're doing? That stuff will melt and stain your clothes."

"No it won't, they're her-met-ic-ally sealed."

"Give them to me."

The old man reluctantly hands over his loot, which his son wraps in a paper napkin and stows away in his briefcase.

"We'll be catering for ourselves, you see," the old man explains to Jeannie. "And who knows whether the shops will be open when we arrive? We might be very glad of a bit of cheese to keep us going. Are you heading for Hawaii yourself, by any chance?"

"No, only as far as L.A.," says Jeannie, perhaps revising her travel plans at that instant, dismayed at the prospect of having to listen to the tiresome old fool for an additional five hours.

He has been a source of distraction and disturbance ever since they began boarding the aircraft at Heathrow. First, he caused a blockage in the gangway leading to the aircraft by refusing to board at all, in a sudden last-minute panic at the prospect of flying, clinging obstinately to the handrail at the end of the ramp, while his son and various airline officials cajoled and scolded him. Then, finally persuaded to board, and strapped into his seat, he groaned and whimpered and muttered prayers under his breath, clutching a holy medal that he had fished out from under his shirt. Then, with a piercing wail of grief, he remembered a bottle of duty-free whiskey that he, or his son, had left under a seat in the air terminal, and had to be forcibly restrained from going back to fetch it, since the plane was already taxiing to the runway. He gaped fearfully at the video-recorded demonstration, by a smiling flight attendant, of how to put on a life-jacket, his attention particularly excited by the apparition of a female signer, relaying the instructions for the benefit of deaf passengers, in a round, haloed insert in the left-hand corner of the screen. "What's that, what's that female thing up there? Is it a fairy or a ghost or what is it?" he cried. As the plane thundered down the runway, he shut his eyes tightly, gripped the arms of his seat with whitened knuckles, gabbled "Jesus, Mary and Joseph," over and over; and then, as they rose into the air, and the undercarriage retracted with a thump, he shrieked, "Oh Mother of God, was that a bomb going off?"

As the plane climbed smoothly through the cloud cover, and sunlight poured into the cabin, and the noise of the engines diminished somewhat, the old man relapsed into a watchful silence, still gripping his seat arms as if he thought he was personally holding the plane aloft by this means, his eyes blinking and swivelling like a caged bird's as he observed the nonchalant behaviour of his fellow-passengers and the cabin crew. Gradually he began to relax, a process greatly accelerated by the appearance of the drinks trolley. He ordered Irish whiskey, and accepted Scotch with a quip that made the stewardess smile and encouraged her unwisely to slip him two Haig miniatures instead of one. Within fifteen minutes he had lost all fear and inhibition, and launched into a non-stop flow of talk, addressed first to his longsuffering son, and then to his neighbour to his right, the Californian student Jeannie, which lasted all through the meal and shows no sign of drying up.

"Yes, my sister Ursula emigrated to the States just after the War, she was a whadyoucallit, a GI bride, married a Yank soldier, but he was no good, ran off with another woman, fortunately there were no children and he had to pay her a lot of whadyoucallit, ali-money, so she could please herself where she lived, and she chose Hawaii, she could hardly get further away from her family, could she, and now she's on her deathbed it's us that has to traipse halfway round the world to see her . . ."

In 1988 approximately 6.1 million tourists visited Hawaii spending 8.14 billion dollars and staying for an average of 10.2 days. This compared with 4.25 million visitors in 1982, and only 0.7 million visitors in 1965. The steep rise in the volume of visitors was clearly related to the introduction of the jumbo jet in 1969. In 1970 the number of visitors arriving by sea had dwindled to 16,735 compared to 2.17 million arriving by air, and became too insignificant to be tabulated after 1975. Roger Sheldrake frowns, trying to concentrate on the statistics and shut out the jabber of the old man's monologue. The fact that he and his son are not ordinary tourists makes the distraction doubly irritating, for it is not as if he is gleaning from it any anecdotal evidence relevant to his research.

"Best student of his year at the English College in Rome, they said . . . He could have been something. A monsignor. A bishop, even. But he threw it all away. A wasted life I call it . . ."

The old man is talking now in a kind of confidential undertone, his head turned away from his son who is evidently the topic of conversation. Jeannie looks embarrassed by these confidences, but Roger Sheldrake pricks up his ears.

"Just a part-time teacher at some whadyoucallit, theological college . . . must be a queer sort of theology they get from the likes of him . . ."

Roger Sheldrake leans forward to peer along the row of seats at the subject of these revelations. The bearded man is asleep, or praying, or meditating – at any rate, his eyes are closed and his hands rest loosely splayed on his thighs. His chest and diaphragm heave and subside rhythmically.

"All the theology you need is in the Penny Catechism, that's what I always say. . . ."

Who made you?
God made me.

Why did God make you?

God made me to know him, love him and serve him in this world, and to be happy with him for ever in the next. (Note: no mention of being happy in this world.)

To whose image and likeness did God make you?

God made me to his own image and likeness. (Awkward, that construction – should be "*in* whose image", surely? Some subtle theological point in the preposition, perhaps.)

Is this likeness to God in your body, or in your soul?

This likeness is chiefly in my soul. (Note the "chiefly." Not "exclusively." God as man-shaped. Father-shaped. Long white beard, white hair, in need of a trim. White face too, of course. Frowning slightly, as if he might fly into a nasty temper if provoked. Sitting on his throne in heaven, Jesus on his right, Holy Spirit hovering overhead, chorus of angels, Mary and the saints standing by. Carpet of cloud.)

When did you cease to believe in this God?

Perhaps when I was still training for the priesthood. Certainly when I was teaching at St Ethelbert's. I can't remember, exactly.

You can't remember?

Who remembers when they stopped believing in Father Christmas? It's not usually a specific moment – catching a parent in the act of putting your presents at the end of the bed. It's an intuition, a conclusion you draw at a certain age, or stage of growth, and you don't immediately admit it, or force the question, *is there a Father Christmas?* into the open, because secretly you shrink from the negative answer – in a way, you would prefer to go on believing that there is a Father Christmas. After all, it seems to work, the presents keep coming, and if they're not exactly the ones you wanted, well, there are ways of painlessly rationalizing the disappointment when they come from Father Christmas (perhaps he didn't get your letter), but if they come from your parents all kinds of difficult implications arise.

Are you equating belief in God with belief in Father Christmas?

No, of course not. It's just an analogy. We lose faith in a cherished idea long before we admit it to ourselves. Some people never admit it. I often wonder about my fellow-students at the English

47

College, and my colleagues at Ethel's . . . Perhaps none of us really believed, and none of us would admit it.

How could you go on teaching theology to candidates for the priesthood if you no longer believed in God?

You can teach theology perfectly well without believing in the God of the Penny Catechism. In fact there are very few reputable modern theologians who do.

So what God do they believe in?

God as "the ground of our being", God as "ultimate concern", God as "the Beyond in the Midst."

And how does one pray to that kind of God?

A good question. There are, of course, answers: for instance, that prayer expresses symbolically our desire to be religious – to be virtuous, disinterested, unselfish, ego-less, free from desire.

But why should anyone wish to be religious if there is no personal God to reward him for being so?

For its own sake.

Are you religious in that sense?

No. I would like to be. I thought I was, once. I was wrong.

How did you find out?

I suppose through meeting Daphne.

Bernard opened his eyes. While he had been dozing, or musing, or dreaming, his mealtray with all its plastic detritus had been removed, and a kind of artificial evening had fallen on the passenger cabin of the jumbo jet. The blinds were drawn down over the portholes and the lights had been dimmed. On the video screen, mounted on a bulkhead further up the cabin, a pastel-coloured film jerked and twitched. A car chase was in progress. Vehicles slewed round corners, leapt into the air, overturned and exploded in flames, with silent, balletic grace. Mr Walsh had fallen asleep, and was snoring loudly with his head lolling forward on his chest like a limp puppet. Bernard moved his father's seat into the reclining position, lifted his head and tucked a pillow under it. The old man groaned protestingly, but stopped snoring.

Bernard had brought with him the monograph on process theology he was reviewing, but felt no inclination to read. He put on his earphones and tuned into the soundtrack of the film. He soon worked out the basis of the plot. The hero was an American policeman on the verge of retirement who, due to a mixup of medical specimens, had been wrongly informed that he was terminally ill, and immediately volunteered for the most dangerous assignments in his last week of service in the hope of getting killed in the course of duty, so that his estranged wife would receive a pension big enough to send their son to college. Not only did the policeman, to his intense exasperation, survive all the dangers to which he exposed himself, but he became a much-decorated public hero, to the astonishment and envy of his colleagues, who had always regarded him as more than usually cautious.

Bernard found himself chuckling at the film even as he despised its slick exploitation of terminal illness. The audience could enjoy the pathos and nobility of the hero's response to his fate, comfortable in the knowledge that he wasn't really ill at all, and confident that the genre ensured his immunity from violent death. Of course, somewhere on the margins of the story there was another character (a black bus driver as it happened – thus doubly marginalized), the donor of the misplaced specimen, who *was* doomed to die, and didn't know it, but out of sight was out of mind in fiction. In the last reel the hero appeared to fall off the top of a high building, and when the next scene presented a funeral in progress it seemed that the filmmakers had turned the tables on the audience in a sudden paroxysm of artistic integrity. But in fact it proved to be their most cynical trick of all: the camera pulled back to reveal the hero on crutches, attending the funeral of the black bus driver, and reconciled with his wife.

As the credits rolled, Bernard got up from his seat and joined a queue for the toilets at the rear of the aircraft, taking his place behind a young man in shirtsleeves and red braces. At the head of the queue, just out of sight, a woman with a loud voice, in which Bernard recognized the tortured vowels of the West Midlands, was telling somebody that she and her husband were on their second honeymoon. The young man made a kind of choked glottal noise in his throat, and turned to face Bernard. "That's rich," he said bitterly.

"I beg your pardon?" Bernard replied.

"Did you hear that? A second honeymoon. Must be gluttons for punishment, that's all I can say."

His hair was tousled and his eyes had a wild gleam in them. Bernard deduced that his father was not the only passenger to have over-indulged in liquor at lunchtime.

"You married?" said the young man.

"No."

"Take my advice: stay single."

"Well, I don't think I'll have any difficulty in doing that."

"Nice, eh, a honeymoon when your wife won't speak to you?"

Bernard inferred that this was the young man's situation. "But surely she can't keep it up indefinitely?" he said.

"You don't know Cecily," said the young man gloomily. "I do. I know her. She's remorseless when she's angry. Remorseless. I've seen her reduce waiters – I mean London waiters, grown men, hardened cynics – I've seen her reduce them to tears." He looked on the verge of tears himself.

"Why. . . ?"

"Why did I marry her?"

"No, I was going to say, why is she not speaking to you?"

"That slag Brenda, wasn't it?" said the young man. "Got pissed at the wedding, and spilled the beans to Cecily about us having it off in the storeroom at the office party last Christmas. Cecily called her a liar and threw a glass of champagne in her face. Oh, it was a lovely reception! Really lovely." The young man twisted his lips into a bitter, reminiscent smile. "They hustled Brenda out of the room, screaming at Cecily: '*Has he or hasn't he got a scar on his bum?*' I have, you see, accident when I was a kid, climbing over park railings." He rubbed his haunch as if the wound were still tender.

"Excuse me, lads!" A middle-aged woman in a bright yellow frock covered with a pattern of red beach umbrellas pushed by them, trailing a waft of powerful scent.

"Er, I think there's a toilet free," Bernard prompted.

"Oh, right, thanks." The young man blundered into one of the narrow cubicles, cursing under his breath as he struggled to close the folding door behind him.

A few minutes later, on his way back to his seat, Bernard picked him out in the gloom by his striped shirt and red braces, slumped in his seat beside a young woman with straight fair hair held back from her pale brow by a tortoiseshell comb and a pair of headphones. Cecily was evidently listening to music because she was also reading, with expressionless concentration, a paperback novel held at an angle to catch the light from the overhead lamp. The young man said something to her, laying a hand on her arm to attract her attention. She shook it off without taking her eyes from her book, and the young man threw himself back in his seat with a scowl.

Bernard also picked out the lady in the yellow frock sitting next to the side-whiskered man with the video camera. He was in a window seat and had raised the blind to film something through the porthole, though Bernard couldn't imagine what it was – they were flying at 30,000 feet, above an unbroken carpet of cloud. He staggered in the aisle as the plane suddenly bucked and lurched. With a warning ping the "FASTEN SEAT BELTS" signs lit up and the muffled voice of the captain requested passengers to return to their seats as they were passing through an area of moderate turbulence. Mr Walsh was sitting bolt upright, gripping the arms of his seat, his eyes wide with terror, when Bernard got back to their row. "What is it, in the name of God? What's happening? Is the plane going to crash?"

"Just a bit of turbulence, Daddy. Air currents. Nothing to worry about."

"I need a drink."

"No," said Bernard. "There's another film starting. Would you like to watch it?"

"I'm dyin' of thirst. Is there any chance of a cup of tea?"

"I doubt it. Not for a while, anyway. I could get you some fruit juice, if you like. Or a glass of water."

"I feel terrible," moaned the old man. "I'm full of wind and my feet are swelled up and my mouth's as dry as the Gobi desert."

"It's your own fault for drinking too much. I warned you."

"I should never have let you talk me into coming on this excursion," the old man whined. "It's madness at my age. It'll be the death of me."

"You'd be perfectly all right if you just did as you were told," said Bernard, stooping with difficulty in the confined space to loosen his father's shoelaces. He straightened up, flushed and breathless from the effort, under the slightly hostile regard of a dome-headed man in a beige safari suit, holding a book and leaning forward in his seat at the other end of the row as if to ascertain the latest cause of disturbance. Bernard glanced at his watch and was dismayed to discover that less than five hours of the eleven-hour flight had passed.

"Do they have a lav on this thing?" said Mr Walsh.

"Yes, of course, d'you want to go?"

"Perhaps I could get rid of some of this wind. God, they don't need a jet engine for this contraption, they could just tie me to the tail and let me fart us all the way to Hawaii."

Bernard sniggered, but was a little shocked. Either the alcohol or the high altitude had released a vein of ribald language in his father's speech that he had never heard before, something that must derive from the rough male world of work and pubs that he had always kept at a distance from his family. For most of his life, Mr Walsh had worked as a despatch clerk for a transport company in the London Docks, retiring as chief shipper. One day in his school holidays, when he was about fourteen, Bernard had invented a pretext to visit his father's place of work, a shabby wooden shed in the corner of a yard full of lorries, driven by men with arms like tattooed hams, who spat on the ground and kicked the huge grooved tyres of the vehicles before they climbed into their cabs. His father had looked up from a steel desk covered with files and spiked invoices, and said, "What the devil are you doing here?" He had not been pleased. "Don't ever come here again," he said, after Bernard delivered his trivial message. Bernard had realized then for the first time that his father was ashamed of his humble job, and of its sordid setting. He had wanted to say something healing and reassuring, but couldn't find the right words. He had slunk off feeling guilty and ashamed himself. It had been a kind of primal scene, very Irish, exposing a secret of status, not sex.

Coming out of the toilet, where she has spent some time trying to remove a sauce stain from her pink and blue tracksuit top, Sue Butterworth comes face to face with the old Irishman she chatted to in the terminal, standing disconcertingly close to the folding door as she opens it. He recoils, equally disconcerted, and says angrily to his son, hovering in the background, "Is this the Ladies you've brought me to?"

"It's all right, Daddy. The toilets are for anybody."

"Did you enjoy the film?" Sue asks, to cover the embarrassment. "I was really taken in at the end, by the funeral."

The old man is silent.

"He's just woken up, he's not feeling too good," says the bearded son. "Can you manage on your own, Daddy?"

"Of course I can."

"What are you waiting for, then?"

By the glare which he directs at herself, Sue infers that he is waiting for her to disappear before he enters the cubicle. She returns to her seat next to Dee, who is reading a courtesy copy of *Cosmopolitan*.

"I just met the old Irishman and his son, coming out of the toilet."

"I wouldn't have thought there was room for the two of them."

"No, silly, I mean *I* was coming out of the toilet. They were waiting. He's rather nice, the son, don't you think? He would suit you, Dee."

"Do you mind? He looks about fifty."

"I wouldn't say that old. Perhaps forty-five. It's hard to tell with a beard."

"I hate beards." Dee gives a little shudder. "When they kiss you it's like walking into cobwebs in the dark."

"He could shave it off. He's very kind to his old Dad. I like a kind man."

"You have him, then, if you fancy him."

"Dee! I've got Des."

"Hawaii's a long way from Harlow."

"Dee! You are awful," Sue giggles.

"Anyway," says Dee, "I expect he's married."

"No, I don't think so, somehow," says Sue. "He might be a widower, though. He has the look of someone who has suffered."

"He's suffering from his old man, all right," says Dee.

Slowly, slowly, the hours passed. Another film began. This time it was a family story, set in Wyoming, centring on a young boy's relationship with his horse. Bernard found it intolerably sentimental, but watched anyway to encourage his father to do the same. Behind the drawn blinds the sun shone brightly. It flooded into the cabin when the blinds were raised and the second meal, a light snack, was served. It was still shining, but dully, through a haze of smog, when they landed in Los Angeles, at four in the afternoon local time, but midnight by the passengers' body clocks. They walked slowly and stiffly through the long carpeted corridors; they stood dumbly on moving walkways, like objects on a conveyor belt; they lined up patiently in a huge, hushed hall, segmented by moveable barriers and braided ropes, to have their passports examined. What was it that these places reminded one of? It was, Bernard decided, those visions of the next world, or of passage to it, that he had seen in films at the Brickley fleapit in his childhood and adolescence, films in which airmen who had just been killed in combat rose serenely on moving staircases to a kind of heavenly reception area of white synthetic surfaces and curved modular furniture, and reported to some officious angelic clerk. The populist *pareschaton*.

"Vacation?" said the official examining Bernard's landing card.

He replied in the affirmative, having been advised to do so by the young man in the travel agency, as being less likely to cause difficulty over the waived visa.

"The old guy with you?"

"He's my father."

The official looked from one to the other, and then at the landing card. "You're staying at the Waikiki Surfrider?"

"Yes." Bernard had found the name of the hotel in his Travelpak.

The official stamped their passports and tore off portions of their landing cards. "Enjoy your stay," he said. "Take care in the big surf."

Bernard smiled feebly. Mr Walsh was oblivious to the irony, and all else. He was beyond fatigue, his arms hanging slackly from his bowed shoulders, his bloodshot eyes glazed. Bernard could hardly bear to look at him, the spectacle made him feel so guilty. Fortunately they were not detained at Customs, though the sandy-haired family had been, much to the father's indignation.

"This is absurd," he was saying crossly. "Do we look like smugglers?"

"If smugglers looked like smugglers, pal, our job would be a lot easier," said the customs official, turning over the contents of a suitcase. "What's this?" He sniffed a packet suspiciously.

"Tea."

"Why isn't it in teabags?"

"We don't like teabags," said the mother of the family. "And we don't like your tea."

A harassed-looking black lady, in the Travelwise livery, came up to Bernard and his father and said, "Hi, how are you today?" Without waiting for an answer, she continued: "Your flight to Honolulu leaves from Terminal Seven. Just follow the signs to the exit and look for the shuttle tram. Take care – it's hot out there today." Bernard and his father passed out of the limbo of the International Arrivals hall, into the noise and bustle of the terminal's main concourse. Here it was palpably a different country, and a different time of day: people dressed in every kind of clothing from business suits to running shorts were moving about, briskly and purposefully, or sitting at tables, drinking and eating, or buying things in shops. Leaning on his luggage trolley, Bernard felt as though he were invisible to them, like a ghost.

"Is this Hawaii?" said Mr Walsh.

"No, Daddy, it's Los Angeles. We have to take another plane to Honolulu."

"I'm not going on another aeroplane," said Mr Walsh. "Not today. Not ever."

"Don't be silly," said Bernard, affecting a light, chaffing tone. "You don't want to spend the rest of your life in Los Angeles Airport, do you?"

As soon as they passed through the automatic doors of the air-

55

conditioned terminal, and stepped out on to the pavement, Bernard broke into sweat all over his body. He could feel the perspiration trickling down his sides underneath his clothing, suddenly intolerably thick and itchy. The air, reeking of aircraft fuel and diesel fumes, was so hot that it seemed in danger of spontaneous combustion. Mr Walsh was opening and closing his mouth like a landed fish. "Mother of God," he gasped, "I'm melted."

As well as heat, there was noise: the swish of tyres on the tarmac, the trombone notes of deep-throated car horns, the thunder of planes taking off overhead. Brightly coloured cars, taxis, vans and buses cruised past in an endless stream, like fish in an aquarium, darting and swerving in and out of each other's way. There were no trams visible, however. Bernard looked around in bewilderment, squinting in the hazy afternoon sunshine, then spotted the girl in the pink and blue tracksuit, with one foot on the runningboard of a small bus parked a short distance away, beckoning to them.

"Come on, Daddy."

"Where are we going now?"

The bus (which seemed for some inscrutable reason to be called a tram) had a cavity in its side for luggage. When Bernard had stowed their suitcases in it, the driver sprang open the door of the vehicle, and snapped it shut on them like a steel trap. Inside, the passengers shivered in a cold blast of air-conditioning. Bernard smiled a thankyou to the girl in pink and blue, whose returning smile turned into a yawn. Her companion, sitting beside her, had her eyes closed and wore a look of suffering. As they passed down the aisle, Bernard nodded to the young man sitting gloomily beside Cecily, his red braces covered by a linen jacket with its sleeves rolled up. Cecily was looking out of the offside window as if the passing traffic were the most fascinating spectacle in the world. The sandy-haired family boarded the bus, the two children red-eyed and wan. Of the Travelwise contingent, only the second honeymooners seemed unaffected by fatigue, conversing animatedly at the back of the bus. When the driver prepared to depart they loudly appealed to him to wait for a missing couple belonging to the Travelwise party – who appeared, at last, flushed and perspiring, the wife in electric-blue jumper and trousers, pushing a trolley piled with luggage, and her paunchy husband limping along behind. They clambered aboard the bus, and were greeted with yelps of encouragement by the cheerful Midlanders, who claimed credit for holding up the bus, and assured them that their dash had been recorded on videotape. It seemed that a kind of acquaintance had been struck up between the two women on the flight from London, which was now extended to their spouses. The four of them sat together on the back seat behind Bernard, who could not avoid overhearing their conversation.

"Phew! We went the wrong way after Customs," said the lady in the blue jumper. "A fine thing if we'd missed our connection, what would Terry have said, turning up at Honolulu airport and us not there?"

"We nearly missed our flight from East Midlands this morning, the traffic was that bad on the Ring Road," said the lady in the yellow frock.

"Terry said he's bringing a very special friend, that he wants us to meet. I expect she'll be at the airport with him."

"Brian wouldn't have gone that way himself, but we took a taxi to save the expense of parking the car, it's shocking what they charge, isn't it?"

"He's doing ever so well at his photography, he works for all the top fashion magazines down under. I said to Sidney, I wouldn't be surprised if his girlfriend's a model."

"Brian's very interested in photography too, only as a hobby of course, he has a business to run."

"Business, eh?" said Sidney.

"Yeah. Sunbeds, rentals and sales," said Brian. "We were doing all right until about a year ago, but business hasn't been so good lately. I put it down to all these scaremongering articles about skin cancer. Written by thickheads who don't even know the difference between UVA and UVB."

"Er, what. . . ?"

"Ultraviolet A and Ultraviolet B. They're the two types of radiation that make you tan."

"Oh."

"UVA reacts with the melanin in the dead cells of your outer skin –"

"Dead cells?" said Sidney uneasily.

"Dead and dying," said Brian. "It goes on all the time. The UVA reacts with the melanin to make you brown. The UVB makes you burn. The sun gives out both types of radiation, but sunbeds are mostly UVA, so they're much better for you. Stands to reason."

"Use one yourself, do you?"

"Me? No, well, I'm allergic, see. It happens to about one in a thousand. For most people, though, they're safe as houses. I could let you have one cheap if you're interested."

"Me? Oh, no thanks. I got to be careful."

"To tell you the truth, I could let you have about a hundred and fifty of 'em cheap. We're thinking of moving into exercise machines instead."

The tram delivered the Travelwise party to Terminal Seven, and they were conveyed by more escalators and moving walkways to the lounge where they were to wait for their onward connection. The two middle-aged couples chattered indefatigably as they were borne along.

"Well it's time he got married, I was only saying to Sidney the other week, it's time Terry settled down, his life seems to be one long round of pleasure, parties, restaurants, surfing, it's all very well but you can wait too long to start a family. Have you got children?"

"Two boys. We've left them in charge of the house, with my mother. Well, you don't want kids with you on a second honeymoon, do you?"

"I've got a married daughter, she lives in Crawley, her husband's in computers. They've got a lovely house, a twenty-foot through living-room, and fitted kitchen in light oak. Sidney did the bathroom for them as a wedding present, circular bath, built-in jacuzzi, gold taps. He was in the trade you see."

"Builder, are you?" Brian asked.

"Was. Plumbing and central heating. Luxury bathrooms. Just me and three men. I had to sell the business."

"Do all right out of it?"

"Just about enough to retire on."

"You're not looking for a little investment opportunity?"

"No thanks."

"The thing about exercise machines is, they're boring. You ever tried one? Well, take my word for it, they're dead boring. That's why people wear Walkmans while they're using them. Now, my idea is, instead of buying say, a rowing machine, and all you do every day is row row row, or a cycle machine, and all you do is pedal pedal pedal, you take out a rental agreement with us and we change your machine every month. Like a travelling library. An exercise-machine library. What d'you think?"

"Wouldn't do for me, I'm afraid. Or, rather, it *would* do for me. Dicky heart, you see. I had to retire early, doctor's orders."

"But they're very good for the heart, exercise machines! Just what you need."

"What you going to do with the sunbeds, then?"

"Flog 'em for what I can get. I thought I'd try some of the hotels in Honolulu."

Sidney laughed uncertainly. "I wouldn't have thought there'd be much call for sunbeds in Hawaii."

"Don't suppose there is. But if I make a few business calls while I'm there, it means I can write the whole trip off against tax, see? Beryl being down as my personal assistant, of course."

"Oh, I see. Clever," said Sidney.

The other Travelwise passengers did not fraternize, but they congregated in the same part of the departure lounge, and kept a watchful eye on each other as a precaution against missing the call for their flight to Honolulu. The lounge overlooked a runway, and from its windows you could watch the planes coming in to land. Bernard gazed, fascinated, at the sky above the horizon. Every minute or so a dot appeared in the middle of this space, a tiny, glowing dot, like a star, and gradually increased in size, until it revealed itself to be a large jet plane, with its flaps down and its landing lights on. It slowly sank towards the ground, its wheels hit the runway with a puff of smoke, and seconds later it raced past, huge, heavy and dangerous, out of his vision; and Bernard looked again at the apparently blank sky until, sure enough, another dot appeared, like a small, glowing seed, and grew into another plane.

"Something interesting out there?"

Bernard turned to find the man in the beige safari suit standing beside him. "Just the planes coming in to land. Every minute or so, regular as clockwork. I suppose this must be one of the busiest airports in the world."

"No, not even in the top ten, actually."

"Really?"

"Chicago's O'Hare is the busiest in terms of traffic movements. Heathrow handles more international flights, and the most passengers."

"You seem to know a lot about it," said Bernard.

"Professional interest."

"You're in the travel business?"

"In a way. I'm an anthropologist, my field's tourism. I teach at South-West London Poly."

Bernard examined him with more interest. He had a bald, domed head, though he looked no more than thirty-five or six, and a heavy lower jaw, now covered with a harsh black stubble, like magnetized iron filings.

"Really?" said Bernard. "I'd no idea that tourism came into anthropology."

"Oh yes, it's a growth subject. We get lots of fee-paying students from overseas – that makes us popular with the admin boys. And there's bags of money available for research. Impact studies . . . Attractivity studies . . . Trad anthropologists look down their noses at us, of course, but they're just envious. When I was starting my PhD, my supervisor wanted me to study some obscure African tribe called the Oof. They have no future tense, apparently, and only wash at the summer and winter solstices."

"How very interesting," said Bernard.

"Yes, but nobody's going to give you a decent grant to study the Oof. And anyway, who'd want to spend two years in a mud hut surrounded by a lot of stinking savages who don't even have a word for 'tomorrow'? In my line of research I get to stay in three-star hotels, at least three-star . . . My name's Sheldrake, by the way, Roger Sheldrake. You may have come across a book of mine called *Sightseeing*. Surrey University Press."

"No, I haven't, I'm afraid."

"Ah. Only I gathered you're an academic yourself. I couldn't help hearing your father – is it? – on the plane . . ." Sheldrake jerked his formidable chin in the direction of Mr Walsh, who was slumped in a seat nearby with the numbed, haggard look of a refugee in a transit camp. "He said you were a theologian."

"Well, I teach in a theological college."

"You're not a believer?"

"No."

"Ideal," said Sheldrake. "I'm interested in religion myself, obliquely," said he. "The thesis of my book is that sightseeing is a substitute for religious ritual. The sightseeing tour as secular pilgrimage. Accumulation of grace by visiting the shrines of high culture. Souvenirs as relics. Guidebooks as devotional aids. You get the picture."

"Very interesting," said Bernard. "So this is a sort of busman's holiday?" He indicated the Travelwise label on Sheldrake's stainless-steel attaché case.

"Good Lord, no," said Sheldrake with a mirthless smile. "I never go on holiday. That's why I moved into this field in the first place. I always hated holidays, even as a kid. Such a waste of time, sitting on the beach, making sandpies, when you could be at home doing some interesting hobby. Then, when I got engaged, we were both students at the time, my fiancée insisted on dragging me off to Europe to see the sights: Paris, Venice, Florence, the usual things. Bored the pants off me, till one day, sitting on a lump of rock beside the Parthenon, watching the tourists milling about, clicking their cameras, talking to each other in umpteen different languages, it suddenly struck me: tourism is the new world religion. Catholics, Protestants, Hindus, Muslims, Buddhists, atheists – the one thing they have in common is they all believe in the importance of seeing the Parthenon. Or the Sistine Chapel, or the Eiffel Tower. I decided to make it my PhD subject. Never looked back. No, the Travelwise package is a

61

research grant in kind. The British Association of Travel Agents are paying for it. They think it's good PR to subsidize a bit of academic research now and again. Little do they know." He grinned mirthlessly again.

"What d'you mean?"

"I'm doing to tourism what Marx did to capitalism, what Freud did to family life. Deconstructing it. You see, I don't think people really want to go on holiday, any more than they really want to go to church. They've been brainwashed into thinking it will do them good, or make them happy. In fact surveys show that holidays cause incredible amounts of stress."

"These people look cheerful enough," said Bernard, gesturing at the passengers waiting to board the flight to Honolulu. There were now quite a lot of them, as the time of departure neared: mostly Americans, dressed in garish casual clothes, some in shorts and sandals as if ready to walk straight off the plane on to the beach. There was a rising babble of drawling, twanging accents, loud laughter, shouts and whoops.

"An artificial cheerfulness," said Sheldrake. "Fuelled by double martinis in many cases, I wouldn't be surprised. They know how people going on vacation are supposed to behave. They have learned how to do it. Look deep into their eyes and you will see anxiety and dread."

"Look deep into anybody's eyes, and that's what you will see. Look into mine," Bernard thought of saying; but instead he said: "So you're going to study sightseeing in Hawaii?"

"No, no, it's a different type of tourism. Sightseeing's not the real selling point of the long-haul beach holiday: Mauritius, the Seychelles, the Caribbean, Hawaii. Look at this –" He whipped out of his briefcase a holiday brochure, and held it up in front of Bernard, concealing with his hand the printed legend on the front cover. It featured a coloured photograph of a tropical beach – brilliantly blue sea and sky, blindingly white sand, with a couple of listless human figures in the middle distance reclining in the shade of a green palm tree. "What does that image say to you?"

"Your passport to paradise," said Bernard.

Sheldrake looked disconcerted. "You've seen it before," he said accusingly, removing his hand to reveal these very words.

"Yes. It's the Travelwise brochure," Bernard pointed out.

"Is it?" Sheldrake examined the brochure more closely. "So it is. Never mind, they're all the same, these brochures. I've got a bundle of them in here, same picture, same caption on every one, more or less. Paradise. It bears no resemblance to reality, of course."

"Doesn't it?"

"Six million people visited Hawaii last year. I don't imagine many of them found a beach as deserted as this one, do you? It's a myth. That's what my next book is going to be about, tourism and the myth of paradise. That's why I'm telling you all this. Thought you might give me some ideas."

"Me?"

"Well, it's religion again, isn't it?"

"I suppose it is . . . What exactly are you hoping to achieve with your research?"

"To save the world," Sheldrake replied solemnly.

"I beg your pardon?"

"Tourism is wearing out the planet." Sheldrake delved into his silvery attaché case again and brought out a sheaf of press-cuttings marked with yellow highlighter. He flipped through them. "The footpaths in the Lake District have become trenches. The frescoes in the Sistine Chapel are being damaged by the breath and body-heat of spectators. A hundred and eight people enter Notre Dame every minute: their feet are eroding the floor and the buses that bring them there are rotting the stonework with exhaust fumes. Pollution from cars queuing to get to Alpine ski resorts is killing the trees and causing avalanches and landslides. The Mediterranean is like a toilet without a chain: you have a one in six chance of getting an infection if you swim in it. In 1987 they had to close Venice one day because it was full. In 1963 forty-four people went down the Colorado river on a raft, now there are a thousand trips a day. In 1939 a million people travelled abroad; last year it was four hundred million. By the year two thousand there could be six hundred and fifty million international travellers, and five times

63

as many people travelling in their own countries. The mere consumption of energy entailed is stupendous."

"My goodness," said Bernard.

"The only way to put a stop to it, short of legislation, is to demonstrate to people that they aren't really enjoying themselves when they go on holiday, but engaging in a superstitious ritual. It's no coincidence that tourism arose just as religion went into decline. It's the new opium of the people, and must be exposed as such."

"Won't you do yourself out of a job, if you're successful?" said Bernard.

"I don't think there's any immediate risk of that," said Sheldrake, surveying the crowded lounge.

At that moment there was a stirring in the waiting area and a surge of passengers towards the gate, as a member of the airline ground staff was observed to pick up a microphone. "Ladies and gentlemen, we shall begin boarding with rows thirty-seven through forty-six," he announced.

"That's us," said Bernard. "I'd better get my father on his feet."

"I'm in row twenty-one," said Sheldrake, examining his boarding pass. "And it looks as if the plane will be full. Pity, I'd like to pick your brains. Perhaps we might get together in Honolulu. Where are you staying?"

"I don't know yet," said Bernard.

"I'm at the Wyatt Imperial. Best hotel in the Travelwise brochure. Thirty pounds a day supplement, or would be if I was paying for myself. Come and have a drink one day."

"That's very nice of you," said Bernard. "I'll have to see. I don't know how busy I'll be. I'm not on holiday either, you see."

"No, so I gathered," said Sheldrake, glancing at Mr Walsh.

4

All day they had been chasing the sun, but while they waited for their connection at Los Angeles it had got well ahead of them, and during the flight to Hawaii darkness overtook the plane. Bernard had a window seat, but could see from it only a black abyss. In the airline's complimentary magazine he found a route map which showed no trace of land between the West Coast of America and the Hawaiian islands, a distance of two and a half thousand miles. What if something went wrong with the aircraft? What if the engines suddenly stopped? It was a thought that didn't seem to be troubling anyone else aboard the plane. The stewardesses, wearing flowers in their hair and brightly coloured floral print sarongs, had been lavish with complimentary drinks before, during and after dinner, and there was a party mood in the cabin. The big American men sauntered up and down the aisles, plastic glasses clamped in their fists, as if they were in a pub or club: they leaned over the backs of seats to gossip, slapped each other's shoulders and guffawed heartily at each other's jokes. Bernard envied their confident demeanour. He always felt as if he should raise his hand and ask permission from the cabin crew to leave his seat. Seeing Roger Sheldrake coming down the aisle on the other side of the plane, he hid his face behind the magazine. He didn't feel ready for another seminar on tourism just yet, and he was anxious not to disturb his father, who was mercifully asleep. Bernard had forbidden him an aperitif, but had allowed him a quarter-bottle of Californian burgundy with his chicken teriyaki, and that had been enough to send him off.

The lights in the cabin were dimmed, and another film began. Bernard was sure he had seen more films in this one day than in the last three years. This time it was a romantic comedy in which two rich and beautiful people, who were obviously destined to fall in love with each other, managed, by dint of a series of improbable misunderstandings, to postpone that conclusion for an hour and forty minutes. This even Bernard recognized as a very old plot. What was novel to him, and slightly shocking, was that both hero and heroine were shown in bed with other lovers while the story unfolded: it had not been thus in the films at the Brickley fleapit. He watched the movie with mildly prurient curiosity, doubly glad that his father was asleep.

After it finished, he too dozed for a while, until awakened by a change in the note of the engines and a sinking sensation. They had begun their descent. Outside and below, the darkness was still total; but after some little while the plane changed course and tilted, he looked out of the window, and there, miraculously, was a shape like a many-stranded necklace of light thrown down on the black velvet of the ocean. He shook his father's shoulder.

"Daddy, wake up! We're nearly there."

The old man groaned and awoke, licking his lips and rubbing his red-rimmed eyes.

"You must see this. It's amazing. Change places with me."

"No thankyou, I'll take your word for it."

Bernard stared, fascinated, out of the porthole, pressing his nose to the glass and cupping his face to screen out the cabin lights, as the plane sank towards what must be Honolulu. As they dropped through the sky, the shimmering strands of light defined themselves as tower blocks, streets, houses, and moving vehicles. How astonishing it was, to discover this brilliantly illuminated modern city, pulsing like a star in the black immensity of the ocean. And how miraculous, really, that their aircraft had felt its way unerringly across the thousands of miles of dark water to this haven of light. There was something mythical about it – the night sea journey – though the other passengers stretching and yawning around him seemed to take it all for granted. The plane dipped and banked again, and the "FASTEN SEATBELTS" signs flashed red.

The night air at Honolulu airport was like nothing Bernard had experienced before, warm and velvety, almost palpable. To feel it on your face was like being licked by a large friendly dog, whose breath smelled of frangipani with a hint of petrol, and you felt it almost instantly on arrival, because the walkways – stuffy glazed corridors in most airports, mere extensions of the claustrophobic aircraft cabin – were here open at their sides to the air. He and his father were soon sweating again in their thick English clothes, but a light breeze fanned their cheeks and rustled in the floodlit palm trees. A kind of tropical garden had been laid out next to the terminal building, with artificial ponds and streams, and naked torches burning amid the foliage. It was this spectacle which seemed to convince Mr Walsh that they had finally arrived at their destination. He stopped and gawped. "Look at that," he said. "Jungle."

As they waited beside a carousel in the Arrivals hall, a beautiful brown-skinned young woman in the Travelwise livery came up to them, smiled brilliantly and said, "*Aloha!* Welcome to Hawaii! My name's Linda and I'm your airport facilitator."

"Hallo," said Bernard. "My name's Walsh and this is my father."

"Right," said Linda, ticking off their names on her clipboard. "Mr Bernard Walsh and Mr John Walsh." She gave them the quick, quizzical appraisal to which Bernard was getting accustomed. "There's no Mrs Walsh?"

"No," said Bernard.

"Okay," said Linda. "When you two gentlemen have collected your bags, will you gather with the rest of the group, please, over by the Information Desk, for the lay greeting."

That was what it sounded like to Bernard. He experienced a sudden spasm of foolish dread, that some garbled version of his personal history had preceded him to Hawaii, and that a committee of parochial worthies had been organized to welcome him, or embarrass him. "Lay greeting?"

"That's correct, it's inclusive. You're staying at the Waikiki Surfrider, right?"

"Yes," said Bernard, who had decided that it was too late, and they were both too tired, to try and locate Ursula's apartment tonight.

"There's a bus waiting outside the terminal to take everybody to their hotels," said Linda, "right after the lay greeting."

While they were waiting for the carousel to deliver their suitcases, Bernard investigated his Travelpak, and found in it two vouchers, each for "One *lei* value US $15.00." It didn't take him long to work out that *lei* was pronounced "lay", and was a garland of flower heads threaded on a string. In the crowded concourse many newly arrived passengers were having these objects flung over their shoulders by friends and professional greeters, with acompanying cries of "*Aloha!*" He passed Sidney the heartcase and his wife Lilian in the act of being thus festooned by two smiling young men with close-cropped hair and neat, furry moustaches. "You shouldn't have, Terry, we get them free, they come with the holiday," Lilian was saying to one of the young men, who replied, "Never mind, Mum, you can have two. I want you to meet my friend, Tony." "Pleased to meet you," said Lilian. She smiled with her false teeth, but her eyes looked anxious.

The other Travelwise passengers gathered dutifully near the Information desk, as instructed. Nearby was a metal rack displaying free newspapers and tourist brochures. The title of one of these publications, *Paradise News*, caught Bernard's eye, and he picked up a copy. Its contents were something of an anticlimax, consisting almost entirely of advertisements, with specimen menus, for various quaintly named local restaurants – the El Cid Canteen, The Great Wok of China, The Godmother, The Shore Bird Beach Broiler, It's Greek To Me. A small advertisement in the bottom right-hand corner of the front page struck a different and less cheery note: "*How to Survive the Break-Up of a Relationship.* Read this book. It will help you stop feeling guilty. It will restore your confidence. It will help you get on with your life." Bernard surreptitiously tore the panel from the newspaper and slipped it into his breast pocket.

"Found something interesting?"

Bernard looked up to see Roger Sheldrake eyeing him.

"It might interest you," said Bernard, indicating the masthead of the newspaper.

"*Paradise News!* Magic! Where did you get it?" Sheldrake hastened over to the rack and helped himself greedily to the free literature.

Linda the facilitator now reappeared, carrying a large cardboard box full of *leis*, which she began to distribute to the passengers in exchange for the vouchers in their Travelpaks. When she came to Cecily and her husband, she said, "You're the honeymoon couple, aren't you? Did you order the Hawaiian Wedding Song?" "No we didn't," said Cecily, quickly. The other members of the party looked with new interest at the young couple. Beryl Everthorpe said, "Fancy that, and us on our second honeymoon," and Lilian Brooks said, "I thought there was something about them," and the girl in the pink and blue tracksuit said, "What a romantic idea for a honeymoon, I must suggest it to Des," and Dee said, "If you ever get a honeymoon, it'll be in a tent halfway up Ben Nevis."

Just before Linda reached Bernard, he was lassooed from behind by a garland of moist, sweet-smelling white blossoms. Startled, he turned to confront a small, brown, wrinkled, elderly lady with pink-rinsed grey hair, wearing a long, loose flowing gown, like a toga, printed with large pink flowers. Her fingertips and toes gleamed with nail polish of the same hue.

"*Aloha!*" she said. "You *are* Ursula's nephew, aren't you?" Bernard admitted that he was. "I knew it, as soon as I set eyes on you, you have her nose. I'm Sophie Knoepflmacher, I live in the same apartment block as Ursula. And this must be her brother, Jack. *Aloha!*" She tossed a second *lei* over the head and shoulders of Mr Walsh, who recoiled a half-step in alarm. "I guess you know what *aloha* means, don't you?"

"Hallo, I presume," Bernard ventured.

"Right. Or goodbye, according to whether you're coming or going." The little lady gave a brief cackling laugh. "Also, I love you."

"Hallo, goodbye, I love you?"

"It's like an all-purpose word. Ursula asked me to give you the keys to her apartment, so I thought I'd better meet you."

"That's very kind of you," said Bernard. "Actually, we have got a hotel room booked . . ."

"Where?"

"The Waikiki Surfrider."

"You'll be more comfortable at Ursula's place. More space. Your own living-room and kitchen."

"Well, all right," said Bernard. Since Mrs Knoepflmacher had taken the trouble to meet them, it seemed the sensible, and the courteous, thing to do.

"Let's go, then. I have my car in the lot outside. You guys must be exhausted, huh?" She addressed the question particularly to Mr Walsh.

"I was exhausted in Los Angeles," said Mr Walsh. "I don't know the word for what I am now."

"It was his first flight," Bernard said.

"No! You're kidding! Well, I think you're just wonderful, Mr Walsh, to come all this way to see your poor sister."

Mr Walsh received this tribute as if it were only his due, but was perceptibly gratified. Bernard explained to Linda that they wouldn't be needing transport, or any more *leis*, and they set off in single file, Mrs Knoepflmacher leading Mr Walsh and Bernard bringing up the rear with a baggage trolley. Mrs Knoepflmacher left them standing on the pavement outside the terminal while she went off to fetch the car, her pink robe rippling in the breeze.

"Nice of her to meet us," said Bernard.

"What's this her name is?"

"Knoepflmacher. I think it means button-maker in German."

"Is she German, then? She doesn't sound it."

"Her family would have been, originally, or her husband's. German Jews, I would guess."

"Oh." It had been a mistake to mention this. There was a certain frigidity in Mr Walsh's voice. "Can I take this thing off?" he said, plucking at his *lei*.

"I don't think so, not yet. It might seem rude."

"I feel like a bloomin' Christmas tree, standing here."

"It's the custom of the country."

"And a daft one, too, if you ask me."

Roger Sheldrake, with a garland of yellow blossoms round his neck like a Lord Mayor's chain, came by, preceded by a man in a peaked cap carrying his luggage. He stopped and turned back to speak to Bernard.

"The Wyatt have sent a stretch limo for me," he said, pointing to a strangely distorted vehicle parked at the kerb, extraordinarily long and low-slung, like something seen in a fairground mirror. "Jolly nice of them. Can I give you a lift?"

"No thanks. Somebody is picking us up," said Bernard.

"Well, see you around. Don't forget to give me a ring." The chauffeur was holding open the door of the limousine. Bernard glimpsed dove-grey carpet and leather upholstery inside, and what looked like a small bar.

Soon after this sumptuous vehicle had driven away, Mrs Knoepflmacher appeared, clinging to the wheel of a racy-looking white Toyota with retractable headlights. She was so small that she had to sit on the edge of the seat to reach the pedals.

"It's nice and cool in here," Bernard commented, when they were settled inside.

"Yeah, it's air-conditioned. Mr Knoepflmacher passed away the day he took delivery," said Mrs Knoepflmacher. "He drove it to Diamond Head and back, and he was so pleased with it, you wouldn't believe. He passed away in his sleep that very night. Brain haemorrhage."

"Oh, I'm sorry," said Bernard.

"Well, at least he died happy," said Mrs Knoepflmacher. "I keep the car as a kind of memento. I don't drive much, to tell you the truth. I can walk to most places I want to get to in Waikiki. What car do you drive, Bernard?" She pronounced his name in the French style, with the stress on the second syllable.

"I don't have one."

"Just like Ursula," said Mrs Knoepflmacher. "She never learned to drive, either. It must run in your family."

"I have a driving licence," said Bernard. "But I don't have a car at the moment. How is Ursula? Have you seen her recently?"

"Not since she left the hospital."

"Ursula has left the hospital?"

71

"Yeah, didn't you know? She's in some kind of private nursing home, out on the edge of the city. It's a temporary arrangement, she said. She didn't seem to want me to visit her. She's a very private lady, your aunt, you know, Bernard. She doesn't give much away. Not like me. Lou always used to say I talk too much."

"Have you got the address?"

"I've got the phone number."

"And how is she?"

"She's not too well, Bernard. Not too well. But it'll do her a world of good to see you two guys. How you doing back there, Mr Walsh?"

"All right, thanks," said Mr Walsh dourly from the back seat.

They were driving sedately along a broad, busy motorway, with the sea distantly visible to their right and steep hills or small mountains, dark humped shapes sprinkled with the lights of houses, to their left. Green exit signs flicked past with names on them that struck Bernard as quaintly genial, like streets in a children's storybook: Likelike Highway, Vineyard Boulevard, Punchbowl Street. Mrs Knoepflmacher pointed out the sky-scrapers of downtown Honolulu before taking a turnoff marked Punahou St. "Seeing as you're *malihinis*, I'll show you Kalakaua Avenue."

"What's a *malihini*?"

"First-time visitor to the islands. Kalakaua is the main drag of Waikiki. Some people think it's gotten tacky, but I think it's still kinda fun."

Bernard asked her how long she had lived in Hawaii.

"Nine years. Lou and I came on a vacation about twenty years ago, and Lou said to me, 'This is it, Sophie, this is paradise, this is where we're going to retire to.' So we did. Bought an apartment in Waikiki to spend our vacations in and rented it for the rest of the year. Then when Lou retired – he was in the kosher meat business, in Chicago – we moved out here."

"And you like it?"

"Love it. Well, I did while Lou was alive. Now I'm kinda lonely sometimes. My daughter says I should move back to

72

Chicago. But can you imagine facing a midwestern winter again, after this? All I need here is a *muu-muu*, the whole year round." She plucked at her flowing pink robe, and glanced at Bernard's tweed sports jacket and worsted trousers. "You and your father will have to get yourselves some Aloha shirts. That's what they call the Hawaiian shirts with the splashy colours and the jazzy patterns, that you wear outside your pants. This is Kalakaua."

They were driving slowly along a crowded thoroughfare, lined with brightly lit shops, restaurants, and vast hotels that towered out of sight. Though it was nearly ten o'clock at night, both pavements, or sidewalks, as Mrs Knoepflmacher called them, were thronged with people, most of them casually and scantily dressed, in shorts, sandals, tee-shirts. They were all shapes, sizes, ages, complexions, sauntering, staring, eating and drinking as they walked, some hand-in-hand or with their arms round one another. A melange of amplified music, traffic noise and human voices penetrated the car windows. It reminded Bernard of the crush around Victoria Station, except that everything looked much cleaner. There were even familiar names on the shopfronts – MacDonalds, Kentucky Fried Chicken, Woolworths – as well as more exotic ones: The Hula Hut, Crazy Shirts, Take Out Sushi, Paradise Express, and signs that he couldn't decipher because they were in Japanese.

"Well? Whaddya make of it?" Mrs Knoepflmacher demanded.

"It's not quite what I imagined," said Bernard. "It's very built-up, isn't it? I had a mental picture of sand, and sea and palm trees."

"And hula girls, huh?" Mrs Knoepflmacher chuckled, and nudged Bernard with her elbow. "The beach is just back of those hotels," she said, waving to her right. "And the girls are inside, doing floor-shows. When we first came here, you could see the ocean between the hotels, but not any more. You wouldn't believe the construction that's gone on since then." She raised her voice and turned her head: "So, do you like it, then, Mr Walsh?"

But there was no reply. Mr Walsh had fallen asleep.

"Poor man, he's exhausted. Never mind, we're nearly there." She turned left off the dazzling thoroughfare, crossed another

73

main road and entered a quiet residential street at the end of which a dark canal glimmered. "This is it, one four four Kaolo Street." She steered the car down a ramp, into a basement car-park beneath the apartment block, and stopped rather abruptly.

Mr Walsh woke in a panic. "Where are we?" he cried. "I won't go in another aeroplane."

"It's all right, Daddy" said Bernard soothingly. "This is where Ursula lives. We've finally arrived."

"Aye, but will I ever get back home alive, that's what I'd like to know," said Mr Walsh piteously, as they eased him out of the back seat of the car.

Ursula's third-floor flat was small, neat and immaculately clean, decorated and furnished in a conventionally "pretty" style, with many knick-knacks and ornaments displayed on shelves and occasional tables. The air inside the living-room was hot and close, and Mrs Knoepflmacher immediately threw open a pair of long windows that gave access to a shallow balcony. "Most of the residents have had air-conditioning installed," she said. "But I guess Ursula thought it wasn't worth the expense, seeing as how she doesn't own the apartment."

This information was a surprise to Bernard.

"No, she rents. It's a shame. One of the big condo developers is interested in this site, and they're going to have to make a very good offer to buy us all out."

Bernard stepped out on to the balcony. "You mean they're going to knock down this perfectly good building and build another one? Whatever for?"

"Build higher, get more money out of the plot. This building is just four storeys. It's nearly twenty-five years old. Almost an ancient monument in Waikiki."

Bernard looked down onto a paved patio, with a bright blue oblong of water embedded in it. "Who does the swimming-pool belong to?"

"The apartment building. It's for the residents."

"Can I swim there?"

"Sure. Any time you like. Shall I show you the kitchen?"

Bernard left the balcony reluctantly. "This breeze is very pleasant."

"The trade winds. It's what keeps the islands cool. Nature's ceiling fan," said Mrs Knoepflmacher with a hoarse chuckle. "We really need the trades in the summer. You've come at the hottest time of the year."

Mrs Knoepflmacher demonstrated how the cooker worked, and the garbage disposal unit in the sink. "I put a few things in the icebox for you: milk, bread, butter, juice, just enough for your breakfast tomorrow. It came to three dollars fifty-five cents, but you can pay me any time. There's an ABC store at the corner of the next block, but you'll do better to stock up with basics at the Ala Moana shopping center, it's a lot cheaper. Here are the keys to the apartment, and here's the phone number of Ursula's nursing home. And this is her doctor at the hospital, if you want to call him. If there's anything else you need, I'm just down the hall, number thirty-seven."

"Thank you very much," said Bernard. "You've been most kind."

"You're welcome," said Mrs Knoepflmacher. Her eyes travelled round the living-room as if in search of something. Then she found it. "Those Dresden figurines are so cute, aren't they?" she said, going up to one of the glass-fronted cabinets. "If anything should happen to Ursula, and you have to dispose of her effects, I'd be glad to have first refusal."

Bernard was surprised, almost shocked by this remark, and it took him a few seconds before he could stammer out a vague reply. But after all, why should he be shocked, he reflected, as he showed her to the door. She was only being realistic. He returned to the living-room where his father was sitting, with his shoes and socks off, staring at his feet. They looked like beached crustaceans, horny and calloused and inflamed; a toe twitched occasionally as if of its own accord.

"Me feet were killin' me," he said.

He declined to take a bath or shower, so Bernard brought a bowl of lukewarm water from the kitchen for him to soak his feet in. The old man closed his eyes and sighed as he lowered them into the water.

"Is there any chance of a cup of tea?" he said. "I haven't tasted a decent drop of tea since we left England."

"Won't that mean you'll have to get up in the night?"

"Sure I'll have to get up anyway," said Mr Walsh. "It's only a matter of how soon and how often."

Bernard found some teabags – Lipton's English Breakfast – in the kitchen, and made a pot of tea. Mr Walsh sucked the brew down thirstily and sighed and wriggled his toes in the water. Bernard knelt to dab the feet dry with a towel. It reminded him of the Maundy Thursday mass of the Last Supper, especially at the parish church in Saddle, where he had often encountered battered, work-coarsened feet like these among the members of the congregation who volunteered to have their feet washed by the celebrant. At the seminary, the young men's feet were white and smooth, carefully pre-washed and pedicured for the occasion. He had an intuition, from his father's grave, thoughtful countenance, that the same association had occurred to him, but neither of them alluded to it.

There was only one bedroom, and one bed – big enough for both of them, but Bernard opted for the studio couch in the living-room, which opened out to make a comfortable spare bed. When his father had retired, he took a shower, left his soiled and sweaty clothing in a heap on the floor, and, not having brought a dressing-gown with him, slipped on a silky robe of Ursula's he found hanging on a hook behind the bathroom door. He thought he would sleep naked – the winceyette pyjamas he had packed would obviously be too warm – but he had an inhibition about walking around the apartment in the nude, even though he could hear his father breathing deeply in sleep. He himself felt strangely untired, perhaps stimulated by the tea, or the novelty of the environment.

He went out on to the balcony and leaned on the rail. There was now no perceptible difference between the air inside and outside the apartment. Although the trade winds were blowing quite strongly, whisking the palm trees to and fro, the air beat warmly against his face. Smudges of cloud raced across the sky, momentarily obscuring the stars, though you could easily imagine that there were no clouds, and that the stars themselves were moving, wheeling across the sky like a speeded-up version of the Ptolemaic spheres. He was filled with wonder at the mere fact of being here, on this tropical island, when only yesterday he had been in Rummidge, with its factories and workshops and arid streets of huddled terraced houses, everything worn and grimy under a low ceiling of grey cloud. He looked down at the swimming-pool, glamorous and seductive in the warm night. Tomorrow he would swim there.

As he levelled his gaze he became aware of two figures, a man and a woman, on the illuminated balcony of a neighbouring building. The man was wearing only boxer shorts, and held a tall glass in his hand; the woman was dressed in a Japanese-style kimono. They seemed to be amused by Bernard's appearance, giggling and pointing. It occurred to him that perhaps the floral patterned housecoat, with its padded shoulders and full skirt, *was* rather incongruous attire, especially with his beard. But their reaction seemed excessive. Perhaps they were drunk. He didn't know how to respond – whether to wave good-humouredly, or stare stonily. As he hesitated, the woman undid the belt of her robe and, with a theatrical gesture, flung it open. She was quite naked underneath. He could see the crescent shadows under her breasts and the dark triangle of her pubic hair. Then, with a final burst of laughter, they turned and went back into their room, drawing a curtain across the window. The light on the balcony went out.

Bernard remained at his station for some moments, leaning on the railing, as if to demonstrate his indifference to the couple's antics. But inwardly he was baffled and disturbed. What did the woman's gesture signify? Mockery? Insult? Invitation? It was almost as if she had had some telepathic knowledge of the sad scene in the Henfield Cross bedsit – Daphne, divested of her blouse and brassière, turning expectantly to face him – and was reminding him of the baggage of guilt and failure he had brought with him to Hawaii.

77

He returned to the living-room, shed Ursula's robe, and lay down on the sofa-bed, naked under a single sheet. In the distance he heard the whoop-whoop-whoop of a police siren. He pushed the image of the couple on the balcony from his mind by rehearsing what he would do next morning: first thing, after breakfast, he would phone Ursula and make arrangements to visit her. But before he got any further, he fell asleep.

5

After the accident Bernard spent many hours trying to reconstruct, in his head, how it had happened. They were crossing the road, he and his father, having just left the apartment – crossing at the wrong place, as the woman and the policemen and the ambulancemen all told him. Apparently you were supposed to cross the street only at intersections. But it was a quiet street, there hadn't been much traffic about, and they hadn't noticed that people weren't crossing the road wherever they pleased, as one did in England. It was their first morning in Honolulu – they were still jet-lagged, woozy from their long sleep. All the more reason why he should have been careful, of course. Ninety per cent of visitors' accidents, Sonia Mee told him in the emergency ward, happened in the first forty-eight hours after arrival.

He could only have taken his eyes off his father for a second, as they stood together on the kerb. He had looked left, and observed a small white car approaching, not very fast. His father must have looked right, as he was accustomed to do at home, seen an empty roadway, and stepped out in front of the car. As it passed Bernard heard a thud and a screech of tyres. He turned and looked incredulously at his father sprawled limp and motionless on the sidewalk, like a stricken scarecrow. Bernard knelt quickly beside him. "Daddy, are you all right?" he heard himself saying. The question sounded foolish, but what it meant was, *Daddy, are you alive?* His father groaned and whispered, "Didn't see it."

"Is he badly hurt?" A woman in a loose red dress stooped over them. Bernard connected her with the white car parked a few yards further up the street. "Are you with him?" she said.

"He's my father."

"What was the idea, trying to cross here?" she said. "I didn't have a chance, he just stepped right out in front of me."

"I know," said Bernard. "It wasn't your fault."

"Did you hear that?" said the woman to a man in running shorts and singlet, who had stopped to stare. "He said it wasn't my fault. You're a witness."

"I didn't see anything," said the man.

"Could I have your name and address anyway, sir?" said the woman.

"I don't want to get involved," said the man, backing away.

"Well, at least go call an ambulance!" said the woman.

"How?" said the man.

"Just find a phone and call 911," said the woman. "Jesus!"

"Can you turn over, Daddy?" Bernard said. Mr Walsh was lying face down with his cheek against the paving stone, and his eyes closed. He looked strangely like a man who was trying to get to sleep and didn't want to be disturbed, but Bernard felt a need to lift the face from its stony pillow. When Bernard tried to help him turn over on his back, however, he winced and groaned.

"Don't move him," said a woman with a tartan shopping trolley, from the small arc of spectators that had now formed around the scene of the accident. "Whatever you do, don't move him." Bernard obediently left his father in his prone position.

"Are you in pain, Daddy?"

"Bit of pain," the old man whispered.

"Where?"

"Down there."

"Where's that?"

There was no answer. Bernard looked up at the woman in the red dress. "Have you got something to put under his head?" he said. If he had been wearing a jacket himself, he could have folded it up to make a cushion, but he had come out in just a short-sleeved shirt.

"Sure." She disappeared, and returned quickly with a cardigan and an old rug with fine grains of sand sparkling in the weave. Bernard put the rolled-up cardigan under his father's head, and covered him with the rug, in spite of the heat, because he had a vague idea that that was what you did to people who had been knocked down. He tried not to think of the potentially awful consequences of what had happened, or the reproaches he would receive, and the guilt he would suffer, for having allowed it to happen. There would be time enough for hand-wringing later.

"You'll be all right, Daddy," he said, trying to sound cheerfully confident. "The ambulance is on its way."

"Don't want to go to hospital," Mr Walsh murmured. He had always had a dread of hospitals.

"You need a doctor to have a look at you," said Bernard. "Just to be on the safe side."

A police car cruising past on the other side of the street did a U-turn and drew up, its lights flashing. The spectators respectfully made way for two uniformed officers. Bernard was aware of their heavy, holstered revolvers at the level of his eyes. He looked up at two plump, brown, impassive faces.

"What happened?"

"My father's been knocked down."

One of the policemen knelt and felt Mr Walsh's pulse. "How ya doin', sir?"

"Want to go home," said Mr Walsh, without opening his eyes.

"Well, he's conscious," said the policeman. "That's something. Where's home?"

"England," said Bernard.

"That's a long way, sir," said the policeman to Mr Walsh. "Better take you to the hospital first." He turned to Bernard. "Somebody call an ambulance?"

"I believe so," said Bernard.

"I wouldn't count on it," said the woman in the red dress. "That wimp in the running shorts never came back."

"I did, too," said a voice from the back of the crowd. "The ambulance is coming."

"Who's the owner of the car?" said the second policeman.

"I am," said the woman in the red dress. "The old guy stepped right out in front of me. I didn't have a prayer."

The expression seemed to trigger a reaction in Mr Walsh, who began to mutter the Act of Contrition under his breath. *"Oh my*

God, I am heartily sorry for all my sins . . ." Kneeling beside him, Bernard felt his hand rising by conditioned reflex to perform the gesture of absolution, and, embarrassed, converted it into a soothing stroke of the old man's brow. "No need for that, Daddy," he said. "You're going to be all right." He turned to the policeman: "He looked the wrong way, I'm afraid. We drive on the left, you see, in England."

A man in a neat lightweight suit stepped forward and said to Bernard, "Take my advice – make no admissions." He took a card from his wallet and offered it to Bernard. "I'm a lawyer. Be glad to act for you on a contingency basis. No fee unless the suit is successful."

"Keep your nose out of this, mister," said the woman in the red dress, snatching the card and tearing it in half. "You people make me sick, you're like vultures."

"That's actionable," said the lawyer calmly.

"Take it easy, lady," said the policeman.

"Listen, I'm driving along the road, minding my own business, and suddenly this old man throws himself under my wheels, out of nowhere. Now I'm being threatened with a lawsuit. And you tell me to take it easy. Jesus!"

"Jesus mercy, Mary help," Mr Walsh muttered.

"Tell them," the woman appealed to Bernard. "You said it wasn't my fault, right?"

"Yes," said Bernard.

"My client is in shock," said the lawyer. "He doesn't know what he is saying."

"He's not your client, asshole," said the woman in the red dress.

"Where's this ambulance?" said Bernard. His voice sounded plaintive to his own ears. He envied the woman her anger and her expletives.

His sense of his own inadequacy did not diminish when the ambulance finally arrived. The paramedics (as he heard someone describe the ambulancemen) seemed admirably professional. They questioned Bernard briefly about the nature of the accident, and coaxed from Mr Walsh an admission that his pain was in the hip region. When the senior man asked Bernard which hospital he wanted his father to be taken to, Bernard suggested the Geyser, where Ursula had been treated, because it was the only one in Honolulu he knew of. The paramedic asked him if his father was covered by a Geyser plan.

"What's that?"

"Health plan."

"No, we're visitors. From England."

"Got medical insurance?"

"I think so." He had certainly paid for some kind of holiday insurance when he collected their tickets, on the advice of the young man in the Rummidge travel agency, but had been too rushed to examine the small print. The documents were in Ursula's apartment, and he could hardly leave his father lying in the gutter while he went to check. A new injection of anxiety and dread coursed through his veins and arteries. One had heard frightening stories about the mercenariness of American medicine, of patients being compelled to sign blank cheques even as they were wheeled to the operating theatre, and uninsured people being ruined by the cost of treatment, or denied treatment altogether because of their inability to pay. Perhaps he would have to pay for the ambulance on the spot, and he had very little cash on him.

Bernard and his father had in fact been on their way to the bank when the accident happened. He had telephoned Ursula as soon as they had breakfasted, and she told him that there were two-and-a-half thousand dollars waiting for him at her bank, to cover the cost of their fares (paid for out of Mr Walsh's savings) and their immediate living expenses. She had suggested that he used some of the money to rent a car – "This place is out in the boondocks, Bernard, you'll never get here by bus." He had set out to do this business, rather looking forward to getting behind the wheel of a car again, taking his father with him because the old man seemed unwilling to be left alone, and they had hardly walked a hundred yards, marvelling at the heat, but in their lightest clothes, feeling considerably more comfortable than the night before, when disaster struck.

"The Geyser's a long way out of town," said the senior paramedic, "if you don't *have* to go there. We could take you to the county hospital, downtown. Or there's St Joseph's, the Catholic hospital."

"Yes," said Mr Walsh in an audible whisper.

"Take him to St Joseph's," said Bernard. "We're Catholics." He used the the plural pronoun instinctively: it was no time to go into the niceties of religious belief and affiliation. If it would make his father feel any better to be treated in a Catholic hospital, he was ready to recite the Creed in public if necessary.

He heard the crackle of a radio telephone as one of the paramedics called up the hospital. "Yeah, we got an emergency here, old man been knocked down, he's in trauma but conscious. Can you take him? Hard to say, could be pelvis, ruptured spleen . . . No, they're visitors . . . the old guy's son is with him, he thinks they have insurance . . . requested a Catholic hospital . . . Right . . . No, no visible bleeding . . . OK . . . 'Bout fifteen minutes." The man turned to his colleague. "OK, we're in business. The doc said to give him an IV just in case there's internal bleeding. Let's get him onto the gurney."

With gentle, practised skill, they eased Mr Walsh onto a wheeled, collapsible stretcher, which they then slid into the back of the ambulance. An intravenous saline drip was attached to his arm from a bottle clipped to the inside wall of the vehicle. One of the men got out and looked enquiringly at Bernard. "You wanna ride with him?" Bernard jumped in and crouched beside the other paramedic. The woman in the red dress, who was being questioned by one of the policemen, broke away from him and came to the rear of the ambulance, just as the driver was about to close the doors. She was olive-skinned, black-haired, aged, he thought, about forty.

"I hope your father'll be OK."

"Thanks. I hope so too."

The driver closed the doors and took his place behind the wheel. The woman remained standing at the kerb, almost to attention, her arms at her sides, frowning thoughtfully at the back of the ambulance as it pulled smoothly away. They had exchanged names and addresses on the advice of the police. He took the piece of paper out from his breast pocket and read her name: Yolande Miller. The address meant nothing to him: something Heights. The ambulance, its siren wailing, turned a corner and she passed from view.

"Has your father got any allergies?" the paramedic asked Bernard. He was filling in a form as they drove.

"Not that I know of. How much does this ambulance cost, as a matter of interest?"

"There's a standard charge of a hundred and thirty dollars."

"I don't have that much money on me."

"Don't worry, you'll be billed."

The tinted windows of the ambulance turned the whole world blue, as if the vehicle were a submarine, and Waikiki built on the seabed. The palm trees waved to and fro like seaweed in the tide and shoals of tourists swam by, goggling and gaping. Traffic was heavy, and the ambulance was frequently forced to a halt, in spite of its wailing siren and flashing lights. At one such stop, Bernard found himself looking into the eyes of the sandy-haired adolescent girl from the Travelwise party, standing on the sidewalk just a few yards away, looking straight at him. He mustered a smile of greeting and a kind of shrugging wave, meant to communicate something like, Look-what-a-pickle-I'm-in-now, but she stared blankly back at him. He realized that, to her, the windows of the ambulance would be opaque, and felt slightly foolish. Then, to his astonishment, she suddenly pulled a gargoyle-like face of derision and contempt, crossing her eyes to an alarming degree and poking out her tongue. Then, as quickly as it had appeared – so quickly that he wondered if he had imagined it – the demonic expression was replaced by the child's usual impassive mask. The ambulance moved on and the girl passed out of his sight.

"Amanda! Don't dawdle!" The clipped, high-pitched male English voice causes several heads to turn on the busy pavement – though not, immediately, Amanda's own. To relieve her feelings, she scowls ferociously at the noisy ambulance, then, adjusting her features, turns and trots after her father.

"You'll get separated, if you're not careful," her mother scolds, as Amanda catches up with them. "Then we'd have to spend the rest of the day looking for you."

"I could find my way back to the hotel."

"Oh, could you, miss, I'm glad to hear it," says her mother sarcastically. "I'm not sure *I* could, we seem to have been walking for hours."

"Eleven minutes, actually," says Amanda's brother, Robert, consulting his digital watch.

"Well, it feels like hours, in this heat. I'd no idea we were going to be so far from the beach. To call that hotel the Hawaiian Beachcomber is downright deceitful."

"I'm going to complain," says Mr Best over his shoulder. "I'm going to write."

The sound of the ambulance siren recedes. *"Cross my fingers, cross my toes, Hope I don't go in one of those,"* Amanda chants under her breath, crossing her toes inside her sandals, as she lopes along, taking care at the same time not to tread on the cracks between the paving stones – anything to block out the all-too-familiar noise of adult whingeing. Are all grown-ups like this? She doesn't think so. It is not her impression that other girls spend their entire lives creased with embarrassment at the spectacle, or imminent threat, of their parents making themselves publicly disagreeable.

Russell Harvey, or "Russ", as he is known to his friends, and to colleagues on the trading floor of the investment bank where he works in the City of London, hears the distant sound of the ambulance siren from the balcony of his room on the 27th floor of the Waikiki Sheriden, where he is breakfasting alone. It looks as if he is going to be doing most things on his own this honeymoon, including sex. Cecily is still asleep, or pretending to be asleep, in one of the two double beds. Russ has just risen from the other one. Apparently every room in the hotel has two double beds, which is one too many from Russ's point of view. Cecily retired first last night, having prepared herself for sleep in the locked bathroom, and when he joined her between the sheets, she simply and silently moved across to the other bed. Russ did not pursue her,

86

having formed the impression that she was quite prepared to play musical beds as long as it was necessary. He feels hard done by. It isn't, of course, a matter of consummating the marriage, or slaking a long-repressed desire – he and Cess have, after all, been living with each other for nearly two years – but a man on his honeymoon is surely entitled to nookie on demand.

Russ stands up, leans on the balustrade and gazes gloomily along the curving palm-fringed shoreline towards a flat-topped mountain sticking out into the sea that the waiter who brought his breakfast told him was Diamond Head. He recognizes that the view is picturesque, but it does nothing to lift his spirits. The noise of the siren grows louder. He looks down at the street intersection below, where a huge five-petalled yellow flower has been painted on the road. They seem to be barmy about flowers round here. There were flower heads on their pillows last night, and another one floating in the toilet bowl, and there was even one on top of his cornflakes this morning, which he might easily have swallowed by accident.

The ambulance appears, crosses the five-petalled flower, and immediately becomes locked in traffic. Its siren noise changes from a wail into a kind of frantic yelping. Then the snagged traffic loosens, the ambulance wriggles through a gap, and away it goes. Russ wonders idly who is inside. Some aged tourist who has pegged out from heatstroke, perhaps (it is already hot as hell on this balcony); some randy second-honeymooner who slipped a disc in mid-fuck; some desperate, spurned lover who –

Russ suddenly has an idea. He stands on a chair at the open patio-style window, with arms extended, the morning sun throwing his crucified shadow into the room, gives a strangled cry, and jumps softly down sideways into the well of the balcony, crouching low beside the wall, out of sight from the bedroom. He squats there for a long minute or so, curled up into a ball, and feeling increasingly foolish. Then he peeps into the room. Cecily has not moved. Either she is really asleep or she saw through his ruse. Or she is an even colder-hearted bitch than he has reckoned with.

Sidney Brooks, standing on a balcony of the Hawaii Palace in his pyjamas, hears the sound of the ambulance, but only faintly, since the hotel is on the oceanfront and their room overlooks the beach (nothing but the best for Terry). Terry and Tony have a room just one level down and three along at a right-angle to their own, and last night they all waved goodnight to each other, but there is no sign of life from the other balcony yet this morning. The ambulance siren stops and then starts again. Sidney feels a faint cold qualm of fear, in spite of the hot sunshine beating on the balcony, remembering recent ambulance rides of his own. He draws some deep breaths, in and out, clasping his paunch before him like a medicine ball. "Lovely view, Lilian," he says over his shoulder. "You should come and take a look. Like a picture postcard. Palm trees, sand, sea. The lot."

"You know I can't take heights," she says. "You should be careful yourself. You'll have one of your dizzy spells."

"No I won't," he says, but comes back into the bedroom. Lilian is sitting up in bed, sipping the cup of tea he has made for her. There is an ingenious little water-heating gadget fixed to the wall of the bathroom, with teabags and sachets of instant coffee thoughtfully provided. Sidney spent quite a few minutes this morning inspecting the bathroom fittings with a professional eye, and was impressed.

"You never went out there like that?" says Lilian. "With all your belongings on show?"

Sidney feels below the overhang of his paunch and pulls the gaping fly of his pyjama trousers together. "Doesn't matter, there's nobody who could see. Terry and Tony don't seem to be up yet."

Lilian frowns into her cup. "What d'you make of it, then?"

"Make of what?"

"This Tony."

"Seems a nice chap. I didn't get much chance to talk to him."

"You don't think there's something funny? Two men on holiday together. At their age? Sharing a room?"

Sidney stares at her. He feels another cold qualm, and shivers. "I don't know what you're talking about," he says, and turns back to the balcony.

"Where are you going?"

"I don't want to talk about it," he says.

When the ambulance passes Brian and Beryl Everthorpe's hotel they are in the middle of shooting "*Waking Up In Waikiki – Day One*". Beryl has in fact been awake for over an hour, has washed and dressed and had her breakfast in the buffet restaurant on the ground floor, leaving Brian still asleep, but when she returned to their room he made her undress again, put on her nightie, and get back into bed. Now Brian is standing on the balcony with his camera focused on the pillow. On his cue Beryl is to sit up, open her eyes, yawn and stretch, get out of the bed, shrug on her negligée, and walk slowly out onto their balcony, where she is to gaze ecstatically at the view. The view is in fact of another hotel across the road, but Brian is confident that by leaning out over the balustrade as far as possible (with Beryl hanging onto his trouser-belt for safety) he can get a long shot of a bit of beach and a palm tree that can be spliced into the sequence at the appropriate point. "Action!" he shouts. Beryl wakes up, gets out of bed, walks towards the open sliding glass door, yawning convincingly, but just as she reaches the balcony the strident bleating of the ambulance's siren rises from the street below. "Cut! Cut!" cries Brian Everthorpe.

"What?" says Beryl, coming to a stop.

"This camera has a built-in mike," says Brian Everthorpe. "We don't want the sound of an ambulance on the sound-track, it would spoil the mood."

"Oh," says Beryl. "You mean I've got to do it all again?"

"Yes," says Brian. "Let's have more cleavage this time. And don't overdo the yawns."

Roger Sheldrake hears but is not distracted by the noise of the ambulance. He has been up for hours, out on the balcony of his room high up in the Wyatt Regency, with his notebook and binoculars and zoom-lens camera, hard at work, observing and recording and documenting ritual behaviour around the swimming-pool in the big hotel across the street. First, in the cool of the early morning, the preparation of the pool by the hotel staff: the hosing down of the poolside area, and the skimming of the water with a long-handled net to remove any debris; then the laying out of the moulded plastic loungers and the moulded plastic tables in neat rows; then the distribution of waterproof mattresses; then the stacking of clean towels at the poolside kiosk. At eight-thirty the first patrons arrived, and claimed their favourite spots. By now, eleven o'clock, nearly all the loungers are occupied, and waiters move between them, bearing drinks and snacks on trays.

The pool, as Roger Sheldrake knows from his researches, is not really designed for swimming. It is small, and irregularly shaped, discouraging the swimming of orderly lengths; in fact it is impossible to swim more than a few strokes without bumping into the sides of the pool or into another bather. The pool is really designed for sitting or lying round, and ordering drinks at. Since the patrons are deterred from swimming for long, they get extremely hot and thirsty, and order a lot of drinks, which come with complimentary salted nuts designed to make them even thirstier and therefore order more drinks. But the pool, however minimal, is a *sine qua non*, the heart of the ritual. Most of the sunbathers take at least a perfunctory dip. It is not so much swimming as immersion. A kind of baptism.

Roger Sheldrake makes a note. The noise of the ambulance fades away.

Sue Butterworth and Dee Ripley do not hear the noise of the ambulance or watch its progress. They are both still asleep, having woken in the middle of the night because of the time change, and drugged themselves with sleeping tablets, and in any case their twin-bedded room in the Waikiki Coconut Grove doesn't have a balcony from which they could have watched, being at the lower end of the Travelwise accommodation scale. A few minutes after the ambulance has passed, however, the telephone beside Dee's bed rings. Sleepily she gropes for the receiver, picks it up and croaks, "Hallo?"

"Aloha," says a lilting female voice. "This is your wake-up call. Have a nice day."

"What?" says Dee.

"Aloha. This is your wake-up call. Have a nice day."

"I didn't ask for a wake-up call," says Dee icily.

"Aloha. This is your wake-up call. Have a nice day."

"Don't you understand, you stupid cow!" Dee screams down the telephone. "I didn't ask for a bloody wake-up call!"

"Whatisit, Dee?" Sue murmurs from the other bed.

Dee holds the receiver away from her ear and stares at it with dawning understanding and impotent rage. The lilting voice carries faintly: "Aloha. This is your wake-up call. Have a nice day."

6

St Joseph's Hospital was a modestly-proportioned building, constructed of beige-coloured concrete and tinted glass, just off a leafy suburban road in the hills above Honolulu harbour. Silver oil storage tanks winked in the sun among warehouses and cranes on the flat industrial landscape far below. The Emergency Department had an air of calm, unostentatious efficiency that Bernard found reassuring. Mr Walsh was wheeled straight into what the staff referred to as the Trauma Room for examination and X-rays, and he himself was taken aside by an administrator, an oriental lady whose name, Sonia Mee, was pinned to her crisp white blouse. She sat him down at the desk, offered him coffee in a plastic beaker, and began to fill in (or, as she said, fill out) yet another form. When the question of insurance came up, Bernard confessed his uncertainty about their cover, but Sonia Mee told him not to worry, they would wait and see if his father needed to be admitted.

A few minutes later a young doctor in pale blue hospital overalls came into the office and reported that Mr Walsh would indeed have to be admitted to the hospital. He had a fractured pelvis. Apparently it could have been worse, and in a worse position. The treatment would probably be just bed-rest for two or three weeks, but a physician would have to be assigned to take responsibility for him. The hospital could contact an orthopaedic specialist on their list, unless Bernard had some other preference. He hadn't, but enquired anxiously about payment. "It would be a great help," said Sonia Mee, "if you could let us have the name of the insurance company at your earliest convenience." Bernard said he would fetch the policy immediately. "That's not necessary," she said. "Just call us with the details. And don't worry about your father in the meantime. At this hospital we believe in treating patients first." Bernard could have kissed her.

He went to the Trauma Room, where his father was still lying stretched out on the gurney, and gave him an account, as brief and reassuring as he could make it, of what was happening. The old man kept his eyes closed, and his mouth shut in a grim, downturned line, but he nodded once or twice and appeared to take in the information. A nurse informed Bernard that a bed was being prepared for him in the main hospital. Bernard said he would return later in the day, and left.

As he stood on the hospital steps, wondering how to get back to Waikiki, a cab drove up to deliver an out-patient, and Bernard hired it. Traffic was heavy on the freeway, and the driver threw up his hands in despair as the stream of vehicles slowed to a halt. "Gets worse all the time," he said. The phrase seemed applicable to Bernard's own situation. He had come to Hawaii to help his sick aunt, and so far all he had achieved was to get his father run over. He hadn't even seen Ursula yet – and by now she must be wondering what had happened to him. But paying off the cab in Kaolo Street with almost his last dollar reminded him that he had to go to the bank before he could see Ursula.

As he stepped out of the elevator on the third floor of the apartment building, Mrs Knoepflmacher was waiting to step in. She cast an inquisitive eye on his flustered, fatherless state, and hovered expectantly, but he did not stop to enlighten her, merely tossing a greeting over his shoulder as he hurried off. Inside the apartment, he went straight to his briefcase and took out the insurance policy. He felt his heartbeat quicken as he scanned the small print – but it was all right: it seemed that his father was covered for medical expenses up to a limit of a million pounds. Presumably not even an American hospital could charge more than that to cure a fractured pelvis. Bernard sank into a chair and blessed the young man in the Rummidge travel agency. He phoned Sonia Mee to give her the details of the policy, and promised to bring the document in with him later.

Then he phoned Ursula's nursing home to leave a message that he had been delayed. Then he went out to the bank.

It was mid-afternoon before he finally came face to face with Ursula. The "nursing home" turned out to be smallish private house, or rather bungalow, in a rather down-at-heel neighbourhood on the outskirts of Honolulu, not very far from St Joseph's, but closer to the the freeway. The street seemed deserted. The distant hum of traffic was the only audible sound in the sultry afternoon, as he parked his rented car and stood for a moment beside it, plucking at the fabric of his shirt and trousers where they had stuck to his shoulders and thighs with perspiration. The car was a biscuit-coloured Honda with 93,000 miles on the clock, plastic-covered seats and no air-conditioning – the cheapest he could get. There was no nameplate outside the house, just a street number hand-painted on a lop-sided mailbox nailed to a rotten post. The house was embedded in a tangle of trees and unkempt shrubbery, built up on brick piers, with three worn wooden steps leading up to the front porch. The front door was open, apart from a wire-mesh insect screen. Somewhere within, an infant was grizzling: the noise stopped abruptly as Bernard pushed the doorbell button and heard it peal at the back of the house. A thin, brown-skinned woman in a brightly coloured housecoat came to the door, and smiled obsequiously as she let him in.

"Mister Walsh? Your auntie been expecting you all day."

"You did give her my message?" Bernard asked anxiously.

"Sure thing."

"How is she?"

"Not well. She don't eat, your auntie. I cook good for her, but she don't eat nutting." The woman had a wheedling, slightly aggrieved tone. It was dark in the hallway, after the blinding sunlight outside, and Bernard lingered for a moment to let his eyes adjust. The figure of a small child aged two or three, wearing only a singlet, materialized in the gloom like a developing photograph. He sucked his thumb and stared up at Bernard with big white eyes. A trickle of snot ran from one nostril into the corner of his mouth.

"I don't suppose she has much of an appetite, Mrs, er. . . ?"

"Jones," said the woman surprisingly. "My name is Mrs Jones. You tell the hospital I cook good for your auntie, OK?"

"I'm sure you do your best, Mrs Jones," said Bernard. The phrase sounded stiff and mechanical to his own ears, but also familiar. If he closed his eyes he could have been back in his days of parish visiting, standing in the hallway of a terraced council house or semi-detached villa, waiting to be shown into the sickroom – except that the cooking smells were different here, sweet and spicy. "Can I see my aunt, please?"

"Sure thing."

He followed Mrs Jones and her child along the hallway, their bare feet slapping the polished wooden floor, wondering whether he should have taken off his own shoes inside the house. The woman knocked on a door and opened it without waiting for a response.

"Missis Riddell, here's your nephew from England come to see you."

Ursula was lying on a low truckle bed, covered by a single cotton sheet. One arm, encased in plaster and held in a sling, was outside the sheet. She raised her head from the pillow as he came into the room, and stretched out her good arm in greeting. "Bernard," she murmured hoarsely. "It's great to see you." He took her hand and kissed her on the cheek, and she sank back on to the pillow, still holding his hand tightly. "Thank you," she said. "Thank you for coming."

"Well, I'll leave you folks alone," said Mrs Jones, retiring and shutting the door behind her.

Bernard pulled a chair up to the side of the bed and sat down. He had ministered to several cancer patients in his time, but it was nevertheless a shock to see the pitifully thin limbs, the dull yellowish skin, the stark ridge of the collarbone under the thin cotton nightie. Only the eyes, bright blue like his father's, gleamed with undiminished life deep in their bruised sockets. He could hardly connect this wasted, white-haired old lady with the vivacious, buxom blonde in her polka-dotted dress who had descended upon his home in Brickley all those years ago,

95

scattering American candies and American vowels to an astonished and mildly scandalized household. But she was unmistakably his aunt. The Walsh head, high-browed, narrow, beaky, was all too recognizable – it was almost a skull. It was like a premonitory glimpse of what his father would look like on his deathbed – or he himself.

"Where's Jack?" said Ursula.

"I'm afraid Daddy's had an accident." Bernard was surprised by the keenness of his own disappointment as he made this admission, and realized that for the past week he had been entertaining a kind of sentimental fantasy, in which he presided proudly over a moving reunion of brother and sister, all tears and smiles and violin music. It was his own vanity, as well as his father's hip, that had been injured by the accident.

"Oh, God," said Ursula, when he had given her an account of the day's events. "This is terrible. He'll blame me for this."

"He'll blame me," said Bernard. "I blame myself."

"It wasn't your fault."

"I should have kept a closer eye on him."

"Jack always was a holy terror about crossing the road. Drove Mammy crazy when we were kids. You're sure the insurance will cover everything?"

"Apparently. Including the fares home – it looks as if we shall overrun our fortnight."

"That reminds me – did you get the money from my bank?"

"Yes." He patted the bulging wallet in the breast pocket of his shirt.

"My God, Bernard, you don't mean to say you're walking around with two-and-a-half thousand dollars in cash?"

"I came straight here from the bank."

"You might have been mugged. Waikiki's full of criminals these days. For heaven's sake, convert it into travellers cheques, or hide it in the apartment. There's a brown cookie jar in the kitchen cupboard that I use."

"All right. But what about you, Ursula? How are you?"

"I'm OK. Well, not too good, to tell you the truth."

"Are you in pain?"

"Not too bad. I have these pills."

"Mrs Jones says you don't eat much."

"I don't like the kind of food she cooks. She's from Fiji or the Philippines or one of those places, they have a different kind of diet from us."

"You must eat."

"I don't have any appetite. I've been constipated ever since I got here. I think it's the painkillers. And it's so darned hot." She flapped the sheet to fan herself. "The trades don't seem to find their way into this bit of Honolulu."

Bernard looked around the small, bare room. The blind on the window was broken and hung down lopsidedly over a view of the back yard, which seemed to be full of abandoned domestic appliances, refrigerators and washing machines, rusting and overgrown. There was a stain on one wall, where rainwater had penetrated and then dried. The wooden floor was dusty. "Is this the best place the hospital could find to put you in?"

"It was the cheapest. My health plan only covers hospitalization, not nursing care afterwards. I'm not a wealthy woman, Bernard."

"But doesn't your husband, your ex-husband . . ."

"Alimony doesn't go on for ever, you know. Anyway, Rick's dead. He died some years ago."

"I didn't know that."

"Nobody in the family knows it, because I didn't tell them. I've been living mainly on social security and it isn't easy. Honolulu has the highest cost of living in the States, you know. Nearly everything has to be imported. They call it the paradise tax."

"But you have some savings?"

"A little. Not as much as I should have. I made some bad investments in the seventies, lost a lot. Now I only have blue-chips, but they took a tumble in eighty-seven." She winced as if from a spasm of pain, and shifted her weight under the sheet.

"Does your specialist visit you here?" Bernard asked.

"The arrangement is that Mrs Jones calls him at the hospital if she thinks it is necessary. But they don't encourage it."

"Has he been here at all?"

97

"No."

"I'll get in touch with him. Mrs Knoepflmacher gave me his number."

Ursula pulled a face. "So you've met Sophie?"

"She seems very nice."

"She's nosy as hell. Don't tell her anything, or it'll be all round the apartment block before you can blink."

"She was very helpful when Daddy and I arrived. She met us at the airport."

"Poor Jack!" Ursula moaned. "It doesn't seem fair. You and Jack make all this effort, travelling halfway round the globe to see a poor sick old woman, and the first thing that happens is one of you gets run over. Why does God allow things like that to happen?"

Bernard was silent.

Ursula cocked a bright blue eye at him. "You do still believe in God, don't you, Bernard?"

"Not exactly," he said.

"Oh. I'm sorry to hear that." Ursula closed her eyes and looked despondent.

"You knew I'd left the Church, didn't you?"

"I knew you'd left the priesthood. I didn't know you'd given up the Faith altogether." She opened her eyes again. "There was a woman you wanted to marry, wasn't there?"

Bernard nodded.

"But it didn't work out?"

"No."

"And I guess they wouldn't let you back after that, would they? As a priest, I mean."

"I didn't want to go back, Ursula. I hadn't had any real faith for years. I'd just been going through the motions, too timid to do anything about it. Daphne was just . . . a catalyst."

"What's that? It sounds like something nasty they do to you in hospital when you can't pass water."

"That's a catheter, I think," Bernard said with a smile. "A catalyst is a chemical term. It's –"

"Don't tell me, Bernard. I can die not knowing what a catalyst

98

is. We have more important things to talk about. I was hoping that you could answer some of my questions about the Faith. There are things I still find difficult to believe."

"I'm afraid I'm the wrong person to ask, Ursula. I'm afraid I'm a great disappointment to you in every way."

"No, no, it's a great comfort to have you here."

"Is there anything else you'd like to talk about?"

Ursula sighed. "Well, there are all kinds of decisions to be made. Such as whether to give up the apartment."

"Perhaps that would be sensible," said Bernard. "If . . ."

"If I'm never going back to it?" Ursula completed the thought for him. "But what will I do with all my stuff? Store it? Too expensive. Sell it? I hate the thought of the likes of Sophie Knoepflmacher picking over my belongings. And where do I go? I can't stay here indefinitely."

"A proper nursing home, perhaps."

"Have you any idea what those places cost?"

"No, but I could find out."

"They're astronomical."

"Look, Ursula," said Bernard, "let's be practical. You've got a certain number of realizable assets, on top of your pension. Let's work out what it all amounts to."

"You mean if I sold my stocks? And lived on the capital? Oh no, I wouldn't want to do that," said Ursula, shaking her head vehemently. "What would happen if the money ran out before I die?"

"We'd try and guard against that," said Bernard.

"I tell you what would happen. I'd end up in a State home. I visited somebody in one of those places once. Way out in the country. Low class of people. Some of them were crazy. And it smelled like some of them were incontinent. All sitting in a great big room, round the walls." She shuddered. "I'd die in a place like that."

The word "die" hung mockingly in the humid air.

"Look at it from another point of view, Ursula," Bernard said. "What's the point in *not* spending your savings? Why not make the rest of your life as comfortable as possible?"

99

"I don't want to die a pauper. I want to leave something to somebody. You, for instance."

"Don't be ridiculous. I don't need your money."

"That wasn't the impression you gave me on the phone last week."

"I don't need it, and I don't want it." He added a fib: "Neither does anyone else."

"If I don't leave a will, I'll be forgotten, I'll leave no trace. I have no child. I've done nothing with my life. What could they put on my tombstone? 'She played a mean game of bridge.' 'At 69 she could still swim a half a mile.' 'Her chocolate fudge was very popular.' That's about it." Ursula fumbled in a box of paper tissues at her bedside, and wiped her eyes.

"*I* won't forget you," Bernard said gently. "I'll never forget the time you visited us at home, in London, when I was a boy, in your red and white dress."

"Hey, I remember that dress! It was white, with red polka dots, right? Fancy your remembering." Ursula smiled reminiscently, pleased.

Bernard glanced at his watch. "I'd better go now. I have to call back at the hospital to see how Daddy's getting on. I'll come back tomorrow." He kissed her bony cheek and left.

Mrs Jones ambushed him in the dark hallway. "Your auntie OK?"

"Well, she's badly constipated."

"That's because she don't eat."

"I'm going to talk to her doctor."

"You tell him I cook good for your auntie, OK?"

"Yes, Mrs Jones," said Bernard patiently, and let himself out.

He had left the car parked in the sun, and the heat inside took his breath away. The plastic-covered seat seared the backs of his thighs through his trousers and the steering wheel was almost too hot to hold. But he was glad to be out of the dark airless house and Ursula's bleak sick-room. He remembered the feeling well from parochial visiting – the selfish but irrepressible lift of the spirits as the front door of the afflicted house closed behind you, the animal satisfaction of being healthy and mobile rather than ill and bedridden.

He put the gear lever into Drive and turned the ignition key. Nothing happened, and several anxious and perspiring moments passed before he discovered that the engine would only start in the Park position. It had been running when he took over the vehicle that morning outside the car-hire firm's premises. He had never driven an automatic car before, and his journey to Mrs Jones's house had been a somewhat nervewracking experience. When accelerating, his left foot had a tendency to depress the brake pedal as if it were a clutch, in preparation for the next gear change, causing the car to screech to an emergency stop, and provoking indignant hornblasts from drivers following close behind. The best way to avoid this, he worked out, was to tuck his left foot under the driver's seat, even though it required him to adopt a rather crippled sitting posture. He adopted it now, as he transferred his right foot from the brake to the accelerator, and the car glided away from the kerb. His lips twitched with an irrepressible grin of childish glee. He had always enjoyed driving, and the magical effortlessness of the automatic gearbox enhanced the pleasure. He wound the window down to let the breeze cool the car's interior.

At St Joseph's, Sonia Mee took Bernard's insurance policy and seemed satisfied with what she read in it. She told Bernard that his father had been transferred to the main hospital, and he found him behind a screen in a two-bed room, asleep, under sedation. The saline drip had been removed from his arm, and he was breathing peacefully. He was wearing a hospital nightshirt. The sister in charge told Bernard what he should bring in the next day by way of clothing and toilet requisites. Recalling the aged pyjamas his father had worn to bed the previous night, faded and clumsily darned, with two buttons missing, Bernard privately resolved to buy him a couple of new pairs on the way home.

The receptionist in the lobby recommended a department store called Penney's and gave him directions to the Ala Moana Shopping Center, a vast complex built over an even vaster car-park, where he wandered, quite lost, for some thirty minutes, among fountains and foliage and glittering musical boutiques that sold everything except men's pyjamas, until he stumbled upon Penney's at the top of an escalator, and made his purchases. He bought himself some lightweight clothing while he was about it: a couple of short-sleeved shirts, khaki shorts, and a pair of cotton trousers. The sales assistant stared as he peeled two hundred-dollar bills off the wad inside his wallet. As soon as he got back to the apartment, he hid most of the money in the cookie jar described by Ursula. He telephoned the Geyser Hospital and made an appointment to speak to Ursula's specialist the next morning. He sat down in an armchair and started to make a list of other things that he had to do – calculate the value of Ursula's assets, inquire about nursing homes – but was suddenly overcome with fatigue. He closed his eyes for a moment and fell instantly asleep.

He was woken by the sound of the telephone ringing. It was eight o'clock, and nearly dark outside: he had been asleep for over an hour.

"Hallo, this is Yolande Miller," said a female voice.

"Who?"

"The accident this morning? I was the driver of the car."

"Oh, yes, sorry, I wasn't thinking straight." He stifled a yawn.

"I just wanted to know how your father's doing."

Bernard gave a her brief résumé.

"Well, I'm glad it's no worse," said Yolande Miller, "but I guess it's ruined your vacation."

"We're not here on vacation," said Bernard, and explained why they had come to Hawaii.

"That's too bad. So your father hasn't even seen his sister yet?"

"No, they're both confined to bed. Only a few miles apart, but it might as well be a thousand. I suppose they'll manage to meet eventually, but it's a bit of a mess."

"You mustn't blame yourself," said Yolande Miller.

"What?" Bernard wasn't sure that he had heard correctly.

"I get the impression that you're blaming yourself for what happened."

"Well, of course I blame myself," he burst out. "This whole

expedition was my idea. Well, not exactly my idea, but I arranged it, I encouraged my father to come. He would never have had the accident if I hadn't brought him here. Instead of being in pain, in hospital, in a foreign country, he would be safe and sound in his own home. Of course I blame myself."

"I could do that. I could say to myself, '*Yolande, you should have guessed the old man was going to step off the pavment, you should never have gone into Waikiki to shop anyway*' – hardly ever do, actually, but I saw an ad in the paper about a sportswear sale . . . I could say all that. But it wouldn't make any difference. These things happen. You have to put them behind you and carry on. You're probably thinking this is none of my business."

"No, no," said Bernard, though the thought had not been far from his mind.

"But I'm a personal counsellor, you see. It's a reflex response."

"Well, thank you for your counsel. I'm sure it's very sensible."

"You're welcome. I hope your father is better soon."

Bernard put down the phone and addressed a surprised "Hmmph!" to the empty room. He discovered, however, that he was more amused than offended by Yolande Miller's presumptuousness. He also felt suddenly ravenously hungry, and realized that he hadn't eaten all day. There was nothing in the fridge-freezer except what Mrs Knoepflmacher had provided for their breakfast, and some packets of frozen vegetables and ice cream. He decided to go out and find a restaurant. At that moment the front doorbell rang. Mrs Knoepflmacher stood on the threshold with a plastic carton in her hand.

"I thought your father might like some home-made chicken soup," she said.

"That's very kind of you," said Bernard, "but I'm afraid my father's in hospital."

He invited her in and gave her a brief account of the accident. Mrs Knoepflmacher listened, enthralled and appalled. "If you need a good lawyer," she said when he had concluded, "I can recommend one. You're going to sue the driver, of course?"

"Oh, no, it was our fault entirely."

"Never say that," said Mrs Knoepflmacher. "It's all insurance money, anyway."

"Well, I have a lot of more important things to think about," said Bernard. "Like my aunt."

"How is she?"

"So-so. I'm not too impressed by the place she's in."

Sophie Knoepflmacher nodded sagely as he described Mrs Jones's establishment. "I know the kind of place. They call it a care home. They're not properly qualified, you know, the women who run those places. They're not proper nurses."

"That was my impression."

"God preserve me from ending my days in one of those places," said Mrs Knoepflmacher, raising her eyes piously to the ceiling. "Fortunately Mr Knoepflmacher left me very well provided for. Maybe you'd like the soup for yourself?"

Bernard took it from her hands, thanked her, and put it in the refrigerator. His hunger demanded more than soup.

He found a restaurant on Kalakaua Avenue called Paradise Pasta which looked inexpensive and reasonably inviting. The waitress, whose name, Darlette, was displayed on a badge pinned to the front of her apron, put a jug of iced water on the table and said brightly, "How are you this evening, sir?"

"Oh, bearing up," said Bernard, wondering if the stress of the day's events had marked him so obviously that even total strangers were concerned for his wellbeing. But he inferred from Darlette's puzzled expression that her enquiry had been entirely phatic. "Fine, thank you," he said, and her countenance cleared.

"Tonight we have a special?" she said.

"I don't know, I'm sure," said Bernard, examining the menu. But apparently the girl's rising intonation did not signify a question, for she proceeded to tell him what the special was: spinach lasagna. He ordered spaghetti Bolognese and salad, and a glass of the house red.

Very soon Darlette set before him an enormous bowl of salad and said, "There you go!"

"Where?" Bernard asked, thinking that perhaps he had to

collect his spaghetti himself, but it seemed that this was a phatic utterance too, and that he was expected to eat all the salad before they would bring him the spaghetti. He munched his way obediently through the heap of crisp and colourful but rather tasteless raw vegetables until his jaw ached with the effort. But the pasta, when it came, was appetizing, and the portion generous. Bernard ate greedily, and ordered a second glass of Californian Zinfandel.

Was it the wine that made him feel less oppressed with guilt and dread than he had been all day, ever since the accident? Perhaps, but it had also been, in an odd and unexpected way, a relief to talk to Yolande Miller on the phone. He felt as if he had confessed, and received absolution. Perhaps counsellors would be the priests of the secular future. Perhaps they already were. Bernard wondered idly in what kind of context she practised her vocation. Yolande Miller. An oxymoron of a name, yoking together the exotic and the banal. He found he had a vivid memory of his last glimpse of her, standing almost to attention in her loose red dress, her brown arms at her sides, black glossy hair falling to her shoulders, frowning thoughtfully as the ambulance pulled away. An olive complexion, with high cheekbones and a deep upper lip. Not a beautiful face, but a strong one.

He paid his bill, left the restaurant, and strolled along Kalakaua Avenue. The night was warm and humid, the sidewalk crowded. It was the same crowd that he had observed the night before from Sophie Knoepflmacher's car (had he been in Waikiki only twenty-four hours? It seemed like a lifetime): a relaxed, sauntering, window-browsing, ice-cream-licking, straw-sucking crowd, most of them lightly and casually dressed in boldly patterned shirts and lettered tee-shirts. Many people had shaped and zippered nylon pouches belted round their stomachs, giving them a faintly marsupial appearance. Popular music poured out of shopping malls and from a brightly lit bazaar called the International Market Place, crammed with cheap jewellery and dubious folk art. The isle was full of noises. Not exactly sweet airs, but

Sometimes a thousand twangling instruments

105

seemed appropriate enough to the ubiquitous whine of Hawaiian guitars.

He paused outside the entrance to a huge hotel, from which amplified music with a loud percussive beat was spilling out into the street. Inside the gates, beside an oval swimming-pool, there was a large open space with tables and chairs set out under coloured lights, like a café-terrace in an Impressionist painting, facing a stage on which two female dancers were performing to the music of a three-piece band. Somebody seemed to be waving eagerly to him from one of the tables. It was the girl in the pink and blue tracksuit, though this evening she was wearing, like her companion, a smart cotton dress.

"Hallo, sit down and have a drink," she said, as he hesitantly approached their table. "You remember us, don't you? I'm Sue and this is Dee." Dee acknowledged his arrival with a thin smile and a slight inclination of her head.

"Well, perhaps a cup of coffee," he said. "Thank you."

"I don't think we know your name," said Sue.

"Bernard. Bernard Walsh. Are you staying at this hotel?"

"Lord, no, it's too pricey for us. But anybody can sit here, as long as you have a drink. We've had two of these each, already," she giggled, indicating a tall glass on the table before her, in which lumps of tropical fruit were submerged in a fizzy pink liquid, with two drinking-straws and a miniature plastic umbrella sticking out of the top. "It's called a Hawaiian Sunrise. Delicious, aren't they, Dee?"

"They're all right," said Dee, without taking her eyes off the stage. Two bosomy blondes in brassières and skirts made of what looked like shiny blue plastic ribbon were gyrating to a kind of Hawaiian rock music. Their fixed, enamelled smiles raked the audience like searchlights.

"Hula hula," Sue observed.

"It doesn't look very authentic," said Bernard.

"It's rubbish," said Dee. "I've seen more authentic hula dancing at the London Palladium."

"Wait," said Sue, "wait till we go to the Polynesian Cultural Center. Don't you know about it?" she said to Bernard when his expression showed curiosity. "You've got a voucher for it in your Travelpak. Polynesian arts and crafts, canoe rides, native dancing. It's like a sort of Disneyland, I think. Well not Disneyland, exactly," she qualified, as if dimly aware that this description did not instantly evoke ethnic authenticity. "But it's in a kind of park, on the other side of the island. You go on a bus. You should take your Dad, he'd enjoy it. We were thinking of going on Monday, weren't we, Dee?"

"I'm afraid my father won't be going anywhere for a while," said Bernard, and told his sorry tale again. He was beginning to feel like the Ancient Mariner. Sue gave little sympathetic cries of pain and dismay as he described the accident and its aftermath: she drew in her breath sharply at the moment of impact, winced as Bernard tried to turn his father over on the pavement, and sighed with relief when the ambulance arrived. Even Dee did not bother to disguise her interest in the story. "Something like that always happens on holiday," she said darkly. "I always do something, twist my ankle, or get a strep throat, or chip a tooth."

"No you don't, Dee," said Sue. "Not always."

"Well if I don't, you do," said Dee. "Look at last year."

Sue acknowledged the truth of this riposte with a rueful smile. "Last year I got some kind of eye infection, swimming in the sea at Rimini. It made me cry all the time, didn't it, Dee? Dee said it put the men off, me sitting there every night in the hotel bar with tears pouring down my cheeks." She giggled reminiscently.

"I'm going back to the hotel," said Dee, standing up abruptly.

"Oh Dee, not yet!" Sue wailed. "You haven't finished your Hawaiian Sunrise. Neither have I."

"You don't have to come."

Bernard stood up. "Are you sure you should walk around here on your own at night?"

"I'll be quite all right, thankyou," said Dee.

At that moment the waiter came up with Bernard's coffee, and demanded immediate payment. When this business was completed, Dee was already threading her way through the tables to

107

the exit, holding her head at a dignified angle and only a little unsteady in her high-heeled sandals.

"Oh, dear," Sue sighed. "Dee's so touchy. You know why she left like that? Because of what I just said about putting off the men at Rimini last year. You know what she'll say to me when I get back? *'That Bernard will think we were laying in wait for him.'* "

Bernard smiled. "Well, you can assure her that no such thought crossed my mind."

As Sue talked, her tongue loosened by the Hawaiian Sunrises, Bernard gradually formed a picture of the curious symbiosis that existed between the two women. They had met at a Teachers' Training College, and taken jobs in the same comprehensive school in a new town near London. They always went on holiday together – first to resorts on the South Coast of England, then more adventurously to the Continent and the Mediterranean – Belgium, France, Spain, Greece. Always, at the back of their minds, was the hope of meeting Someone Nice. Their holiday routine was simple and repetitive. Each morning they put on their swimming-costumes and went down to the beach or the pool to acquire the statutory tan. Each evening they changed into cotton frocks and got mildly tiddly over cocktails and a shared bottle of wine at dinner. They were frequently approached by men, either natives of the country in question or fellow-tourists. But somehow they never met Anyone Nice. Inexperienced as Bernard was in such matters, it seemed to him that while they laid themselves out to attract men, they distrusted the sort of men who made overtures to women in holiday resorts. He visualized them, when they were accosted, turning their backs haughtily, or hobbling away on their high-heels, giggling and nudging each other.

So it went on, year by year: Yugoslavia, Morocco, Turkey, Tenerife. Then suddenly, Sue met Someone Nice at home, in Harlow. Desmond was a junior manager at the local branch of the building society where Sue had a savings account. They moved in together. "I expect we'll get married one day, but Des says he's not in a hurry. When the question of the next holiday came up, I asked Des if Dee could come along with us, she was on her own of course, and he said it was either him or her, I'd have to choose. Des never hit it off with Dee, unfortunately. So there was only one solution."

Ever since that time, it appeared, Sue Butterworth had taken two holidays every summer – a package holiday with Dee, and a camping holiday with Des. It was fortunate that Desmond's tastes in this department were simple and inexpensive, but even so the double vacation was a considerable drain on Sue's income, especially as Dee's choice of destinations became more and more ambitious. "Florida last year, Hawaii this. I don't know where it will end. When she meets Someone Nice, I suppose." Sue sucked on a straw and looked hopefully at Bernard from under her fluffy curls.

Bernard glanced at his watch. "I think I'd better be going."

"Me too," said Sue, groping under her seat for her handbag. "It's a shame, Dee's ever so nice, really, but she puts people off."

As they left their table, the two buxom blondes were still swaying their hips and grinning indefatigably, though they had changed into green plastic skirts, or perhaps it was the lighting that had changed. A pomaded male singer, wielding a hand microphone like a whip, was leading the audience in the chorus of a song called, "I Love Hawaii."

"Nice here, isn't it," said Sue. "Lively."

Bernard hesitated on the sidewalk outside the gates, wondering whether he should offer to escort Sue back to her hotel. Politeness seemed to require it, but he did not wish to be misinterpreted. Fortunately it turned out that the hotel was on his own way home. Three youths tumbled hilariously out of a bar in their path, pushing and shouting at each other. One of them wore a tee-shirt inscribed, *"Get Lei'd in Waikiki."* Sue shrank closer to Bernard as they ran past. "I hope Dee got back all right," she said.

"I'm sure she can look after herself," said Bernard, filled with wonder at this young woman's self-sacrifice. She had sentenced herself to an unwanted second holiday every year, for life, it seemed, simply because Dee could not find anyone else to keep her company.

109

"Have you ever thought of shaving off your beard?" she said suddenly.

"No," he said, smiling with surprise. "Why do you ask?"

"Oh, nothing, I just wondered. This is our hotel. The Waikiki Coconut Grove."

Bernard stared up at the façade of a white concrete tower, honeycombed with a thousand identical windows. "Where's the grove?" he wondered aloud.

"I dunno. Dee says they must've built the hotel on top of it."

Bernard shook Sue's hand and bade her goodnight.

"See you again, I hope," she said. "Waikiki's quite a small place, really, isn't it?"

"It seems to be," he said. "Horizontally, anyway."

"Isn't that the man from the plane, the one with the old man that made such a fuss about getting on at Heathrow?" says Beryl Everthorpe to her husband. They are sitting in a coach locked in traffic on Kuhio Avenue, on their way back from the Sunset Cove Luau. The brochure for this attraction, open seven days a week including holidays, lies open on her knees. *"Nightly at Sunset Cove, guests are greeted with an exotic Mai Tai (Hawaiian fruit punch with rum), songs, dances, chants of Old Hawaii, with an Imu ceremony where the Royal Court oversees the preparation of the pig for roasting in the fire pit. Plus a beautiful Hukilau (traditional shoreline fish-gathering ceremony in which guests lend a hand to pull in the huge net). Then a sumptuous Luau including gorgeous hula dancers, intrepid fire-eaters, steel-guitar music and much much more!"* It had been a bit of shock at first to discover that something like a thousand people had been bussed to Sunset Cove for the evening, to be seated at plastic-topped refectory tables, laid out in rows as if in some kind of refugee camp; but fortunately they were only fifty yards from the stage for the floor show, so Brian had plenty of scope for his video camera. Most of the food looked as if it was cooked in microwaves rather than the fire pit, and was not noticeably exotic in character, but you could eat as much as you liked.

Brian Everthorpe belches, and says, "Who?"

110

"That man over there, with the beard." Beryl points across the wide, traffic-filled avenue at the entrance to a big hotel.

Brian Everthorpe shoulders his video camera, and aims it across the road. He picks out the figures of a man and a woman in his viewfinder, and zooms in. "Yeah," he says. "He looks familiar. So does the bird he's with. She wore a jogging suit on the plane."

"Oh yes, I remember. I didn't think they were together."

"Well, they are now," says Brian Everthorpe. He pushes the record button on his camera and the motor whirrs.

"What are you filming them for? What are they doing?"

"Shaking hands."

"Is that all?"

"You never know," says Brian Everthorpe. "They might be passing drugs." He is only half-joking. He lives in hope of being on the spot with his video camera when some crime or other public drama is occurring – a bank robbery, say, or a fire, or a suicide leap from a bridge. He has seen such sequences on the television news, fuzzy, jerky, but hypnotically gripping, with the caption "*Amateur Video*" across them. "After all, what's he doing in Hawaii with his old man? You can't tell me they're on holiday together. They could be Mafia."

Beryl snorts incredulously. The bus moves forward, removing the bearded man and the girl from their vision. "Seeing them reminds me: you remember the honeymoon couple on the plane?" she says.

"The Yuppie and the Ice Maiden?"

"I saw them on the beach today, while you were filming those girls."

"What girls?"

"You know what girls. She said hallo. *He* didn't look too cheerful, I must say."

"Probably got frostbite in his dick."

"Ssh!"

"Speaking of which," says Brian Everthorpe, running a hand along Beryl's thigh, "what about starting this second honeymoon properly tonight?"

111

"All right," says Beryl. "As long as you're not planning to film it."

Back in Ursula's apartment, Bernard opened the French windows to let the breeze blow through the living-room, and stepped out on to the balcony. The balmy night air beat gently against his face; the palm trees swayed in the wind, rustling their skirts like hula dancers; a crescent moon sailed across the sky, towing a bright star. He scanned the façade of the neighbouring block, half hoping, half-fearing to see the mysterious couple of the previous night. He could see into several of the rooms, where the lights were on and the blinds not drawn. In one, a fat woman dressed only in her underwear was hoovering the carpet. In another, a man was eating a meal from a tray on his knees, staring the while at what must be a television, just out of Bernard's sight. In a third, a woman in a bathrobe was drying her hair, flicking it from side to side like a horse's tail under the hairdryer's nozzle. It was shiny black hair, and reminded him of Yolande Miller's. The couple of the previous night were not, however, to be seen, and he couldn't even be sure which balcony they had occupied.

The telephone rang inside the room and he gave a start. As he went back inside, a strange conceit sprang into his head that the call was from the couple, who had been watching him from behind their curtains in the building opposite. He would pick up the phone and a mocking voice would drawl . . . What? And how would they know the number, anyway? He shook his head as if to clear it of such nonsense, and picked up the receiver. It was Tess.

"You promised to phone to say you'd arrived safely," she said accusingly.

"It's difficult, because of the time difference," he said. "I didn't want to wake you up in the middle of the night."

"How's Daddy? Has he recovered?"

"Recovered?"

"From the journey."

"Oh! Yes, I think so."

"Can I speak to him?"

"I'm afraid not."

"Why?"

Bernard paused for thought. "He's in bed," he said at length.

"Why? What's the time?"

"Ten-thirty, at night."

"Oh well, don't disturb him, then. How's Ursula? Was she glad to see Daddy?"

"She hasn't seen him yet. I went on my own today. Ursula's been moved out of the hospital to a rather unsatisfactory place called a care home." He went on at some length about the unsatisfactoriness of the care home, and the financial constraints on Ursula's freedom of choice in this respect.

Tess was clearly put out. "Do you mean to tell me that Ursula is *poor?*" she said at length.

"Well, not exactly poor. But she isn't at all well-off. She certainly couldn't afford a posh private nursing home for long. The question is, how long will she need it for? It's a rather delicate matter to discuss with her."

"I must say," said Tess crossly, "that I think Ursula has given us all a very misleading impression of her style of life."

"Don't you think we constructed it for our own purposes?"

"Oh, I can't split hairs with you now, Bernard," said Tess. "This call is costing a fortune." She rang off with a final injunction to him to phone her again, "when I can speak to Daddy."

Bernard stared at the receiver in his hand as if at a smoking gun, appalled by his own duplicity. He had completely forgotten his promise to phone Tess, and although the question of how he would break the news of his father's accident to her had hovered darkly at the perimeter of his consciousness all day, he had been too preoccupied with more urgent problems to give it proper thought. Presented with an opportunity, he had funked it. He had lied to Tess – or if, according to a certain kind of casuistry, he had not quite done that, he had certainly deceived her.

He felt a powerful impulse to phone Tess back immediately, and confess all. He actually lifted the receiver, and got halfway through dialling the long sequence of digits, before clapping it down on the cradle again. He got up and paced around the apartment. Of course, she was bound to find out about the accident sooner or later. On the other hand, there was nothing she could do about it, so why not wait until their father was definitely on the mend? The logic seemed impeccable, but he was left with a residue of guilt to add to to the heap he had already accumulated.

To distract himself, he sat down on a spindly upright chair at Ursula's bureau, and searched, as she had instructed him, for her bank statements and stock portfolio. He found these documents without difficulty; but while he was looking through the drawers he also came across an exercise book, or writing book, unused, pristine, its stiff board covers bound in dark blue cloth. The empty, ruled pages opened easily, invitingly, and lay flat before him. They were smooth and silky to the touch. It was the kind of book, Bernard thought, in which you might write a journal. Or a confession.

He yawned suddenly, and felt another wave of tiredness course through his limbs. He closed the bureau, and went to bed, taking the writing book with him.

In other rooms in Waikiki other visitors are preparing themselves for bed, or are already asleep. Dee Ripley seems to be asleep, her sharp features gleaming with moisturizer against the white pillow, as Sue Butterworth tiptoes past on her way to the bathroom. Amanda Best is listening to Madonna on her personal stereo, under the bedclothes so as not to disturb her mother, who is asleep in the adjoining bed. Since Amanda and Robert are too old to share a bedroom, and Mr Best considers the single-occupancy supplement exorbitant, he is sharing a twin room with his son, and Mrs Best another with Amanda. Robert has speculated to Amanda that their parents may be particularly ill-tempered because these sleeping arrangements prevent them from having sexual intercourse. Amanda finds it difficult to imagine her parents having sexual intercourse under any circumstances, and it is only the second night of the holiday, but they have certainly been abnormally stroppy, even for them, so perhaps there is something to his theory. Lilian and Sidney Brooks have just returned to their room after dining with Terry and Tony to find the lights turned on beside their beds and the radio playing soft music. The bedclothes have been turned down to expose a triangle of crisp white sheet; their humble Marks and Spencer's nightwear, which they rolled up and shoved under their pillows earlier in the day, has been smoothed and spread out across the beds; and on each pillow reposes an orchid blossom and a chocolate wrapped in gold foil. Lilian looks nervously around the room as if fearing that the perpetrator of these attentions may be hiding in a closet, waiting to spring out at them with a cry of "Aloha!" or whatever the Hawaiian for "Goodnight" is. Roger Sheldrake is sitting up in his enormous bed, underlining occurrences of the word "paradise" in *This Week in Oahu*, sipping a glass of champagne poured from a bottle generously sent to his room with the manager's compliments. Brian and Beryl Everthorpe are enjoying vigorous sexual intercourse, positioned on the bed so that Brian can watch his performance in the wardrobe mirror, even if he cannot replay it. And Russell Harvey is gloomily watching an adult movie on the hotel's video channel, while Cecily breathes deeply in sleep from one of the room's double beds.

It has been a trying day for Russ. Cecily showed considerable ingenuity in avoiding direct communication with him. In the morning, she called the concierge from their room to say, "We're going to the beach, which part would you recommend?" so that when she prepared to go out, Russ knew where they were going. When they were settled on the crowded beach, she struck up an acquaintance with a woman sitting on a raffia mat nearby and chattered away to her, saying, "What a good idea those mats are, where do you get them?" so that Russ knew he had to go and buy them a couple of mats; and then, "I think I'll go for a dip now," so he knew it was time for a swim; and, after an hour or so, "I think we've had enough sun for our first day," so that he knew it was time to collect up their belongings, and traipse back to the hotel. And at the hotel she asked the bell-captain the way to the zoo, so that he knew what they were going to do in the afternoon. The zoo! Whoever heard of honeymooners going to the zoo, on their first day, and in Honolulu of all places. Apart from anything else, it must niff to high heaven in this heat. When Russ expressed this opinion, Cecily smiled sweetly and said to the bell-captain, "Well, he doesn't have to go, does he?" But of course Russ did go, and it did niff.

So it went on all day. And all evening. At the end of dinner, Cecily yawned in the waiter's face and said, "Oh, excuse *me*! Jet-lag I suppose. We'd better have an early night," so Russ knew they were going to bed. But not to the same one. When the housemaid knocked on the door to ask if they wanted their bed turned down, Cecily smiled sweetly and said, "Yes, both of them please." Then she locked herself in the bathroom for about an hour. Then she took a sleeping tablet and passed out.

Yes, it has been a trying day, and now even the adult movie channel seems to have joined the conspiracy to drive him mad with frustration. Not only does it have the usual imbecilic plot and robotic actors, but he has been watching it for a good three-quarters of an hour and so far there hasn't been a single bonking scene. A bit of striptease, a coy hint that the heroine was touching herself up in the bath, but not a single bout of simulated sexual intercouse, which is after all the whole point of watching these films and the only justification for charging you $8.00 a throw. Whenever it looked as if the heroine was finally going to make it with one of her admirers, the image faded out and the next thing you knew, she was dressed again and in another scene. He has seen sexier things at home on BBC2. It dawns on Russ that the film must have been cut. Censored. As if to confirm this suspicion, the movie ends abruptly, after only fifty-five minutes. Russ is outraged. He considers phoning the reception desk to complain, but cannot think of a suitable form of words. He paces up and down the room. He stops and glowers at Cecily. She is lying on her back, with her fair hair fanned out over the pillow. Her bosom rises and falls rhythmically under the sheet. Russ slowly peels back the sheet. Cecily is wearing a long white nightdress of chaste design. He lifts its skirt and looks under-neath. Things are much as he remembers them under there, except that the thighs are a little red from the sun. He contemplates marital rape, but decides against it. He lets the skirt of the nightdress fall, pulls the sheet up to Cecily's chin and returns to the television. He slumps into the armchair, and presses a button on the remote control at random. An enormous blue-green wave fills the screen, a moving cliff of water, smooth and glassy at the bottom, foaming and boiling at the top, like an inverted waterfall, propelling before it, clinging to his surfboard by his toes, balanced at an impossible angle, with arms extended and knees bent, a tiny triumphant human figure. Russ sits up.

"Fucking hell," he murmurs admiringly.

PART TWO

And dark scents whisper; and dim waves creep to me,
  Gleam like a woman's hair, stretch out, and rise;
  And new stars burn into the ancient skies,
Over the murmurous soft Hawaiian sea.

And I recall, lose, grasp, forget again,
  And still remember, a tale I have heard, or known,
An empty tale, of idleness and pain,
  Of two that loved – or did not love – and one
Whose perplexed heart did evil, foolishly,
A long while since, and by some other sea.

Rupert Brooke:
"Waikiki"

I

Saturday 12th

Drove to the Geyser Hospital this morning to see Ursula's oncologist, by appointment. The Geyser is a huge medical citadel, much bigger and grander than St Joseph's, recently constructed in curvilinear concrete and mirror glass on a site about ten miles outside Honolulu. Apparently it used to be situated down by the shore just outside Waikiki, next to the Marina, but a few years ago the site was sold to developers, the hospital demolished and a high-rise luxury hotel was constructed in its place. In fact the reception area of the new hospital is itself a bit like the lobby of a luxury hotel, carpeted and upholstered in tasteful tones of grey and mauve, with examples of Hawaiian folk art on the walls – an indication of how profitable the change of location was. Dr Gerson assures me that it also has all the state-of-the-art medical technology, but it must seem a long ambulance ride if you happen to be knocked down in Waikiki.

Gerson admits to missing the view he used to have, from his old office, of the yachts going in and out of the marina. He is a keen windsurfer, and I should think he is good at it – he is lean, wiry, youngish. As he leafed through Ursula's file he tilted his swivel chair as far it would go as if balancing a sailboard against the wind. His forearms, thrust from the short sleeves of his starched white tunic, were tanned and muscular, covered with fine gold hairs.

He thanked me for coming to Honolulu – "Frankly, it makes my task easier if there's family around to take care of the practical problems in a case like this." He was brisk, forthright and, I thought, a little cold. Perhaps you have to be in his line of

121

medicine. The mortality rate of his patients must be pretty high. He confirmed what Ursula had told me about her condition: malignant melanoma with secondary cancers of the liver and spleen. "Caused by too much exposure to the sun, I'm afraid, in the days when the danger wasn't appreciated. People came here because of the climate and lay about in the sun all day. It was asking for trouble. I always wear a sunblock with a fifteen per cent protection factor when I go windsurfing. I advise you to do the same on the beach." I said I doubted if I would have any time for sunbathing.

Prognosis was difficult, he said, especially with elderly patients. His own estimate was that Ursula would live for about six months, but it could be more, or much less. The condition was incurable. "This type of cancer doesn't respond well to radio-therapy or chemotherapy. I offered them to Mrs Riddell because they can give some remission in certain cases, but she declined, and I respect that. She's a tough old lady, your aunt. She knows her own mind."

When I criticised the accommodation she was in, he answered, as I knew he would, that she had insisted on the cheapest available. "But I agree with you, it's not appropriate for a patient in her condition, and will become even less so as time goes on." He said there were several private nursing homes in and around Honolulu, costing anything from $3000 a month up, according to the type of care and degree of luxury they offer, and gave me a list compiled by the hospital's Nursing Co-ordinator. He explained that Ursula's medical plan covered her for something called Skilled Nursing Care, i.e. 24-hour attendance by registered nurses, such as you get in hospital, but not Intermediate Nursing Care, which is all she needs at present – or so he says. I deduced that there was a certain pressure on him not to admit patients to hospital lightly, since they then become a charge on the Geyser Foundation. I said I thought Ursula ought to be in hospital while I looked for a suitable nursing home, and pressed him to visit her. He said he was very busy, but when I told him how badly constipated she was, he agreed to try and call on her today.

Drove back along the freeway to visit Daddy at St Joseph's. He is in some pain, and was fretful and surly. He turned his nose up at the pyjamas I had bought for him because they didn't button at the neck. I pointed out that in this climate you didn't need pyjamas that buttoned at the neck, and he said, "What about when I go home – or don't you think I'm ever going to get home?" I told him not to be silly. I described my visit to Ursula yesterday, but he didn't seem very interested. Illness, I'm afraid, makes people even more selfish and ill-natured than they are normally. In all my time as a parish priest, visiting the sick in hospital and at home, I could count on the fingers of one hand the number of patients I met who "rose above" their suffering. I'm pretty sure I wouldn't be one of that number myself.

Daddy asked me if I had telephoned Tess to tell her about his accident. I said I thought it was pointless to worry her unless it was absolutely necessary. He was displeased and said she had a right to know, the whole family had a right to know. What he meant was that he had a right to know they were all worrying themselves sick on his behalf, and blaming me. He said slyly, "You're afraid of Tess, aren't you?" *Touché.*

On my way out, I met Daddy's physician, Dr Figuera, a cheerful, portly man of about sixty, who assured me that Daddy was making a good recovery, and that he didn't anticipate any complications. "Good bones, good bones," he said. "Don't worry about him. He'll mend."

Drove to Mrs Jones's. A white BMW with a sailboard on the roofrack was parked outside, and proved to belong to Dr Gerson, who was just leaving as I arrived. We conferred in the street, through the open window of his car. His tanned, golden-haired arm was jack-knifed to grip the roof. "You were right to call me in, she's in bad shape," he said. "I'm readmitting her to treat the constipation. That should give you a few days to fix up a nursing home, OK?" I asked him when Ursula would be moved, and he said, "When can you bring her in?" I pointed to my old Honda and said, "You mean, in that? Can't she have an ambulance?" He said, somewhat irritably, "You don't seem to realize I have to

123

operate within certain financial constraints. I have to make a medical case for every ambulance I authorize. If your aunt can walk to the bathroom, she can walk to your car."

I pointed out that the cast on her arm would make this difficult. "She can sit in the back."

"It's a two-door car. She could never climb into the back."

He sighed and said, "OK. You get your ambulance."

I stayed with Ursula until the ambulance came, and helped her pack her few belongings. Mrs Jones, who had given me a very frigid reception at the front door, didn't come near us. "She thinks it's your fault that I'm being moved," Ursula said. "Well," I said, "she's right," and we giggled conspiratorially.

Ursula was delighted to be escaping from that dreary house. For the first time since I got to Hawaii – for the first time in a long while – I felt a glow of satisfaction at having achieved something, at having bent circumstances to my will, at having been of some use. Ursula has also been busy on her own account. She had Mrs Jones bring her a cordless phone, and made calls to her bank, her stockbroker and her lawyer. It seems that I must obtain power of attorney before I can consolidate her various bank accounts and sell her stocks and shares.

Re-reading that sentence, I sound like a man of business. In fact I have only the foggiest idea of what is entailed. I have never managed personal finances more complex than a current bank account and a Post Office Savings Book in my life. When I was parish priest of St Peter's and Paul's my curate Thomas did all the accounts. He had a head for figures, fortunately. I'm just about the least qualified person in the world to help Ursula settle her affairs. But I suppose I can learn, if only from Ursula. Perhaps she learned from Rick. It surprises me that she has any investments at all, good or bad. The Walshes never were any good at money. We don't understand its abstract workings – interest, inflation, depreciation. Money to us is cash: coin and banknotes, kept in jamjars and under mattresses, something necessary, coveted, but vaguely disreputable. Family gatherings – weddings, funerals, visits from or to relatives in Ireland – were always marked by people furtively pushing screwed-up, low-denomination banknotes into each other's hands or pockets by way of presents. We never had enough money at home, and what we had was badly managed. Mummy would send one of the girls out to the shops every day, for little bits of this and that, instead of buying in bulk. Daddy never had any savings to speak of. I think he bet on horses secretly. Once, when I was still at school, I borrowed a raincoat of his and found a betting slip in the pocket. I never told anybody.

The ambulance came at three. The men moved Ursula out in a wheelchair, which they carried down the front steps, and I brought up the rear with her little holdall. Mrs Jones put on an oily display of sympathetic concern for the benefit of the ambulancemen, patting Ursula's hand as she was carried over the threshold. The ambulance drove sedately and sirenless along the freeway to the Geyser, and I followed in my car. I took Ursula's belongings up to her ward, but did not linger. She is in a room with three other women, but the beds are placed in the middle of the floorspace at oblique angles, so that the occupants don't have to stare at each other across the room, as they do in a British hospital.

Before I left I told Ursula about finding this writing book in her bureau, and asked her if I could have it. She said, "Of course, Bernard, take anything you like. All I have is yours for the asking." She bought the book a long time ago to write down recipes in, but she had never used it and had forgotten all about it.

Called in again at St Joseph's on my way home, and was pleasantly surprised to find Mrs Knoepflmacher sitting beside Daddy's bed, in a bright yellow *muu-muu* and gold sandals. (She seemed to have re-tinted her hair ash blonde to match – is that possible? Perhaps she wears a wig.) There was a small basket of fruit on the bedside table, gaudy and artificial-looking as millinery. I suppose I must have mentioned the name of the hospital to her yesterday evening, and she decided to visit Daddy. This was a kind gesture, even though Ursula would probably ascribe it to nosiness. I thanked her warmly, and after a few minutes of empty chat, she left us alone.

"Begob, I thought she'd never go," Daddy said. "I'm bursting. Will you tell the nurse I need a bottle, for the love of Jesus. They never answer when I press this thing." He indicated the bell push on his bedside table. I found a pretty Hawaiian nurse, who brought him a bottle and drew the curtains round his bed, and I hung about a little selfconsciously outside the screen while he relieved himself. The nurse returned and carried off the bottle.

"A nice thing to be doing at my time of life," he said bitterly. "Pissing into a bottle and handing it to a strange black woman, wrapped in a towel like it was vintage champagne. And don't even ask me about the other business."

I brought him up to date on Ursula, and mentioned that the driver of the car had phoned to enquire about him.

He said, "The other one, Mrs Buttonhole or whatever she is, she thinks we ought to sue her."

"Daddy, you know it was your fault – our fault. We were crossing in the wrong place. You looked the wrong way."

"Mrs Whatsername says the lawyers don't charge you anything unless they win the case." He looked at me with a gleam of avarice in his eye. I said I had no intention of getting involved in litigation which was bound to cause anxiety and stress for someone I regarded as entirely innocent, and we parted on bad terms. I felt guilty about this as I drove home. Why had I taken such a high moral tone? I could have humoured Daddy instead of browbeating him. The thought of a lawsuit, however fanciful, might have taken his mind off bottles and bedpans. Failed again.

Stayed in this evening and cooked myself a packet of frozen canelloni I discovered in Ursula's freezer – but not for long enough, or perhaps the temperature of the oven was wrong. At any rate, it wasn't quite cooked through: steaming and bubbling on the outside, still frozen at the core. It could be a symbol of something. I hope I don't get food poisoning. All three Walshes in hospital at the same time would be too much. I have a vision of us lying helplessly in three different Honolulu infirmaries while Mrs Knoepflmacher scurries round from one bed to another in various wigs, bringing us chicken soup and baskets of fruit.

126

I was washing up after this meal, and wondering whether Tess would be getting suspicious at not having heard from me, when the telephone rang. I gave a guilty start, and nearly dropped the plate I was mopping. It wasn't Tess, though; it was Yolande Miller, enquiring about Daddy again. She must have registered the anxiety in my voice, because she asked me if I was all right. I explained my dilemma, and then on impulse I said, "Do you think I should tell my sister about the accident now? What's your professional opinion?"

"Is there anything she can do to help?"

"No."

"And you say he's recovering OK?"

"Yes."

"Then I don't see why you need rush to tell her . . . unless it would make you feel better."

"Ah, there's the rub."

She gave a little snicker of recognition, and then there was an awkward silence between us. I didn't want to terminate the conversation, but I couldn't think of anything else to say, and neither, it seemed, could she. Then she said, "I was wondering whether you'd like to come to dinner some time."

"Dinner?" I repeated the word as if I had never heard it before.

"You must be kind of lonely in the evenings, after you've done your hospital rounds . . ."

"Well, er, it's very kind of you, but, well, I don't know . . ." My mumbled words concealed total panic. Analysing this reaction later, I realized that the invitation had stirred up painful memories of Daphne. Our relationship – our personal relationship – had started that way. After she had been to the presbytery for instruction for several weeks, as she got up from the other side of the parlour table to leave one evening, she said, "Would it be proper for me to invite you to lunch one day?" and I laughed and said, "Of course, why not, thank you very much." Though of course it wasn't quite proper, and I didn't tell my housekeeper or my curate where I was going on that fateful Saturday.

"How about tomorrow?" said Yolande Miller. "We usually eat

127

around seven o'clock." I smiled with relief at the plural pronoun, realizing that it was a family meal I was being invited to share, not an intimate repast *à deux*. I thanked her and accepted the invitation.

Sunday 13th

This morning I visited two of the cheapest private nursing homes on the list Dr Gerson gave me. They weren't keen for me to come on a Sunday, but I explained that the matter was urgent. (Gerson won't keep Ursula in the Geyser a day longer than necessary, and if I haven't found a nursing home by then, she'll have to go back to Mrs Jones, or some similar place.) It was a deeply discouraging experience – worse, somehow, than a geriatric ward in an NHS hospital at home, though God knows they can be bad enough – perhaps because of the contrast between the outside and the inside.

You drive through impressive gates, tyres purring on the smooth tarmacadam, park your car in the landscaped car-park, and enter the lobby with its polished wood and comfortable sofas. The receptionist smiles and takes your name and asks you to be seated. Then a lady comes to show you round the establishment. Her smile is less ready, her greeting less fulsome, than the receptionist's: she knows what it is like behind the locked double doors on the far side of the lobby.

The first thing that hits you is the ammoniac stench of urine. You comment on this. The lady explains that many of their residents are incontinent. Many of them are evidently senile, too. They shuffle to the doors of their rooms in pyjamas and dressing-gowns, staring at us as if trying to place our faces, grinning with toothless gums, or muttering incomprehensible questions. Long threads of spittle dangle from their chins. Some scratch their ribs or rub their crotches absent-mindedly. Many are propped up in bed, their limbs twitching feebly like dying insects, staring listlessly at the passing scene, or asleep, their eyes closed, their mouths open. The beds are close together, two or four to a room.

The walls are painted with glossy institutional paint, green and cream. There is a kind of lounge with high-backed chairs, upholstered (for obvious reasons) with shiny plastic, where the more mobile residents sit and read magazines, or watch TV, or just stare vacantly into space. The staff, mostly coloured women in cotton overalls and flapping slippers, humour and cajole the residents as they move through the wards and corridors, pushing trolleys of medicines before them like soft-drink vendors.

Ursula could not possibly tolerate such conditions, nor would I dream of subjecting her to them. But this is evidently where the old and the sick end up in Paradise, if they have no families to look after them, and are not rich enough to buy themselves decent nursing care, or poor enough to qualify for State Welfare. This is the bargain basement of private geriatric nursing homes. My escort knows it, and lets me know it. Her expression and her tone of voice say to me: if we had both been more successful in life, I wouldn't be working in this dump and you wouldn't be thinking of putting your aunt in it. At the end of the tour, I thank her and take my leave, accepting a brochure and tariff for politeness' sake.

The second home was only marginally superior, and they didn't have a vacancy anyway. Hard to believe there could be a *waiting* list to get into such a dismal and depressing place.

Feeling pretty dismal and depressed myself, I drove back into Waikiki, and sat on the beach. A mistake. The sun was fierce, and the few patches of shade under the palm trees at the back of the beach were occupied. The sea was a blinding dazzle, and the sand painful to walk on in bare feet. Most of the people around me wore rubber flip-flops with thongs between the toes, and had straw mats to lie on, though how they can bear to spreadeagle themselves under this brutal sun baffles me. Sweat trickled down my sides from under my armpits, but I dared not take off my shirt for fear of getting sunburned. I rolled up my trouser bottoms in traditional British-seaside-style, and paddled for a while at the edge of the ocean. The water was warm and cloudy. Scraps of paper and plastic rubbish lapped against the coarse sand. A continuous procession of people trying to keep cool in the same way trudged up and down the margin of the sea, all ages, shapes and sizes, many of them clasping drinks, ice-creams or hot-dogs in their hands. Americans seem to like to eat on the move, like grazing cattle. Most of them, of course, were dressed in swimming-costumes, which do not flatter the elderly and obese. The young men seem perversely to favour rather baggy knee-length bathing shorts, that cling uncomfortably to their thighs when wet, while the young women's swimsuits are sleek and cut very high at the hip. Twice in half an hour very professional-looking beachcombers came past, festooned with bags and pouches, wearing headphones and wielding electronic metal-detectors with which they tested the sand for buried valuables.

The breeze was light and wavering. Out to sea, the swimmers bobbed up and down in the swell, trying without much success to bodysurf on the sluggish rollers, and, further out still, serious surfers sat astride their boards, waiting for a big wave to break. A large catamaran with a yellow sail, crewed by Polynesians with skins like oiled teak, was moored a little further up the beach, announcing its imminent departure for a cruise with blasts on what sounded like an amplified conch shell. Out to sea, in the direction of Diamond Head, people were paddling, or being paddled, in outrigger canoes, and a tiny figure dangling from a parachute was being towed across the sky by a speedboat. It was hard to connect this scene of harmless if mindless pleasure with my mental images of the nursing homes I had just visited, the swimmers and the sunbathers in all the pride of their flesh with the drooling, emaciated figures haunting the dreary wards and corridors just a couple of miles away. I felt like a tongue-tied prophet who had come back from the kingdom of the dead, as if I should give a message or utter a warning, but did not know what to say – except perhaps, "Use a sunblock with a protection factor of fifteen," and most of the people on the beach seemed to know that already, since they spent so much time smearing their dead and dying skin cells with various creams and lotions.

As I was standing in the tepid shallows, squinting out to sea, a swimmer suddenly surfaced a few yards away like a submarine, and then reared out of the water. He wore a glazed rubber mask and a plastic tube protruded from his mouth. He stumbled and waved his arms urgently, so that at first I thought he was in distress; but then he removed his mask and I recognized Roger Sheldrake. He staggered towards me, impeded by enormous webbed rubber flippers on his feet, a very land-fish. He seemed excessively glad to see me.

"Snorkelling," he said explanatorily, as he divested himself of his equipment. "All part of the fieldwork."

I asked him if he had seen any interesting fish and he said no, only plastic bags, but conditions were not good off this beach – the water was too murky. There was a place on the other side of Diamond Head that had been recommended to him, Hanauma Bay. "Perhaps you'd care to join me one day?" I said I had my hands full at present, and gave him a résumé of my experiences since we arrived in Hawaii. He clucked his tongue sympathetically. "Still, you must need a bit of relief from geriatric duty – come back to my hotel and have a drink. The management keep sending up bottles of champagne to my room. I've got quite a stockpile." I excused myself, as I had still to make calls at both hospitals before my dinner engagement with the Millers, so he bought me, from a kiosk at the back of the beach, a huge paper cup full of fruit-flavoured slush, apparently a local delicacy known as shave-ice. Mine had melted under the broiling sun long before I got to the bottom of the container. Everything is too big in this country: the steaks, the salads, the ices. You weary of them before you can finish them.

We sat side by side on a straw mat where Sheldrake had left his clothes, eating our shave-ice, and I asked him how his research was going. He said quite well, he had collected quite a lot of Paradise references already. He took a notebook out of his shirt pocket and ran through the list: "Paradise Florist, Paradise Gold, Paradise Custom Packing, Paradise Liquor, Paradise Roofing, Paradise Used Furniture, Paradise Termite and Rat Control . . ." He had spotted these names on buildings or the sides of vans or in newspaper advertisements. I asked him if it wouldn't be simpler to look up the Honolulu telephone directory under "Paradise", and he seemed rather offended. "That's not the way we do fieldwork," he said. "The aim is to identify totally with your subjects, to experience the milieu as they experience it, in this case to let the word 'Paradise' impinge on your consciousness gradually, by a slow process of incrementation." I inferred that it would be improper for me to pass on any Paradise motifs I happened to come across, but he seemed prepared to stretch a point, so I told him about Paradise Pasta and he wrote it down in his little book with a ball pen that was leaking in the heat.

He is working on the theory that the mere repetition of the paradise motif brainwashes the tourists into thinking they have actually got there, in spite of the mismatch between reality and archetype. The beach we were sitting on certainly didn't bear much rememblance to the one on the front of the Travelwise brochure. "As a matter of fact," he said, when I commented on this, "Waikiki is now one of the most densely populated places on earth. It's only one-seventh of a square mile, that's smaller than the main runway of Honolulu airport, but at any one time there are a hundred thousand people living here."

"Yet it's also one of the most isolated places on earth," I said, remembering the lights of Honolulu suddenly appearing out of the black abyss of the Pacific night. "That's what makes it a rather mythical place, in spite of all the crowds and the commercialism."

Sheldrake pricked up his ears at the word "mythical".

"Like the Gardens of the Hesperides, or the Fortunate Isles, in classical mythology," I elaborated. "The winterless home of the happy dead. They were supposed to be on the extreme western rim of the known world."

He got rather excited at this, and asked me for references. I told him to look up Hesiod and Pindar, and he wrote down these names in his notebook with inky fingers.

"Come to think of it," I said, "the idea of paradise as an island is essentially pagan rather than Judaeo-Christian. Eden wasn't an island. Some scholars think the *Insulae Fortunatae* were really the Canaries."

"Oh God," he said. "You wouldn't call them fortunate today. Have you been to Tenerife lately?"

When I asked him whether he ever took his wife with him on

his research trips, he said rather curtly that he wasn't married. "My mistake," I said, in some confusion, "pardon me."

"I was engaged once," he said, "but she broke it off, after I started my PhD. She said I spoiled her holidays, analysing them all the time."

At that moment I was startled to be hailed by a female voice crying "Hallo, Bernard!" and looked up to find the young woman called Sue smiling down at me, with her friend Dee in attendance. They were wearing shiny one-piece swimming-costumes and straw hats, and carrying the usual beach paraphernalia in plastic shopping bags. I struggled to my feet and made introductions. Sue said that they were on their way to purchase tickets for a sunset cruise, and invited Sheldrake and myself to join them. She gave me a conspiratorial wink, while Dee looked away as if to dissociate herself from this proposition. I excused myself, but encouraged Sheldrake to go. He did not appear unwilling. He seems to be as lonely as me, and to mind it more.

Drove to St Joseph's in the afternoon to visit Daddy. When I got to his room he was in the act of receiving Communion from a hospital chaplain. An awkward moment. I hovered at the doorway, wondering if I could retreat without being observed, but Daddy noticed me and said something to the priest, who smiled and beckoned me to approach. He was a youngish, plumpish man, with a short haircut, wearing the stole over a grey clerical shirt and black trousers. A bored-looking teenager in jeans and running shoes was in attendance as acolyte. It was strange to watch them going through the familiar motions, like watching a previous incarnation of myself (why do I so often have the feeling of being a ghost these days?). Daddy closed his eyes and extended his tongue to receive the host in the traditional manner. He never had any time for the post-Vatican II practice of receiving it in the hand – a disrespectful Protestant dodge, he used to say of it scornfully.

When he had closed the lid of the ciborium, the priest put his hand on Daddy's head and began to pray aloud for his recovery. I recognized the trademark of the charismatic. Daddy, taken by

133

surprise, shook his head like a startled horse, but the chaplain pressed his scalp firmly down into the pillow and continued with his prayer. I suppressed a temptation to smile at Daddy's discomfiture. When the priest had finished, he turned to me and asked me if I would like to pray. I shook my head. Then it was Daddy's turn to give a faint, sardonic smile.

The priest introduced himself to me as Father Luke McPhee. He said he was deputizing for one of the regular chaplains who was in California attending a course, and that it was a great privilege because the sick seemed to appreciate the Eucharist so much more than parishioners at an ordinary Sunday mass. I mumbled some appropriate reply, but perhaps I looked unconvinced, or unconvincing, for he looked at me keenly, like a uniformed officer who suspects a deserter in disguise.

Drove on to the Geyser to visit Ursula. I didn't go into detail about the nursing homes – just said they weren't suitable, and that I was looking at another two tomorrow. She asked anxiously about Daddy. Apparently she'd tried to speak to him by phone earlier, and someone at St Joseph's had told her he wasn't available. She had left a message, but he hadn't called back. I said that he didn't have a bedside telephone and she said that they would bring one to him if he asked. She fretted at being just a few miles away from her brother – "so near and yet so far – it would be something if we could just talk." I said that Daddy had never been a great one for chatting on the telephone, which is true enough, perhaps because he spent almost his entire working life with telephone bells shrilling in his ears. But he had said nothing to me about getting a message from Ursula.

She was envious when I told her about his receiving communion. She said the Catholic chaplain came round the Geyser once in a blue moon. She would like to be in a Catholic hospital, but her health plan is tied to the Geyser. I said I was sure that Father Luke would visit her, but she would have to put up with being prayed over. She said she didn't go much for that kind of stuff, it was what she called Billy Graham religion. "But it seems to be creeping into the Catholic Church. When I started going to mass again, a few years ago, I hardly recognized the service. It seemed more like a concert party to me. There was a bunch of kids up at the altar, with tambourines and guitars, and they were singing jolly camp-fire type songs, not the good old hymns I remember, 'Soul of My Saviour' and 'Sweet Sacrament Divine'. And the mass was in English, not Latin, and there was a *woman* on the altar reading the epistle, and the priest said the mass facing the people – I was quite embarrassed watching him chewing the host. When I was a girl, at the convent, we were told never to touch the host with your teeth. You had to sort of fold it over with your tongue and swallow it."

An old superstition, I assured her, that had been dropped from First Communion preparation years ago. I gave her a brief rundown on modern eucharistic theology: the importance of the shared meal in Jewish culture, the place of the *agape* or love-feast in the lives of the early Christians, the misguided scholastic effort to provide an Aristotelian rationale for the eucharist, leading to the doctrine of transubstantiation and the superstitious reification of the consecrated host. I could hear myself sounding more and more like a St John's College lecturer, and see Ursula getting more and more restive, but somehow couldn't shift into a more appropriate register. When I had finished, she said, "What've the Jews got to do with it?" I said that Jesus was a Jew. She said, "I suppose he was, but somehow I never thought of him as Jewish. He doesn't look Jewish on the shroud of Turin." I said the shroud of Turin had recently been exposed as a medieval forgery. She was silent for a moment, then she said, "Is that Sophie Knoepflmacher still poking her nose into my affairs?"

There are times when it is quite hard to love ignorant, prejudiced old people, even if they are sick and helpless.

Drove back to the apartment to get ready for my visit to the Millers. By 5.15 I was ready: showered, beard trimmed, shirt changed. I wondered whether I should wear a tie, but decided against it: too hot. To kill time, I wrote up this journal for today. It is now 6.15. I feel strangely nervous, excited, expectant. Why? Perhaps because I haven't told anyone about the invitation – not

135

Daddy, not Ursula, not even Mrs Knoepflmacher, who knocked on my door just now with some tuna-fish salad, which I received with thanks and put in the fridge. I feel a little bit as if I am truanting, or fraternizing with the enemy. That must be it.

10.00 p.m.

Just returned from dinner with Yolande Miller. An interesting evening, and mostly enjoyable, though it ended rather abruptly and unsatisfactorily. My fault entirely. I feel restless and dissatisfied; also curiously wide-awake – an effect of jet-lag, no doubt. I know that if I go to bed, I won't sleep, so I might as well write down my impressions of the occasion while they are still fresh.

The Millers' house is one of many small, square, one-storey wooden structures stuck into the flanks of a damp, narrow cleft at the end of a valley in the hills above the University, which is itself above Waikiki. The road climbed steadily, and towards the end became so steep and twisty that I wondered more than once whether my ageing Honda was going to make it round the next bend. It's a different climate from Waikiki up there, wetter and more humid. The vegetation is dense and lush. "Welcome to the rainforest!" Yolande called out from the porch as I climbed the stepped path from the road, slippery with trodden leaves and hibiscus petals. She says it rains almost every day, though seldom for long. The clouds graze the tops of the hills and every now and then they let fall a gentle precipitation. "Out of habit," she said, "like a dog peeing against a post." Appliances rust, books become mildewed, wine turns sour. "I loathe it," she said, "but I'm stuck here."

It wasn't raining this evening, however, and from the verandah (or *lanai*, as Yolande called it, with a certain droll emphasis, as if to disown by self-parody any ethnic affectation) there was a stunning view of the sun setting behind Waikiki, tinting the clustered tower blocks pink and mauve. From up there, you can see just how compact and improbable Waikiki is. It looks like a mini-Manhattan, clean and pristine as an architect's model,

136

magically sprouted from a tropical beach. Yolande pointed out to me the line of the Ala Wai canal which contains it on the inland side. "They built the canal to drain the marshes – that was what made Waikiki habitable. Before that it was infested with mosquitoes. But it was a stroke of planning genius, because as well as attracting the tourists it keeps them corralled in one place, so they have to spend all their money in the Waikiki hotels and the Waikiki shops, and don't interfere too much with the rest of us. My husband explained that to me. He's a geographer."

I soon ascertained that she is separated from her husband, and that the "we" of the invitation referred to her sixteen-year-old daughter, Roxy, to whom I was introduced as "Mr Walsh, whose father had the accident." Roxy looked at me curiously and inquired politely about Daddy's state of health. Her own father, it seems, left Yolande a year ago for a younger woman, an instructor in his Department at the University. Divorce proceedings have been delayed by disputes about the financial settlement, disputes that Yolande admits to prolonging.

"He would like me to move away, out of his life, to give him his divorce as quickly as possible, take my share of the value of the house and move back to the mainland. But I'm not going to give him an easy out. Why should I? I want to embarrass him. I want to shame him. I want to hurt him. I want him to know that he can't go to the supermarket or the drugstore or to a faculty party without the risk of running into me. I have a special baleful stare I keep ready for him – or her. I practise in front of the bathroom mirror. Not very mature behaviour, you may think, especially for a therapist, and you'd be right. But I was hurt. I felt betrayed. I knew the girl, you see. She was one of Lewis's graduate students. She used to come to the house. I thought of her as a sort of friend."

I should say that she had put away a fair amount of drink by the time she reached this degree of candour. A stiff gin and tonic before dinner (if the one she mixed for me was anything to go by) and more than half the bottle of Beaujolais I had brought with me. We were sitting over cheese and fruit. The rise-and-fall lampshade, pulled down low over the dining-table, cast a circle of bright light on the yellow puddle of melting Camembert, but left her face in shadow. We were alone. Roxy had gobbled down her salad and lemon chicken casserole and departed with some friends to a drive-in movie. ("Don't be late," Yolande said to her, as a car horn cleared its throat in the road below the house, and Roxy leaped to her feet. "How late is late?" "Ten o'clock." "Eleven." "Ten thirty." "Ten forty-five," Roxy yelled from the porch, as the screen door slammed behind her. Yolande sighed and grimaced. "It's called family negotiation," she said.)

Roxy (short for Roxanne), a pretty girl with her mother's dark colouring and glossy black hair, is another factor in the marital deadlock. Although, according to Yolande, she disapproves of her father's behaviour, she sees him regularly and does not want to lose touch with him. There is another child, an older boy called Gene, who is at college in California, and at present doing a vacation job in a State park, but Roxy is the focus of Yolande's concern. "I'm afraid if I take her away from Hawaii, she'll resent it. I think she secretly hopes Lewis and I will get together again one day."

"Is that likely?" I was bold enough to ask.

"No," she said, pouring the last of the Beaujolais into her glass. "I don't think so. What about you, Bernard, are you married?"

I shook my head.

"Divorced? Widower?"

"No, just a bachelor." Something, I don't know what – I suppose that I too had imbibed more alcohol than I am used to – prompted me to add: "I'm not gay, either."

She laughed and said, "I didn't think you were. Otherwise I wouldn't have invited you up here to work my feminine wiles on you."

"What wiles are those?" I said hoarsely. My larynx had contracted in panic. Please don't let her throw herself at me, I prayed inwardly – (to whom?) – please not that. I was enjoying the evening, the excellent food, the wine, her company, the sense of being on holiday from the responsibilities of Ursula and Daddy. Now I feared she was going to spoil it all by making some sexual overture that I would not be able to respond to, and she would be hurt, and I would have to leave, and we would never see each other again. I wanted to see her again. I feel she could be a friend, and I ache for a friend.

"Oh, the food, the table linen, the soft lights . . . You don't know how lucky you are to get a genuine French Camembert in Honolulu. And to tell you the truth, I thought I looked pretty good in this dress. Roxy said it was a knockout."

"It's a very nice dress," I said lamely, not looking at it. I had a vague impression that it was predominantly dark red, and silky.

She laughed again. "OK. Let's come to the main business of the evening. Are you or are you not going to sue?"

It took me a second or two to catch her meaning. Then *I* laughed, with relief. "Of course not. It was our fault. We were crossing the road in the wrong place."

"Well, I know. But the cops tested my brakes after you left in the ambulance, and they didn't seem too impressed. I probably shouldn't be telling you this, but it wouldn't have made any difference to the accident, trust me. Your father walked into my fender before I had time to hit the brakes."

"I know," I said, remembering the sequence of events, the sickening thud and the squeal of tyres.

"But it's the sort of thing lawyers exploit. I haven't had the car serviced in quite a while. Things have been difficult, with Lewis dragging his feet over maintenance and so on, and I just haven't gotten round to it. The last thing I want is to get involved in more litigation. I can't afford it. Haven't people been telling you you should sue?"

I admitted that they had, but repeated that I had no intention of doing so.

"Thanks," she said, with a smile. "Somehow I could tell you were an honest man. There aren't so many left."

Her face is transformed by a smile. In repose the deep upper lip gives her a somewhat truculent, almost sullen expression, but when she smiles the whole face lights up with the curl of her full mouth over the crescent of white teeth, and her dark brown eyes seem to sparkle.

Over coffee she told me her life-story, in brief. She was born

139

and brought up in an affluent outer suburb of New York, daughter of a lawyer who commuted daily to Manhattan. "And is called Argument, believe it or not. That was my maiden name, Yolande Argument. Lewis used to say it was all too appropriate. It's some kind of Huguenot name, originally." She went to college in Boston in the mid-60s, was very radical in the approved style of the day, majored in psychology, went on to do post-graduate work and met Lewis Miller, another graduate student, doing a PhD in Geography. They lived together and, when Yolande became accidentally pregnant, married. In the early years of the marriage Yolande worked in an office to support Lewis, and consequently never completed her own PhD. "You'd think the son-of-a-bitch would be grateful, wouldn't you? The hell he is." One of the points of legal dispute between them at present is that Yolande is claiming financial compensation for the non-completion of her PhD, and consequent loss of professional earnings, as part of the divorce settlement. "My attorney – she's a woman – is all fired up about it."

In the 1970s Yolande was swept up in the Women's Liberation Movement. "I was ripe and ready for it. But instead of applying its lessons and going back to school, I threw all my energy into the movement itself – meetings, demos, workshops. For a time I thought I was going to be a feminist artist. I made collages out of diapers and tampons and pantyhose and pages torn out of women's magazines. Jesus, the time I wasted! Lewis was cunning. While I let off steam with the sisters, he put his head down and got on with his career. As soon as he finished his PhD, he was appointed assistant professor in his Department. He didn't have any problem with women's lib. The other women in my group used to envy me, he seemed so housetrained. He would always do his share of the cooking and the shopping. Well, he *liked* cooking, he *liked* shopping."

One day Lewis came back from a big convention in Philadelphia and said he had been offered a good job, associate professor with tenure, at the University of Hawaii. "He was desperate to take it. It was a promotion, and the place suited his research interests – he's a climatologist. To me the idea of moving

140

to Hawaii seemed bizarre – I mean, it didn't sound like a serious place, where anyone would do serious work. It was somewhere you went for vacations, or your honeymoon, if you were kind of corny and had the money and didn't mind long airplane trips. It was a resort. The last resort. It is, you know. This is where America ends, where the West ends. If you keep going past Hawaii, you wind up in the East, in Japan, Hong Kong. We're out on the rim of Western civilization here, hanging on by our fingertips . . . But I could tell Lewis was desperate to accept the offer, and would hold it against me for ever afterwards if I refused to go. And it was the middle of a New England winter, and I had a cold, and the kids had colds, and Hawaii didn't seem such a bad idea for a few years – Lewis promised he would stay for five at the most. So I agreed.

"As soon as we got here, I knew it was a mistake – for me, anyway. Lewis loved it. He liked the climate, he liked the Department – the faculty were much less competitive than back East, and the students were in awe of him. Our kids loved it – swimming and surfing and picnicking all year round. But I was never happy here. Why? Basically because it's boring. Yeah, that's the bad news. Paradise is boring, but you're not allowed to say so."

I asked her why. She said: why is it boring, or why are you not allowed to say so? I said, both.

"One reason it's boring is that it has no real cultural identity. The original Polynesian culture has been more or less wiped out, because it was oral. The Hawaiians didn't have an alphabet until the missionaries invented one for them, and it was applied to translating the Bible, not to recording pagan myths. There are no buildings older than the nineteenth century, and not many of them. All there is to show for a thousand years of Hawaiian history before Captain Cook are a few fishhooks and axe heads and pieces of *tapa* cloth in the Bishop Museum. I exaggerate, but not much. There's a lot of *geography* here, wonderful volcanoes, waterfalls, rainforests – that's why Lewis loves it – but not much history, history in the sense of continuity. What you've got is a lot of disparate elements who came here at different times for different reasons – *haole*, Chinese, Japanese, Polynesian, Melanesian, Micronesian – all bobbing up and down like flotsam in a lukewarm sea of American consumer culture. Life here is incredibly bland. Nothing important has happened in Hawaii since Pearl Harbor. The sixties passed almost unnoticed. News from the rest of the world takes so long to get here that by the time it arrives it isn't news anymore. While we're reading Monday's newspaper, they're already printing Tuesday's headlines in London. Everything seems to be happening so far away that it's hard to feel involved. If World War Three broke out, you'd probably find it on an inside page of the *Honolulu Advertiser*, and the lead story would be about a hike in local taxes. It makes you feel out of time, somehow, as if you've fallen asleep and woken up in a kind of dreamy lotus land, where every day is the same as the one before. Perhaps that's why so many people retire to Hawaii. It gives them the illusion that they won't die, because they're kind of dead already, just by being here. It's the same with the absence of seasons. We have a lot of weather, a lot of climate, but no seasons, not so you'd notice. Seasons remind you that time is passing. I can't tell you how much I miss the New England fall. The maple leaves turning red, yellow, brown, dropping off the trees till the branches are black and bare. Then the first frost. Snow. Skating out of doors. Then the spring, shoots appearing, buds, blossom . . . here it's blossom all fucking year. Excuse me," she said, perhaps seeing me blink at the expletive. "It's my rock fever speaking. That's what they call it, rock fever, the panic at being stranded here, two and a half thousand miles from the nearest landmass, the desperate longing to escape. It's like a social disease among the senior faculty here, people avoid you if you've got it, because implicitly it's a judgment on them, for settling here. Or perhaps they think it's catching. Or perhaps they've already got it, but are hiding their symptoms. Officially we're all supposed to be terribly lucky to be here, in this wonderful *climate*, but sometimes you can catch people off their guard, and there's a kind of glum, faraway look in their eyes. Rock fever.

"I did my best to adapt. I took courses in Hawaiian culture, I even learned a bit of the language, but I soon got bored, bored and depressed. There's so little left that's authentic. The history of Hawaii is the history of loss."

"Paradise lost?" I said.

"Paradise stolen. Paradise raped. Paradise infected. Paradise owned, developed, packaged, Paradise sold.

"So, anyway, I thought of going back to school to escape the boredom, finishing my doctorate, but you know, I felt too old, too much time had passed, I just couldn't see myself becoming a student again, sucking up to professors, and there was nobody here in my field worth sucking up to anyway. I wanted a job. I wanted to earn some money of my own, not to be dependent on Lewis for everything. Maybe I had a premonition. One day I saw this ad for a part-time counsellor at the Center for Student Development at UH. I wasn't really qualified, I had no clinical training, but they were quite impressed by my paper qualifications, and I could cite a lot of experience on the mainland with, like, self-help therapy workshops and T-groups, in the women's movement, and anyway the University wasn't paying much so they couldn't be choosy. So I got the job, and learned it as I went along. I pity the poor kids I counselled in my first year, it was the blind leading the blind."

I asked her what kind of problems she had to deal with.

"Oh, the usual ones: love, death, money. Plus race – that's more local. They say this is a multi-racial society, a melting-pot. Don't you believe it. More coffee?"

I declined, and said that I would have to be going.

"Oh, but you can't go yet!" she cried. "I've told you *my* life-story. Now it's your turn." She said it lightly, but she wasn't entirely joking. And it was a fair point. It was precisely because I feared I might be expected to repay her fascinating disclosures in kind that I had made a move to leave. I smiled feebly, and said mine was a very boring story.

"Where do you live in England?" she said.

"A place called Rummidge, it's a big industrial city in the middle of the country. Very grey, very dirty, mostly very ugly. It's about as different from Hawaii as anywhere on the face of the earth."

"Do you have fog there?"

"Not very often. But the light is always hazy in summer, thick and soupy in the winter."

"I used to have a raincoat called London Fog. I bought it for the name, it sounded romantic. It made me think of Charles Dickens and Sherlock Holmes."

"There's nothing romantic about Rummidge."

"I never wore it here. Even though it rains all the time, it's always too hot to wear a raincoat, so I gave it to the Goodwill. Is Rummidge your home town?"

"No, no. I've only been there a couple of years. I teach theology at a non-denominational college."

"Theology?" She gave me a look I was used to receiving: it expressed in rapid and overlapping succession, surprise, curiosity and anticipated boredom. "Are you a minister?"

"I was once," I said. "But not any more." I stood up to leave. "Thank you so much for inviting me. It's been a most enjoyable evening, but I really must go. I have a lot to do tomorrow."

"Sure," she said, with a shrug and a smile. If she felt rebuffed, she didn't show it. We shook hands on her front porch, and she sent her best wishes to Daddy, "if he can bear to hear from me."

I drove rather recklessly back down the steep twisting road, tyres squealing and headlights ricocheting off the roadsigns, venting my irritation with myself. I felt I had behaved clumsily and churlishly. I still feel that. I should have repaid her confidence. I should have told her the whole story. Something like this:

I was born and brought up in South London, one of four children in a family of second-generation Irish immigrants. Our parents were lower-middle-class, just a notch above working-class. My father was a despatch clerk in a road-haulage firm. My mother worked for many years as a school dinner-lady. It was their children who lifted them above their peers. We were all bright, academic kids, who passed public examinations with flying colours. We went to state-aided Catholic grammar schools or convent schools. My elder brother went to University, my sisters to Teachers' Training Colleges. There was always a vague expectation in the family that I might become a priest. I was a rather pious boy – an altar-boy, a regular server at early-morning mass, a collector of indulgences and performer of novenas. I was also a bit of a swot. At the age of fifteen, I decided I had a vocation. I think, now, that it was a way of coping with the problems of adolescence. I was troubled by the things that were happening to my body, and the thoughts that were straying into my mind. I was very worried about sin, about how easily you could commit it, and what the consequences would be if you died in a state of it. That's what Catholic education does for you – did for you in my day, anyway. Basically I was paralysed with fear of hell and ignorance of sex. There was the usual smutty talk in the playground and behind the bicycle sheds, but I was never included. It was as if the other boys sensed I was marked out for a celibate life, or perhaps they were afraid I would tell on them. Anyway, I couldn't spontaneously break into the little huddles where dirty jokes and dirty magazines were sniggered over, and perhaps some know-ledge was passed on amid the smut. I couldn't talk to my parents:

they never mentioned the subject of sex. I was too shy to ask my elder brother, and anyway he was away at University at the crucial time. I was astonishingly ignorant, and afraid. I suppose I thought that by committing myself to the priesthood, I would solve all my problems at a stroke: sex, education, career, and eternal salvation. As long as I fixed my aim on becoming a priest I couldn't, as they say, "go wrong." According to my lights, it was a perfectly logical decision.

On the advice of our parish priest, and of a Monsignor responsible for vocations in the diocese, I left school after taking my O-Levels, and went to a junior seminary, a kind of boarding-school attached to the seminary proper. The idea was to protect the young aspirant to the priesthood from dangerous secular influences and temptations, especially girls, and it worked pretty well. I went straight from the junior seminary to the senior seminary, and from the senior seminary to the English College in Rome – a reward for being top of my class in theology and philosophy. I was ordained in Rome, then sent to Oxford to do a doctorate in Divinity, living in a Jesuit house, working under a Jesuit supervisor, not having much to do with the life of the University at large. I was being groomed for an academic role in the Church, but normally I would have been sent to work as a curate in a parish for at least a few years after finishing my studies. It happened, however, that the distinguished theologian who had taught me at my old seminary suddenly upped and left in the wake of the row over *Humanae Vitae*, and shortly afterwards excommunicated himself by marrying a former nun, so there was a vacancy at St Ethelbert's which they hastily plugged with me.

I was back where I had started, at Ethel's (as we called our *alma mater*), and I stayed there for twelve years. Add those to my years of training and you will realize that I spent most of my adult life insulated from the realities and concerns of modern secular society. It was rather like the life of a mid-Victorian Oxford don: celibate, male-centred, high-minded, but not exactly ascetic. Most of my colleagues could order a decent wine, or discuss the merits of rival malt whiskys, when they got the chance. The building itself was a kind of imitation of an Oxbridge college, a dignified neo-Gothic edifice standing in a small park. Inside, the ambience was less impressive, halfway between a boarding-school and a hospital: tiled floors, gloss paint on the walls, lecture rooms named after the English martyrs, *Aula More, Aula Fisher,* etc. On Sunday mornings, the smell of roasting meat and boiling cabbage crept out of the kitchens and mingled in the corridors with the odour of incense from the college chapel.

Life was regular, ordered, repetitive. One rose early, did half an hour's meditation, concelebrated mass in the chapel at eight, had breakfast (a meal the staff took separately from the students, and therefore particularly relished) gave one's lectures, seldom more than two a day, and met students individually for tutorials by arrangement. Lunch was a communal meal, and so was supper, but afternoon tea was served in the staff common-room. On reflection, we ate rather excessively, though the food was stodgy and unexciting. Afternoons were generally free. You could walk in the park, or catch up on your marking, or work on an article for a theological journal. After supper we usually congregated in the staff common-room, and watched television, or retired to our rooms to read. (My colleagues favoured detective stories or biographies for recreational reading, but I indulged a taste for poetry that I had acquired from A-Level English. I often think I might have taught English in a Catholic secondary school if I hadn't become a priest.) When somebody important, like the bishop, visited, we had drinks. Occasionally we treated ourselves to a discreet blowout at a local restaurant. It was a civilized, dignified, not unsatisfying existence. Students looked up to you. There was, after all, nowhere else for them to look. We were masters of our tiny, artificial kingdom.

Of course, we couldn't entirely ignore the fact that vocations were declining, students dropping out more and more frequently, and ordained priests leaving the priesthood or the Church in ever-increasing numbers. When it was someone you knew personally, someone you had been trained with, or taught by, or whose work you had read and admired, it was always a shock. It was as if in the middle of a party, or an animated meeting, with everybody talking at the tops of their voices, the door suddenly slammed, and the gathering fell silent, and everybody turned to look at the door, and realized that one of their number had left the room and would not be returning. But after a little while, the conversational roar would resume, as if nothing had happened. Most of the defectors seemed to get married sooner or later, with or without the benefit of laicization, and those of us who remained attributed their departure to problems about sex. It was easier to blame sex than to think about the credibility of what we were teaching.

As our numbers dwindled, those of us who remained had to stretch ourselves further and further across the range of theological disciplines. I found myself having to teach biblical exegesis and ecclesiastical history, in neither of which I was properly qualified, as well as dogmatic theology, which was supposed to be my speciality. In the training I had received there was something called apologetics, which consisted in a tenacious defence of every article of Catholic orthodoxy against the criticism or rival claims of other churches, religions and philosophies, employing every available device of rhetoric, argument, and biblical citation. In the climate generated by the Second Vatican Council a more tolerant and ecumenical style of teaching developed, but Catholic seminaries in England – St Ethelbert's anyway – remained theologically conservative. We were not encouraged by our episcopal masters to disturb the faith of the ever-dwindling number of recruits to the priesthood by exposing them to the full, cold blast of modern radical theology. The Anglicans were making all the running in that direction, and we derived a certain *Schadenfreude* from contemplating the rows and threatened schisms in the Church of England provoked by bishops and priests who denied the doctrine of the Virgin Birth, the Resurrection, and even the divinity of Christ. I had a little joke which I used to make each year in my Introduction to Theology lectures, about the demythologizers having thrown the infant Jesus out with the bathwater, which always drew a resounding laugh. And there was a story about an Anglican vicar who had called his three daughters Faith, Hope and Doris, having read Tillich in between numbers two and three, that kept the staff room in fits for a week.

Come to think of it, my abiding memory of Ethel's is of overhearty laughter, in the lecture-rooms, in the common-rooms and the refectory. Honking guffaws, heaving shoulders, grinning teeth. Why do clerics laugh so much at the simplest jokes? To keep their spirits up? Like whistling in the dark?

Anyway, we played the theological game with a straight bat. We stonewalled against the difficult questions, or watched them fly past without offering a stroke. The easy ones we whacked to the boundary. And we were never out lbw, because we also acted as umpires. (I would have had to explain this metaphor to Yolande, of course.)

You don't have to go very deep into the philosophy of religion to discover that it is impossible either to prove or to disprove the truth of any religious proposition. For rationalists, materialists, logical positivists, etc., that is a sufficient reason for dismissing the entire subject from serious consideration. But to believers a non-disprovable God is almost as good as a provable God, and self-evidently better than no God at all, since without God there is no encouraging answer to the perennial problems of evil, misfortune, and death. The circularity of theological discourse, which uses revelation to apprehend a God for whose existence there is no evidence outside revelation (*pace* Aquinas), does not trouble the believer, for belief itself is outside the theological game, it is the arena in which the theological game is played. It is a gift, the gift of faith, something you acquire or have thrust upon you, through baptism or on the road to Damascus. Whitehead said that God is not the great exception to all metaphysical principles to save them from collapse, but unfortunately, from a philosophical point of view, that is exactly what He is, and Whitehead never found a convincing argument to the contrary.

So everything depends upon belief. Grant the existence of a personal God, the Father, and the whole body of Catholic doctrine hangs together reasonably well. Grant that, and you can bat all day. Grant that, and you can afford to have a few mental reservations about the odd doctrine – the existence of Hell, say, or the Assumption of the Virgin Mary – without feeling insecure in your faith. And that was what I did, precisely – I took my belief for granted. I didn't seriously question it, or closely examine it. It defined me. It explained why I was who I was, doing what I did, teaching theology to seminarians. I didn't discover that my belief had gone until I left the seminary.

Stated so baldly, that sounds incredible. After all, I had what we called a "prayer life", of sorts. In fact, I was rather more conscientious than most of my colleagues in doing the statutory half-hour's meditation first thing in the morning. Whom did I think I was praying to? I can't answer that question, except by saying that prayer was part of the taken-for-grantedness of my faith, connected by an unbroken continuum to the simple acceptance of religious ideas that began when my mother first pressed the palms and fingers of my infant hands together at bedtime, and taught me the "Hail Mary". Undoubtedly it had something to do with my exclusively academic career within the Church. Lévi-Strauss says somewhere that "the student who chooses the teaching profession does not bid farewell to the world of childhood: on the contrary he is trying to remain within it."

In the early 1980s, there was a rationalization of Catholic ecclesiastical education in England and Wales, as a result of which Ethel's was closed down. Some of the staff were re-deployed to other academic institutions. But my bishop called me in for a chat and suggested that I might find it useful to get some experience of pastoral work for a while. I think the word must have got through to him that I was a rather uninspired and uninspiring teacher, unable to motivate the students for the ministry for which they were preparing. Well, it was true, though the syllabus was partly to blame. Because of the chance circumstance that had propelled me straight from the status of student to that of teacher, I knew little or nothing about the day-to-day life of an ordinary secular priest. I was like a staff officer who had never seen combat, sending young recruits out to fight a modern war with weapons and tactics handed down from the Middle Ages.

The bishop sent me to St Peter and Paul's, at Saddle. It's one of those rather amorphous places about twenty miles north-east of London, a village that has swollen to the size of a small town since the War. It has a working-class council estate and a middle-class executive estate and a light industrial estate and some horticulture, but most of the working population commute daily to London. There is an Anglican parish church with an Early English tower, a redbrick neo-Gothic Methodist chapel, and a flimsy-looking Catholic church built out of breeze-block and coloured glass in reach-me-down Modern style. My parishioners were a typical cross-section of the English Catholic community: mostly second- or third-generation Irish, with pockets of more recent Italian immigrants, imported after the war to work in the horticultural nurseries, and a sprinkling of converts and pukka Old Catholics who could trace their ancestry back to the Penal Days.

It was a fairly prosperous community, as English Catholic communities go. Unemployment caused less havoc in that part of the country than elsewhere in the early 1980s. The cost and scarcity of housing made life difficult for young married couples, but there was no real poverty, or the serious social problems that go with it: crime, drugs, prostitution. It was a respectable, modestly affluent society. If I had been sent to a parish in Saō Paolo or Bogota, or even one of the more depressed areas of Rummidge, things might have worked out differently. I might have thrown myself into the cause of social justice, made what the liberation theologians call a "preferential option for the poor" – though I doubt it. I was never cast in a heroic mould. But in any case, this was Metroland, not South America. My parishioners did not need or want political or economic liberation. Most of them had voted for Mrs Thatcher. My role was clearly designated, "supernatural reassurance". They looked to the Church to provide a spiritual dimension to lives outwardly indistinguishable from those of their secular neighbours. Perhaps fortunately for me, the great row about birth control and *Humanae Vitae*, which dominated Catholic pastoral life in the sixties and seventies, had died down by the time I came on to the parochial scene. Most of my parishioners had settled the question in their own consciences, and tactfully avoided raising it with me. They wanted me to marry them, to baptize their children, to comfort them in bereavement, and to relieve them from the fear of death. They

151

wanted me to assure them that if they were not as prosperous and successful as they might have wished, or if their spouses deserted them, or their children went off the rails, or they were stricken with fatal illnesses, it wasn't the end, it wasn't a reason to despair, there was another place, another time out of time, where everything would be compensated for, justice done, pain and loss made good, and we would all live happily ever after.

That, after all, is what the language of the Mass promised them every Sunday. *"Have mercy on us all; make us worthy to share eternal life with Mary, the virgin Mother of God, with the apostles and with all the saints who have done your will throughout the ages. May we praise you in union with them, and give you glory for ever and ever."* The Second Eucharistic Prayer. Dip into the Missal at random (I have just tried the experiment on the missal in Ursula's bureau, a newish-looking copy bound in white leatherette, with "holy pictures" between the gold-edged pages) and you will encounter the same theme, endlessly repeated. *"God our Father, may we love you in all things and above all things and reach the joy you have prepared for us beyond all imagining."* (Opening Prayer, 20th Sunday in Ordinary Time, Year A.) *"Lord, we make this offering in obedience to your word. May it cleanse and renew us, and lead us to our eternal reward."* (Prayer over the Gifts, 6th Sunday in Ordinary Time, Year C.) *"Almighty God, we receive new life from the supper your Son gave us in this world. May we find full contentment in the meal we hope to share in your eternal kingdom."* (Prayer after Communion, Holy Thursday, Mass of the Last Supper.)

This has always been the basic appeal of Christianity – and no wonder. The vast majority of human lives in history have not been long, happy and fulfilled. Even if progress should one day achieve such a Utopia for everyone, which seems unlikely, it cannot compensate retrospectively for the billions of lives already thwarted, stunted and damaged by malnutrition, war, oppression, physical and mental illness. Hence our human longing to believe in an afterlife in which the manifest injustices and inequalities of this life would be redressed. It explains why Christianity spread so rapidly among the poor and underprivileged, the conquered and the enslaved, in the Roman Empire of the first century. Those early Christians, and, it would seem, Jesus himself, expected that the end of history, and with it the end of injustice and suffering, was imminent, in the Second Coming of Christ, and the inauguration of His Kingdom – an expectation that continues to inspire fundamentalist sects to this day. In the teaching of the institutional Church, the Second Coming and the Last Judgment were indefinitely postdated, and emphasis put on the fate of the individual soul after death. The appeal of the Gospel message, though, remains essentially the same. The Good News is news of eternal life, Paradise news. For my parishioners, I was a kind of travel agent, issuing tickets, insurance, brochures, guaranteeing them ultimate happiness. And looking down at their faces from the altar, as I pronounced these promises and hopes week after week, looking at their patient, trusting, slightly bored faces, and wondering whether they really believed what I was saying or merely hoped that it was true, I realized that I didn't, not any longer, not a word of it, though I couldn't put a finger on exactly when I had passed from one state to the other – so fine, it seemed, was the membrane, so slight the distance, that separated belief from unbelief.

All the radical demythologizing theology that I had spent most of my life resisting suddenly seemed self-evidently true. Christian orthodoxy was a mixture of myth and metaphysics that made no kind of sense in the modern, post-Enlightenment world except when understood historically and interpreted metaphorically. Jesus, insofar as we could disentangle his real identity from the *midrash* of the early Gospel-writers, was clearly a remarkable man, with uniquely valuable (but enigmatic, very enigmatic) wisdom to impart, infinitely more interesting than comparable apocalyptic zealots who were characteristic of that period of Jewish history; and the story of his crucifixion (though not historically verifiable) was moving and inspiring. But the supernatural machinery of the story – the idea that he was God, "sent" by himself as Father from heaven to earth, born of a virgin, that he rose from the dead and returned to heaven, from whence he would return again on the last day to judge the living and the

153

dead, etc., well, that too had its grandeur and symbolic force as a narrative, but it was no more credible than most of the other myths and legends about divinities that proliferated in the Mediterranean and Middle East at the same time.

So there I was, an atheist priest, or at least an agnostic one. And I didn't dare to tell anyone. I went back to the radical Anglican theologians, John Robinson, Maurice Wiles, Don Cupitt and Co., whom I used to deride in my Introduction to Theology lectures, and re-read them with more respect. In their work I found a kind of justification for carrying on as a priest. Cupitt, for instance, talked about "people who are quietly agnostic or sceptical about Christian supernatural *doctrines*, while neverthe-less continuing to practise the Christian *religion* to striking effect." I thought I would be one of those people. Cupitt, who was less than quiet about his own scepticism, and had been publicly denounced as an "atheist priest", particularly fascinated me as, in a series of books, he grimly sawed away at the branch he was sitting on, until there was nothing left between him and thin air except a Kierkegaardian "religious requirement": "There is as far as we are concerned no God but the religious requirement, the choice of it, the acceptance of its demands, and the liberating self-transcendence it brings about in us." I used to amuse the students at Ethel's by turning that sort of language into a Creed: *"I believe in the religious requirement . . ."* Now even Cupitt seemed to me to presume a lot. Where was this liberating self-transcendence? I didn't feel it. I felt lonely, hollow, unfulfilled.

It was at this point that Daphne came into my life. The circumstances were ironic. She was a senior nurse at a local hospital which I used to visit, in charge of a woman's ward. We used to chat occasionally about the patients in her little cubbyhole of an office. There was one patient we both took a particular interest in, a nun, Sister Philomena, aged about forty, who was dying of some virulent form of bone cancer. She was in and out of the hospital over many months, often in considerable pain. They amputated a leg, but it didn't stop the spread of the disease. There was nothing more they could do. She accepted her fate calmly and courageously. She had tremendous faith. She was quite confident

154

that she was going to meet her Maker, or, as the liturgy of her Final Vows had put it, her bridegroom. Naturally I didn't disturb her with my own doubts, but reflected her faith back to her with simulated fervency. It seems that Sister Philomena told Daphne what a source of comfort and inspiration I was to her, and I had to put up with the embarrassment of receiving this totally undeserved accolade at second hand.

After Sister Philomena had left the ward for the last time, and returned to her convent to die (which she did a couple of months later) Daphne said that she had been so impressed by the experience of nursing her that she wanted to find out more about the Catholic faith. She asked me if she could come to me for Instructions (a phrase she had obviously got from Sister Philomena). I tried to pass her on to my curate, but she insisted that it had to be me. That perhaps should have been a warning signal. But I could see no way of refusing that wouldn't have seemed both rude and irrational. So every Thursday evening, or on Friday afternoons when she was on night duty, Daphne came to the presbytery and we would go into the front parlour, with its ticking clock and massive plaster crucifix over the mantelpiece, and gaudy mission posters on the walls, and sit down on opposite sides of the polished table, on straight-backed chairs whose upholstered rexine-covered seats had long ago collapsed into shallow, uncomfortable craters, and work our way through the articles of the Catholic faith. What a farce.

At first, I aimed to get the whole business over as soon as possible, so when Daphne raised some objection or expressed some bafflement about a particular doctrine, leaning forward and gazing earnestly into my eyes, I would shrug and look away and say, yes, it did present problems from a purely rational point of view, but you had to put it in the context of the Faith as a whole; and then pass on to the next doctrine. But soon I began to look forward to her weekly visits. I was, God knows, lonely. I missed the donnish companionship of the staffroom at Ethel's. My curate, Thomas, was a good lad, a young Liverpudlian not long ordained and seconded to our priest-starved diocese, but his secular interests were mainly football and rock music (he took a

155

keen interest in the Youth Club and conducted a hugely popular folk mass on Sunday evenings) – subjects about which I knew nothing. Our housekeeper was a wizened and arthritic widow called Aggie whose main topics of conversation were the cost of food and the aches in her joints. Daphne was not the world's greatest brain, but she took an intelligent interest in the news, she watched the more serious programmes on television, she read novels that won literary prizes, and went up to London occasionally to see a play or an exhibition. She had been educated at a good girls' boarding-school (her father had been a professional soldier, often stationed abroad) and acquired there a rather genteel accent and style of speech that was off-putting to many people (I overheard staff mimicking her behind her back at the hospital) though not to me. We formed the habit of chatting a little about secular topics after we had gone through the prescribed bit of instruction. Gradually the instruction became more cursory and the chat more extended. I began to suspect that Daphne was no more likely to become a Catholic than I was to recover my belief, and that she too was prolonging the course of instruction for personal reasons.

What did she see in me? I often asked myself that, later. Well, she was thirty-five, and desperate to marry, perhaps to have children. And she was not, one has to say, physically attractive in the modish modern way, or perhaps any way, though it was not something that had occurred to me when we first met, for I had trained myself long ago not to regard women as sexual objects. She was tall and matronly in figure, and looked more impressive in her uniform than when off duty. Her complexion was pale and her face jowly, with a hint of a double chin. She had a sharp nose, and a small, thin-lipped mouth which she usually kept buttoned in a severe straight line, especially on duty (she ran her ward with autocratic authority, and the young nurses in her charge regarded her with respect and, I couldn't help noticing, a degree of dislike). But when we were together she would sometimes permit herself a smile, exposing two neat rows of rather sharp white teeth, and a pink pointed tongue, which she would pass rapidly across her lips in a way that, as our intimacy grew, I found rather sensually

156

arousing. But she was not an obviously desirable woman, any more than I was a desirable man. Neither of us would score very high in what Sheldrake calls attractivity. Perhaps that was what encouraged her to think that we were made for each other.

So came the day of the lunch, the fateful lunch, in her flat, a small apartment in a purpose-built private block, the kind occupied by childless couples and young single professionals, with a rubber plant in the lobby and carpeted corridors where the loudest noise is the whine of the lift. It was a raw February day, with a cold drizzle falling from low, grey clouds. The interior of Daphne's flat looked warm and inviting as she opened the front door – and so did Daphne. She was wearing a soft velvet dress I hadn't seen before, and her hair, which she usually wore in a rather severe chignon, was loose and freshly washed, smelling of scented shampoo. She seemed pleasantly surprised by my own appearance: I was dressed in a pullover and corduroys, and it was the first time she had seen me out of clerical black. "It makes you look younger," she said, and I said, "Do I normally look old, then?" and we laughed, and her pink tongue flickered over her lips in that feline, coquettish way she had.

We were both a little self-conscious, but a glass of sherry before lunch eased our stiffness and a bottle of wine with the meal removed it entirely. We talked more freely, more personally, more interestingly than ever before. I can't remember what we ate, except that it was light and palatable and a vast improvement on Aggie's greasy stews. After lunch we had coffee, sitting side by side on a sofa that Daphne pulled up to face the fire, one of those gasfires with remarkably convincing simulated coal, and we talked. We talked on as the winter afternoon turned to dusk and the room became darker and darker. At a certain point Daphne moved to turn on a lamp, but I stopped her. I was seized by a powerful impulse to tell her the truth about myself, and it seemed easier to do it in the semi-darkness, as if the room had become a confessional. "There's something I have to tell you," I said, "I can't go on giving you instruction any more, because, you see, I no longer believe any of it myself, it would be wrong to continue,

157

bad faith in every sense of the word. There, it's out, and you're the only person in the world that I've told."

In the light from the fire I saw her eyes widen with excitement. She took my hand and squeezed it. "I'm deeply moved, Bernard," she said (we had been on first-name terms for some weeks). "I know how important this is for you, how much it matters. I feel really privileged to receive your confidence."

We sat in solemn silence for a few minutes, staring into the fire. Then, with Daphne still clasping my hand, I told her the whole story, more or less as I have told it here. At the end I said, "So I'll have to hand you over to Thomas, now. He's a bit callow, but his heart is in the right place."

"Don't be silly," she said, and leaning across, kissed me on the mouth, as if to silence me, which it certainly did.

Monday 14th

A meeting this morning with Ursula's lawyer, a Mr Bellucci. His office is in what is called downtown Honolulu, the financial and business district. Like Waikiki, it has a slightly unreal quality, as if it was all built yesterday, and might be dismantled and cleared away overnight for something quite different to be erected tomorrow. You take a turnoff from a rather scruffy stretch of the Ala Moana Boulevard, a mile past the Shopping Center, park in a multi-storey, and walk out on the other side into a maze of pedestrianized streets and plazas linking sleek tower blocks that look confusingly alike, all built of the same stainless steel, smoked glass and glazed brick. The offices, or "suites", are lavishly furnished with wood panelling and fitted carpets, chilled by relentless air-conditioning, and screened by venetian blinds lowered over tinted windows, so that minutes after you have stepped inside off the hot bright pavement it is hard to believe that you are still in Hawaii. Perhaps it is a deliberate effort to create an artificial microclimate conducive to work, and to overcome the lethargy of the tropics. Bellucci and his staff certainly seemed to be playing parts in a simulation of office life in some commercial capital of the northern hemisphere. He wore a three-piece suit and tie; his secretary a severe long-sleeved frock, stockings, and high-heeled shoes. I felt sloppy and unbusinesslike in my slacks and sports shirt.

Mr Bellucci greeted me gravely at the door of his room and gestured me to sit down in a green buttoned-leather armchair that, like the rest of the furnishings, looked brand-new and curiously inauthentic. "How you doing, Mr Walsh?' he said. I told him briefly of my problems, Daddy's accident, etc., and he clucked his tongue sympathetically. "Sticky wicket," he said. "Isn't that what you say in England? Sticky wicket?" I told him the meaning of the phrase in cricket. "No kidding?" he said with mild incredulity. "You gonna sue the driver?" He seemed disappointed when I said no.

He called his secretary to bring in the power-of-attorney document, and smoked a cigar while I read through its four pages. The text was written in typical legal jargon designed to cover every possible eventuality – "*to purchase, sell, bargain, or contract for, encumber, hypothecate, or alienate any property, real, personal or mixed, tangible or intangible* . . ." But the drift was clear enough. It had to be signed by Ursula in the presence of a notary public. I asked how that could be managed, since she was confined to bed, and Bellucci told me the notary would come to the hospital. "The hospital social worker will set it up for you." Which indeed she did. To my astonishment the business was all completed by three o'clock this afternoon, after a brief little ceremony at Ursula's bedside. I now have total power to manage her affairs. My first task was to pay Mr Bellucci's not inconsiderable bill, $250.00.

Between my appointment with Bellucci and the signing of the document, I fitted in visits to two more nursing homes on the list Dr Gerson gave me. The first was Makai Manor, which is in a posh residential district on the coast on the far side of Diamond Head. As soon as I drove through the gates I knew it was going to be wonderfully attractive and impossibly expensive. The building is colonial in style, painted pristine white, with a long verandah where the more mobile patients can sit in the shade and enjoy the sights and scents of the lush, immaculately landscaped gardens. The air smells just as sweet inside. Everything is sleek and comfortable and clean. All the residents have their own bright, comfortably furnished private rooms, with personal TV, bedside telephone, etc. The nursing staff are smiling, neatly dressed and well-groomed, dispensing meals and medicine to the patients with the studied poise of air hostesses. Ursula would love Makai Manor. Unfortunately it costs $6500 per month, not including charges for drugs, physiotherapy, occupational therapy, etc. Her pleasure in being there would be vitiated by anxiety about having to leave if her money ran out. As if reading my mind, the administrator who showed me round, a tall, statuesque blonde lady in a spotless linen suit, discreetly intimated that they required certain financial guarantees when a terminally ill resident was admitted, "to pre-empt any difficulties that might eventuate should the prognosis prove overly pessimistic," as she periphrastically put it. She could tell from my wistful demeanour, and probably from my creased Penney's Levis, that I was out of my class. So that was that.

The second place I saw is called Belvedere House, a somewhat pretentious name for a plain, one-storey building made of pastel-coloured concrete, that looks rather like a small school from the road. The site is exposed and shadeless, just off a broad straight main road in a rather barren, anonymous suburb on the north-western outskirts of the city. After the luxury of Makai Manor, it was a bit of a come-down, but on reflection it was considerably better than either of the two institutions I saw yesterday. Only a faint pong of urine, which I hardly noticed by the time I concluded my visit, and a friendly, caring atmosphere among the staff. There are still some things about it that Ursula won't like: she would have to share a room with another lady, and the beds are very close together (I suspect the rooms were originally designed for single occupancy); some of the residents are plainly gaga, and the communal recreational facilities are very limited. On the other hand it's only $3000 per month. And they have a vacancy.

Tomorrow I must go to Ursula's bank in Waikiki and get her share certificates from her safe-deposit box, and then take them to her stockbroker in downtown Honolulu so that the shares can be

160

sold. I must also close down the safe-deposit box to save the rental, and wind up a small deposit account, and cash a $3000 moneymarket bond administered by the bank. Then all this money must be consolidated into an interest-bearing checking account, as they call a current account here. At the last valuation, which was fairly recent, Ursula's stock portfolio was worth about $25,000, and her other savings and assets amount to about $15,000, giving a total of $40,000, plus her pension. Suppose she sets aside the pension for out-of-pocket expenses and unforeseen contingencies, and pays her nursing-home fees out of the capital. If she went into Belvedere House, that would cover her for just over a year, that is to say, for twice as long as Gerson expects her to live, which leaves an acceptable margin for error in his estimate. A somewhat morbid calculation, but one must face facts.

Ursula seems prepared to face them. I told her about my latest research into nursing homes, without lingering too much on the unattainable attractions of Makai Manor. She accepted my judgment that Belvedere House was probably the best place we could hope to find within her price range, and agreed that I should begin the procedure to get her admitted as soon as possible. Gerson still hasn't sorted out her constipation, which is proving remarkably stubborn, but it's only a matter of time and then she'll have to leave the hospital. Ursula has taken a keen interest in the business of the power of attorney, and the calculation of her assets. Paradoxically all this activity seems to have given her back the will to live. She asked me to bring her some additional nightwear and underwear from the apartment, and tomorrow she is going to have her hair done. The time seems to fly when I visit her, there is so much to discuss.

I wish I could say the same for Daddy. All he can do is to moan about the pain in his hip, and about the indignity of bedpans, and about me for having got him into this scrape in the first place. He longs to get home, and asked me again about Tess. I think perhaps I had better phone her this evening and get it over with, but it's too early yet – they're still asleep in England. I think I'll go for a swim. I feel the need of some exercise after driving around

Honolulu all day in my plastic-lined car, and sitting in offices and hospital rooms.

I've just returned from my swim, having narrowly escaped a minor disaster, and so pleased with myself that I can't stop grinning, even laughing out loud occasionally to vent my ridiculous sense of triumph. Mrs Knoepflmacher caught me chortling to myself as I came out of the lift and gave me a suspicious stare. She came so close to me as she enquired about Daddy and Ursula that I think she was trying to sniff my breath. But I'm quite sober.

I had intended to swim in the pool here, but when I went to inspect it from the balcony it was in deep shadow, quite deserted and somehow uninviting. So I put on a pair of bathing trunks under my shorts and drove down to the beach that fronts Kapiolani Park, which begins where the hotels of Waikiki end. I found a place for my car under the trees of the park without difficulty, for the hour was late and the beach relatively empty. The holidaymakers who jostle for sunbathing space here during the day had rolled up their towels and straw mats and flip-flopped back to their tower-block hatcheries to feed. The scattering of people still on the beach mostly looked like locals who had come down at the end of a working day, with a few beers or Cokes, to take a swim, relax, and watch the sun go down.

It was a perfect hour for a swim. The sun was low in the sky and had lost its fierce daytime heat, but the sea was warm and the air balmy. I swam vigorously for about a hundred yards in the general direction of Australia, then floated on my back and gazed up at the overarching sky. Long shreds of mauve-tinted cloud, edged with gold, streamed like banners from the west. A jet droned overhead, but could not disturb the peace and beauty of the evening. The hum of the city seemed muted and distant. I emptied my mind, and let the waves rock me as if I were a piece of flotsam. Occasionally a bigger wave surged past, swamping me or lifting me into the air like a matchstick, leaving me spluttering in its wake, laughing like a boy. I decided I would do this more often.

Some keen surfers were taking advantage of the last light. At the distance I had swum from the beach, I was better placed than before to observe them, and to appreciate their grace and skill. When a big wave comes along they glide diagonally along its glassy surface, just under the overhanging crest, knees bent and arms extended, and by swivelling their hips they are able to change direction and even reverse, leaping through the spray to the trough on the other side of the wave. If they ride the wave till it spends itself, they gradually stand erect. Sometimes, from my angle of vision, their boards were invisible, and as they approached me they seemed to be walking on the water. Then, as they lose momentum, they sink to their knees, as if in thanksgiving, before turning and paddling back towards the open sea. Watching them, I half-recalled some lines from *The Tempest*, which I have just looked up in Ursula's Book Club edition of Shakespeare's plays. It's Francisco on Ferdinand:

> *Sir, he may live.*
> *I saw him beat the surges under him,*
> *And ride upon their backs.*

Is that, I wonder, the first description of surfing in English Literature?

Back on the beach, I dried off and sat down to watch the sunset. The last surfers shouldered their boards and departed. Out to sea, the sails of catamarans and schooners on "Cocktail Cruises" leaned in silhouette against a backdrop of shimmering gold. Somewhere under the trees in the park at the back of the beach an invisible solo saxophonist was improvising long jazz arpeggios. The instrument wailed and sobbed with a throaty timbre that seemed the very voice of the evening. For perhaps the first time I understood how Hawaii could cast a spell upon the visitor.

Then, as I thought about returning home, my tranquil mood was shattered: I discovered that my keys were missing. Somehow they had fallen out of the pocket of my shorts, into the soft dry sand. I froze, conscious that any movement I made might bury them irretrievably, if they were not buried already. I rotated slowly, the spoke of my shadow lengthening and contracting on the sand, and scrutinized every ridge and hollow around me, without spotting the keys.

I uttered a low whinny of despair, and literally wrung my hands in anguish; for it was not only the keys to the car and the apartment that were missing, but also the key to Ursula's safe-deposit box, which she had entrusted to me that afternoon, and which I had attached to the car-hire firm's key-ring on which I also kept the apartment key. No doubt all these keys would be replaceable, but at the cost of inordinate effort, inconvenience and consumption of precious time. I had, I thought, been doing so well in my management of Ursula's affairs; now, by a stupid act of carelessness, I had jeopardized the expeditious conclusion of the business, and surrendered my newly-won self-esteem. For it *was* stupidly careless to bring a bunch of keys down to the beach in an open pocket. It is so easy to lose a small object in the sand – that's why professional beachcombers go up and down the Waikiki beaches all day with their metal detectors. I squinted along the length of the beach in the hope of seeing such a person, and seriously contemplated standing stock still where I was, until next morning if necessary, until one came along, so that I could enlist his help.

A couple of dark-haired, brown-skinned youths were sitting about ten yards from me, dressed in faded sawn-off jeans and singlets, sipping beer from the can. They had come down to the beach while I was in the water, and with forlorn hope I called across to them to ask if they had by any chance seen a bunch of keys in the sand. They shook their heads pityingly. I wondered whether to fall on my knees and risk raking through the sand with my fingers. In another phase of my life I might have fallen on my knees to say a prayer. My shadow on the sand was now grotesquely long and thin, like one of Giacometti's anorexic statues, and seemed expressive of my impotent grief. I turned again to face the sea, towards which the golden disc of the sun was rapidly sinking. Soon there would not be light enough to search for the keys. That thought gave me an idea.

It was a far-fetched idea, but it seemed to me that it was my only chance. I walked down to the water's edge, about fifteen yards away, in a perfectly straight line. The sun was now almost touching the horizon and its beams were level with the surface of the ocean. I stopped, turned, and squatted on my heels. I looked back up the gently sloping beach to the spot where I had changed for my swim, and there, a yard or two to the right of my towel, something gleamed and glinted, something reflected back the light of the setting sun, like a tiny star in the immensity of space. When I straightened up, it vanished. When I bent my knees again, it reappeared. The two youths watched these exercises with mild curiosity. Keeping my eyes fixed on the spot where the spark of light had gleamed, I marched back up the beach, and there, sure enough, was the tip of Ursula's safe-deposit key, protruding a mere half-inch out of the sand. With a "Ha!" of triumph, I swooped and plucked the key, with its attachments, from the sand and held it up for the admiration of the two youths, who grinned and applauded. At that moment the sun slipped beneath the horizon, and the beach darkened like a stage on which the lights are suddenly dimmed. Clutching the keys tightly – the indentations in my palms have not yet faded – I made my way back to my car in the purple gloaming, light-hearted and gleeful. Tomorrow I must get one of those little marsupial pouches.

I've been looking over the "story of my life", as far as I got with it last night, scribbling furiously into the small hours in a prolonged spasm of self-revelation, or self-examination. I began by imagining myself talking to Yolande Miller, but I was soon talking to myself. And I stopped when I did, not because I was tired, or not just because of that, but because I could hardly bear to go on. It is so painful to recall the sequel, to try and unravel the tangle of momentous spiritual decisions and absurd physical fumblings that followed. That, of course, was why I got up and left Yolande's house so abruptly: because I feared a repetition of events. I had reached the same point, last night, in Yolande's living-room, as I reached with Daphne, in her flat, that dark, drizzly February afternoon. That was why I panicked and ran away. I'll finish the story as briefly as possible.

165

I left our hero, as it were, pinned to the back of the sofa, his lips warmly pressed by those of a woman for the first time in . . . I do believe, my entire life, at least from adolescence onwards. There was a little girl in our road called Jennifer, whom I was rather sweet on when I was about seven, and I dimly remember kissing her on the lips in some game of forfeits at a children's birthday party, with confused feelings of pleasure in the touch of her lips, soft and moist like a peeled grape, and of shame and embarrassment at having to exchange the kiss in public. But after the onset of puberty I never embraced a woman other than my mother and sisters, and those hugs and pecks on the cheek were, needless to say, entirely non-sexual. So it was for me an extraordinarily novel sensation to feel Daphne's mouth against mine. I didn't have a beard in those days, so there was no cushioning insulation at the point of contact. She kissed me firmly, carefully, I might almost say reverently, as some of my female parishioners, usually well-turned out, matronly women like Daphne, used to kiss the feet of the crucified Christ in the Good Friday liturgy, with a graceful genuflection and a confident, well-aimed inclination of the head, as if to demonstrate to others how it should be done. (As celebrant, standing beside the big cross held out by two acolytes on the altar steps, wiping the plaster feet with a white linen cloth after each veneration, I couldn't help noting and mentally classifying the various styles in which different people performed this pious act – some shy and embarrassed, as if at a game of forfeits, some clumsy but fervent and unselfconscious, others cool and poised and self-regarding.)

I sat stock still as Daphne kissed me, astonished, but unresisting – indeed, I was enchanted. I discovered in an instant how deprived I had been of human physical contact, of the animal comfort of touch, during all the long years of my training and work as a priest – deprived, especially, of the mysterious physical otherness of women, their soft, yielding amplitude, their smooth satiny skin, their sweet-smelling breath and hair. It was a long kiss. I had time to notice that Daphne's eyes were closed and, anxious to conform to the rubric of this unfamiliar proceeding, closed my own. Then she detached her lips from mine, withdrew her face and said archly, "I've been wanting to do that for ages. Have you?"

It seemed unchivalrous to say no, so I said yes. She smiled, and lowered her eyelids and pursed her lips and tilted her chin, more or less obliging me to lean across and kiss her again, which I did. When I left the flat, hurrying (Oh, sacrilege!) to get back to the church in time to hear six o'clock Confessions, though no further intimacies had taken place and nothing had been explicitly declared, I was emotionally committed to a relationship with Daphne and morally committed to leaving the priesthood. It would not be fair to say that she had pressured me into this course of action. I was ready to make the break with the Church – indeed secretly longing to do so, to end the contradictions of my ministry, to be frank and open and honest at last about what I believed, or did not believe – but I lacked the courage to do it alone. I needed a provocation and I needed support. Daphne supplied both. A sceptical priest who concealed his doubts and went on doing his job out of timidity or a sense of duty was one thing (I believe there are many such); but a Catholic priest canoodling on a couch was another – a scandal, an anomaly, which couldn't be allowed to continue. Daphne's kiss and my reciprocation of it had set a seal on my loss of faith – or, I should say, had broken the seal on my concealed doubts. I felt no guilt, only relief and exhilaration as I drove away from the block of flats, glancing up at the window of Daphne's living-room, where a curtain was pulled back, and a bulky shape, silhouetted against the light within, seemed to wave a hand. For only the second time in my life I had taken a decisive step to change it. The first had been a leap into the stern but reassuring embrace of Mother Church; the second had been into the arms of a woman and a life of unpredictable risk. I felt more alive than I had done for years. I was "high" on the experience, and I truly believe that I was never a more effective confessor than I was that evening – compassionate, caring, encouraging.

Saying mass and preaching the next morning was a different matter. I was nervous and distraught. I stumbled

167

uncharacteristically over the readings and avoided eye contact with individual members of the congregation when I distributed communion, as if I feared they could look into my eyes and see there, as in a peepshow, some scandalous tableau of myself and Daphne embracing. At lunch I could hardly sustain an intelligent conversation with Thomas, who looked curiously at me once or twice, and asked me if I was feeling all right. In the afternoon I drove round to Daphne's flat, and we had another long talk, this time about the future.

My main concern was to minimize as far as possible the shock and pain my change of life would inevitably cause my parents. So, instead of publicly renouncing the priesthood, the Catholic Faith, and celibacy, all in one stroke, I thought I would apply first for laicization, presenting my decision to Mummy and Daddy as a crisis over my vocation; then, when they had got used to that, I might be able to explain the theological doubts that lay behind it, and in due course prepare them to accept the idea of my marrying. I thought that in the meantime I would look for a teaching job somewhere in the north of England, and that Daphne might join me up there in due course, so that we could get to know each other better in calm and privacy before we took the decisive step of marrying. But it was a naive and ill-thought-out plan, which soon collapsed.

I went to see the auxiliary bishop under whom I served in the diocese, told him of my loss of faith, and asked to be laicized. He predictably urged caution, delay, reflection. He asked me to make a private retreat to consider the matter in a peaceful and spiritual atmosphere. To show willing, I went to a Carmelite monastery for a two-week retreat, but left after three days, half-mad from the silence and solitude, and returned to the bishop to repeat my request for laicization. He asked me if it had anything to do with difficulties over celibacy, and I replied, somewhat casuistically, that my doubts about the Catholic faith were entirely intellectual and philosophical, though it was obviously quite likely that, once laicized, I would, like most laymen, marry. He said he would take further counsel with himself, hoping that we could find some mutually acceptable way of delaying an irrevocable step. He said he would pray for me.

There followed a hiatus of a week or two, during which my mind was in a turmoil of indecision and contradictory impulses. The bishop had dispensed me from the obligation to say mass: officially I was unwell, suffering from stress, resting under doctor's orders. I had a room in a convent just up the road from St Peter's and Paul's. Daphne and I continued to meet surreptitiously. I think she rather enjoyed the illicit and conspiratorial character of our relationship – it gave it a spice of the romantic. Our talk was all of my doubts, my decision, the bishop's procrastination, but our physical closeness grew. Her kisses when we parted were long and lingering, and once she startled me by pushing her wet, warm tongue between my lips and teeth. Inevitably, a parishioner spotted us one evening, holding hands in a little country pub miles from Saddle, and the cat was out of the bag.

Next day the parish vibrated with gossip. Aggie goggled at me when I called at the presbytery to pick up my mail as if I had horns growing from my forehead and hoofs protruding from my trouser cuffs. I was reported to the bishop, who summoned me to an interview and accused me of deceiving him. We exchanged angry words, as a result of which I resigned from the priesthood there and then, and effectively excommunicated myself. I travelled to South London and had a painful meeting with Mummy and Daddy to report what I had done and planned to do. It was a terrible shock to them. Mummy wept. Daddy was haggard and speechless. It was a hellish experience. I didn't attempt to explain the reasons behind my decision – it would only have aggravated the pain. Their simple faith was as vital to them as the circulation of their blood; it had kept them going through the trials and disappointments of life, and would do even through this one. Mummy said, as I left, that she would say the rosary every day of her life for the return of my faith, and I am sure she did. All that wasted breath . . . it makes me unspeakably sad, still, to think of her kneeling night after night in that vain endeavour, in her chilly bedroom, beneath the statue of Our Lady of Lourdes on the mantelpiece, her eyes screwed tight shut, and the rosary beads twisted round her knuckles like bonds, at a time when she was far from well herself. The break-up of my brief relationship with Daphne gave her hope, however. It still left the way back to the priesthood theoretically open.

I hastily moved out of the presbytery at Saddle, and rented a bedsitter in Henfield Cross, a drabber, less affluent place about eight miles away on the outskirts of Greater London (the irony of the vestigial Christian allusion in the name did not escape me). Daphne had invited me to move into her flat, which had a tiny guest-bedroom, but it was too close to the parish for my comfort. The local press had got hold of the story, and once a young reporter ambushed me in the lobby of Daphne's block, requesting an interview. In any case, I shrank from so sudden a plunge into total intimacy, total commitment. Somehow, in the space of a few weeks, an embrace had turned into a relationship, a vague possibility of marrying had turned into a discussion of practicalities: where, when, and under what auspices. I felt I needed some quiet interval in which to collect my thoughts, adjust to the lay life, and get to know Daphne better. Then there was the unresolved question of how I was to earn my bread. I was living off my small savings, which wouldn't last for long. I signed on at the Social Security Office for unemployment benefit, and put my name down on the Professional register at the local Job Centre. The clerk looked somewhat nonplussed when I gave my occupation as "theologian". "We don't get many requests for them," he said. I believed him. I began to haunt the local public library, reading the small ads in the newspapers, especially for educational posts, where I thought my best chance of employment lay.

Meanwhile I saw Daphne regularly. Often we ate a meal out at a pub or an Asian restaurant, or she came over to Henfield Cross and cooked us a meal on my gas-ring. I was reluctant to visit her at her flat for the reasons just given. Also she had a car, and I didn't. The Ford Escort I drove as parish priest had been bought with a loan from the diocese, and I had to surrender it on leaving St Peter's and Paul's. That car is the only thing I genuinely

170

I was interrupted in mid-sentence by the telephone ringing. It was Tess. I had completely forgotten my intention of phoning England this evening. That Tess had had to call *me* again naturally put me still deeper in the wrong, and at a still greater moral disadvantage when it came to admitting that she couldn't speak to Daddy because he was in hospital. She hit the roof, of course. I almost conformed to the cartoon stereotype of holding the receiver at arm's length from my ear, as she berated me for my carelessness and incompetence in looking after Daddy, and folly in dragging him to Hawaii in the first place. Fuelling her anger, I knew, was a guilty consciousness that she herself had encouraged him to go, for mercenary motives that had proved to be ill-founded. I gave as encouraging an account as I could manage of Daddy's injury and his progress towards recovery, and craftily emphasized that the hospital was not only highly efficient but Catholic. I also claimed a little credit (which properly belonged to the young man in the travel agency) for having taken out insurance to cover the medical expenses. (The Walshes were never very prudent in such matters: I recall that our house was burgled twice in the nineteen-fifties before Daddy got round to insuring the contents.) I promised to arrange for Daddy to phone her from his hospital bed, so that she could satisfy herself that I was telling the truth, and that he wasn't ("for all I know," as she darkly hinted) concussed, unconscious or in intensive care.

I tried to steer her off the subject of Daddy by describing the difficulties of finding a suitable nursing home for Ursula. Tess asked me how much Ursula was worth, and grunted in a dissatisfied sort of way when I told her. When I mentioned that I had persuaded Ursula to pay for a private nursing home out of her capital, Tess said, "Don't you think, Bernard, that you're acting a little high-handedly in all this? After all, it's Ursula's money, even if you have got this power of whatever-it-is. If she would *prefer* to go into a state home, and have the comfort of knowing she's got a bit of money behind her –"

"For God's sake, Tess," I interrupted, "she's only got a matter of months to live. And in any case, it doesn't make any difference.

171

If she went into a state home now, they'd claw back the cost from her private means, until it got down to a threshold of a few thousand dollars." (I had discovered this in the course of my research).

"Oh well, I give up," said Tess crossly. "It's all a mess and a muddle. And," she concluded irrationally, "it's all your fault," and slammed down the phone.

Back to Daphne: I want to finish with this sad story and go to bed. Essentially the situation was that I wanted to delay marrying, to give us both time to get to know each other better. Daphne was in more of a hurry: she was thirty-five, and she wanted a family. I needed her companionship and support, but deep down I was terrified of the sexual side of marriage. We had never got beyond kissing and cuddling, in a cosy, decorous sort of way that I found comforting rather than arousing. Only when Daphne's tongue squirmed against mine did I experience some sexual excitement, and then, by a kind of conditioned reflex, I immediately backed off, and sought some mental distraction from the "occasion of sin". I trusted this indicated that I was at least capable of performing the sexual act, but how I would set about it when the time came I could hardly imagine. One evening when we were sitting together in my bedsitter, I hinted at my anxieties and doubts, so vaguely and obliquely that it took Daphne some time to grasp what was worrying me. When she did, she said, with characteristic briskness, "Well, there's only one way to find out," and proposed that we went to bed together there and then.

Well, it was a disaster, a fiasco, that night and the other occasions on which we tried – whether it was in my room, or in her flat, or (once, a desperate last resort) in a hotel. Daphne wasn't a virgin, but her sexual experience had been limited to a couple of brief, unsatisfactory affairs in her student years. From what she told me of these episodes, they sounded like sad stories of a plain fat girl who, desperate for affection, gave herself too easily to unscrupulous young men, who took their pleasure, gave her little, and quickly moved on. After qualifying, she had fallen in love with a surgeon at the first hospital where she worked, but it was a

172

purely platonic relationship because he was a happily married man. She told me this as if to solicit my admiration for her self-control and self-denial, but I wonder whether the surgeon wasn't quite content with a platonic relationship with Daphne, and whether he didn't in due course accept a teaching appointment in New Zealand partly to get away from her oppressive devotion. So she was sexually inexperienced, or at least unpractised, but also curiously shameless – the worst possible combination to set at ease an ageing novice like me. Fifteen years of nursing men and women of all ages and shapes had made her totally indifferent to the naked human body, its functions and its imperfections, while I was acutely selfconscious about exposing my own body, and ultra-sensitive to the spectacle of hers. Daphne disrobed was a very different creature from Daphne in the crisply starched carapace of her nurse's uniform, or sheathed in her ladylike frocks and invisible foundation garments. My image of the naked female form, inasmuch as I had one at all, was something chaste, classical and ideal, derived I suppose from icons like the Venus de Milo and Botticelli's Venus. Daphne in the nude was more like a life-sized version of one of those female fertility figurines you find in museum collections of ethnic exotica, with huge breasts, swelling bellies and jutting buttocks, crudely carved or shaped out of wood and terracotta. A more virile and confident lover might have revelled in this abundance of flesh, but I was intimidated.

Some people imagine, I think, that a man released from twenty-five years of compulsory celibacy must be quivering with priapic appetite, ready and eager to couple with the first willing woman he encounters. Not so. There had been a time, in my student days, when, like any normal young man, I could be surprised into almost unbearable feelings of lust by inadvertently glancing at a lewd picture in a magazine, or finding myself staring down the gaping neckline of a pretty girl seated beneath me as I hung from a strap in a crowded Underground train. And for (I suspect) rather longer than most young men, I was troubled by nocturnal emissions, as the accumulated juice of generation, denied the normal means of relief, spilled over in sleep and dream. (It was a common problem: I once overheard a couple of women who did the laundry at Ethel's making coarse jokes about "maps of Ireland on the sheets" and "no wonder they call it a seminary".) But that was a long time ago. Gradually involuntary sexual arousal become rarer, and easier to control. Celibacy became less of a sacrifice, and more of a habit. The sap slowly sank.

Even with men who have led a normal sexual life, I believe, there comes a time when sexual intercourse is an act of will rather than a reflex response. I read somewhere recently a witticism attributed to a Frenchman, a typical piece of worldly Gallic wisdom, to the effect that "Fifty is a good age, because when a woman says, 'Yes', you are flattered, and when she says, 'No', you are relieved." Well, I wasn't fifty, I was only forty-one when Daphne said Yes to a question I had hardly formulated, but, like muscles that are not exercised, instincts that are not indulged tend to atrophy. Neither Daphne nor I possessed the skill or the tact to revive my long-suppressed libido. I could not, as I believe the vulgar phrase goes, "get it up". Or, if I did get it up, I couldn't keep it up long enough to get it inside Daphne; and her well-intentioned attempts to assist me only increased my shame and embarrassment. Every failure foredoomed the next attempt, by making me more nervous and apprehensive. One day Daphne gave me a sex manual to read, full of erotic drawings and descriptions of perverse practices, but it was like giving a gourmet menu to a man who had been living on bread and water all his life (the book was in fact divided into sections facetiously entitled Appetizers, Starters, Main Courses, etc.). It was like giving a Do-It-Yourself handyman, who aspired only to mend a fuse, a textbook on nuclear physics. All it did was to intensify my sense of inadequacy and anticipatory panic as the next test approached.

Although Daphne was tolerant and good-humoured at first, her patience became strained, and it was more and more difficult to disguise the fact that we were unlikely ever to make happy sexual partners. She naturally felt rejected, while I felt humiliated. The difficulties of this side of our relationship began to infect the rest of it, which Heaven knew was already vulnerable and stressful enough. We bickered about trivia, and quarrelled about some-

174

thing important – whether I should accept the part-time job at St John's College which had been offered to me. She didn't want to move to Rummidge – a nasty, dirty, industrial slum as she called the city, though she had never done more than drive through it on the motorway, hardly the most flattering viewpoint. She wanted me to spend more time looking for a job in the south-east, perhaps in the religious-education department of a secondary school. But I knew in my heart that I could never control a class of no doubt bored and resentful teenagers in a state comprehensive, while the post at St John's, meagre as the salary was, sounded congenial. Besides, I was anxious to move away from the South, away from London and environs, to somewhere where there would be less chance of bumping into former students and colleagues, and less occasion to meet members of my family. So, sadly, miserably, wretchedly, a couple of months after I left the priesthood, I left Daphne – or she left me. We parted, anyway, by mutual agreement. The failure of the relationship weighed on my mind for many months. Had I used her, or had she used me? I don't know, perhaps neither of us really understood our true motives. I was enormously relieved to learn last year that she is married. I hope it is not too late for her to have children.

Tuesday 15th

An extraordinary and wonderful thing happened today. In another phase of my life I might have called it providential, or even, as Ursula did today, "miraculous". Now I suppose I must call it fortunate or lucky, though "fortunate" sounds too restrained, and "lucky" too flippant an epithet for an event that has a satisfying poetic justice about it. And the key! The lost and found key! A more superstitious person might well have interpreted that little episode as a favourable omen. For without the key I couldn't have gone to the bank this morning to open Ursula's safe-deposit box, and without opening the safe-deposit box I couldn't have collected her share certificates, and without the share certificates I wouldn't have gone to the stockbroker's office in downtown Honolulu and discovered that Ursula is very much better off than she ever dreamed. Indeed, rich!

Because there was a joker in the pack, an extra share certificate that Ursula had completely forgotten about, in a plain, un-marked, rather cheap envelope, slipped between the folds of her marriage certificate (which she had never felt inclined to inspect since her divorce) at the bottom of the box, under a copy of her will, and under the little bundle of the share certificates she *did* know about, each in its transparent plastic wallet, acquired since she settled in Honolulu, through the firm of Simcock Yamaguchi, with whose Mr Weinburger I had an an appointment this morning. It appears that she had purchased the share (for that was all it was, a single share) at the time of the break-up of her marriage, on the recommendation of a friend, or her attorney, or possibly even her ex-husband (she can't be sure, it is all so long ago), a very small investment of two hundred and thirty-five dollars, for just one share in a then little-known company. She had stowed away the certificate of ownership, forgotten it, failed to inform the company of her numerous changes of address at that period of her life, so that she never received dividends, and eventually the company would have given up trying to contact her, according to Mr Weinburger.

He frowned as he drew the certificate from its flimsy envelope. "What's this?" he said. "There's no record of this in Mrs Riddell's portfolio."

Ursula's shareholdings were listed on one of his computer screens, amber letters and numbers on a brown background. He had been going through the items one by one, summoning up other lists and tables on another screen, white letters on green, to demonstrate, with a display of professional expertise that was quite wasted on me, for I could understand nothing of it, the market value of each share at that moment, before punching in an instruction to sell.

It is a strange, troglodytic life that Mr Weinburger leads. The New York Stock Exchange closes at ten a.m. Hawaiian time, so he rises in the dark, and comes to work at five o'clock every morning, to spend eight hours in a large, windowless open-plan room crammed with rows of desks at which men in dark suits and striped shirts frown at computer screens and mutter into telephones trapped under their chins like violins. The dealing room of Simcock Yamaguchi is a more convincing simulation of Wall Street than Mr Bellucci's suite, and even more effective in making one forget that outside the building the sun is flashing in the surf, and the palm trees bending in the trades. The wealth of Hawaii presumably depends on such people as Mr Weinburger, working away under electric light, indifferent to the blandishments of the tropical climate. By one o'clock, I gathered, he would have finished his day's work, but he didn't look as if he spent his afternoons on the beach. His complexion was pale, like a miner's, under his premature five-o-clock shadow. I imagined him eating lunch with his cronies in some ice-cold, dimly lit basement restaurant in a nearby shopping mall, then driving home in his air-conditioned, tinted-glass automobile, to watch TV in his shuttered house.

"Jesus Christ," he said, as he examined the share certificate. "Where in hell did this come from?"

I explained where I had found it.

"Have you looked at it, Mr Walsh?"

"Yes. It's only one share, isn't it?"

"One share, but that was in 1952, and did you notice that the company is called International Business Machines?" He tapped the keyboard of his computer, peered at the green-and-white screen, where a new list of figures appeared. "There's been a whole lot of stock splits and stock dividends since 1952, so your aunt's single share has multiplied into two thousand four hundred and sixty-four shares, and the current price of IBM being one hundred and thirteen dollars, your aunt's investment is worth approximately . . ." (he did a rapid calculation) ". . . two hundred and seventy-eight thousand dollars."

I gaped at him. "Did you say, two hundred and seventy-eight *thousand*?"

"Not including the dividends and accumulated interest on the dividends, which IBM would have banked in your aunt's name for a certain number of years, while they tried to trace her."

177

"My God," I breathed in an awed whisper.

"A hundred thousand per cent profit on the original investment," said Mr Weinburger. "Not bad. Not bad at all. What d'you want me to do with these shares?"

"Sell them!" I cried. "Sell them now, before they lose their value."

"Not much risk of that," said Mr Weinburger.

Three-quarters of an hour later I walked, or rather floated, out of the building, with a cheque in my wallet for $301,096.35c., the total sale value of Ursula's shares, less the commission of Simcock Yamaguchi. I jumped into a taxi and sped to the Geyser in a daze of incredulous delight. All Ursula's problems were solved at a stroke. There was no need for her to worry about money ever again. Forget Belvedere House and its ilk. She would move into Makai Manor as soon as it could be arranged. What a pleasure it is to be the bearer of good news! What an irrational proprietory pride one feels. I ran into the lobby of the Geyser, and fretted as I waited for an elevator. I burst through the swing doors into Ursula's wing, brushed past a nurse who protested that it wasn't a visiting hour, and rushed up to Ursula's bed. Curtains were drawn round it, and there was an appalling stench in the air. A pale-faced nurse appeared from behind the curtains with something under a towel in her hand and hurried away, followed by Dr Gerson, who swivelled me round with a hand on my shoulder and guided me to the door.

"We finally fixed her bowel," he said. "It took a real Molotov cocktail of an enema. I was beginning to think we'd have to operate."

"Is she all right?" I said.

"She's OK, but it wasn't very pleasant. She's resting. Come back in an hour or so."

I said I had important news to deliver, and that I would wait. Sitting on a mauve banquette in the ground-floor lobby, I calmed down and put the events of the morning in perspective. Ursula's financial problems were solved, but she was still dying, in some discomfort and distress. Nothing could alter that fact. Rejoicing was hardly in order.

178

But of course Ursula was delighted when I finally got to see her. She was scarcely able to believe in her suddenly acquired fortune, and I think it was only the sight of the cheque that convinced her. She had completely forgotten having purchased the share – it had been suppressed along with painful memories connected with the break-up of her marriage. "It's a miracle," she said. "If I'd known that I had that stock, I'd have sold it years ago, and probably frittered the money away. Now it's turned up when I need it most, like buried treasure. God has been very good to me, Bernard – and so have you!"

"Somebody was bound to find it, eventually," I said.

"Yes, but maybe not till after I was dead," she replied. The word "dead" put a damper on our spirits momentarily. Ursula broke the silence. "Don't tell Sophie Knoepflmacher about this, whatever you do. Don't tell anybody." When I asked her why, she muttered vaguely about burglars and spongers, but it hardly made sense. I put it down to the ingrained Walsh secretiveness and defensiveness about money. I asked her if I could tell Daddy, and she said, yes, of course. "And tell him to call his sister, will you? I still haven't managed to talk to him."

I went straight to St Joseph's to give Daddy the news, only to find a silver-haired Mrs Knoepflmacher stationed by his bedside in a white *muu-muu* with big blotchy flowers of pink and blue printed on it. A little posy of orchidaceous blossoms of the same hues lay on Daddy's night table. "Your father's been telling me about the Catholic religion," she informed me. "Oh, really?" I said, trying to conceal my amusement. "What aspect of it?" "Oh, the difference between . . . what were those two things?" she said, turning to Daddy, who looked slightly sheepish. "Calumny and detraction," he muttered. "That's right," said Mrs Knoepflmacher. "Apparently it's worse to say something bad about a person that's true than to say something bad that's untrue." "Because if it's true you can't retract it," I said, "without telling a lie." "That's right," said Mrs Knoepflmacher. "That's exactly what Mr Walsh said. I'd never have thought of that. Mind you, I'm still not *quite* sure I understand it." "I'm not sure I do, either,

179

Mrs Knoepflmacher," I said. "It's the kind of thing moral theologians amuse themselves with on long winter evenings."

After a few minutes further chit-chat, Sophie Knoepflmacher left us alone. "You have to talk about something," Daddy said, as if in self-defence, "if the bally woman insists on coming to see you. *I* don't invite her."

"I think it's very nice of her," I said. "And if it takes your mind off your hip –"

"Nothing takes my mind off that," he said.

"Ursula has had some news that should do the trick," I said. "Why don't you phone her now, and let her tell you herself. I'll have a phone brought here to your bed."

"What news?"

"If I tell you, it'll spoil the surprise."

"I don't like surprises. News about what?"

"Money."

He considered for a moment. "Well, all right. But I don't want you staring at me while I talk to her."

I said I would wait outside. The conversation didn't last long, considering that they hadn't spoken to each other for decades. When I put my head round the door after a few minutes, Daddy had already put the phone down.

"Well?" I said with a smile.

"It seems she's a rich woman after all," he said flatly. "Not that it will do her much good now, poor soul."

"It will buy her the best nursing care available," I said.

"Aye, there's that, I suppose." There was a thoughtful, faraway look in his eyes. I realized that Ursula's news had revived the hope of inheriting her fortune. It's a depressingly selfish response, but if it takes the edge off his resentment at having been brought to Hawaii, I shan't complain.

"I expect Ursula was glad to hear your voice at last," I prompted.

He shrugged. "So she said. She was threatening to hire an ambulance to bring her here to see me."

"Well, it may come to that," I said. "You didn't speak for long on the telephone."

"No," he said. "A little of Ursula always went a long way with me."

Just before I left Ursula today she said wistfully, "It would have been great, wouldn't it, if you and I and Jack could have gone out and painted the town red tonight? You'll have to celebrate for us, Bernard. Have a slap-up dinner somewhere."

"What, all on my own?" I said.

"Don't you know anyone you could ask?"

I immediately thought of Yolande Miller. It would have been an opportunity to return her hospitality, but since I hadn't mentioned my Sunday-night supper to Ursula I couldn't very well introduce her name now without provoking surprise and unwelcome curiosity. "I could always invite Sophie Knoepflmacher," I said.

"Don't you dare!" Ursula exclaimed. When she saw I was teasing, her features relaxed. "I tell you what you could do, Bernard – it's what I would do this evening, if I was able. Go to the Moana for a champagne cocktail. It's the oldest hotel in Waikiki –and the finest. You must have seen it on Kalakaua where it joins Kaiolani. They restored it recently, it was badly run down. It has a huge old banyan tree in the courtyard at the back, looking on to the ocean, where you can sit out and have drinks. They used to broadcast a famous radio programme from there, 'Hawaii Calls', to the mainland. I used to listen to it when I first came to America. Go there for me tonight. Tell me tomorrow what it was like."

I said I would. It is now 4.30 in the afternoon. If I'm going to invite Yolande Miller, I must do it now.

Wednesday 16th

Today was slightly less frantic than the preceding ones. I have arranged for Ursula to move into Makai Manor on Friday, "subject to satisfactory financial guarantees," which shouldn't be a problem. I drove over there to fill out the necessary forms ("fill out" – I am learning American English fast) and brought back a brochure to show Ursula. I also took into the hospital the fresh

181

supply of lingerie she had requested. I must say that I found it an odd and slightly uncomfortable task to rifle her bedroom drawers for these intimate articles of feminine attire, holding them up to determine their function, fingering the delicate fabrics to discriminate between silk and nylon; but then this whole expedition to Hawaii has plunged me into unfamiliar experiences from the very beginning.

At the bottom of one of the drawers I found an unsealed, unmarked manila envelope, and thinking that it might contain another forgotten share certificate or similar treasure, I looked inside. All it contained however was an old photograph, a sepia snapshot that had been torn nearly in half at some time and then repaired with Sellotape. It showed three young children, a girl aged about seven or eight, and two older boys aged about thirteen and fifteen. The girl and the younger boy were sitting on a fallen tree-trunk in the middle of a field, squinting up at the camera, and the older boy lounged behind them, with his hands in his pockets, and a cocky grin on his face. Their clothes were drab and old-fashioned, and they all wore clumsy laced boots, though the season seemed to be summer. I immediately recognized Daddy as the younger boy. The little girl with the mass of ringlets and the shy smile was Ursula, and the older boy must be another sibling – Sean, perhaps: I thought I recognized the jaunty pose from the photo of the drowned hero on Daddy's dresser.

I took the photo with me to the hospital, thinking that it might provoke some interesting memories of Ursula's childhood. She glanced at it and gave me an odd look. "Where did you find that?" I told her. "It got torn once and I tried to mend it. It's not worth keeping." She gave it back to me. "Throw it away." I said that if she didn't want it, I would have it. She confirmed my identification of the children in the picture, but seemed uninterested in discussing it further. "It was taken in Ireland," she said, "when we lived in Cork, before we moved to England. A long time ago. Did you go to the Moana last night?"

I told Ursula all about the Moana – everything except that I had been accompanied by Yolande.

I finally summoned up the courage to ring her at five o'clock yesterday afternoon. Roxy answered the phone. I heard her calling to her mother, who was evidently outside the house: "Mom! Call for you, I think it's that guy who was here the other night." Then Yolande came on the phone, sounding rather cool and guarded, as well she might after my abrupt departure on Sunday evening. Gabbling breathlessly from embarrassment and self-consciousness, I summarized the exciting events of the day, and explained Ursula's wish to celebrate vicariously with cocktails at the Moana. I asked Yolande if she knew the hotel.

"Of course I know it, everybody knows it. I'm told they've done a beautiful job on the restoration."

"You'll come, then?"

"When?"

"This evening."

"*This* evening? You mean, like *now*?"

"It has to be this evening," I said. "I promised my aunt."

"I'm out in the yard," she said, "cutting back the jungle. I'm covered in dirt and sweating like a pig."

"Please come."

"Well, I don't know . . ." she said hesitatingly.

"I'll be there in half an hour," I said. "I hope you'll join me."

I don't know where I got this nonchalant, almost rakish "line" from, for it isn't at all my style; but it worked. Forty minutes later, I was sitting in a cane armchair and a clean white shirt at a table for two on the verandah that runs round the Moana's Banyan Courtyard, and saw Yolande come through the rear doors of the hotel's lobby and look around, shading her eyes against the evening sun. I waved, and she strode towards me with a bounding, athletic gait. Her black hair bounced about her shoulders, still damp from the shower. She was wearing a full-skirted cotton dress that looked cool and comfortable. As I rose from the table and shook her hand, she regarded me quizzically.

"Surprised to see me?"

"No," I said. Then, thinking that this sounded rather arrogant, amended it to "Yes," and finally to, "Well, let's say, relieved. Thank you very much for coming."

She sat down. "You must think my social life is pretty arid if I can drop everything and rush out for a drink at a moment's notice."

"No, I –"

"Well, you'd be absolutely right, as it happens. Besides, I can't resist a date with a man who knows how to use the word 'vicariously'."

I laughed, feeling a slight thrill of danger, not disagreeable, at the word "date."

The waiter arrived. I asked him what a champagne cocktail was, and when he told me I suggested to Yolande that we drank straight champagne, to which she readily assented. I ordered a bottle of Bollinger, the only name I recognized on the list the waiter rattled off.

"Have you any idea how much that's going to cost in a place like this?" Yolande said, when the waiter had departed.

"I'm under orders to be extravagant this evening."

"Well," she said, looking round, "this is elegant."

And indeed it was. The Moana is quite unlike any other building I have seen in Waikiki – not kitsch, not a three-quarter scale reproduction like the strange little Victorian shopping precinct I stumbled upon the other day (Burger King housed behind sash windows, a mock English pub called the Rose and Crown) – but the real thing, a Beaux Arts building in wood of real grandeur and distinction, now beautifully restored, with polished hardwood floors and William Morris textiles. The pale grey frontage is imposing, with Ionic columns and an arcaded porch. The courtyard at the back, overlooking the beach, is dominated by an immense and ancient banyan tree, tethered to the ground by its curious aerial roots. In the shade of the banyan a string trio played Haydn – Haydn in Waikiki! – as the sun slid down the sky towards the sea in an apricot haze. I cannot remember when I felt so happy, so carefree, when life seemed so enjoyable. I was drinking vintage champagne, listening to classical music, watching the sun set over the Pacific, and conversing with an intelligent, amusing and personable companion. " 'How pleasant it is to have money, heigh-ho, how pleasant it is to have money!' " I chanted.

184

"Is that a song?"

"It's from a poem by Arthur Hugh Clough. One of those Victorian honest doubters with whom I feel a kind of kinship."

"Honest doubters," said Yolande. "I like it."

" 'There lives more faith in honest doubt, believe me, than in half the creeds.' Tennyson. *In Memoriam*." Why was I showing off in this ridiculous fashion? It dawned on me that I must be a little drunk. Yolande didn't seem to mind, or even notice. Perhaps she was a little drunk too. She came to that conclusion herself when she knocked over her last half-glass of champagne.

"How am I going to drive myself home in this state?"

"You'd better have something to eat," I said. We had eaten nothing with the champagne except a small dish of potato crisps, a speciality from the island of Maui, thick and gnarled like tree bark.

"OK. But not here. It'll be far too grand and I might disgrace us by knocking over another glass. D'you like sushi?"

I confessed that I didn't know what it was. Yolande said it was time I found out, and that there was a good Japanese restaurant in a hotel across the road.

The restaurant was crowded, so we sat up at a bar on high stools. A smiling Japanese chef put before us exquisitely fashioned morsels of raw fish which one dipped into various delicious sauces. Yolande said the fish had to be absolutely fresh. The chef, who overheard us, said it was so fresh it was swimming a few minutes ago, gesturing with his knife at the glass tank behind him. Well, I thought, this is living. I felt worldly and sophisticated.

Most of the diners in the restaurant were Japanese tourists, and when the chef was out of earshot, Yolande claimed that she could pick out at least two honeymoon couples among them. "They come here for a Western-style wedding, after they've been married in a traditional ceremony at home; they come for the long white dress, the stretch limo, the wedding cake, all recorded on video to show the folks back home. This is Fantasyville, you know? Nothing is real. I wandered into the Kawaiahao mission church the other day – it's one of the oldest buildings in

Honolulu, which isn't saying very much, but it's kind of nice – and there was a Japanese couple getting married. It gradually dawned on me that not only the minister, the organist, the usher, the photographer and the chauffeur were hired, so were the best man and the bridesmaids. I was the only person present who wasn't being paid to be there, except the bride and groom – and I had my doubts about them." I asked her how she could tell the couples in the restaurant were honeymooners. "You can tell because they're not speaking to each other, they're shy. They don't know each other too well – they still have arranged marriages in Japan. With us it's the other way round; it's the middle-aged couples who eat in silence." She was silent herself for a moment, perhaps reminded of the doldrums of her own marriage. I said I had met an English honeymoon couple on the plane who weren't speaking to each other, and told her the story of the young man in braces and his Cecily. She said she didn't know whether it was terribly funny or terribly sad. I said it was terribly British.

I was reminded of a married couple I had known at Saddle, pillars of the parish and weekly communicants, who always chatted animatedly with me when I called on them, but who, I was reliably informed, had not spoken to each other in private for five years, ever since their only daughter got pregnant by her boyfriend and left home. I contrived to tell this story without revealing my relationship to the couple. We got talking about the permissive sexual mores of the ancient Polynesians, which Yolande described as "the kind of sexual Utopia we were all pursuing in the sixties – free love and nudity and communal childrearing. Only with them it wasn't a pose, they really lived it. Until the *haoles* came along with their hang-ups and bibles and diseases." The sailors gave the beautiful amorous women of Hawaii the pox, and the missionaries made them wear *muu-muus* even in the sea so they sat about in damp clothes and caught cold. In seventy years the population of the islands declined from 300,000 to 50,000. "And now Hawaiians suffer from the same sexual hang-ups as people anywhere else. Read the agony column in the *Honolulu Advertiser* if you doubt me. But one mustn't

186

idealize the Polynesians. After all, they invented the word taboo. They just attached it to different things. If you happened to eat dinner in the wrong place or with the wrong person, it could be fatal. If the king picked up your baby and it weed on him he had to either adopt it or have its brains bashed out. Human beings seem to take a perverse delight in making life more difficult for themselves than it is already." Yolande looked at her watch. "I should go."

I was surprised to find how late it was. We hadn't sobered up completely, no doubt because we drank some sake, warm rice wine, in tiny handleless porcelain cups, with the sushi. Perhaps she should take a taxi home, I suggested, as I settled the bill, tipping the chef generously.

"No, I'm fine," she said. "And I had to park the car so far away, I'll walk off any remaining effects of the booze."

I offered to escort her to her parking place, which was near the Zoo.

"That would be nice," she said. "It's kind of dark over there by the park."

Indeed it was, and as we walked under the trees, where couples sauntered hand in hand, or with their arms round each other's waists, it struck me that to them we must look like just such another couple, and I sensed from Yolande's momentary, pensive silence, that the same thought had struck her. Suddenly the companionable ease of the evening was spoiled. I felt a rush of the old familiar panic, a premonition that at any moment Yolande would suddenly stop, and pull me into her arms, and kiss me, and push her tongue between my lips, and then what, then what? So that when a few moments later she stopped and laid a hand on my arm, I jumped away as if burned. "What's the matter?" she said. "Nothing," I said. "I was only going to say, look at the moon." She pointed through a gap in the trees at the bright crescent moon. "Oh," I said. "Yes. Very nice."

She walked on in silence for a few moments, then stopped and rounded on me. "What's the matter with you, Bernard? Do you think I'm trying to seduce you, or something? Hey? Is that it? You think I'm a sex-starved deserted wife whose tongue is hanging out for a screw? Is that it?"

187

"No, of course not," I said weakly. One or two couples had stopped in the shadows nearby, their interest aroused by this outburst.

"Let me remind you that *you're* the one who set this up tonight, *you're* the one who pleaded with me to come out, at a half-hour's notice."

"I know," I said. "And I'm very grateful."

"Well you have a funny way of showing it. Like the other night, I thought we were getting on fine together, and suddenly you rushed out of the house leaving me wondering what I'd said."

"I'm sorry," I said. "It wasn't your fault. It was me."

"OK. Forget it." She closed her eyes and took some deep breaths. I watched her bosom rising and falling under her cotton dress. The people who had stopped nearby melted away. Yolande opened her eyes. "You needn't come any further," she said. "I can see the car from here. Goodnight, and thanks for the champagne and dinner."

She stuck out her hand, and like a fool I shook it, and stood rooted to the spot, watching her walk away, her skirt twirling from her hips with the energy of her stride. Like a fool I let her go, when what I should have done was to run after her, take her hand, and try to explain why I find it so difficult to have an ordinary, friendly relationship with a woman. And that for most of this evening, I came closer to achieving it than ever before in my life.

I have had an idea, a rather wild idea. It is now half-past midnight. I am going to drive up to Yolande's house in the Heights, and leave this journal, or confession, or whatever it is, wrapped in brown paper, in Yolande's mailbox, or, if it's too big to go in, propped up on her porch outside the front door. I must do it now, before I have time to change my mind, or am tempted to go through the text first, editing it and improving it. I shall write on it: *"Whoso readeth, let her understand."*

2

Dear Gail,
   The beach is usually more crowded than it looks in
this picture. The water is nice and warm, but just
swimming is boring and Dad won't let me and Robert
try surfing because he says it's dangerous. There's not
much else to do. It was more fun at Center Parc last
year.
                    Best wishes,
                    Mandy

Dearest Des,
   Well, here we are in Hawaii! Phew is it hot! Hotel
clean and quite comfortable but you have to wait about
ten minutes to get into a lift at rush hours. The beach is
lovely, though a bit crowded. We've found a nice place
to drink in the evenings, outdoors with a floor show.
We met an English man called Bernard on the plane
who I thought would do for Dee, but he's very shy and
she doesn't fancy him anyway. Hope you're behaving
yourself.
                    All my love,
                    Sue

Dear Mother,
    Well, we got here, but I'm not sure it was worth the journey. Waikiki is overrated – crowded and commercialized. All Macdonalds and Kentucky Fried Chicken, just like Harlow Shopping Centre. We should have gone to one of the other islands, Maui or Kauai, but it's too late now. Love,
                                    Dee

Dear Denise,
    Arrived safely. This is our hotel, I have marked our balcony with a cross. It overlooks the sea. Such a beautiful place, flowers everywhere. Nothing but the best for my Mum, Terry says! Unfortunately his girl friend couldn't come after all, so his friend Tony is keeping him company. V. hot here, doesn't really agree with your father.
                    Love,
                    Mother

Dearest Des,
    Met that Bernard I told you about on the beach with a friend, another English chap called Roger who I thought would do for Dee. He is bald but you can't have everything. We went out on a Sunset Cruise with him (Bernard couldn't come), on this sailing boat, sails set by computer, ever so romantic, but Dee got seasick and I had to talk to Roger all the time, or rather listen to him, he's a university lecturer, likes the sound of his own voice. Better luck next time. Wish you were here,
                    Lots of love,
                    Sue

Dear Greg,
　　This is the famous Waikiki beach. Haven't seen much of it yet – been catching up on our sleep (nudge, nudge). How did you make out with the chief bridesmaid after the reception? Or were you too p----d?
　　　　Cheers,
　　　　Russ

Paradise Bakery
Paradise Dental
Paradise Jet Ski
Paradise Redicab
Paradise Yacht Sales
Paradise Erectors
Paradise Chapel
Paradise Ferrari and Lamborghini
Paradise Antique Arts
Paradise Video
Paradise Pets

Dear Sir,

I am currently enjoying, if that is the *mot juste*, which I venture to doubt, a holiday provided by your company at the Hawaiian Beachcomber Hotel, Waikiki.

Your brochure states quite unambiguously that the hotel is "five minutes" from Waikiki beach. I have explored every possible route between the hotel and the beach, and my son and I have independently timed these journeys on digital stopwatches. The fastest time either of us achieved was 7.6 minutes, and that was carried out at a brisk pace, early in the morning, when the pavements were comparatively uncrowded, and the traffic lights at pedestrian crossings favourable.

A normal family, carrying the usual accoutrements for a day on the beach, would take at least twelve minutes to get from the hotel lobby to the nearest point on the beach. The brochure is deeply misleading and

191

seriously inaccurate, and I hereby give you notice of my intention to claim an appropriate rebate on the cost of the holiday. I will correspond with you again on my return to the UK.

> Yours faithfully,
> Harold Best

Dearest Des,

We went snorkelling here with Roger yesterday. You can hire the equipment and a little waterproof camera to photograph the fish. There are thousands of fish, but also thousands of snorkellers, and a lot of bread floating about in the water, that they give you to feed the fish. Dee said it was disgusting and refused to go in, so I ended up feeding the fish while Roger took pictures. Better luck next time.

> Much love,
> Sue

Draft intro: The categorization of tourist motivation into either "wanderlust" or "sunlust" (Gray, 1970) is unsatisfactory, as is Mercer's suggestion of a taxonomy of holidays based on "monotony reduction" (Mercer, 1976). A sounder typology is based upon the binary opposition culture/nature. Two basic types of holiday may be discriminated, according to whether they emphasize exposure to culture or nature: the holiday as pilgrimage and the holiday as paradise. The former is typically represented by the bussed sightseeing tour of famous cities, museums, châteaux, etc. (Sheldrake, 1984); the latter by the beach resort holiday, in which the subject strives to get back to a state of nature, or prelapsarian innocence, pretending to do without money (by signing chits, using credit cards or, as in Club Med villages, plastic popper beads), indulging in physical rather than mental pursuits, and wearing the minimum of clothing. The first type of holiday is essentially mobile or *dynamic*, and strives towards fitting the maximum number of sights into the time available. The latter is essentially *static*, striving towards a kind of timeless, repetitive routine typical of primitive societies (Lévi-Strauss, 1967, p. 49).
[*Note*: Apparently Club Med failed to establish itself in Hawaii. Why?]

Dear Joanna,

What can I say? I was so ashamed and embarrassed, I couldn't even bring myself to phone you afterwards. You must regret ever having agreed to be my chief bridesmaid. I shall never forgive Russ, never. Our marriage is over before it began. I haven't spoken to him since the reception. When we get back to England, I shall begin divorce proceedings.

You are probably surprised to get this letter from Hawaii, but it isn't really a honeymoon. We sleep in separate beds and communicate by note or through third parties. I look on it as a holiday, one I saved for and looked forward to for months. I didn't see why I should give it up as well as have my wedding ruined. And to have cancelled it at the last moment would have meant losing most of what we paid in advance. I looked up our holiday insurance, but it doesn't cover cancellation for adultery. Well, I know it wasn't strictly speaking adultery, since we weren't married at the time, but we *were* engaged, and living together.

How could he do it, and with that slut Brenda of all people? *And then invite her to the wedding.* That was the last straw.

We go our different ways each day. I spend most of my time by the hotel pool – I prefer it to the beach, it's less crowded and there's more shade and you can order drinks and snacks. I don't know where he goes, and I don't care. Perhaps he's picked up another little tart somewhere, another Brenda, but I don't think so. He stays in most evenings and watches TV.

Write back if this gets to you in time. Don't suppose it will.

      Love,
        Cecily

Dear Stuart,
   Thought it would make your day to find this dusky beauty on your desk. Fine pair, eh? Reminds me of Shirley's Tracey, in the old days at Pringle's. Actually, Hawaii's a bit of a sell as far as tit goes. Not a patch on Corfu. The Yank talent believe in keeping their bikini tops on. Pity. Waste of videotape. But hotel is comfortable, grub generous and weather hot. Don't work too hard.
                              Brian

Dear Gail,
   We went snorkelling here yesterday. Lots of brightly coloured fish, very tame, they come right up to you. Daddy got sunburned all down his back and the backs of his legs. He can't straighten his knees and has to walk about with them bent. It hasn't improved his temper.
                    With love,
                    Mandy

Dear Sir,
   May I suggest that, in future, when the *soi-disant* instructor in charge of snorkelling equipment hire under your auspices informs customers of the dangers of sunburn, he makes clear that it is possible to get burned *in* the water as well as out of it?
                    Yours faithfully,
                    Harold Best

Paradise Finance Inc.
Paradise Sportswear
Paradise Supply Inc.
Paradise Beauty and Barber Supplies
Paradise Beverages
Paradise Puppets
Paradise Snorkel Adventures
Paradise Tinting
Paradise Cleaning and Maintenance Service
Paradise Parking

Dear Pete,
     This is the best bit of Hawaii so far. First you get
to see a film about the Jap bombing of Pearl Harbor
(that's how they spell it here). Old newsreel, but quite
interesting. Then you take a naval boat out to the wreck
of the *Arizona*. You can look down through the water at
the gun turrets. It's called a war grave, so you're not
allowed to eat food there.
                         Best wishes,
                         Robert

Dear Jimmy,
     What d'you know, an English pub in Hawaii!
Proper draught pulls, but unfortunately they're
connected up to American beer, all gas and no flavour,
and bottled Guinness costs about £2 a half-pint. Still,
it's a home from home. And in this heat you work up
quite a thirst.
                         Cheers,
                         Sidney

195

Dear Boys,

Having a good time in Hawaii. We've been too a luau, that's a kind of Hawaiian barbecue, and on a Sunset Cruise, and visited the Polynesian Cultural Center (v. interesting) and Waimea Falls Park (lovely trees and birds) and Pearl Harbor (v. sad). Your father is using up lots of videotape, as you can imagine. I hope you are remembering to lock up every night – and remember, *no parties*.

Love from,
Mum and Dad

Dear Stuart,

Funny, I'd forgotten Pearl Harbor was in Hawaii. Very instructional tour. Did you ever see that film, *Tora! Tora!*? Apparently it cost the Americans more to make it than it cost the Japs to actually bomb the place. Thought you'd like to know the little yellow buggers were undercutting us even that long ago.

Best,
Brian

Dear Mum and Dad,

Having a lovely time here, apart from a few niggles about the hotel (Harold is writing to the company). Waikiki is more built-up than we expected, but quite nice. Cleaner than Marbella. Spotless toilets. The children love the water.

Love,
Florence

Dear Stuart,

Thank Christ there's a fax machine in this hotel. You know I was joking about trying to sell our surplus sunbeds here? Well, believe it or not somebody wants to buy them. Don't ask me why. I suppose it must be some kind of tax dodge for him too. Or else he's setting up a tanning parlour as a cover for a brothel, he seems a shady sort of character. Name of Louie Mosca. I met him in a topless bar called Dirty Dan's down by the docks – me and another British bloke, Sidney, ditched our wives and sloped off for a bit of a stag night, or rather stag afternoon. I was in a mild state of tit-starvation, to tell you the truth, they don't even have page three girls in the newspapers out here. He was sitting at the end of the catwalk, knocking back beers from the bottle and stuffing ten-dollar bills down the girls' knickers like there was no tomorrow. We got talking, and I told him what line of business I was in, and how I was in Hawaii to sell off the sunbeds – somehow I didn't want to admit to being a tourist, not in a dive like that – and he said how much? Not thinking for a moment that he was serious, I quoted him a silly price, shipping included, and he shook hands on it there and then. I suppose I'd had a fair number of jars myself. Now I look into it, we wouldn't even recover the shipping costs. So send us a fax, sharpish, will you, saying that we can't get an export licence, so I can cancel the deal. Thanks.

                    Yours ever,
                    Brian

Dear Joanna,

Well, I've discovered where he goes every day. I followed him yesterday, without his knowing. I wore dark glasses and a big floppy hat bought specially for the purpose. He went down to the beach, to a place

197

where they have surfboards for hire. He met a couple of men whom he seemed to know there, and they all put these great surfboards on their shoulders and went into the sea. I watched from the beach through a slot-machine telescope. The other two men were much better at it than Russ. He seemed to find it difficult to get going, the waves kept sweeping past him, leaving him paddling frantically behind, looking a bit silly. But once he managed to catch a big wave, and he actually stood up on the board for a few seconds and I could see him grinning all over his face with triumph before he overbalanced, and fell into the water with a splash. For those few seconds I almost forgot what a pig he is.

> Love,
> Cecily

Dear Greg,
　　I've discovered surfing! Fantastic! Better than sex!! Met two great Australian guys who are teaching me how to do it.

> Best,
> Russ

There has been a steady rise in the percentage of tourists staying in Waikiki who make excursions to one or more of the Neighbor Islands: 15% in 1975, 22% in 1980, 29% in 1985, 36% last year. Whether this is because the charm of Oahu is wearing increasingly thin due to overdevelopment, or because organized excursions to the other Islands have been more effectively marketed and advertised, is uncertain.

Went to Kauai yesterday on one-day tour advertised as "Paradise Quickie". Wakeup call at 5.15. Minibus collected me, and various other red-eyed, yawning tourists waiting outside their Waikiki hotels, among them Sue and Dee, the two British girls who have a habit of popping up wherever I happen to be. I suppose I must have mentioned that I was taking the tour and they thought it sounded interesting.

Transferred from minibus to coach which took us to Honolulu airport, against the early morning rush-hour traffic already clogging the freeway. At airport, tour rep distributes boarding passes and instructions. Kauai veiled in rain as we approach. Pilot has to make two attempts to land. Sue has white knuckles. Dee yawns impatiently. We look through streaming windows at drenched airport, apprehensive in our shorts and trainers. Kauai has been christened "The Garden Isle" by Hawaiian Vistors Bureau, which is a euphemism for "rains a lot." Somewhere in the middle of it is Mount Waialeale, the wettest place on earth (annual rainfall 480 in.)

The day trippers are herded into groups and various tour company minivans. Our guide is Luke. He introduces himself from the driver's seat via a microphone. "My friends call me Lukey, which means you are Lukey's groupies," he chortles. Sue laughs. Dee groans. We drive out of airport, along newly macadamed road. Still pissing down. Palm trees thrash furiously to and fro like windscreen wipers.

We stop at various hotels to pick up more passengers, then commence tour of the island. It seems necessary to drive for hours along very boring roads in order to get to any place of even modest interest: medium-sized waterfalls, a large but ugly canyon, a waterspout hole in the rocks by the sea. (Busloads of tourists waited in vain, with cameras cocked, for the spout to do its stuff, like waiting for rhinoceroses to mate.) The highspot of the tour is a trip up the Wailua river. This is the only navigable river in Hawaii. Otherwise it is of no particular interest or scenic beauty. However a considerable fleet of riverboats has been established to ferry people up and down it. On the boat we are entertained by a rather jaded troupe of Hawaiian musicians and hula dancers. The terminus of the trip is the so-called Fern Grotto, allegedly a historic site for the celebration of weddings, and certainly a popular gathering place for mosquitoes. The musicians sang the "Hawaiian Wedding Song" for us, and at the end of it you were supposed to kiss the person next to you. I manoeuvred myself next to Sue, who is the prettier of the two girls, but at the last moment she changed places with Dee, so I had to kiss her instead.

The only really attractive feature of Kauai is its coastline. We kept getting glimpses of beautiful beaches, especially tantalizing in the afternoon, when the sun came out, but we were never allowed to get out of the minibus and explore them because we were always tearing off to another bloody waterfall. And Luke became quite stroppy if, when we got to it, we didn't all get out and photograph it. The whole excursion has made me rethink the opposition between pilgrimage and paradise. *The holiday paradise is inevitably transposed into a site of pilgrimage by the innate momentum of the tourist industry.* Trivial or totally spurious sights are fabricated or "marked" (MacCannell, 1976) in order to construct an itinerary along which the tourists can be conveniently transported and "serviced" (by shops, restaurants, riverboats, entertainers, etc.). Dee seemed quite impressed with this theory. I sat next to her in the minibus for the latter part of the trip. It seemed only polite after kissing her. Sue may be prettier, but Dee is cleverer.

Dearest Des,

    Just got back from wonderful tour of Kauai, they call it the Garden Isle because of all the lovely flowers growing wild there. Amazing waterfalls. This waterspout wasn't actually working when we stopped, perhaps the tide was out. Big news is that Dee has got this Roger bloke interested at last. She tells him all her holiday disaster stories and he writes them down in his little book.

Fingers crossed,
Sue

Dear Denise,

I'm sorry to tell you that your father had one of his turns yesterday, and had to be rushed to hospital. They kept him in overnight, under observation, but said he could come home today. I say home, I mean hotel, how I wish it *was* home. I thought about phoning you but there didn't seem any point with you so far away. I reckon you should receive this just before we return so you will be prepared if Dad is not up to scratch when you meet us at the airport. Of course I will phone if anything sudden happens.

I'm telling everybody here it was the heat, but really it was the shock of finding out something about Terry. I don't know how to tell you, Denise, but your brother is a homo. There, I've said it. Did you have any idea when you were younger? I'm sure I didn't, but it's been so long since he lived at home. I knew there was something wrong as soon as he met us at the airport and his "special friend" turned out to be a man, this Tony. He's really very nice, but Sidney couldn't stomach it. Just refused to talk about it.

Terry can't do enough for us, ferries us about in a huge hire car, meals in the best restaurants, I can't eat half of it, we've been everywhere, seen everything,

Pearl Harbor, hula dancing, and the hotel's beautiful, but Sidney wasn't enjoying himself, kept sloping off to a so-called pub he'd discovered, the Rose and Crown, trust him, just behind the sea-front. Then, the night before last, after dinner, Terry announced that he and Tony were going to get married. Apparently there's a gay minister down under who will marry them, a sort of marriage anyway. Well, your Father nearly had a fit there and then. He went very white and then very red. Then he just walked out without saying a word.

I knew he'd have gone to the Rose and Crown, so after a little while I went out and fetched him. He was there, sure enough, drinking with a man called Brian Everthorpe we met on the plane, rather a loud type, I don't care for him much, though his wife's all right. They made me have a gin and orange, and then I brought Sidney back to the hotel. He kept muttering under his breath, What did we do wrong? I said we didn't do anything wrong, Terry is just made that way. He said, do you know what they do, men like that? And I said, no, and I don't want to, it's none of my business and none of yours either, I said. You're going to make yourself ill over this if you're not careful, and sure enough the next morning he had one of his turns, and had to be rushed to hospital. We were on our way to the National Memorial Cemetery when it happened, the bus made a detour to the nearest hospital, a Catholic one but they were very nice. Terry is ever so upset, of course. So all in all, it's not the happy holiday we looked forward to. I just hope your Father keeps going till we get back home.

Your loving Mother

Dear Travelwise Customer,

On behalf of Travelwise Tours, I hope you are enjoying your vacation in Waikiki. As your stay on the beautiful island of Oahu draws to a close, we hope that we will have the pleasure of welcoming you to Hawaii again one day.

In the spirit of traditional Hawaiian hospitality, Travelwise Tours, in conjunction with Wyatt Hotels, invite you to cocktails and *pupu* at 6 p.m. on Wednesday 23rd, at the Wyatt Imperial Hotel on Kalakaua Avenue (in the Spindrift Bar on the Mezzanine Floor).

This invitation card entitles you to one complimentary cocktail and one plate of *pupu* per person. Cash bar also available. There will be a short video presentation of other Travelwise holidays available on the Neighbor Islands, including the fabulous new resort of Wyatt Haikoloa.

Aloha, Sincerely Yours,
Linda Hanama
Resort Controller

Dear Miss Hanama,

Thank you for your invitation, which is accepted. May I point out, however, that only three invitation cards were enclosed, and my party numbers four. I would be grateful if you would forward an additional card to obviate any possible unpleasantness at the door.

Yours sincerely,
Harold Best

Paradise Gems
Paradise Cruise
Paradise Plants
Paradise Record Productions
Paradise Home Builders
Paradise Upholstery
Paradise Puzzle Company

PART THREE

Ho'omākaukau No Ka Moe A Kāne A Moe Wahine:
To learn to be expert at man and woman sleeping. Thus,
preparation for sex; sex education.

Ho'oponopono:
Setting to right; to make right; to correct; to restore and
maintain good relationships among family and family-and-
supernatural powers. The specific family conference in
which relationships were "set right" through prayer,
discussion, confession, repentance and mutual restitution and
forgiveness.

– Nānā I Ke Kumu (Look To The Source)
A source book of Hawaiian cultural practices,
concepts and beliefs, by Mary Kawena Pukui,
E. W. Haertig, MD, and Catherine A. Lee.

I

"Do you believe in anything at all, Bernard?" said Ursula. "Do you believe in an afterlife?"

"I don't know," he said.

"Come on now, Bernard. Give me a straight answer to a straight question. What's the point of being a college teacher if you can't do that?"

"Well, modern theologians tend to be a bit shifty about the afterlife, I'm afraid. Even Catholic ones."

"Really?"

"Take Kung's *On Being a Christian*, for example, one of the modern classics. You won't find anything in the index under 'Afterlife' or 'Heaven'."

"I don't see the point of religion if there's no heaven," said Ursula. "I mean, why be good, if you're not going to be rewarded for it? Why not be bad, if you're not going to be punished in the long run?"

"They say that virtue is its own reward," said Bernard, with a smile.

"The hell with that," said Ursula, and chuckled hoarsely at her own choice of expletive. "And what about hell? Has that gone down the tubes too?"

"Very largely, and good riddance, I'd say."

"And purgatory with it, I guess?"

"Oddly enough, modern theologians, even non-Catholic ones, are rather more sympathetic towards the idea of purgatory, though there's very little scriptural warrant for it. Some see analogies between purgatory and the idea of reincarnation in oriental religions, which are rather fashionable nowadays, especially Buddhism. You know, expiating in one life for your sins in a previous one, until you reach *nirvana*."

"What's that?"

"Hmm . . . well, roughly speaking it means the extinction of the individual ego, its assimilation into the eternal spirit of the universe. Release from the Wheel of Being into nothingness."

"I don't think I like the sound of that," said Ursula.

"Do you really want to live for ever?" Bernard risked teasing her. These theological discussions, which had become a regular feature of his visits to Makai Manor, struck him as treading on very thin ice, considering Ursula's condition; but she was always the one who initiated them, and she seemed to derive a quirky satisfaction from tapping his professional expertise and probing his scepticism.

"Sure," she said. "Doesn't everybody? Don't you?"

"No," he said. "I'd be quite glad to be rid of this self of mine."

"You might not think so in a better place."

"Ah, place," said Bernard. "That's the difficulty, isn't it? Thinking of heaven as a place. A garden. A city. Happy Hunting Grounds. Such solid things."

"I always used to think of heaven as a kind of huge cathedral, with God the Father up on the altar, and everybody worshipping him. That was the idea we got from Religious Instruction at school. It sounded kind of boring, like a High Mass going on for ever and ever. Of course the nuns told us we wouldn't find it boring when we got there. They seemed quite excited at the prospect, or they pretended to be."

"There's a contemporary theologian who has suggested that the afterlife is a kind of dream, in which we all achieve our desires. If you have rather low-level desires, you get a rather low-level heaven. More refined desires and you get a more refined heaven."

"That's a neat idea. Where'd he get it from?"

"I don't know. I think he made it up," said Bernard. "It's remarkable how many modern theologians who have rejected the orthodox eschatological scheme feel free to invent new ones that are just as fanciful."

"Gee, you sure know some jaw-breakers, Bernard. What's that word? Escha. . . ?"

"Eschatological. Pertaining to the Four Last Things."

"Death, Judgment, Hell and Heaven."

"You learned your Catechism well."

"The nuns used to strap us if we didn't," said Ursula. "But I think this guy has got something."

"It's a bit elitist, though, don't you think? A heaven of beer and skittles for the *hoi polloi*, while the better educated get – what shall we say, command performances by Mozart, and drawing lessons from Leonardo da Vinci? It sounds too much like this world, where some get to stay at the Moana, and others at the Waikiki Surfrider."

"What's the Waikiki Surfrider?"

"Oh, it's the hotel where Daddy and I were supposed to stay, as part of our package holiday. It's one of those huge, anonymous eggboxes, several blocks from the beach."

"Have you been there, then?"

"Er, yes, I have," said Bernard, slightly embarrassed. "I went to see if I could get a rebate for the room."

"Any luck?"

"No."

"No, I'm not surprised . . . If you *could* have the heaven of your desire, what would it be?"

"I don't know," said Bernard. "I think I'd like the chance to live my life over again. Not decide at the age of fifteen to become a priest, and see what happened."

"You might have made a lot of different mistakes."

"Quite right, Ursula. But I might have had better luck, too. One can't tell. Everything is connected. I remember, some years ago, I was watching a football match on television, England against some other country. Apparently it was a very important match – some kind of cup. My young curate, Thomas, had the set switched on, so I watched to be companionable. England lost the game by a penalty in the second half. Poor Thomas was tearing his hair at the final whistle. 'If only we hadn't given away that penalty,' he said, 'we'd have got a draw and been through to the finals.' I pointed out to him that this assertion was based on a fallacy, namely, that you could extract the penalty from the game without altering it. In fact, of course, if the penalty hadn't been awarded, the game would have continued without interruption, and every movement of the ball from then onwards would have been different from the match we watched. England might have won, or lost, by any number of goals. I pointed this out, but it didn't seem to console him. 'You have to go by the run of the play,' he said. 'On the run of play we deserved to draw.' "

Bernard chuckled reminiscently, then became aware that Ursula had fallen asleep. She did this not infrequently, little catnaps in the middle of a conversation, which he hoped were attributable to tiredness rather than boredom.

She blinked and opened her eyes again. "What were you saying, Bernard?"

"I was saying, sometimes things can happen in a life quite against the run of play. Like my being here in Hawaii."

Ursula groaned. "How I wish you'd come before, when I was well! And before the place was spoiled. When I came here in the sixties, it was so beautiful, you've no idea. There was hardly a highrise hotel in Waikiki, and I could walk in a straight line from my apartment to the beach. Now there's a wall of hotels all along the shore, and just one narrow passage you have to squeeze through to get to the sea. I used to go for a swim every day of my life, there was a little gang of us wrinklies who used to meet at the same spot. We used to use the showers beside the Sheriden pool, the attendants knew us and turned a blind eye. But one day a man turned us away, such a rude man, and that was the beginning of the end. Waikiki wasn't like a village any more. It was like a city. So many people on the beach, in the street. The rubbish. The crime. Even the climate doesn't seem to be what it was. It's too hot for comfort in the summer now. They say it's because of all the construction. It's so sad."

"Don't you think," said Bernard, "that Hawaii is one of those places that was always better in the past? I expect the people who lived here before the jumbo jets, before you came yourself, Ursula, look back on those days as a golden age, and likewise the

208

people who lived here when you could only get here by steamship, and so on, right the way back to the Hawaiians who lived here before Captain Cook discovered them."

"Yeah, maybe," said Ursula. "But that doesn't mean that it isn't actually getting worse."

"No," Bernard smiled. "You're quite right, it doesn't."

"I think you've enjoyed being here, haven't you? I mean apart from Jack's accident and everything. You look different than when you arrived."

"Do I?"

"Yeah, brighter, less hangdog."

Bernard blushed. "It's been satisfying, getting things organized for you."

"You've done wonders," said Ursula, extending her good arm and squeezing his hand. "How's Jack? When am I going to see him?"

"The doctor is pleased with his progress. He should be out of bed soon."

"How are we going to get together? As soon as he's able, he'll want to get back home. Why can't I hire an ambulance and just go see him at St Joseph's?"

"That's what I was thinking myself. I've asked Enid to try and set it up."

Every resident at Makai Manor had a social worker allocated to them, and Ursula's was a quietly efficient young woman called Enid da Silva. She demonstrated her efficiency once more by intercepting Bernard on his way out of the lobby to tell him that she had arranged for Ursula to be transported to St Joseph's Hospital the following Wednesday afternoon. He thanked her and asked her to pass on the information to Ursula.

He drove back along the scenic coast road to Waikiki. Out to sea, underneath Diamond Head, brightly coloured triangular sails flickered in the sun like butterfly wings. As he had plenty of time before his next appointment, he pulled into a parking place at the edge of the cliff and watched the windsurfers at their sport. Perhaps because it was a Sunday afternoon, there were scores of them, and they made a thrilling spectacle. Tensed and balanced, knees flexed, backs arched, hands grasping the curved steel bows that harnessed their bellying sails, they careered towards the shore under the curling crests of the rollers and then, to avoid being beached, with incredible dexterity they swivelled round, turned, and leaped like salmon through the spume of the oncoming waves. Some, miraculously, even turned somersaults, without being parted from their boards. Then they used their sails to tack back towards the open sea, to catch another wave. They seemed to have discovered the secret of perpetual motion. They seemed, to Bernard, like gods. He could not conceive of the skill, strength, and daring required to perform such feats. He wondered if Dr Gerson was among them, obliterating the grim realities of the cancer ward in the rush of foam, the sting of salt, the dazzle of sun and sea. No problem guessing what a windsurfer's heaven would be like. If you could do that, Bernard thought, you would want to do it all the time, for ever.

He drove to Kaolo Street, and parked the car in the basement parking lot, in the space allocated to Ursula's apartment. Then he walked the three blocks to the Waikiki Surfrider. He was getting used to the landmarks on this route: the Towel Factory, the Wacko Gift Shop, the Hula Hut, 24-Hour Hot-Dogs, First Interstate Bank, ABC Store. Not that the ABC was much of a landmark. There was an ABC Store every fifty yards or so in Waikiki, all selling the identical range of groceries, drinks, and holiday gear – flip-flops, swimming costumes, straw mats, suntan products and postcards. Inside, bemused-looking tourists browsed through the merchandise as if hoping to discover something different from the stock in the last ABC Store they had patronized. There was always that sense of unspecified lack or longing in the warm humid air of Waikiki. The visitors strolled up and down Kalakaua and Kuhio Avenues, up and down, up and down, in their novelty tee-shirts and knee-length shorts and little marsupial pouches, and the sun shone and the palm trees waved in the trade winds and the steel guitar music twanged from the shop doorways, and the faces looked contented enough, but in the eyes there seemed to be a half formulated question: well, this is nice, but is this all there is? Is this it?

The lobby of the Waikiki Surfrider was large, bare and functional. A heap of luggage was stacked near the door, waiting to be distributed or transported, and on a banquette nearby sat an elderly couple who themselves looked a little like unclaimed baggage. They glanced hopefully at Bernard as he came in, and the man rose to his feet and asked him if he was Paradise Island Tours. Bernard said he was sorry, he wasn't. He went to the desk, presented his room card, and asked for the key to 1509. With the key the clerk handed him an envelope addressed to himself and his father. He opened it while he waited for the elevator, and discovered inside an invitation from the Travelwise company to a cocktail party on the following Wednesday.

The hotel was quiet. It was mid-afternoon. Everybody was out – on the beach, or on the street, or driving round the island in buses and minivans and hire cars. His only companion in the elevator was a solemn little Japanese girl aged about seven, wearing a tee-shirt over her swimming-costume with the injunction *SMILE* written on it, who got out at the tenth floor. The corridor of the fifteenth floor was empty and silent, the uniform doors of the rooms closed and inscrutable. He opened the door of 1509, hung the *Do Not Disturb* sign on the outside, and went in.

The room was as functional, characterless and antiseptic as the Trauma Room at St Joseph's hospital. There were two beds, some drawer units and a wardrobe veneered with marbled melamine, a minibar, two chairs and a coffee table, and a TV mounted on the wall. There was a small windowless bathroom with shower and WC. Bernard was fairly sure that every other room in the building was identical, down to the colour of the ribbed nylon carpet. The hotel was a factory for mass-producing package holidays. There were no frills, no pretensions to personal service, and therefore no personal inquisitiveness. Admittedly, some curiosity had been aroused when he turned up, a week late, to claim his room, but after he had spun some story about being delayed by an accident, and produced his reservation slip, the Assistant Manager had shrugged his shoulders and said he guessed he was entitled to the room for the unexpired portion of the holiday.

At some time in the morning, anonymous and invisible hands

serviced the room and re-stocked the minibar. What the chambermaid made of occupants who appeared to possess no clothes or other luggage, who used two bathtowels but only one bed, he couldn't imagine, but no doubt she didn't complain of the light workload. Whoever it was, she invariably left the air-conditioning on "Hi". Bernard adjusted the control to a more comfortable temperature, and a quieter hum, and undressed, hanging his clothes in the empty wardrobe. He took a shower, and wrapped himself toga-style in one of the large bathtowels. Then he opened the minibar, took out a half-bottle of Napa Valley Chardonnay, and poured himself a glass. He recorked the bottle and put it back in the fridge to keep cool. He sat on the bed with his back against the headboard and sipped the wine, glancing at his watch from time to time, until there was a knock on the door.

He let Yolande in, and quickly closed the door behind her. She was wearing the same red cotton dress that she had worn the first time he set eyes on her. She smiled and kissed him on the cheek.

"Sorry I'm late, Roxy needed a ride someplace."

"Not to worry," he said. "Glass of white wine?"

"Sounds great," said Yolande. "I'll just take a quick shower."

While she was in the bathroom, Bernard took the bottle from the minibar and poured a second glass of wine, setting it down on the night table beside the bed. He went to the window, which looked onto the blank side wall of another hotel, and pulled the heavy, lined curtain across, leaving a narrow gap through which just enough daylight squeezed to diffuse a dim illumination inside the room. When Yolande came out of the bathroom he was surprised to see that she was still dressed. "Haven't you showered yet?" he asked, handing her her drink.

"Sure," she said, smiling at him with her eyes over the rim of her glass. "But today you get to undress me."

The day after he had delivered his journal to Yolande's house in the middle of the night, she had appeared at the door of Ursula's apartment, carrying it under her arm. She arrived unheralded by any phone call. "Oh," he said, as he opened the door. "It's you."

"Yeah. I brought your book back. Can I come in?"

212

"Of course."

He glanced up and down the corridor as he admitted her, and glimpsed Mrs Knoepflmacher's head withdrawing into the doorway of her flat like a tortoise into its shell. Yolande stood in the middle of the living-room and looked around. "This is nice," she said. "It must be worth a fortune in this location."

He explained that Ursula didn't own the apartment. "She could probably afford to buy it now, but there wouldn't be any point. I've given notice that she'll be leaving. Would you like a cup of tea?"

She followed him into the kitchenette, and sat down at the little Formica-topped breakfast table. When he had put the kettle on to boil he sat down opposite her. The journal lay on the table between them like an agenda.

It appeared that Yolande had been woken by the noise of his car driving up to her house. She had heard the flap of her mailbox bang shut and gone out to investigate. She had taken the journal back to her bed and read it straight through to the end. "And then this morning I read it again. It's the saddest story I ever heard."

"Oh, I wouldn't say that," he demurred.

"I mean the English part," she said. "The stuff about Hawaii was more fun. I loved the story of the lost keys. And reading about myself . . ." She smiled. "That was the most interesting part of all, of course."

"I never intended you should read any of it when I wrote it."

"I know. That's why it seems so truthful. It's not written for effect. It's completely honest. I always knew you were an honest man, Bernard. Well, I say so in the book, don't I?" She tapped the stiff blue covers. " '*Somehow I could tell you were an honest man. There aren't so many left.*' " She laughed again. "It's like reading about yourself as a character in a novel. Or seeing yourself in a home movie, when you didn't know you were being filmed. Like the way you describe me coming into the Banyan Courtyard at the Moana, and looking around, and then walking towards you with, what was it, '*A bounding athletic stride*'. I never realized I bound when I walk, but I guess you're right. And I'll tell you another

213

thing, that bit at the end, about when we were walking under the trees by the Zoo –"

"That was stupid of me," said Bernard. "I wanted you to read that so you could understand why I acted so strangely."

"No, you were right," said Yolande. "I did want you to kiss me."

"Oh," said Bernard. He dropped his eyes and examined his hands. "But the moon – you said you wanted me to look at the moon."

"That was just an excuse to touch you," said Yolande, and stretching out her hand she placed it over one of Bernard's.

There was a longish silence, broken by the preliminary wheeze of the kettle's whistle. Bernard looked appealingly at Yolande, and she smiled and released him. As he turned off the gas, he was aware that she had got to her feet also, and when he turned she was standing erect facing him, as he remembered seeing her from the back of the ambulance on that first morning in Waikiki, except that she wasn't frowning this time, and her arms were not at her sides but extended towards him. "Come over here, Bernard," she said, "and give me that kiss."

He took a hesitant step or two, and she took his hand and drew him close. He felt her arms around his shoulders, and her fingers caressing his neck. Timidly he clasped her round the waist and she fitted her body snugly against his. He felt the heat of her bosom through his thin shirt and her cotton dress. He felt his penis stiffen. They kissed.

"There, that wasn't so bad, was it?" Yolande murmured.

"No," he said hoarsely, "it was very nice."

"Would you like to make love?"

He shook his head.

"Why not?"

"You know why."

"I could teach you. I could show you how. I could heal you, Bernard, I know I could." She took his hands in hers and squeezed them.

"Why do you want to?"

"Because I like you. Because I'm sorry for you. Showing me your diary was a cry for help."

"I didn't think of it like that. I thought of it as a kind of . . . explanation."

"It was a cry for help, and I can help you. Trust me."

There was another long silence. He looked down at their linked hands, conscious that she was gazing intently into his face.

"And I need some loving too," she said, in a softer voice.

"All right," he said at last.

It was as if all his life he had been holding his breath, or clenching his fist, and now at last he had decided to exhale, to relax, to let go, not caring about the consequences, and it was such a relief, such a violent metabolic change, that he felt momentarily dizzy. He swayed on his feet and staggered slightly as Yolande hugged him.

"But not here," he said.

"Well we can't go to my place, Roxy'll be home soon. What's wrong with here?"

"Not in Ursula's apartment. I wouldn't feel comfortable. It wouldn't seem right."

Yolande seemed to understand this scruple. "Then we'll have to take a hotel room," she said. "Shouldn't be difficult to find in Waikiki, but it might be expensive."

"I've already got a hotel room," said Bernard, remembering the reservation slip in his Travelwise Travelpak.

They went straight round to the Waikiki Surfrider, and Yolande waited in the basement coffeeshop while he negotiated with the Reception Desk. "I hope you don't think we're going to have sex this afternoon," was the first thing she said to him when they were alone together in room 1509, and she laughed at the expression on his face, halfway, she said, between disappointment and relief, "like the Frenchman's wisecrack in your diary."

"If we don't," he said, "I'm not sure that we ever shall. The awful daring of a moment's surrender is not something you can turn on at will."

"The awful what?"

"It's a line from a poem."

"Forget poetry for a while, Bernard. Poets are romantics. Let's be practical. The reason you and Daphne didn't make it together, well, one reason anyway, is that you rushed at it. You tried to go from total chastity to hands-on fucking in one move. Sorry, does that word bother you?"

"It does a bit."

"OK, I won't use it. Standard practice in sex therapy is to advise the person, or the couple, who are having problems, to build up to full intercourse in easy stages, one step at at time. Even if they've been having sex for years, they're told to go back to the beginning and start again, as if they've never had sex before. First non-erotic kissing and touching, then sensuous massage, then heavy petting and so on. Ideally it should be spread over several weeks, but as we don't have that sort of time we're going to have to do it day by day. OK?"

"I think so," Bernard said.

So that afternoon they just lay on the bed, fully clothed apart from shoes and socks, and stroked each others faces, and hair, and ears, and kissed gently, and fingered each other's palms and massaged each other's feet. He felt very silly at first, but Yolande made it not disablingly embarrassing by not betraying the slightest hint of embarrassment herself.

The second afternoon, after they had both showered, she pulled the heavy blackout curtain across the window and then, as they stood on opposite sides of the bed, wrapped in towels, turned off the lights from the bedside console so that the room was totally dark. "I think maybe you're a little bit afraid of women's bodies, Bernard," she said. "I think maybe you should learn your way around by touch first." He heard the faint sound of her towel dropping to the floor, and then felt her hand reaching for him. So he first learned the composition of her body as if he were a blind man; the firm, muscular arms, the smooth wings of her shoulder blades, the supple, notched rod of her backbone, the soft, elastic roundness of her buttocks, and the smooth tender skin on the inside of her thighs. When she turned over on her back he felt the weight of her breasts slide to each side of her rib-cage, and the

216

steady beating of her heart and the sudden hardening of her nipples, and traced the ridge of an old appendectomy scar across her belly down to the soft, springy nest of pubic hair, where she gently stayed his hand. She seemed like a tree to him: her bones were the trunk and branches, and the rounded shapes of her flesh were like ripe fruit to his hands. When she asked him how he was feeling, he could only quote more poetry to her:

> *"I cannot see what flowers are at my feet*
> *Nor what soft incense hangs upon the boughs*
> *But in embalmed darkness guess each sweet*
> *Wherewith the seasonable month endows*
> *The grass, the thicket, and the fruit tree wild . . ."*

She laughed and said he was incorrigible. "Tomorrow we'll have more light," she said. "Tomorrow will be raunchier. But now it's my turn to find out what your body feels like."

"It's nothing to write home about, I'm afraid."

"It's OK. Some loss of muscle tone around here," she said, pinching his abdomen. "Do you work out?"

"I walk a lot at home."

"Walking's good exercise, but you should do something a little more strenuous."

"What do you do? You don't seem to have an ounce of surplus flesh."

"I play a lot of tennis. Lewis and I used to be Faculty Mixed Doubles champions. Now I play with Roxy."

He wished she hadn't mentioned Lewis and Roxy. These names reminded him that she had a real life, complex and particular, beyond the confines of this room and bed. But her hands gradually massaged his anxieties away. Slowly, methodically, Yolande worked over every inch of his body except his private parts. It was as if she were sculpting his body in the darkness, making him aware of its contours and limits for the first time. For so long he had treated it like a suit of shabby but serviceable clothes, which he put on in the morning and took off at night, living entirely in his mind. Now he realized that he also lived in this strange forked flawed amalgam of flesh and bone, blood and sinew, liver and lungs. For the first time since childhood, he felt alive from his fingertips to his toes. Once she brushed his erect penis with her hand, and murmured an apology. "Shall we make love?" he said.

"No," she said, "not yet."

"Tomorrow?"

"No, not tomorrow."

Tomorrow there was more light in the room, and they split a half-bottle of white wine from the minibar before they began. Yolande was bolder and more loquacious. "Today is still touching only, but nowhere is off-limits, we can touch where we like, how we like, OK? And it needn't be just hands, you can also use your mouth and your tongue. Would you like to suck my breasts? Go ahead. Is that nice? Good, it's nice for me. Can I suck you? Don't worry, I'll squeeze it hard like this and that'll stop you coming. OK. Relax. Was that nice? Good. Sure I like to do it. Sucking and licking are very primal pleasures. Of course, it's easy to see what pleases a man, but with women it's different, it's all hidden inside and you've got to know your way around, so lick your finger, and I'll give you the tour."

He was shocked, bemused, almost physically winded by this sudden acceleration into a tabooless candour of word and gesture. But he was elated too. He hung on for dear life. "Are we going to make love today?" he pleaded.

"This is making love, Bernard," she said. "I'm having a wonderful time, aren't you?"

"Yes, but you know what I mean."

"Are we going to make love today?" he asked, as he unbuttoned her red dress. "I mean really make love."

"No, not today. Tomorrow."

"Tomorrow?" he wailed. "What in the name of God is there left to do between yesterday and tomorrow?"

"Well this, for one thing," she said, stepping out of her dress. She was wearing a one-piece undergarment of white lace-trimmed satin.

He shut his eyes and shook his head. "Yolande, Yolande . . ."

"What's the matter? Doesn't this turn you on?"

"Of course it does."

"Then help me take it off."

He plucked clumsily at the shoulder straps and she freed her arms. The garment fell to her hips and exposed her breasts. He kissed them tenderly and groaned, "Yolande, Yolande, what are you doing to me?"

"You could call it sex education. It's the American way, Bernard. Everything can be taught. How to be successful. How to write a novel. How to have sex."

"Have you taught anyone else before?"

"No. It wouldn't be ethical."

"Ethical!" He giggled a little hysterically. "Why is it ethical with me?"

"Because you're not a client. You're a friend."

"You seem so expert at it."

"If you must know, Lewis had a potency problem about eight years ago. We went to a therapist together. It worked."

The undergarment slithered to the floor, and she stood before him, compact, shapely, tawny as a Gauguin nude except for the pale outline of a two-piece swimming-costume across her bosom and loins. He fell to his knees and pressed his face against her belly, stroking her flanks. "You're so beautiful," he said.

"Mmm, that's nice," she said, gently massaging his scalp with her fingers. "It's wonderful to have someone hold you in their arms again."

"Has there been anyone else since Lewis left?"

"No, there hasn't. When I get horny, I make do with a vibrator. Does that shock you?"

"Nothing shocks me any more," said Bernard. "Sometimes I think you must be a witch, a beautiful dark-eyed witch. How else could I do these things without dying of shame and embarrassment? And with the woman who nearly killed my father, too."

"If I was a Freudian," said Yolande, drawing him to his feet, "I might say that was part of the attraction. You were attracted to me from the very beginning, weren't you, Bernard?"

"Yes, I was. I remembered you so vividly after the accident, in your red dress. I never dreamed that one day I would be helping you take it off."

"There you are. Life is full of surprises. Lie face down."

"Quite against the run of play."

"What?" She began her methodical sensuous massage of his neck and shoulders.

"Oh, nothing. It was a phrase that came up in conversation with Ursula today."

"What do you two talk about?"

"Today we were talking about heaven."

"But you don't believe in heaven!"

"No, but I know a lot about it."

Yolande laughed. "There speaks the true academic."

"What about you?"

"I think we have to make our own heaven on this earth," said Yolande. "And answer our own prayers. Like you did when you found your key on the beach. Turn over, will you?"

"Can't we make love now?" he pleaded.

"What we're going to do today," said Yolande, "is you're going to practice coming inside me without coming, if you follow. If you feel yourself coming, you've got to tell me, OK? Now we know you can't possibly have any nasty sexual diseases – in fact, come to think of it, Bernard, you must be the safest lay in Honolulu. You could sell your body to the rich widows at the Royal Hawaiian for a fortune. And in case you've been wondering, I had an HIV test the day after I discovered Lewis had been cheating on me, and it was negative –"

"It never crossed my mind," said Bernard.

"Well, it should have, and just to be absolutely safe I'm going to put a condom on you . . . OK? I'm going to kneel astride you like this, and very gently take you inside me, like this, and we're just going to stay like this for a minute or two, quite still, OK? How does it feel?"

"Heavenly," he said.

220

"How about that? Feel that?"

"God, yes."

"Pretty good muscle tone, huh? I read somewhere Hawaiian grandmothers used to teach their granddaughters how to do that. They called it *amo amo*. It means 'wink, wink,' literally. I'm talking my head off like this to stop you coming."

"I love, I love."

"What?"

"*Amo* is Latin for 'I love'."

"Oh, it is? Now I'm just going to move gently up and down a few times, like that, OK? Then I'm going to raise myself off you."

"No," said Bernard, holding her down by her hips.

"Then in a few minutes we'll do it again."

"No," said Bernard. "Don't go away."

"The idea is that you get a sense of control over your erection."

"I've been controlling my erections for the last three days," he said. "What I want to do now is lose control."

"You can bring yourself to climax afterwards," said Yolande. "I'll help you, if you like."

"No thankyou," he said. "I haven't lost all sense of shame, you know. I still draw the line somewhere. Let's stop the lessons, Yolande. Let's make love, I love you, Yolande."

"I think we should talk about this," she said, trying to lift herself off him. But he arched his back and held her. "Don't go away," he sobbed, losing control. "Don't go away, don't go away, don't go away!"

"OK! OK! OK! Oh!" she gasped.

Afterwards they pulled a sheet over themselves and slept, curled up close together like spoons. Yolande woke him by switching on the bedside lamp. It appeared to be dark outside. "My God!" Yolande exclaimed, screwing up her eyes at her watch. "Roxy will be wondering where the hell I am."

She made a quick phone call to her daughter, sitting naked on the edge of the bed. When Bernard began to stroke her shoulder, she grasped his hand and held it still. She put down the phone and began rapidly to dress.

"Same time tomorrow?" he said.

221

She gave him a strange, shy smile. "The course is over, Bernard. Congratulations. You graduated."

"I thought I failed," he said. "I thought I jumped the gun."

"You flunked the sex education," she said, "but you passed in Assertiveness Training."

"I love you, Yolande."

"Are you sure you're not confusing gratitude with love?"

"I'm not sure of anything," he said. "Except that I want to see you again."

"OK. Tomorrow afternoon, then."

She darted her head forward to give him her usual friendly kiss of goodbye, but he put his arms round her and kissed her long and passionately. "I never knew till today what 'to sleep with' someone really meant," he said.

"That's nice, Bernard, but I have to run."

As was their usual practice, Bernard allowed a few minutes to elapse after Yolande's departure before he followed her down to the lobby. It was thronged with guests returning from their day's excursions, or preparing to go out for the evening. He looked benevolently upon their garish casual clothes, their sunburned faces and empty chatter. He dropped his key in the slot provided and sidled unnoticed through the crowd, out into the balmy evening. A few drops of warm rain sprinkled his face agreeably. Pineapple juice, the locals called these evanescent wind-borne showers, according to Sophie Knoepflmacher. He let himself be carried along by the stream of humanity on the sidewalk, floating rather than walking. He felt rested, refreshed, renewed. He felt serenely happy. He felt hungry.

Finding himself near Paradise Pasta, he went inside and asked for a table. Darlette brought him iced water and asked him how he was this evening. "I'm fine," he said. Feeling that this epithet scarcely did justice to his state of mind, he added, "Over the moon." It had been a favourite phrase of Thomas's.

"That's great," said Darlette, with a wide unfocused smile. "Tonight we have a special? Seafood Tagliatelli? Shrimp, clams and flaked swordfish in a cream sauce?"

"I'll have it," said Bernard. And he did, and it was delicious. He had two glasses of white wine with the meal, and hummed the tune of "I Love Hawaii," which was being belted out again by the pomaded singer in the open-air floorshow, as he walked back to the apartment. He was still humming to himself as he came out of the elevator. Mrs Knoepflmacher seemed to have been lying in wait for him, for she sprang out of her apartment as he passed the door.

"Western Union delivered a cable for you this afternoon," she said. "I told the man he could leave it with me, but he put it under your door."

"Oh, right, thankyou," said Bernard.

"I hope it isn't bad news," said Mrs Knoepflmacher.

"So do I," said Bernard.

The envelope was lying just inside the door of the apartment. Bernard stooped to pick it up.

"Is it there?" said Mrs Knoepflmacher, over his shoulder, making him start. She had followed him silently up the corridor.

"Yes, thankyou, Mrs Knoepflmacher," he said. "Quite safe. Goodnight." And he closed the door.

The cable said: "ARRIVING HONOLULU MONDAY 21ST FLIGHT DL 157 AT 8.20 P.M. PLEASE MEET ME AT AIRPORT TESS."

Bernard flopped into an armchair and stared at the piece of paper. He felt his euphoria rapidly draining away. The free, independent, secret life he had led for the last ten days would come to an end. Tess would take over – take over his father, take over Ursula, take over the management of the apartment. She would hustle and scold and issue orders. She would requisition Ursula's bedroom and make him sleep on the couch and fold it away first thing in the morning, and wash up directly after every meal. She would send him out with shopping lists. She would be suspicious if he continued his assignations with Yolande, and scandalized if she discovered their relationship.

He telephoned Yolande, and read out the cable to her.

"Is this is a surprise?" she said.

"A complete surprise. Tess always claims she can't do this sort of thing because of her family responsibilities." He explained to her about Patrick.

"Perhaps she's bringing Patrick with her."

"No, they never fly with him. He's subject to fits."

"Why did she cable? Why didn't she just call?"

"So I couldn't put her off. It's a *fait accompli*. It's Monday morning already in England. She'll have left home by now."

"And you have no idea why she's coming?"

"I suppose she's worried about Daddy . . . though she spoke to him on the phone just the other day." An idea struck him. "He would have told her about Ursula's windfall, that's probably it."

"She wants to get hold of Ursula's money?"

"She wants to stop me getting hold of it," said Bernard. "She thinks I'm intriguing to inherit Ursula's fortune. She's thought that all along."

"It doesn't sound as if you two get along too well," Yolande said.

"No, we don't, I'm afraid."

"You should stop saying that, Bernard."

"Saying what?"

" 'I'm afraid.' "

Mr Walsh was delighted to hear, the next morning, that Tess was coming out to Honolulu. "That's grand," he said. "Now we'll see some action around here. She'll get a grip on these doctors and nurses, I'm telling you." He persisted in thinking that the medical staff of St Joseph's were detaining him in hospital unnecessarily in order to extract maximum profit from his medical insurance. "Tess will tell them what's what. She'll have me out of here in no time. She'll take me home."

"Did you ask her to come and fetch you?" Bernard said accusingly.

"No, I did not," Mr Walsh replied emphatically. "It never crossed my mind that she could get away from home, not to mention the cost. But Ursula will see her right, won't she? She can afford to, now."

"If Tess needs any help with the fare, I'm sure Ursula will gladly give it," said Bernard. "But nobody asked her to come. I don't see the point of it."

224

"At a time like this," Mr Walsh said piously, "families should rally round. It will be a comfort to Ursula to see Tess."

"I'll be very glad to see Tess, of course," said Ursula. "But right now I'm more excited at the prospect of seeing Jack next Wednesday. Nervous, too, now it's actually going to happen."

"Nervous?"

"It's been such a long time. And when he speaks to me on the phone, which isn't all that often, he seems so cold, so defensive."

"You know Daddy. He doesn't express emotion very easily. Neither do I, come to that. It's a family trait."

"I know." Ursula relapsed into a somewhat gloomy silence. When she broke it, it seemed a reversion to their conversation of the previous day. "That man who said heaven was like a dream in which everybody gets what they desire . . . Did he include sex?"

"I don't know," said Bernard, startled. "I can't recall whether he mentioned it. I don't see why it wouldn't be included."

"Our Lord said there was no marrying or giving in marriage in heaven, didn't He?"

"Many Christians have found that a hard saying, and tried to find ways around it," said Bernard. "Swedenborg, for instance."

"Who was he?"

"A Swedish mystic of the eighteenth century. There's a lot of stuff in his books about heavenly nuptials. He thought you would marry your true soul-mate in heaven and have a rather ethereal kind of sexual intercourse. He wasn't married himself, but he had his eye on a certain Countess, whose husband was conveniently going to be a cat in the next world."

"A cat?"

"Yes, Swedenborg thought that spiritually undeveloped souls would be cats in the afterlife."

"He wasn't a Catholic, then."

"No, a Lutheran. There's a sect that based itself on his writings, called the Church of the New Jerusalem. Come to think of it, Protestants have always been keener on sex in heaven than Catholics. Milton, for instance. Charles Kingsley. There was a Catholic theologian in the sixteenth century, I can't remember

225

his name now, who thought that a lot of kissing went on in heaven. He said the saints could exchange kisses at a distance, even if they were separated by thousands of miles."

"Kissing wasn't my problem," said Ursula. "I always liked kissing and cuddling. It was the other business I couldn't get on with."

Bernard's flight of donnish wit faltered and stalled. He was silent, uncertain how to respond.

"I never satisfied Rick that way. I could never let myself go. That's what he said when we broke up."

"I'm sorry," Bernard mumbled.

"I could never bring myself to touch his . . . his thing, you see. Just couldn't do it." She was talking in a kind of weary drawl, her eyes closed, like someone making their confession. "He used to make me hold it and then stuff like catarrh would squirt out of the little hole in the top, over my hand."

"Rick made you do that?" Bernard whispered.

"No, not Rick. Sean. That's why I could never touch Rick that way."

Bernard recalled the photograph, almost torn in half, of the three children sitting in the field, the two younger ones squinting up at the camera, and the older boy grinning behind them, his hands in his pockets. An appalling thought struck him. "Ursula," he said, "Daddy didn't ever . . . did he?"

"No," said Ursula. "But Jack knew about it."

"It seems that it happened one summer when the family still lived in Ireland," Bernard said to Yolande later. "They lived on the outskirts of Cork, then. It was the school holidays. A relative was dying and my grandmother was away from the house a lot, helping the family. My grandfather was out at work all day. The children were left to their own devices. Sean was the eldest, sixteen, Ursula thinks. She was seven, Daddy about twelve. Sean took advantage of the situation. He took Ursula out for walks, gave her sweets, made her his favourite. At first she was flattered. The first time he exposed himself, he made out it was a joke. Then it became a regular thing, a secret between them. When he started masturbating she knew it was wrong, but she was too frightened to do anything about it."

"Did he do anything to her – I mean, assault her sexually?"

"No, nothing, she was quite definite about that. But he left her with a disgust of physical sex that she was never able to overcome. It ruined her marriage, she said. It put her off thinking of marrying again. She had plenty of flirtations, plenty of male admirers, she said, but as soon as they started to get physical, she would back off."

"What a sad story," said Yolande. "Even sadder than yours."

"Mine isn't sad any more," he said fondly, stroking the dune-shape of her naked hip. They were lying on the bed in room 1509, having made love as soon as they came together, urgently and passionately this time, like lovers, it seemed to Bernard, not teacher and pupil. (Though Yolande had found an opportunity to inform him that he had adopted the missionary position – "and what could be more appropriate?" she said mischievously.) "But I agree with you," he said, with all the fervour of a recent convert to sexual candour, "I mean, what's a penis, what's a bit of semen" – he lifted his sticky, detumescent member from his thigh and let it drop again – "that the sight of them should blight a woman's entire life?"

"The physical acts are not necessarily important in child abuse. It's the fear, the shame, that leave the scars."

"You're right," said Bernard. "Ursula was convinced that *she* was in a state of mortal sin, never mind Sean; and since she couldn't bring herself to mention it in Confession, for years she was in terror of sudden death, convinced she would go straight to hell."

"Did she ever confront Sean about it in later life?"

"Never. And then he was killed in the war, and canonized by the family, and it was impossible to mention it. She's never mentioned it to a single soul till today, can you believe that? It must be why she wanted Daddy to come out here in the first place, why she asked me to persuade him to come. She wanted to exorcize the memory, lay Sean's ghost, by talking to Daddy. But now that the moment has come, she's scared, and I don't blame

227

her. I don't know how he's going to take it. And on top of everything, Tess is coming out to complicate matters further."

"What did Ursula mean, that your father 'knew'?"

"Apparently one day he caught them in the act. Sean used to take her to an old outhouse at the bottom of their garden. Daddy went in there one day, looking for something, and they didn't hear him coming. She remembers him blundering through the door, and stopping suddenly on the threshold, and smiling and opening his mouth to speak, and then the smile fading on his face, as he realized what they were doing. Then he turned and ran out without a word. Sean was frantically buttoning himself up. He said to Ursula – she remembers the words to this day – '*Don't worry about Jack, he'll never spy.*' And he didn't. He never said a word to anyone. At first Ursula was relieved, for she was in mortal terror of their parents finding out. But later, when she was grown up, she blamed Jack. He could have stopped it, she said, by just threatening to tell on Sean."

"You mean, it went on after that?"

"Yes. It went on all that summer, and Daddy knew it was going on. Ursula blames him for that."

"I'm not surprised."

"She wants an apology. She wants an act of contrition. I'm not sure that she'll get it."

"You'll have to help," said Yolande.

"What d'you mean?"

"You'll have to set it up. Prepare your father. See that they're left alone at the right moment."

"I'm not sure I could talk to Daddy about this. Anyway, Tess won't let me. She'll interfere."

"You'll have to get her co-operation."

"You don't know Tess."

"Well, I will soon, won't I?"

He raised himself on one elbow to stare at her. "You mean, you want to meet her?"

"Well, you weren't planning to keep me under wraps, were you?"

228

"No . . ." he said, "of course not." But his expression betrayed him.

"I think you were!" Yolande said teasingly. "I think you were planning to keep me a secret, the little piece of ass that you meet in the afternoons for illicit sex." She pinched him sharply enough to make him cry out.

"Don't be ridiculous, Yolande," he said, blushing.

"Have you told anybody that you're seeing me? Your aunt? Your father?"

"Well, no. Have you told Roxy?"

"She knows I'm seeing you. She doesn't know we're sleeping together, but why should she?"

Bernard considered. "You're quite right, as usual," he said. "I've been afraid to tell them. Have lunch with Tess and me tomorrow."

2

Following the signs to Arrivals at Honolulu airport, Bernard drove past a row of half a dozen kiosks selling *leis*, each with its own parking bay. On impulse, he stopped and purchased a sweet-smelling garland of yellow blossoms that the vendor, a cheerfully fat Hawaiian lady with a gap-toothed smile, told him were called *ilima*. He waited inside the terminal near the baggage carousels with other *lei*-bearing greeters, marvelling that it was only twelve days since he and his father had landed here, sweating in their thick fibrous English clothes. He felt as if he were hardly the same person, and not just because he was wearing shorts. The feeling was reinforced when Tess came into view and peered at the waiting crowd, plainly not recognizing him. She looked hot and lumpish, in a crumpled linen jacket and skirt, carrying a raincoat over her arm. He pushed his way forward and called her name. "Tess! *Aloha!*" He tossed the *lei* over her head, but it snagged in her wiry hair, and she had to distengangle herself.

"What's this?" she said crossly, as if suspecting a practical joke.

"It's called a *lei*. It's a local custom."

"It seems a shame to treat flowers like that," she said, examining the threaded blossoms. "But they do smell nice, I must say. You've shaved off your beard, Bernard. You look younger without it. I didn't recognize you. How's Daddy?"

"He's fine, and looking forward to seeing you. How was the journey?"

"It seemed to go on for ever. If I'd known what it would be like, I probably wouldn't have come."

"Why *did* you come, Tess?" he asked.

230

"I'll tell you later," she said.

"I came for a break," Tess said, to Bernard's surprise. "I came to get away from home, away from Frank, away from the family. To indulge myself for once. Sit about on the beach, or round a swimming-pool, without having to plan the next meal. I hope you're not expecting me to keep house for you while I'm here?"

"No, no," he said. "We can eat out. I do, a lot."

They were sitting on the balcony of Ursula's apartment, overlooking the swimming-pool, a brilliant sapphire rectangle set in the dark patio. Tess had surprised him by insisting on swimming in it as soon as they arrived home. She had cavorted in the water like a happy porpoise, emitting little sighs and cries of pleasure. While she showered afterwards, he made a pot of tea. She joined him on the balcony wearing Ursula's flowered silk housecoat, and pronounced herself a new woman. "Of course, I wanted to see for myself that Daddy was all right," she said. "That was the pretext. But it wasn't the main reason why I came. Or to see Ursula. It was to please myself."

"What about Patrick?" Bernard asked.

"Let Frank take care of him," said Tess curtly. "*I* have for the last sixteen years."

Bernard inferred that there must be some trouble between Tess and her husband, and it wasn't long before she poured out the story.

"He's got a girlfriend, can you imagine? Frank? My God, when he was young he was so shy he could hardly look a woman in the face. Now he fancies himself as a great romantic hero, *Brief Encounter* isn't in it. It's someone he met through the church – nice that, don't you think? He's always been a great one for the lay apostolate, of course, Frank. Chairman of the Parish Council. Organizer of the Covenant Scheme. Pillar of the Knights of St Columba. Out two or three evenings a week on parish business. I thought I shouldn't complain, since it was all in a good cause, though it put more strain on me, having to look after Patrick on my own in the evenings as well as half the day. I know the girl, a silly moon-faced primary teacher, much younger than him – I

231

suppose that's part of the attraction, that and the adoring looks she gives him with her big cow-eyes. She baby-sat for us a few times, you see, before I found out what was going on. I thought it was rather amusing, the moony way she followed him about with her eyes. They met through the covenant scheme – she volunteered to be a canvasser, and did the rounds with him, to see how it was done. He says they haven't slept together, and I don't suppose they have, he hasn't the gumption, but I know he kisses her, because it was in the letter. I found a letter in his jacket, when I was taking it to the cleaners – corny, isn't it? A lovey-dovey love letter. He says she's had a hard life – well, who hasn't, I'd like to know? A broken home, parents divorced, she's a convert, became a Catholic on the rebound from a broken love affair – a lonely heart, in other words, just looking for a shoulder to cry on. And Frank fell for it, hook, line and sinker. After doing the covenant circuit, they would go to a pub and she'd tell him all her troubles. During the school holiday, it appears, she's been going up to the City and meeting him in his lunch hour. He's swears it's innocent, that he's just sorry for her, but he won't break it off. He says he's afraid she'd do something desperate. Well, I thought I'd do something desperate instead, so I went out and booked a flight to Honolulu. He didn't believe me until I showed him the ticket – an open one, he went pale at the price of it. He said, 'What about Patrick? You can't just leave him with me. I have to go to work every day.' I said, 'You'll have to work something out, won't you, like I have for the last sixteen years. I'm sure Bryony will lend a hand.' That's her name, Bryony."

"I'm sorry," said Bernard, when she seemed to stop, or pause. "These things are very painful."

"What gets me," Tess said, "is that he's never shown a spark of pity for me in all the years of our marriage. It was always a hearty, cheerful, down-to-earth sort of relationship, ours. Practical. Commonsense. Coping with Patrick and the other children. Sex was something silent and physical, done in the dark – and there hasn't been a great deal of that lately. Yet when he talks about her, his eyes fill with tears. Tears!" Tess seemed to stifle a sob herself, or maybe it was a scornful laugh – he couldn't be sure, for her face

232

was in shadow. "I said to him, 'You never showed me a fraction of the compassion you have for that girl.' He said I seemed so strong, he thought I didn't need his compassion."

"It's so difficult to know what other people are really like," said Bernard. "What they really want, what they really need. It's hard enough to know it about oneself."

Tess blew her nose on a paper tissue. "How warm it is, even at night," she said, in a different, calmer voice. She stood up and leaned on the balcony rail. "There are two people waving over there, do they know you?"

Bernard looked, and saw the strange couple of his first evening, rather smartly dressed this time, with glasses in their hands. They looked perfectly normal. He wondered whether he had hallucinated the woman exposing herself.

"No," he said. "I think I excited their attention once by wearing that robe. I should sit down, if I were you."

"Needless to say, I don't want Daddy to hear a word of this."

"If you say so. But is that a good idea?"

"What d'you mean? Why burden him with my marital problems, especially when he's not well?"

"Daddy's nearly better. He's made an excellent recovery, his physician says. He's already walking with a Zimmer frame for ten minutes a day."

"I don't want to upset him unnecessarily."

"That's always been the way in our family, hasn't it? Don't upset Daddy. Don't upset Mummy. Don't tell anybody anything unpleasant. Pretend everything's all right. I'm not sure it's such a good way. Things that are suppressed tend to fester."

"What are you getting at, Bernard?" Tess said.

So he told her about Ursula and her two brothers, that summer in Ireland long ago, and his theory that it was the main reason why Ursula had wanted to see their father before she died. Tess was silent for some moments after he had finished. Then she exhaled, a long, whistling breath. "Uncle Sean. I never knew him, of course, but everybody in the family always spoke of him as if the sun and moon shone out of his eyes. They said he was a wonderful man."

233

"Well, maybe he was a wonderful man," said Bernard. "But he was a disturbed adolescent, and Ursula suffered for it."

"It will kill Daddy to have this brought up now," she said.

"Nonsense," said Bernard. "He's as tough as old boots. Anyway, it's not as if he abused Ursula himself."

"No, but he connived at it. He'd die of shame if he thought we knew."

"Well, that's tricky, I agree. But I don't know whether Ursula can handle it on her own. I'll have to ask Yolande's advice." The name slipped out unintentionally.

"Who's Yolande?"

"A friend of mine. I'd like you to meet her. We could have lunch together, tomorrow."

"You mean someone you met here, in Hawaii? Who is she?"

Bernard could not suppress a nervous giggle. "Well, actually, she was the driver of the car . . ."

"The car? You mean, the car that knocked Daddy down? You've become friendly with a woman who nearly killed him?"

"I think I'm in love with her, as a matter of fact," said Bernard.

"In *love*?" Tess gave a shrill laugh. "What's come over you men, suddenly? Is it the male menopause or something they've put in the water, or what?"

"I don't think it can be the water supply," said Bernard. "Frank being in England, and me being in Hawaii."

Tess slept till he woke her the next morning at ten, and after breakfast he drove her to St Joseph's. Their father was exercising with the Zimmer frame when they arrived, taking slow hesitant steps in the middle of the room, with a physiotherapist in watchful attendance. Tess burst into tears as she embraced him. When she recovered her composure, the first thing she said was, "Your hair needs cutting, Daddy."

"We can arrange that," said the physiotherapist. "There's a barber who visits the hospital."

"No," said Tess, "I always cut his hair. If you would bring me a pair of scissors and something to put round his shoulders, I'll do it now."

So they brought her a pair of scissors, and a disposable paper cape that did up at the back, and drew the curtains round Mr Walsh's bed, and Tess began to trim his hair. The task seemed to soothe them both equally.

After a few minutes Bernard left them alone together, and went to sit outside the hospital entrance, on a stone bench in the shade. A taxi drew up and deposited two people whom he recognized as Sidney the heartcase and his wife Lilian. When Bernard hailed them, they looked at him with puzzled alarm, until he reminded them who he was.

"Oh yes, I remember you," said Lilian. "You had your father with you. How is he enjoying Hawaii?"

Bernard told them about the accident, and received their commiserations.

"Sidney's been in the wars too, haven't you, love?" Lilian said.

"I'm all right," said Sidney, unconvincingly.

"He had one of his turns."

"Angina," Sidney interjected.

"Had to be rushed to hospital," said Lilian. "That's why we're here. Come back for a check-up. How has your holiday been otherwise?"

"I'm not really here on holiday," said Bernard. "We came to see my father's sister. She lives here."

"Does she really? I don't think we could stand the heat, could we Sidney, day in day out. But it's what you're used to, isn't it? Now my son, Terry, he's treating us to this holiday, he lives in Australia normally, and he's in his element. Down at the beach every day, surfing. He's there now, him and his friend, Tony. Mr Everthorpe – d'you remember him on the plane? – he wants to get them on his video. Terry was going to bring us up here in his hire car, but I said, no, you go and have a surf, Terry, let Mr Everthorpe take your picture, and we'll have a cab. Does your auntie like it here?"

"She certainly used to. I'm afraid she's not very well now. She's in a nursing home."

"Well, it never rains but it pours, does it?" said Lilian. She began to edge away from Bernard, towing her husband by his sleeve, as if Bernard's family misfortune might be contagious.

235

"Going to the party tomorrow evening?" Sidney asked him.

"Party?"

"The Travelwise do."

"Oh, that. Maybe. I did get an invitation."

"Come on, Sidney, we'll be late for your appointment," said Lilian.

"Yes, please don't let me detain you," said Bernard. "I hope all is well."

"What I dread is, if they say he's not fit to fly on Thursday," said Lilian. "I can't wait to get back to Croydon."

After about three-quarters of an hour, Bernard went back inside the hospital. His father and Tess were deep in conversation, their heads close together and their voices low to avoid being overheard by the other occupant of the room, an elderly man called Winterspoon who was recovering from a hip-joint replacement.

"It's time to go, Tess," Bernard said. "We're meeting someone for lunch, Daddy."

"Daddy says he doesn't know anything about this friend of yours," said Tess with a mischievous smirk.

"No, I didn't get round to telling him," said Bernard, wishing he still had a beard with which to conceal his blushes. "Her name's Yolande Miller, Daddy. She was the driver of the car. D'you remember a lady in a red dress standing over you in the street?"

"I do not," said the old man sulkily. "I don't remember anything after that car hit me. No wonder you didn't want to sue the woman."

"I made that decision long before we became friends, Daddy. It wasn't her fault. The police are not taking any further action, so that proves it."

Mr Walsh sniffed.

"Naturally Yolande was very upset about it. She'd love to come and see you, if you would like her to."

"I have enough women visiting me, thank you very much," said Mr Walsh. "That Sophie never misses a day. By the way, d'you think you could pick up a Penny Catechism for me

236

somewhere? She's always pumping me about the Catholic faith, and I'd like to be sure I was giving her the certified stuff. I don't want to be passing on a lot of heresy by mistake."

"I'll see what I can do," said Bernard.

"Who is Sophie?" Tess enquired.

"I call her that because I can't pronounce her last name," said Mr Walsh defensively.

Bernard explained who Sophie Knoepflmacher was.

"Well, you fellows certainly haven't let the grass grow under your feet," Tess said. "You both seem to have fixed yourselves up with girlfriends."

Bernard laughed over-heartily, and avoided meeting his father's eye.

"So tomorrow's the great day, Daddy," he said.

"What's great about it?"

"Ursula's coming to see you."

"Oh, yes." He did not look thrilled at the prospect. "I hope she's not planning to stay too long. I get tired easily."

"She's a very sick woman, Daddy, you should be prepared for that. And she has an enormous amount of emotion invested in this meeting. It won't be easy for either of you. Just be kind to her."

"Kind to her? Why shouldn't I be kind to her?" said the old man, bridling.

"I mean, be patient, be understanding. Be gentle."

"I don't need you to tell me how to behave towards my own sister," said Mr Walsh. But he asked some questions about the arrangements for the visit, and Bernard felt that he had at least focused the old's man's mind upon its importance for Ursula. They left him looking thoughtful.

Yolande had booked a table at a Thai restaurant a few blocks north of the Ala Wai canal. The district, like most of Honolulu outside Waikiki and the downtown area, had a scruffy, improvised character, and the restaurant looked unpromising from the outside: an L-shaped arrangement of clapboard sheds, with corrugated roofing and ugly air-conditioners protruding from the walls. But inside it was a cool oasis, with a tinkling fountain, oriental wall-hangings, ceiling fans and bamboo screens. The clientele did not look like tourists.

Yolande was waiting for them at a corner table. The two women regarded each other warily as Bernard introduced them. Yolande expressed her regrets over the accident, and Tess stiffly declared that she understood it had not been Yolande's fault. Tess had never had Thai food before, and seemed irritated or intimidated by Yolande's knowledgeability. "You two order for me," she said, closing her menu. "I don't really go in for exotic food."

Yolande's face fell. "Oh, I'm sorry. If I'd known, I wouldn't have suggested this restaurant."

This skirmish did nothing to relieve Bernard's misgivings about the wisdom of bringing the two women together. But after they had ordered, Tess asked the way to the Ladies, and Yolande went with her. They were gone long enough for Bernard to drink most of a Thai beer, and he presumed that some confidences had been exchanged, some mutual appraisal satisfactorily accomplished, in the interval, for when they returned to the table they seemed more relaxed and at ease with each other. The lunch was a surprising success. Tess pronounced the food delicious. The conversation, in which Bernard took a minor role, was mainly about bringing up children. Yolande deftly drew Tess out on the subject of Patrick's problems, a topic of which she never tired.

They separated in the restaurant car-park, for Bernard was to drive Tess to see Ursula. He kissed Yolande on the cheek with studied casualness, painfully aware of Tess's sardonic observation, and she murmured into his ear, "Your sister's OK, I like her." She got into her rusting white Toyota and rattled away.

"Well, I must say you've got better taste than Frank," said Tess, as they walked to his car. "Though what she sees in you, Bernard, I can't imagine."

"It must be my beautiful body," he said. Tess laughed, but gave him a shrewd glance, as if trying to assess exactly how facetious he intended to be.

They drove to Makai Manor along the coast road, and he stopped at the lookout point near Diamond Head to let her watch the windsurfers. There weren't so many of them as there had been at the weekend, and Tess regarded them with only mild, unfocused interest. She seemed to have something else on her mind.

"Has Ursula said anything to you about her will?" she asked, when they were back in the car.

"No," said Bernard. "Well, not since she came into all this money. Before that, she did say something about wanting to leave something, to somebody, perhaps me, so that she would be remembered. I persuaded her to spend whatever she had on making the rest of her life as comfortable as possible."

"That was unselfish of you, Bernard," said Tess. "And now she's rich, she'll probably reward you by leaving you her fortune. Well, you deserve it, I suppose. And God knows, you could use the money. But I have to say that I don't think it would be right. The money should go to Daddy, and then in due course to all four of us, you, me, Brendan, Dympna, and not necessarily in equal proportions. After all, what have Brendan and Dympna done for Daddy or Ursula? And they're both comfortable enough as it is."

Bernard mumbled something non-committal.

"But after what you told me last night, I can't see Ursula leaving her money to Daddy, not all of it, anyway. I'll be quite open with you, Bernard – I've been thinking over what you said last night, and I think you're right, so here's my contribution to *glasnost* in the Walsh family circle: I want a fair share of that money for Patrick, or better still, an unfair share. At the moment we can cope, more or less. He goes to a special school every day, during term, by taxi. But he can't live at home indefinitely. He needs physically looking after, and I won't be able to do it much longer, with or without Frank. He'll have to go into some kind of residential care eventually, and the best ones are private. If we could set up some kind of Trust Fund, it would make all the difference . . ."

"I understand your feelings," Bernard said. "But really, Tess, it's Ursula's business. I have no idea what she intends to do with her money."

"But you could influence her. You're managing her affairs for her now, aren't you?"

239

"Not to that extent, no." He paused for thought. "If we'd had this conversation two weeks ago I would have said: You can have all Ursula's money, as far as I'm concerned, and welcome. But since then, I've become involved with Yolande. I've got nothing to offer her at the moment. No house, no savings. I haven't even got a proper job. I can't deny it's crossed my mind that a substantial legacy would be very useful."

"D'you mean you want to marry her?"

"If she'd have me, yes. But I don't know what her feelings are about me, really. I haven't dared to discuss the future of our relationship, in case she says it hasn't got one."

"I gather that she's getting divorced."

"Yes."

Tess slowly shook her head. "You've come a long way from chief thurible bearer at Our Lady of Perpetual Succour, Bernard."

"Yes," he said. "I have."

Enid da Silva was waiting for them in the entrance hall of Makai Manor as they came in, her normally serene brow creased by a frown. "Oh, Mr Walsh, I've been trying to call you all morning. Mrs Riddell is not very well, I'm afraid. She vomited a little blood this morning and it upset her. Dr Gerson has been out to see her. He said you were to call him. Mrs Riddell is afraid he's going to say she can't visit her brother tomorrow. She's very agitated. Here's the number."

Bernard phoned Gerson at once. "She had a small haemorrhage," he said. "I didn't think it was necessary to bring her back into hospital. She didn't lose a lot of blood. But it's not a good sign."

"Can she travel to Honolulu by ambulance tomorrow?" Bernard explained the arrangement that had been made, and its importance to Ursula.

"Can't your father come to *her*?"

"I could ask Dr Figuera, but I doubt it. He's only just been allowed out of bed, for a few minutes a day."

"You're probably right." Gerson deliberated for a moment.

240

"Strictly speaking, I should say no. She ought to rest tomorrow. But from what you tell me, she's only going to fret if she doesn't see her brother, right?"

"Correct," said Bernard.

"Then we might as well let her go, and accept the risk."

It was the first topic Ursula raised, as soon as she had greeted Tess. Bernard saw in his sister's eyes the shock of encountering Ursula's wasted appearance; he supposed that he himself had got used to it, though she did look particularly frail and sallow today, scarcely able to lift her head from the pillow to meet Tess's kiss. "Not too good," she whispered, when he asked her how she was. "I brought up a little blood this morning. They called Dr Gerson out to see me. I'm afraid they won't let me go to see Jack tomorrow."

"It's all right, Ursula," Bernard said. "I just checked with Dr Gerson, and he says you can go."

"Thank God for that," Ursula sighed. "I don't think I could have stood another delay." She stretched out her good arm to clasp Tess's hand. "Now I can relax and enjoy your being here, Tess. It's wonderful. The last time I saw you, you were in pigtails and a gymslip."

"You shouldn't have stayed away so long, Aunt Ursula," said Tess, leaving her hand in Ursula's. "You should have come home before . . ."

"Before it was too late? Yeah, of course I should. But I wasn't sure I would be welcome. My last visit wasn't exactly a success. In fact it ended with a tremendous row between myself and your mother, and Jack. I forget how it started now, something very trivial, about bathwater or something. That was it, I used all the hot water in the cistern, unintentionally – I was already Americanized by then, you see, I took constant hot water for granted, but in your house in Brickley it was heated by some complicated system . . ."

"A solid-fuel boiler in the kitchen," said Tess. "It never worked properly. We had an immersion heater put in eventually."

"Well, anyhow, I used to take a bath every morning, because it

241

was what I was used to, a tub or a shower every day, and there wasn't a shower in your bathroom . . . Monica used to give out little hints that she considered this routine excessive – the rest of you only had one bath a week. I pretended that I didn't understand what she was talking about, and I guess she brooded about it and got more and more resentful, until one morning I accidentally overfilled the tub and all this precious hot water was spilling out the overflow pipe into the back garden, and when I was through there was none left for the washing. It was washday. Well, that was the last straw for Monica. She exploded. I don't blame her, looking back. She had a hard time making ends meet in those days, and I must have seemed a spoiled, inconsiderate houseguest. But it was an ugly scene, and unforgivable things were said, on both sides. Jack did nothing to calm things down when he came home from work. He made them worse, if anything. I left the house the next morning, a week earlier than I'd planned, and never went back. Too proud to say sorry, I guess. Sad, isn't it, to think that a few gallons of hot water could keep a family divided for a lifetime."

Exhausted by this long narrative, Ursula closed her eyes.

"Of course, it wasn't just the hot water, was it Ursula?" Bernard gently prompted. "There were other things dividing you. Other resentments. Like what you told me yesterday, about yourself and Daddy and Uncle Sean, when you were children."

Ursula nodded.

"We were wondering – I've told Tess about it, by the way, I hope you don't mind –"

Ursula shook her head.

"We were wondering whether you intend to bring it up with Daddy tomorrow."

Ursula opened her eyes again. "You think I shouldn't?"

"I think you have every right. But don't be too hard on him."

"He's an old man, Aunt Ursula," said Tess, "and it all happened a long time ago."

"To me, it's as if it happened yesterday," said Ursula. "I can still smell the smells in that old shed back of our house: turpentine and creosote and cat pee. It comes back to me like the memory of a bad dream. And Sean smiling at me, with his teeth but not with his eyes. I can't forgive Sean, you see, because I can't talk to him about it, any more than I can ask Monica to forgive me for wasting the bathwater. I left it too late. They're both dead. But I feel that if I could talk to Jack, if I could tell him how much unhappiness it caused me, in later life, that summer in Cork, and feel he understood, and accepted some responsibility for it, then I would be free from the memory, once and for all. I could die in peace."

In silent acquiescence Tess patted Ursula's fragile hand.

"Of course, there's always the possibility that he's entirely forgotten it, erased it from his memory," said Bernard.

"I don't think so," said Ursula. And, recalling how reluctant his father had been, all along, to be reunited with Ursula, neither did Bernard.

"One more thing," Ursula said, as they were preparing to leave. "I think maybe I should receive the Last Sacrament."

"That's a good idea," said Tess. "Only we don't call it that any more. Or Extreme Unction. It's called the Sacrament of the Sick."

"Well, whatever it's called, I think I could use it," said Ursula drily.

"I'll speak to Father Luke at St Joseph's," said Bernard. "I'm sure he'd be glad to come out here."

"Perhaps he could do it tomorrow afternoon, at the hospital," Tess said. "When we're all together, as a family."

"I'd like that," said Ursula. So Bernard made a telephone call there and then to the Chaplain's office at St Joseph's, and arranged it.

"My God, Bernard," Tess said, when they were outside Makai Manor, "she looks terrible. She's just skin and bone."

"Yes. I suppose I've got used to it. But it is a cruel disease."

"Oh, life, life!" Tess shook her head. "What with mental suffering and physical suffering . . ." The sentence trailed away, unfinished. "I need a swim," she said abruptly, straightening her shoulders, and lifting her face to the sun. "I need a swim in the sea."

243

They returned to the apartment to change into their swimming-costumes, and then Bernard drove them down to Kapiolani Beach Park. He told Tess the story of the lost and found keys as they slipped off their outer clothes. She looked heavy-hipped and ungainly in her plain black swimming-costume, but she was a strong, graceful swimmer, and he had some difficulty keeping up with her as she struck out towards the open sea. When they were about a hundred yards from the shore, she rolled over onto her back and kicked her feet luxuriously. "It's ridiculously warm," she cried as he came puffing and blowing up to her. "You could stay in all day, and never get cold."

"Not like Hastings, eh?" he said. "Remember how your fingers used to turn blue?"

"And your teeth used to chatter," she said, laughing. "Literally. I'd never heard it before, or since."

"And the agony of stepping on those pebbles in your bare feet."

"And trying to take off your wet cossie, and put on your knickers, under a towel that was far too small, while balancing on one foot on a hill of sliding shingle . . ."

It was a long time since he had felt so at ease with Tess. The word "knickers", at once homely and faintly naughty, seemed to evoke a state of playful and unreflective happiness that he associated with childhood, though he couldn't actually remember Tess ever pronouncing it in his hearing. As they lay on the sand, drying off after their swim, he remarked on this.

"No, well, I would have got my ears boxed if I had, wouldn't I? Mummy and Daddy were very strict with Dympna and me, as far as you were concerned. We had to be very modest, for fear you'd be distracted from your vocation."

"Really?"

"Of course. 'Bra' and 'knickers' were considered dirty words. If we were washing or ironing our underwear, and you happened to come into the kitchen, it was whisked out of sight for fear it would inflame your senses. And as for sanitary towels . . . well, I don't suppose you even knew when we started our periods, did you?"

"No," said Bernard. "I never gave it a thought, till this moment."

"You were marked out for the priesthood from an early age, Bernard. I could almost see the halo growing round your head, like the rings of Saturn. You had a very privileged life at home."

"Did I?"

"You mean you don't remember? Never asked to wash up because you were supposed to have more homework than anyone else, or it was supposed to be more important. Always getting the choicest cut of the Sunday roast."

"Don't be ridiculous."

"It's true. And if you needed new clothes or shoes, they appeared without your having to ask. Whereas with us . . . Look at that toe." She raised her foot in the air and pointed to a deformed big toe joint. "That came from wearing shoes that I'd grown out of, for far too long."

"But that's awful! You make me feel terrible."

"It wasn't your fault, it was Mummy and Daddy. They walked around putting screens between you and the real world."

" 'They fuck you up, your mum and dad/They may not mean to, but they do.' "

"I *beg* your pardon!" Tess sat up and stared at him.

"It's a poem. Philip Larkin."

"Nice language for a poet."

" 'They fill you with the faults they had/And add some extra, just for you.' "

Tess sniggered and sighed. "Poor Mummy. Poor Daddy."

"Poor Ursula," Bernard said. "Poor Sean."

"Poor Sean?"

"Yes. We shouldn't withhold our pity from Sean. Who knows what made him act as he did? Who knows what remorse he felt afterwards?"

When they returned to the apartment to shower and change, Bernard proposed going out to eat, but Tess, suddenly stricken with jet-lag, demurred. She found in the fridge some eggs and cheese he had bought from the ABC Store at the corner of the block, and ended up cooking for them after all, a cheese omelette,

245

with some coleslaw that Sophie Knoepflmacher had left a couple of days earlier.

While they were eating, Frank phoned from England. Bernard made a move to leave the room, but Tess gestured him to stay where he was. She answered Frank's questions briefly and expressionlessly. Yes, she had arrived safely. Yes, she had seen Daddy, who was making a good recovery. Yes, she had seen Ursula, who was not at all well. The weather was hot and sunny. She had been swimming twice already, once in a pool and once in the sea. No, she didn't know when she would be coming back. He was to give her love to the children. Goodbye, Frank.

"How is he coping?" Bernard asked, when she put down the phone.

"He sounds . . ." Tess searched for a word. "Chastened. No mention of Bryony."

Tess retired to bed soon after supper. Bernard called up Yolande and asked her to meet him at the Waikiki Surfrider. She said she had to stay in to make sure Roxy got home by ten-thirty, as she had promised. Bernard glanced at his watch. It was twenty past eight. "Just for an hour," he pleaded.

"Just for an hour! What d'you think I am, a call girl?"

"It's not for that," he said. "I want to talk."

But it was, in the event, for "that", too.

"So, what d'you want to talk about, Bernard?" she said, afterwards.

"Do you have to call me 'Bernard' all the time?"

"What d'you want me to call you?" she said, startled. "Bernie?"

He giggled. "No, I'd hate that. But lovers call each other 'darling', or 'sweetheart' or something like that, don't they? And there's an American word . . ."

"Honey?"

"Yes, that's it. Call me 'honey'."

"I used to call Lewis, 'honey.' I'd feel married to you."

"That's why I'd like it. I'd like to be married to you, Yolande."

"Oh? How, or rather where, were you thinking of doing that?"

"That's what I wanted to talk about. But how do you feel about it in principle?"

246

"In principle? In principle I think it's the craziest idea I ever heard in my life. I've known you for less than two weeks. I'm in the middle of a long and complicated divorce proceeding. I have a teenage daughter at school in Hawaii, and a job that, even if it isn't exactly at the pinnacle of the psychiatric profession, satisfies me. You, as I understand it, have only visitor's papers and a job in England that you have to get back to, not to mention a convalescent father you have to return to his home."

"Obviously we couldn't get married right away," he said. "But I could apply for an immigrant's visa in England, and come back to Hawaii, and try and get a job here. Teaching. Or something in the tourist trade."

"Dear God, no," said Yolande. "The only reason I'd marry you is to get out of Hawaii."

"I'm serious, Yolande."

"So am I."

He levered himself up from the mattress into a semi-recumbent position, the better to see her face in the dimly illuminated room. "You mean you *will* marry me?"

"I mean I'm serious about getting out of Hawaii."

"Oh," said Bernard.

"Don't look so dejected." She smiled and reached up to stroke his face. "I really like you, Bernard. I don't know whether I want to marry you – I don't know whether I want to marry anyone, again. But I'd like to continue our relationship."

"How? Where?"

"I'll come and stay with you at Christmas – how's that for starters? Lewis can have the kids."

"Christmas?" Bernard thought with dismay of Rummidge in late December, and St John's College in the Christmas vac: a skeleton service in the Refectory, homesick African students mooning about the half-lit corridors, his own cramped study-bedroom, with its narrow single bed.

"Yeah. D'you realize I've only spent a few days in England, in London in the summer?"

"I'm not sure you'll like the English winter."

"Why, what's it like?"

"The days are very short. It doesn't get light till eight o'clock in the morning and it's dark again by four in the afternoon. There's a lot of cloud. Sometimes you don't see the sun for days."

"Sounds great," said Yolande. "I'm sick to death of the frigging sun. We can draw the curtains and pile up the logs on the fire."

"I don't have a log fire, I'm afraid," said Bernard. "In fact I only have a single room in College, with a one-bar electric fire and a gas-ring. We'd have to go and stay in a hotel somewhere."

"That would be great. One of those country hotels where you can have a traditional English Christmas. I've seen them advertised."

"You'd have to pay for yourself, I'm afraid."

"That's OK. You've started saying 'afraid' again. Are you sure you want me to come?"

"Of course I want you to come. It's just that I don't want you to be disappointed. The fact is I don't have enough money to look after you properly. And I never will have, unless . . ."

"Unless what?"

"Well, to be blunt, unless I inherit it from Ursula."

"Well, that's likely to happen, isn't it? After all, you discovered the IBM money."

"She did talk of leaving me something, before that ever happened. But now there's so much money, it's become more fraught. I have a feeling that the family is drawing together around Ursula. Old wounds are being healed. We're talking to each other, honestly, at last. I don't want that to be jeopardized by ill-feeling about Ursula's will. You know what families are like. Daddy is the next-of-kin. And now Tess wants me to persuade Ursula to set up a trust fund for Patrick."

"Don't, Bernard," said Yolande forcefully. "Don't do it. Don't make yourself a doormat. Leave it to Ursula to decide what to do with her money. If she wants to give it to Patrick, fine. If she wants to give it to your father, fine. If she wants to give it to cancer research, that's fine too. But if she wants to give it to you, accept it. It's her choice. Patrick will be OK. Tess will be OK. She's a survivor. She told me how she just walked out on her husband,

248

what's his name, Frank? Frank's obviously been using that handicapped kid like a ball and chain for years, to keep her trapped in the home. She had to cut loose, and she did. That took guts. I respect her for it. But on the other hand, what about Frank? Why is he having his thing with the little schoolteacher? Perhaps Tess hasn't given him enough. She's obsessed with that kid. She'd take on the whole world, to protect his interests. She'll trample all over you, if you give her the chance. And if you're thinking to yourself while I'm talking that there's some resemblance between her marital situation and mine, don't think it hasn't occurred to me."

The next day, after they had shared an early lunch together, Tess took a cab to St Joseph's, and Bernard drove out to Makai Manor. The plan was that he would leave his car there and ride in the hired ambulance with Ursula, to and from the hospital, while Tess kept their father company. It wasn't a fully equipped ambulance like the one in which Bernard had accompanied his father to St Joseph's on the day of the accident, but a high-sided vehicle used for transporting patients in wheelchairs, with an electrically operated lift at the rear end. Ursula was excited and nervous. Her hair had been washed and waved that morning; her withered, yellow face was heavily powdered and her lips outlined with lipstick: the effect was well-intentioned but somewhat gruesome. She wore a silky blue and green *muu-muu*, and a fresh sling for her arm. A rosary of amber beads on a silver chain was wound around her wasted fingers.

"This was my mother's," she said. "She gave it to me when I left home to marry Rick. I think she thought of it as a kind of leash that would bring me back into the fold one day. She had a great devotion to Our Lady, like your own mother, Bernard. I thought Jack might like to have it."

Bernard asked if she didn't want to keep the rosary for herself.

"I want to give Jack something, something to remind him of today, when he goes back to England. I couldn't think of anything else. Anyway, I won't be needing it much longer."

"Nonsense," Bernard said with forced cheerfulness. "You're looking miles better today."

"Well, it feels good to be outside Makai Manor for a change, nice as it is. The sea looks so beautiful. I miss the sea."

They were running along the cliff-top road near Diamond Head at this point. Bernard asked her if she would like to stop somewhere and look at the view.

"Maybe on the way back," said Ursula. "I don't want to keep Jack waiting." Her fingers nervously twisted and untwisted the strands of the rosary. "Where are we meeting him? Has he got a private room?"

"No, he shares it with another man. But there's a nice sort of terrace outside, where patients can walk up and down, or sit in the shade. I thought we'd go there. It will be more private."

When they arrived at St Joseph's, the driver lowered Ursula, strapped into her wheelchair, to the ground, and pushed her up a ramp into the hospital's elevator. When they reached the right floor, Bernard asked the man to wait for them below, and took over the wheelchair. He went first to his father's room, but the bed was empty. Mr Winterspoon looked up from his miniature TV to say that Mr Walsh and his daughter were outside on the terrace. Bernard pushed the wheelchair down a corridor and through a pair of swing doors, out into the open air, round a corner – and there they were, at the end of the terrace. Mr Walsh was also seated in a wheelchair, and Tess was stooping to adjust his dressing-gown round his knees.

"Jack!" Ursula croaked, much too quietly for him to have heard, but he must have sensed her presence, for he looked round sharply, and said something to Tess. She smiled and waved and began to push the wheelchair towards Bernard and Ursula, so that they all met, almost collided, in the middle of the terrace, in a clamour of laughter and tears and exclamations. Mr Walsh had obviously decided to control the emotion of the situation with a determined jocularity.

"Whoa!" he exclaimed, as the two wheelchairs converged, "Not so fast! I don't want another traffic accident."

"Jack! Jack! It's wonderful to see you at last," Ursula cried, leaning across the interlocked wheels to clutch his arm and kiss his cheek.

"You too, Ursula. But aren't we a sight for sore eyes, propped up in these contraptions like a couple of Guy Fawkes dolls?"

"You look marvellous, Jack. How's your hip?"

"It's mending well, I'm told. I don't know whether I'll ever be the same man again, mind you. And how are you, my dear?"

Ursula shrugged. "You can see for yourself," she said.

"Aye, you're very thin. I'm very sorry about your illness, Ursula. Don't cry, don't cry." He patted her bony hand nervously between his own.

Bernard and Tess parked the wheelchairs in a quiet, shady corner of the terrace, which was a kind of paved cloister, shaded by flowering vines growing over an open latticed roof. It had for Mr Walsh the attraction that he was allowed to smoke there, and he immediately broke out a packet of Pall Malls and offered them round. "No takers?" he said. "Well, I'll force myself, to keep the flies off the rest of you."

After some animated chatter about Ursula's ambulance ride, Mr Walsh's opinion of St Joseph's hospital, the view from the terrace, and similar trivia, a silence fell.

"Isn't it silly," Ursula sighed. "There's so much to talk about, you don't know where to start."

"We'll leave you two alone for a little while," said Bernard.

"There's no need," said his father. "You and Tess aren't in the way – are they, Ursula?"

Ursula murmured something non-committal. Tess supported Bernard's proposal, however, and they wandered off, leaving the two old people facing each other in their wheelchairs. Mr Walsh looked after them with a faintly cornered expression.

Bernard and Tess walked to the end of the terrace, and leaned on the balustrade, looking out over the roofs of suburban houses shimmering in the heat, at the freeway with its unceasing currents of traffic, and in the distance the hazy flat industrial landscape around Honolulu harbour. A jumbo jet, small as a child's toy, rose slowly into the sky and circled over the ocean before heading eastwards.

"Well," said Bernard. "We made it. We finally brought them together."

"It's nice of you to say 'us', Bernard," said Tess. "You're the one who made it happen."

"Well, I'm very glad to have you here, anyway."

"As you know, my first reaction was that it was a mad idea, bringing Daddy all this way to see Ursula, and when I heard that he'd been knocked down, I thought it was a judgment on me for having changed my mind," said Tess, with the air of someone who had something she had decided to get off her chest. "But now I'm here, and knowing what I know now about their relationship in the past, I think you were right. It would have been terrible if Ursula had died alone, unreconciled, all these thousands of miles from home."

Bernard nodded. "I think it would have preyed on Daddy's mind, as he gets older. When he faces death himself."

"Don't," said Tess, clutching her arms, and hunching her shoulders. "I don't like to think of Daddy dying."

"They say," said Bernard, "that when your second parent dies, you finally accept your own mortality. I wonder if it's true. To accept death, to be ready for death whenever it happens, without letting that acceptance spoil your appetite for life – that seems to me the hardest trick of all."

They were silent for a few moments. Then Tess said: "When Mummy died, I said an unforgivable thing to you, Bernard, at the funeral."

"You're forgiven."

"I blamed you for Mummy's death. I shouldn't have. It was very wrong of me."

"That's all right," he said. "You were upset. We were all upset. I shouldn't have walked out. We should have talked. We should have talked a lot more, on many occasions."

Tess turned and gave him a quick kiss on the cheek. "Well, *they* seem to have found plenty to talk about at last," she said, nodding over his shoulder in the direction of Jack and Ursula, who were, indeed, deep in conversation.

They went for a rather aimless walk around the hospital's grounds, mostly car-park, and then sought out Father Luke. He showed them the chapel, a cool, pleasant room, its white walls and polished hardwood furniture splashed with blotches of colour from the modern stained-glass windows. "I thought, as your aunt is in a wheelchair, we'd administer the sacrament in here," he said. "Of course, it's usually done with the patient in bed, but in this case . . . After the anointing, will you all be taking communion with Mrs Riddell?"

"Yes," said Tess.

"No," said Bernard.

"I could give you a blessing, if you like," said the priest. "I always invite people at mass who can't communicate for any reason, divorce for instance, to come to the altar for a blessing."

Bernard hesitated, then acquiesced. He was beginning to feel better disposed towards Father McPhee, who had put himself out to be helpful.

When they went back to the terrace, they found Mr Walsh smoking reflectively, gazing out over the balustrade at the sea, and Ursula asleep in her wheelchair.

"How long has she been asleep?" Bernard exclaimed, afraid that it had been for the duration of their absence.

"About five minutes ago," his father said. "She just nodded off in the middle of something I was saying."

"She does that occasionally," said Bernard. "She's very weak, poor thing."

"Did you have a nice talk, before that, Daddy?" Tess asked.

"Yes," he said. "There was a lot to talk about."

"There sure was," said Ursula. She seemed to have no awareness that she had been asleep.

On the way back to Makai Manor, Bernard asked their driver to pull into the clifftop parking place near Diamond Head and lower Ursula's wheelchair to the ground. Then he pushed her to the parapet, so that she could look out over the blue and emerald sea, and at the dozen or so windsurfers scudding across its surface.

"What a wonderful day it's been," she said. "I feel so at peace. I could die now, quite happily."

"Don't be silly, Ursula," he said. "You've plenty of life in you yet."

253

"No, I mean it. I daresay it won't last for long, this feeling. I expect the fear and depression will come back tonight, as usual. But just now . . . I read in a magazine, the other day, that the old Hawaiians believed that when you died, your soul jumped off from a high cliff, into the sea of eternity. They had a special word for it, I can't remember it now, but it means, 'jumping-off place.' D'you think this was one?"

"I wouldn't be surprised," said Bernard.

"I have the strangest feeling that if I threw myself over the edge of this cliff now, I wouldn't feel any pain or terror. My body would fall off me like clothing, and flutter gently down to the beach, and my soul would fly up to heaven."

"Well, please don't try it," Bernard joked. "I think it would upset the people here." He gestured at the tourists who stood nearby, clicking and whirring with their cameras.

"I feel so strangely . . . light," said Ursula. "It must be the effect of unburdening myself to Jack. Unburden is a good word. That's just what it feels like."

"So you talked about Sean, then?"

"Yes. Jack remembered that summer, of course. Perhaps not as vividly as I do, but as soon as I mentioned that old shed at the bottom of our garden in Cork, I could see from the expression on his face that he knew what I was going to say. He said that, at the time, he was frightened to report Sean to our Father and Mother, because Sean had got up to some dirty games with him, too, a couple of years before, and he was afraid it would all come out and all of us would be thrashed within an inch of our lives. Maybe he was right. He was a frightening man, when he was angry, I can tell you, our Father. Jack said he honestly thought I was too young to know what Sean was doing, too young to be harmed by it, and he assumed that in time I forgot all about it. He seemed genuinely shocked when I told him it had destroyed my marriage and pretty well ruined my life. He kept saying, 'I'm sorry, Ursula, I'm sorry.' I believe he is, too. I guess that's why he asked Father Luke if he could go to confession this afternoon, before he took communion. It was a beautiful service, wasn't it, the anointing? Some of the words were so beautiful, I wish I could remember them."

"I think I probably can," said Bernard. "I said them often enough. *'Through this holy anointing, and through his own loving mercy, may the Lord forgive all the faults that you have committed through your eyes.'* And then the same for the nose, mouth, hands and feet."

"As matter of interest, how can you sin with your nose?"

Bernard guffawed. "Oh, that was a favourite teaser in Moral Theology, when I was a student."

"And what was the answer?"

"The textbooks suggested that you could overindulge in smelling perfumes and nosegays. It didn't seem very convincing. And there was a dark hint about lust being excited by bodily scents, but they didn't go very deeply into that in the seminary, for obvious reasons." He had a sharp memory-picture of himself kneeling at Yolande's feet with his face buried in her crotch, inhaling what smelled like the salty air of a tidal beach.

"That wasn't the bit I was thinking of, anyway," she said. "There was a lesson . . ."

"The Epistle of St James. *'Is any of you sick?'* "

"That's it. Do you know how it goes?"

"Is there any of you sick: let her call for the elders of the Church, and let them pray over her, annointing her with oil in the name of the Lord; and the prayer of faith will save the sick woman, and the Lord will raise her up; and if she has sinned, she will be forgiven. Therefore confess your sins to one another, and pray for one another, that you may be healed."

"That's it. What a pity you aren't a priest any more, Bernard, you say the words so beautifully. Did Father Luke say 'woman' when he read that this afternoon?"

"No," said Bernard. "I changed it, for you."

Ursula was exhausted by the time they got back to Makai Manor. "Exhausted, but content," she said, when she was back in her bed. She stretched out her hand to clasp his. "Dear Bernard! Thankyou thankyou thankyou!"

"I'd better leave you to rest," he said.

"Yes," she said, but she did not release his hand.

255

"I'll come tomorrow."

"I know you will. I've come to count on it. I dread the day when you'll walk out that door for the last time. When I'll know you won't be coming back the next day, because you'll be in an airplane, on your way back to England."

"I don't know yet when I'll be leaving," he said, "so there's no point upsetting yourself about it. It all depends on Daddy's progress."

"He told me he expects to be discharged from the hospital next week."

"Tess could take him home, perhaps. I could stay on a few extra days."

"You're very sweet, Bernard. But sooner or later you'll have to go. You have a job to go back to."

"Yes," he admitted. "There's an induction course at the College, for African and Asian students, coming up soon. I said I'd run it. It's supposed to introduce them to life in Britain," he elaborated, hoping to distract Ursula from her melancholy train of thought. "We have to demonstrate how to light a gas ring and how to eat a kipper, and take them to Marks and Spencer's to buy winter underwear."

Ursula smiled wanly. "I just hope I don't live too long after you've gone."

"You mustn't say that, Ursula. It's upsetting for me as well as for you."

"Sorry. I'm just trying to condition myself to doing without you. I've been spoiled these last couple of weeks, having you here, and then seeing Jack and Teresa. When you've all flown away, I'm going to feel terribly lonely."

"Who knows, I may come back to Hawaii."

Ursula shook her head. "It's too far, Bernard. You can't just hop into an airplane and fly halfway round the world because I'm feeling lonely."

"There's always the telephone," he said.

"Yes, there's always the telephone," Ursula said drily.

"And there's always Sophie Knoepflmacher," he joked. "I'm sure she'd be glad to visit you, when Daddy has gone."

Ursula made a grimace.

"There's somebody else who lives in Honolulu," he said. "Someone I know who would love to visit you – and I know you'd like her." A vivid proleptic image flashed into his head, of Yolande in her red dress, bounding into the room, swinging her brown tennis-player's arms, radiating health and energy, smiling at Ursula and pulling up a chair to talk. They would talk of himself, he thought fondly. "I'll bring her out to meet you tomorrow. Her name's Yolande Miller. She was the driver of the car that knocked Daddy down – that he walked into, I should say. That's how we met. We've become quite friendly since. Well, very friendly, actually." He blushed. "You remember when you asked me to go to the Moana for cocktails, to celebrate the discovery of your IBM shares? Well I didn't tell you at the time, but I invited Yolande." Without going into explicit detail, he made clear that they had been seeing a lot of each other since.

"Well, Bernard, you're a dark horse!" said Ursula, highly amused. "So you have another motive for coming back to Hawaii, apart from seeing your poor old aunt."

"Absolutely," said Bernard. "The only problem is the fare."

"I'll pay your fare, any time you want to come," said Ursula. "After all, I'm leaving you all my money, anyway."

"Oh, I wouldn't do that," said Bernard.

"Why not? Who deserves it more than you do? Who needs it more than you?"

"Patrick," said Bernard. "Tess's Patrick is completely helpless."

257

3

With Yolande's agreement – indeed, encouragement – Bernard had planned to devote the evening to entertaining Tess. He proposed taking her first to the Travelwise cocktail party at the Wyatt Imperial, staying just as long as its entertainment value seemed to warrant, and then dining out somewhere – Yolande had suggested a Hawaiian garden restaurant with carp pools and strolling musicians, just outside Waikiki. When he returned to the apartment just before six, however, he found Tess lounging on the balcony in the flowered silk robe, having just returned from a swim in the pool. She said she didn't want to go out in the next hour or two, in case Frank phoned. It was early in the morning in England, and she thought he might phone just before he left home to go to work, as he had the previous day. Bernard sensed some softening in Tess's attitude to Frank, perhaps connected with the events of the afternoon. She had the quiet, contemplative air of a devout communicant just returned from the altar rail. He gave her a résumé of what Ursula had told him about her conversation with their father, and Tess seemed satisfied. It had been a good day's work, she said. She urged him to go to the party, and although he had no particular inclination to do so, he acquiesced. He had the impression that she wanted to be on her own. Also it was slightly on his conscience that he had never taken up Roger Sheldrake's invitation to have a drink at the Wyatt Imperial, and Sheldrake would presumably be at the cocktail party. It was agreed that he would return later to ascertain whether Frank had phoned and what she wanted to do about the evening meal.

The Wyatt Imperial was built on Babylonian scale. Two high

tower blocks were joined by an atrium that enclosed shopping arcades, restaurants and cafés, a 100-foot waterfall, palm groves, and a sizeable stage, on which, providing a striking change from the usual twangling guitar music, a Bavarian band dressed in Lederhosen and kneesocks was performing for the entertainment of patrons sitting at the café tables or promenading nearby. The Wyatt Imperial didn't seem like a hotel at all at ground level, and if it hadn't been for the carpet underfoot, he might have assumed that he was still in the street, or in some public square. After wandering about for some minutes, deafened by the amplified yodelling and accordion-squeezing of the suspiciously swarthy Bavarian musicians, Bernard found an escalator that took him to the Registration desk on the mezzanine floor, from which he was directed to the Spindrift Bar.

The decor of the Spindrift Bar had a heavy marine accent, with fishing nets draped across the roughcast walls, portholes for windows, and wall lamps in the form of navigation lights. Linda Hanama, the author of the invitation, standing just inside the door, smiled brilliantly and ticked off Bernard's name on a list. He recognized her as the airport facilitator of their first evening; it seemed that in the meantime she had been promoted to resort controller. She introduced a slim, eager young man with Chinese features, wearing a black silk suit, as Michael Ming, Director of Public Relations for the hotel. He shook Bernard's hand and thrust into it a tall glass brimming with fruit, ice-cubes, plastic bric-à-brac and a rum-flavoured fruit punch. "Welcome. Have a Mai Tai. Help yourself to some *pupu*." He gestured to a table laid out with finger snacks.

There were only about twenty people present, but the decibel level was high. The first person he focused on was the young man of the red braces. What caught Bernard's eye this evening, however, was the thick white bandage round his head. He also had a *lei* round his neck, and his arm round the waist of Cecily, who wore a strapless white dress and was similarly garlanded. They looked flushed and happy and appeared to be the centre of attention, together with a couple of broadshouldered young men

259

with neat furry moustaches, who were also vaguely familiar to Bernard. A professional-looking photographer was taking flash-photos of this quartet, and Brian Everthorpe was pointing his video camera at them.

"You made it, then!"

Bernard felt a hand on his arm, and turned to find Sidney and Lilian Brooks grinning at him.

"I thought I'd look in," said Bernard. "What has that young man done to his head?"

"Don't you know? Haven't you heard? Didn't you see the local paper this morning?" they exclaimed, interrupting and over-lapping with each other in their eagerness to tell him the story. It appeared that the previous day – "just about the time when we were chatting with you at the hospital it must have been, Sidney's all right, by the way, passed fit to fly" – the young man had sustained the injury while surfing, struck on the head by his own surfboard, and the Brookses' son Terry, and his Australian friend Tony, had saved him from drowning – carried him bleeding and unconscious from the sea, and laid him at the feet of the distraught Cecily, who had given him the kiss of life. Brian Everthorpe had been on hand to record the whole drama on videotape. "He's going to show it when this thing is over," said Sidney, jerking his thumb in the direction of a large television on a mobile stand. Bernard became aware that part of the noise level in the room was contributed by a voice-over commentary for what was presumably the video presentation promised in his invitation.

"*Wyatt Haikoloa,*" drawled a mellow American baritone, "*the new resort on the Big Island, where your wildest dreams come true . . .*" Between the heads of Sidney and Lilian, Bernard glimpsed luridly coloured images of a massive marble staircase and colonnade rising out of a lagoon, tropical birds stalking through a hotel lobby, rope bridges slung across swimming-pools, monorail trains snaking between palm trees. It looked like the set for a Hollywood epic that hadn't quite decided whether it was to be a sequel to *Ben Hur*, *Tarzan of the Apes* or *The Shape of Things to Come*.

"Terry and Tony knew him, you see," said Lilian. "They saw him down at the beach every day, trying to learn how to surf."

260

"Gave him a few tips, you know," said Sidney. "There's a knack to it, like everything else."

"They had no idea he was on the same package as us, though," said Lilian.

"Here," said Sidney. "Have a look at this. This morning's paper." He took a folded newspaper cutting from his wallet and handed it to Bernard.

Underneath a smudgy photograph of the two young men with moustaches smiling at the camera, and a headline, "AUSSIE WIZARDS OF SURF SAVE BRITISHER," was a short report of the incident.

> Terry Brooks and his buddy Tony Freeman, from Sydney, Australia, rescued surfing novice Russell Harvey, of London, England, from drowning off Waikiki beach Tuesday morning. Russ, 28, is in Honolulu honeymooning with his blonde wife Cecily, who was watching him through a dime telescope when he was struck on the head by his surfboard. "I was horrified," she said later. "I saw the board fly up in the air, then Russ disappeared under a huge wave, and when he came up, he was lying face down in the water. The surfboard was floating beside him. I was completely frantic, and began running towards the sea, screaming for help, but of course he was much too far out for anybody on the beach to get to him. Thank God those two Australian boys spotted him and pulled him out of the water. They brought him in on one of their surfboards. I think they deserve a medal."

"Very nice," said Bernard, returning the cutting to Sidney. "You must be proud of your son."

"Well, it's only natural," said Sidney. "I mean, it's not everybody who could react to an emergency like that, is it?"

"Not so much a hotel as a whole resort. Not so much a resort as a way of life. So extensive, that after checking in you will be transported to your room by monorail tram or canal barge . . ."

Bernard caught sight of the Best family sitting against the wall, eating *pupu* from paper plates balanced on their knees, and glancing furtively at the video show. He gave a little wave to the freckled girl and she smiled timidly in response. "No indeed," he said to Sidney. "And I'm delighted to see that the honeymooners are back on good terms with each other. They seemed to be having a bit of a tiff on the plane coming over."

"More than a tiff, by all accounts," said Lilian. "But apparently the accident has brought them together. Cecily says she discovered she really loved him when she thought he was lost."

"They got married again this afternoon," said Sidney.

"Really?" said Bernard. "Is that allowed?"

"It's called a Renewal of Vows," said Linda Hanama, who was passing with a tray of *pupu*. "There's a chapel at the other end of Kalakaua that does a special deal, with the Hawaiian Wedding Song performed by authentic local artists. It's very popular with second honeymooners, I don't think we've ever had a request from first-timers before, but Russ and Cecily felt they wanted to mark his narrow escape in a special way."

"Another Mai Tai?" Michael Ming was coming round with a jug.

"Could I have mine without the fruit juice?" said Sidney.

"Sorry, the complimentary drinks are pre-mixed."

"I thought we were only entitled to one," said Lilian holding out her glass.

"To tell you the truth, we over-catered, but what the hell, this is a very unique occasion." Michael Ming turned to address the photographer, who was on his way to the door. "Don't forget to mention us in the caption." The man nodded. "Great publicity for the company," Michael Ming said complacently. "Human interest. You can't beat it. Have you folks seen the video? It's really something. I told Mr Sheldrake he just had to see it." Michael Ming pronounced the name of Sheldrake with peculiar unction.

"*Wyatt Haikoloa covers 65 acres, boasts two golf courses, four swimming-pools, eight restaurants and ten tennis courts . . .*"

Bernard picked out the domed head of Sheldrake, watching the television with Sue and Dee, and edged towards them, pausing to greet the Bests. "Have you enjoyed your holiday?" he said sociably to the freckled girl. She blushed and lowered her eyes. "It was all right," she murmured.

"We'll be glad to get home, though," said Mrs Best.

"Best part of a holiday, I always think," said her husband. "No pun intended." He bared his teeth and gums in a rare smile. "When you push open the front door, pick up the letters, put the kettle on for a cup of tea, go out and see how the garden's survived. And you think to yourself, well, that's that for another year."

"It seems a long way to come for the pleasure of getting back home," Bernard said.

Mr Best shrugged. "Florence saw a programme about Hawaii on the box."

"Well, we've been to the usual places, Spain, Greece, Majorca," said Mrs Best. "We went to Florida once. Then we came into a bit of money, so we thought we'd try something more adventurous this year."

"Not a lot of money," said Mr Best. "Don't get the idea we're rich."

"No, no," said Bernard.

"I took a fancy to Hawaii," said Mrs Best. "But things always look different on the television, don't they? Like this video. I don't suppose it's a bit like that really."

They all looked at the screen.

"Bask in the sun on sparkling sandy beaches, frolic amid waterfalls and fountains, or let yourself be carried along by the current of a meandering riverpool . . ."

"I wish we could have gone there instead of Waikiki," said the young boy. "It looks good fun."

"Yeah," said the girl. "It looks like Center Parc."

Bernard enquired what Center Parc was and the girl explained, in a sudden spasm of volubility, that it was a holiday village in the middle of Sherwood Forest. She had gone there the previous summer with her friend Gail's family. You lived in a little house in the woods and cars were not allowed, everybody rode about on bicycles. There was a huge covered swimming-pool in the middle, with water chutes and a wave machine and palm trees and a Jungle River. It was called a Tropical Paradise.

"You should talk to that man over there," said Bernard, pointing to Roger Sheldrake. "He's writing a book about tropical paradises. I'll introduce you, if you like."

"I don't think so, thank you very much," said Mr Best. His smile had vanished.

"No, we don't want to be in a book," said Mrs Best.

Bernard wished them a safe journey home and moved on to where Roger Sheldrake stood in front of the television, flanked by Sue and Dee, though perceptibly closer to Dee. "Hallo, old man," said Sheldrake. "Do you know these two young ladies?"

Bernard reminded him that he himself had introduced Sheldrake to them. Sue asked after Mr Walsh, and Dee bestowed upon him a smile that might almost have been described as warm. "Sorry I didn't manage to call in before," Bernard said, "but I've been rather busy. What's it like staying here?"

"Wonderful service," said Sheldrake. "I recommend it. This is their latest venture." He gestured at the TV screen. "It put them back three hundred million dollars."

"Enjoy the mile-long museum walkway lined with antique art treasures of Oriental and Polynesian cultures. Stroll along the flagstone paths with brilliantly plumaged tropical birds as your companions . . ."

"Must have had their wings clipped," said Dee.

"Oh don't, Dee! Isn't it lovely though?"

"It's what they call a fantasy resort hotel," said Sheldrake. "Very popular with big corporations who want to reward their top managers and salesmen. Incentive vacations, they're called. The wives get invited along."

"That's not what I'd call an incentive," said Brian Everthorpe, who was standing nearby, and was playfully punched by his wife for this witticism. She was resplendent in a flounced cocktail dress of some shiny purple material. He was wearing a Hawaiian shirt covered with blue palm trees on a pink ground, and smoking a green cigar.

"A complete health spa offering everything from aerobics to

meditation counselling to aromatherapy . . . Dine privately on your own lanai *to the soothing sound of waves caressing the shore, or sample the menus of our eight gourmet restaurants . . ."*

"I don't care what they call it," said Sue wistfully. "It looks like heaven to me."

"And you can sign up for a whole range of fantasy excursions and activities: the Lauhala Point Fantasy Picnic, on a clifftop site accessible only by helicopter, . . the Sunset Sail and Secluded Beach Fantasy . . . The Kahua Ranch Fantasy, with authentic 'Paniolo' cowboys . . the Big Island Hunting Safari: hunt wild Russian boar, Mouflon and Corsican sheep, pheasant, and wild turkey, depending on season . . ."

"Sheep?" said Dee. "Did he say, hunt sheep?"

"Wild sheep," said Michael Ming, recharging their glasses from his jug. "Which have been proven to be detrimental to the environment due to over-grazing. But if you have any conscientious objection to shooting the animals you can photograph them instead. Mr Sheldrake, another Mai Tai? Or can I get you something from the bar?"

"No, this stuff is fine," said Roger Sheldrake, extending his glass.

"I wouldn't mind something from the bar," said Brian Everthorpe, but Michael Ming didn't appear to hear him.

"And the most popular of our special attractions – the Dolphin Encounter."

"Oh, this is unbelievable," said Linda Hanama. They watched spellbound as swimsuited holidaymakers fraternized with tame dolphins in the resort's lagoon: chucking them under the chin, stroking them behind the eyes, and gambolling in the water with them. A young boy grasped a dorsal fin and was towed through the water, laughing ecstatically.

> *"Straddling each a dolphin's back,*
> *And steadied by a fin,*
> *Those Innocents re-live their death,*
> *Their wounds open again,"*

Bernard recited, as much to his own surprise as everyone else's.

He was, however, on his third Mai Tai, and supposed he was a little tipsy.

"Did you say something, old man?" said Sheldrake.

"It's a poem by W. B. Yeats," said Bernard. " 'News For The Delphic Oracle.' In neoplatonic mythology, you know, the souls of the dead were taken to the Fortunate Isles on the backs of dolphins. You might find it a useful footnote for your book."

"Oh, I've re-jigged the thesis of that, to some extent," said Sheldrake. "I've decided that the paradise model is inevitably transformed into the pilgrimage model under the economic imperatives of the tourist industry. It's a sort of marxist approach, I suppose. A post-marxist marxism, of course."

"Of course," Bernard murmured.

"I mean, take an island, any island. Take Oahu. Look at the map. What do you see, nine times out of ten? A road going round the edge, forming a circle. What is it? It's a conveyor belt, for conveying people from one tourist trap to the next, one lot leaving as the other lot arrives. The same applies to cruise itineraries, charter flights –"

"Just in time," said Brian Everthorpe.

"I beg your pardon?" said Sheldrake, not particularly pleased at being interrupted in full flow.

"It sounds like what we call just-in-time in industry," said Brian Everthorpe. "Each operation on the assembly line is buffered by a card that instructs the operative to supply the next operation precisely when needed. Eliminates bottlenecks."

"That's very interesting," said Sheldrake, taking out his notebook and ball pen. "Can you give me a reference?"

"Invented by a Dr Ono, a Jap of course. He worked for Toyota. Hence the expression, 'Oh no, not another Japanese car.' " Brian Everthorpe guffawed at his own joke and held up a video cassette. "Now that the promotional video seems to have run its course, I'm going to show you lucky people a home movie, so perhaps you'd like to pull up some chairs and make yourselves comfortable."

"Oh Gawd!" said Dee under her breath.

"I haven't had time to edit this properly, or dub any music on,"

266

said Brian Everthorpe, as the guests gathered round with more or less enthusiasm. "It's what we call a rough cut, so bear with me. It's provisionally entitled, *Everthorpes in Paradise.*"

"Oh, get on with it, Bri," said Beryl, smoothing her purple flounces under her haunches as she sat down.

The film began with a picture of two teenage boys and an elderly lady waving goodbye from the porch of a mock-Jacobean house with leaded windows and integral garage. "Our boys and my mother," Beryl explained. There followed a long static close-up of a notice board saying *"East Midlands Airport"*, and then a jerky sequence with a painfully high-pitched whine on the soundtrack showing Beryl, in her red and yellow dress and gold bangles, climbing a steep flight of mobile steps into the cabin of a propeller plane. She stopped suddenly at the top and swept round to wave at the camera, causing the passengers behind and beneath her to cannon into each other and bury their faces in each other's bottoms. An orange bounced down the steps and rolled across the tarmac. There followed a blurred and tilted view of the outskirts of West London, seen through the aeroplane's porthole, and then a wide shot of the crowded Departures Concourse at Heathrow's Terminal Four. The camera zoomed in on two couriers in Travelwise Livery, one tall, straightbacked and middle-aged, the other young, slight, scowling at the camera. Recognizing these figures, the hitherto bored viewers sat up and began to take notice.

"Ooh, I remember him," Sue exclaimed. "The older one. He was nice."

"The younger one wasn't," said Cecily. "And he had shocking dandruff."

The scene shifted to the long perspective of one of Heathrow's interminable walkways, with passengers, their backs to the camera, streaming towards the numbered gates. A small wheeled vehicle like a golf-cart appeared in the middle distance, travelling in the opposite direction, and suddenly, to the accompaniment of shouts and laughs from those around him, Bernard beheld himself, bearded and grim-faced, and his father, grinning and waving jauntily, on the back seat of the buggy. They filled the screen for a second, then passed out of the frame. It was an extraordinary and disconcerting apparition, like a fragment of a broken dream, or a scene from one's past life reviewed at the moment of drowning. How staid and depressed he looked! What dingy clothes he wore, and what a mangy, unconvincing beard it had been.

They reappeared, he and his father, along with other members of the Travelwise party, who saluted themselves with hoots of laughter, cheers and jeers – sitting in the waiting area beside the gate, queueing for toilets on the flight to Los Angeles, and undergoing the *lei* greeting at Honolulu airport. "Hey," said Linda Hanama. "That's neat. Can I have a copy of that? We could use it for training."

Then the film became more exclusively Everthorpian, beginning with a slightly embarrassing sequence depicting Beryl rising from her hotel bed, clad in a diaphanous nightdress. There were whoops and wolf-whistles from the spectators. Beryl reached across and punched her husband in the small of the back. "You never told me that nightie was so see-through," she said.

"Hey, Brian, are you going into the blue-movie business?" Sidney enquired.

"Well I've seen worse on our hotel's adult video channel," said Russ Harvey. "Much worse."

"But you won't be watching that any more, will you, darling?" said Cecily, with just the hint of an edge to her voice.

" 'Course not, pet." Russ squeezed his wife's waist and kissed her on the nose.

On the screen, Beryl donned a negligée and sauntered towards the balcony, yawning affectedly. The murmur of traffic coming from the open french windows was suddenly augmented by the penetrating wail of an ambulance siren. The voice of Brian Everthorpe was heard crying, "Cut!" Beryl stopped sauntering and turned to frown at the camera. Then she appeared to get back into bed and to wake up all over again.

"Had to do two takes of this, because of the ambulance," said Brian Everthorpe. "I'll cut the first one out of the finished film, of course."

"What day was that?" Bernard asked.

"Our first morning."

Bernard felt the hairs on the back of his neck rise.

There was a very thorough coverage of the Sunset Beach Luau floorshow, with hula dancers and fire-eaters performing energetically on a stage in front of a vast crowd seated in rows that seemed to stretch to infinity. Then a blurred but unmistakable shot of Bernard shaking hands with Sue outside the Waikiki Coconut Grove hotel, at night.

" 'Allo, 'allo!" said Sidney, nudging Bernard. "You're a dark horse."

"Didn't know you were being watched, did you?" said Brian Everthorpe.

"Don't take any notice, Bernard," said Sue. "He was just escorting me home," she explained to the company, "like any gentleman would." She gestured airily with her hand, forgetting that it was holding her glass, and spilled some Mai Tai over her dress. "Oops! Never mind, going home tomorrow."

The film then became tedious again as it began to trace the Everthorpes' peregrinations around Oahu. Since Brian was always operating the camera, Beryl was required to provide the point of human interest in most of these sequences, posed against beaches, buildings and palm trees, smirking into the lens or gazing raptly into the distance. As if sensing the audience's restiveness, Beryl herself requested Brian to "gee it up a bit", and he rather reluctantly pressed the fast-forward button on his remote control. This certainly had the effect of making the film more amusing. At Pearl Harbor, a naval cutter surged out towards the *Arizona* with the speed of a torpedo boat, and disgorged a cluster of tourists who swarmed all over the Memorial for a few seconds before being sucked back into the vessel and returned abruptly to shore. At the Sea Life Park, killer whales burst from the surface of the pool like Polaris missiles. The coastline of Oahu and its pleated volcanic mountains flashed past in a blur. The Polynesian Cultural Center erupted in a frenzy of ethnic activity: weaving, woodcarving, war-dancing, canoeing, pageantry, music and drama.

The scene shifted to a sandy beach, and Brian Everthorpe switched the video machine back to normal speed. He had evidently persuaded someone else to hold the camera for this sequence, for it depicted himself and Beryl in swimming-costumes, stretched out at the water's edge. The recorded Everthorpe winked at the camera and rolled over on top of his spouse. There were more whoops and whistles from the viewers.

"Remind you of anything?" he quizzed them, as a wave spent itself on the sand and broke over the entwined Everthorpes.

"Burt Lancaster and Deborah Kerr," said an Australian voice from the back of the room. *"From Here To Eternity."*

"Bingo!" said Brian. "And this is the very beach where they shot that scene."

> *"Belly, shoulder, bum*
> *Flash fishlike; nymphs and satyrs*
> *Copulate in the foam,"*

Bernard murmured.

"What was that, old man?" said Sheldrake.

Bernard didn't know why Sheldrake had taken to addressing him in this slightly condescending manner, unless it was the effect of Michael Ming's obsequiousness, or the admiring way Dee looked at him every time he opened his mouth.

"It's the same poem," said Bernard. " 'News For The Delphic Oracle.' "

"It sounds a bit rude to me," said Dee.

"The Neo-platonists assumed there was no sex in heaven," said Bernard. "Yeats thought he had news for them." It occurred to him that he should have quoted the lines to Ursula; on second thoughts, perhaps not.

"Bonking on the beach, eh?" said Brian Everthorpe. "A much overrated pastime, in my opinion."

"What would you know about it?" Beryl demanded.

"Every engineer will tell you sand is very bad for moving parts," said Brian Everthorpe, skipping nimbly out of Beryl's reach.

At an order from Mr Best, the Best family stood up and began to file out of the room.

270

"Oh, don't go now!" Brian Everthorpe called out. "The best bit is just coming up. Aussies to the rescue. The drowned bridegroom restored to his bride."

The young Best girl hung back and looked wistfully at the screen.

"Come along Amanda, don't dawdle."

Amanda pulled a face at her father's back and, seeing that she was observed by Bernard, blushed. He smiled and waved, sad to see them go, forever self-excluded from life's feast.

The scene of the film now shifted to Waikiki beach, with the familiar blunted peak of Diamond Head in the background, and long shots of Terry, Tony and Russ surfing. The Australians were skilful and exhilarating to watch. Russ managed quite well when kneeling on his board, but tended to overbalance when he tried to stand up.

There was a distracting confabulation at the door of the room, where someone was saying, "No, I haven't got an invitation. We're friends of Mr Sheldrake, he's a guest here," and Michael Ming was heard to reply, "Oh, come in, come in, any friend of Mr Sheldrake's is welcome."

Roger Sheldrake said, "Ah, good, they've come," and hurried across to the door to shake hands with the new arrivals. On the TV screen the images began to lose cohesion as the aim of the camera swung wildly between beach, sky and sea.

"Bit of camera wobble here, I'm afraid," said Brian Everthorpe. "I was running with it, see?"

Roger Sheldrake ushered his guests, a middle-aged man and a young woman, into seats just in front of Bernard. "So glad you could make it. Dee, this is Lewis Miller, the chap I was telling you about."

"Hi," said the man. "And this is Ellie."

"Hi," said Ellie, listlessly.

Handshakes were exchanged. Seeing Bernard staring at the new arrivals, Sheldrake drew him into the introductions. "Lewis is an old conference crony of mine," Sheldrake explained. "I ran into him this morning in the University Library. I'd completely forgotten he taught here. Let me get you both a drink. I believe they're called Mai Tais."

"God, no," said Ellie. "I'll have a vodka martini."

"Bourbon on the rocks, please Roger," said Lewis Miller.

The picture on the TV screen had stopped swaying violently about. There was a close-up of Cecily screaming and gesticulating at the water's edge, pictures of people running to and fro on the beach, and long shots of heads and surfboards bobbing up and down in the sea in the distance. It was dramatic footage, but Bernard's attention kept wandering to the two new arrivals. Lewis Miller was not as he had, for some reason, imagined him –tall, handsome and athletic – but surprisingly small and slight, with yellowy-grey hair brushed across his scalp to cover a bald patch, and a long-chinned, slightly lugubrious countenance. His companion was several inches taller, a handsome, haughty young woman with long reddish-brown hair, plaited like a heavy rope, falling down over one breast.

"This looks exciting," said Lewis Miller. "What's going on?"

Russ Harvey leaned across to explain. "That's me, being carried out of the sea by Terry and Tony, here. And that's Cecily, my wife, giving me the kiss of life. Wouldn't let anyone else touch me, bless her heart."

"I learned how to do it in a first-aid course," said Cecily. "I was in the Rangers. I've got a badge."

"First thing I remember when I came round, was Cess bending over me, trying to kiss me."

"Far out," said Lewis Miller. "Good as a soap, isn't it, Ellie?"

"Could I have that vodka martini?" Ellie said to no one in particular.

"Coming up!" Roger Sheldrake cried, pushing forward with a trayful of drinks. "Anyone for another Mai Tai?"

"Then I threw up," said Russ.

"God, how gross," Ellie muttered, averting her eyes from the screen.

"I wish I'd known you were in Honolulu earlier, Roger," said Lewis Miller. "You could have talked to my graduate students."

"Are you an anthropologist too, then?" Dee asked him.

"No, a climatologist. Roger and I met at an interdisciplinary conference on tourism."

Someone tugged at Bernard's sleeve. It was Michael Ming. "Excuse me," he hissed, "but do you get the impression from this conversation that that guy" – he jerked his head in the direction of Sheldrake – "is a college professor?"

"I know he is," said Bernard. "Why, what's the matter?"

"Only that I don't usually send college professors complimentary champagne and fruit on a daily basis," said Michael Ming. "Or send a stretch limo to meet them at the airport. Or have fresh flowers put in their room every evening. I thought he was a journalist." He wandered away like a man who had been hit on the head by a sock filled with wet sand.

"Lewis is very big in impact studies," Sheldrake was explaining to Dee. "He wrote a famous paper showing that the mean temperature of Honolulu rose by 1.5 degrees Centigrade between 1960 and 1980, because of all the trees that were felled to clear the ground for parking lots."

"Then Joni Mitchell set it to music," Lewis Miller joked.

"Oh, I know that song," said Sue. She snapped her fingers and sang:

" 'Paved paradise and put up a parking lot . . .' "

"Very good!" cried Lilian Brooks, clapping her hands. "What a lovely voice!"

"Concrete reflects the heat of the sun, you see. Foliage absorbs it."

"Took all the trees and put 'em in a tree museum,
Charged all the people a dollar and half just to see 'em . . ."

Sue closed her eyes and swayed to the rhythm of the song until she fell off her seat. She sprawled on the floor and laughed up at them.

"You've had one Mai Tai too many," said Dee reprovingly, pulling Sue to her feet.

"Hey, could you be a little bit quieter?" said Russ. "I want to hear this."

On the screen he and Cecily, dressed as they were this evening, were standing with hands joined in front of a smiling Hawaiian man in a white suit. "Do you, Russell Harvey . . ." he was saying.

273

"Did they get married here in Hawaii?" Lewis Miller whispered.

"No, they renewed their vowels," said Sue.

"Vows," said Dee. "It's the Everthorpes who ought to renew their vowels."

Sue shrieked with laughter – whether at Dee's witticism or her own mistake was unclear – and fell off her chair again.

Ellie drained her drink and stood up. "I have to go now," she said. "Are you coming, Lewis?"

"Oh, but you've only just come!" Sheldrake protested. "Have another drink. Try a Mai Tai."

"I did," said Ellie. "Once was enough. Lewis?"

"Roger is leaving tomorrow, Ellie," Lewis said in a coaxing tone. "We have a lot to talk about."

"I thought the four of us might go out to dinner," said Sheldrake. "Dee and I and you two."

"Hawaiian wedding song coming up!" said Brian Everthorpe. Three elderly Hawaiians in matching Aloha shirts appeared on the screen, plucking ukeleles and wailing piteously.

Sue sat down beside Bernard. "You have to kiss the person next to you at the end," she confided.

"I'm sorry, but I have work to do," said Ellie. "I'll see you later, Lewis." She swung her plait over her shoulder, like a lioness swinging its tail, and stalked out of the room.

"Sorry about that, Roger," said Lewis Miller. He picked up one of the spare Mai Tais and sucked unhappily on the straw. "Ellie and I had a fight before we came out. Things aren't too good between us at the moment."

"Looking forward to going home?" Sue said to Bernard.

"Well, I'm not going just yet," Bernard said. "My father's still in hospital. But to be honest, I'm in no hurry to get back to Rummidge."

"Rummidge! Brian's business is in Rummidge," Beryl Everthorpe exclaimed.

With extraordinary speed, and without apparently moving his hands, Brian Everthorpe produced a business card. "Riviera Sunbeds," he said. "Any time you want a discount, let me know."

"What part of Rummidge?" Beryl asked Bernard, and he was obliged to explain while trying to eavesdrop on Lewis Miller.

"I think she's getting ready to dump me," he was saying, "and to level with you, Roger, it'll be a relief. I miss my kids. I miss my home. I even miss my wife."

"We should all exchange addresses, shouldn't we?" said Beryl. "Could you lend us a pencil and paper?" she asked Linda Hanama, who came up to them at that moment.

"Sure." Linda slipped a sheet of blank paper from her clipboard. "I came over to say that you're being paged, Mr Everthorpe. There's somebody at Reception to see you. A Mr Mosca?"

Brian Everthorpe went pale under his ruddy tan and pressed the stop button on the video machine. Sue gave a little squeak of disappointment as the Hawaiian singers disappeared from the screen.

"Time we were off, love." Brian smartly ejected his cassette from the video machine.

"Oh, but we haven't exchanged addresses," said Beryl.

"And we're not going to," said Brian Everthorpe, snatching his business card from between Bernard's fingers. "Goodnight, all." He bustled the protesting Beryl out of the room.

"I must be going too," said Bernard, getting unsteadily to his feet. "Our revels now are ended."

"Aren't you going to give us a kiss?" Sue asked him, so he did. "If I didn't have Des, I could fancy you, Bernard," she said. "Give my best wishes to your Dad."

Bernard found himself in the foyer of the Waikiki Surfrider without any clear recollection of how he had got there. He went up to the desk and collected his key. The clerk gave him an envelope containing a printed message from the hotel manager, expressing the hope that he had enjoyed his stay, and reminding him that checkout time was 12 noon.

"If I wanted to stay on for another year, would you have a room?" Bernard asked.

"A year, sir?"

"Sorry, I mean a week." Bernard shook his head, and banged on it with his fist. The clerk consulted his computer and confirmed that he could be accommodated for another week.

In room 1509, Bernard took off his shoes and sat on the bed. From the bedside console he turned off all the lights except the lamp over the telephone. He dialled the number of Ursula's apartment.

"Where have you been?" Tess said.

"I'm sorry. I lost track of the time. What is it?" He peered at his watch. "Good Lord, half-past eight."

"You sound squiffy. Are you?"

"I am a bit. They were very generous with the Mai Tais."

"I couldn't wait any longer to eat. I made myself an omelette."

"God, I'm terribly sorry, Tess. That's omelette two days running."

"It doesn't matter. I didn't want to go out anyway. I'm packing."

"Packing? What for?"

"I'm flying home tomorrow. I got a seat on a flight at 8.40 in the morning. Can you run me to the airport?"

"Of course. But you've only just got here!"

"I know, but . . . I'm needed at home."

"Frank phoned, then?"

"Yes. Bryony has been sent about her business. Patrick keeps waking Frank up in the middle of the night to ask him where I am."

"It seems hard. I thought we could be tourists together for a few days. See Pearl Harbor. Go snorkelling. I have a wallet stuffed with discount vouchers for all kinds of things."

"That's nice of you Bernard, but I must go back before Patrick has a fit. You'll have to bring Daddy home on your own. I spoke to his doctor at the hospital this afternoon, after you left. He thinks Daddy should be able to travel in about a week's time." She proceeded to give him detailed advice about travel arrangements until she suddenly stopped herself. "I don't know why we're discussing this on the phone. Where are you, anyway?"

"I stopped somewhere on the way home. I won't be long."

He rang off and dialled Yolande's number.

"Hi," she said. "How was your day?"

"I don't know where to begin."

"How did the reunion go?"

"Rather drunkenly."

"*Drunkenly?* You mean they let you drink booze at St Joseph's?"

"Oh, you mean Daddy and Ursula? That went fine. Sorry, I'm a bit confused. I've just been to a party, I thought that was what you meant, a party for all the people on the package holiday. They're going back tomorrow. Probably on the same flight as Tess, come to think of it."

"Tess is going back to England tomorrow?"

"Yes." He gave her a brief account of Tess's reasons.

"Well, it's her life," said Yolande. "Personally, I think she's putting it back in hock. But Ursula and your father got on OK?"

"Yes. All reconciled, all forgiven. Ursula is content. I told her you would visit her at Makai Manor when I've gone. I hope that was all right?"

"Sure, I'd be glad to."

"And I told her she should leave her money to Tess's Patrick."

There was silence at the other end of the line. Then Yolande said, "Why did you do that?"

"I know you said I shouldn't. But somehow it was such an extraordinary day, such a satisfying achievement to bring Daddy and Ursula together again, that it seemed important that I shouldn't benefit materially from it. It's probably very silly of me."

"It's probably why I love you, Bernard," Yolande said with a sigh.

"In that case, I'm glad I did it," said Bernard. "Oh, and by the way, I met your husband tonight."

"*What?* You met Lewis? How? Where?"

"At this party. He'd been invited by a chap called Sheldrake."

"I don't believe it. Did you speak to him?"

"We were introduced, by Sheldrake. I didn't let on that I knew you, of course. He seemed to be having a row with his girlfriend."

277

"She was there too? Ellie?"

"For a while. Then she walked out in a huff."

"Tell me more!"

"There isn't much more to tell. He said he thought she was getting ready to leave him."

"He said that?"

"Yes. And he said he missed you. And the house. And the children."

There was another silence at the other end of the line. "Is your sister listening to this, Bernard?" Yolande said at length.

"No, no. I'm calling from the Waikiki Surfrider. Which reminds me, I have to extend my reservation on the room, or check out, by tomorrow morning. What do you think? I mean, it's been exciting meeting you here, secretly, anonymously, but I wonder, now that, you know, now that our relationship is more . . . well, normal, I wonder whether it wouldn't feel a bit queer going on meeting here . . . It's been like a kind of capsule, a bubble in time and space, this room, where there's no gravity, where the normal rules of life are suspended. Do you know what I mean? And now that Tess is going home, perhaps we could use the apartment. I don't think I'd feel awkward about that now. What do you think?" He came breathlessly to a halt.

"I think we'd better cool it, Bernard," said Yolande.

"Cool it?"

"Put our thing on hold. I need time to absorb what you've just told me."

"So shall I check out of the room?"

"Yeah. Do that."

"All right, I will then."

"Look, this doesn't mean I don't want to go on seeing you."

"Doesn't it?"

"Not at all. We can do other things together."

"Like Pearl Harbor and the Polynesian Cultural Center?"

"If you insist. Bernard, you're not crying, are you."

"Of course not."

"I believe you're crying, you big booby."

"I've had rather too much to drink, I'm afraid."

"Bernard, you must understand. I've got to think about this new stuff about Lewis. I wish you hadn't met him. I wish you hadn't told me."

"So do I."

"But you did, and I can't just ignore it. Shit, now you've got me crying too. It's that incorrigible honesty of yours that's the trouble."

"Is that what it is?"

"Look, I can't talk any more. Roxy has just come in. I'll call you tomorrow, OK?"

"All right."

"Goodnight, then, dearest Bernard."

"*Aloha*," he said.

She laughed uncertainly. "Are you going native on me?"

"Hallo, goodbye, I love you."

4

"The question facing the theologian today is, therefore, what can be salvaged from the eschatological wreckage?

"Traditional Christianity was essentially teleological and apocalyptic. It presented both individual and collective human life as a linear plot moving towards an End, followed by timelessness: death, judgment, hell and heaven. This life was a preparation for eternal life, which alone gave this life meaning. To the question, 'Why did God make you?' the Catechism answered, 'God made me to know him, love him and serve him in this world, and to be happy with him *for ever in the next.*' But the concepts and images of this next world which have come down to us in Christian teaching no longer have any credibility for thoughtful, educated men and women. The very idea of an afterlife for individual human beings has been regarded with scepticism and embarrassment – or silently ignored – by nearly every major twentieth-century theologian. Bultman, Barth, Bonhoeffer, Tillich, for example, even the Jesuit Karl Rahner, all dismissed traditional notions of personal survival after death. For Bultmann, the concept of 'translation to a heavenly world of light, in which the self is destined to receive a heavenly vesture, a spiritual body,' was 'not merely incomprehensible by any rational process' but 'totally meaningless.' Rahner said in an interview, 'with death it's all over. Life is past and it won't come again.' In print he was more circumspect, arguing that the soul would survive, but in a non-personal, 'pancosmic' state:

> the soul, by surrendering its limited bodily structure in
> death, becomes open towards the universe and, in some

way, a co-determining factor of the universe precisely in the latter's character as the ground of the personal life of other spiritual corporeal beings.

This, however, is mere metaphysical doodling. It expresses a preference for a decently abstract concept of the afterlife over a crudely anthropomorphic one, but it is not an afterlife that anyone would eagerly look forward to, or be martyred for.

"Of course, there are still many Christians who believe fervently, even fanatically, in an anthropomorphic afterlife, and there are many more who would like to believe in it. Nor is there any shortage of Christian pastors eager to encourage them, some sincerely, some, like the TV evangelists of America, with more dubious motives. Fundamentalism has flourished precisely on the eschatological scepticism of responsible theology, so that the most active and popular forms of Christianity today are also those which are the most intellectually impoverished. The same seems to be true of other great world religions. In this, as in so many other areas of twentieth-century life, the lines of W. B. Yeats hit the nail on the head:

> *The best lack all conviction, while the worst*
> *Are full of passionate intensity.*"

Bernard glanced up from his script to check whether the twenty-odd students in the room were still listening. He was not a good lecturer, he knew that. He could not maintain eye contact with his audience (the slightest flicker of doubt or boredom on their faces would bring him to an abrupt halt in mid-sentence). He could not improvise from notes, but had laboriously to write out the entire lecture in advance, which meant that it was probably too densely packed to take in easily through the ear. He knew all that, but he was too old a dog to learn new tricks; he just hoped that the careful preparation he put into his lectures compensated for the dullness of their delivery. This morning only three or four of the students looked as if they had switched off. The others were looking attentively at him, or writing on their notepads. They were the usual mixed bag of diploma students and casual auditors: missionaries on sabbatical, housewives doing Open University degrees, RE teachers, some African Methodist ministers, and a couple of worried-looking Anglican nuns who, he was pretty sure, would soon be switching to another course. It was only the second week of term, and he knew hardly any of their names yet. Fortunately, after this introductory lecture, the course would proceed in seminar format, which he much preferred.

"Modern theology therefore finds itself in a classic double bind: on the one hand the idea of a personal God responsible for creating a world with so much evil and suffering in it logically requires the idea of an afterlife in which these things are rectified and compensated for; on the other hand, traditional concepts of the afterlife no longer command intelligent belief, and new ones, like Rahner's, do not capture the popular imagination – indeed, they are incomprehensible to ordinary laypeople. It is not surprising that the focus of modern theology has turned more and more upon the Christian transformation of *this* life, whether in the form of Bonhoeffer's 'religionless Christianity,' or Tillich's Christian existentialism, or various types of Liberation Theology.

"But if you purge Christianity of the promise of eternal life (and, let us be honest, the threat of eternal punishment) which traditionally underpinned it, are you left with anything that is distinguishable from secular humanism? One answer is to turn that question around and ask what secular humanism has got that isn't derived from Christianity.

"There is a passage in Matthew, Chapter 25, which seems particularly relevant here. Matthew is the most explicitly apocalyptic of the synoptic gospels, and this section of it is sometimes referred to by scholars as the Sermon on the End. It concludes with the well-known description of the Second Coming and the Last Judgment:

> When the Son of Man comes in his glory, escorted by
> all the angels, then he will take his seat on the throne of
> glory. All the nations will be assembled before him and
> he will separate men one from another as the shepherd

separates sheep from goats. He will place the sheep on his right hand and the goats on his left.

Pure myth. But on what grounds does Christ the King separate the sheep from the goats? Not, as you might expect, fervency of religious faith, or orthodoxy of religious doctrine, or regularity of worship, or observance of the Commandments, or indeed anything 'religious' at all.

> Then the King will say to those on his right hand, 'Come, you whom my Father has blessed, take for your heritage the kingdom prepared for you since the foundation of the world. For I was hungry and you gave me food; I was thirsty and you gave me drink; I was a stranger and you made me welcome; naked and you clothed me, sick and you visited me, in prison and you came to see me.' Then the virtuous will say to him in reply, 'Lord when did we see you hungry and feed you; or thirsty and give you drink? When did we see you a stranger and make you welcome; naked and clothe you; sick or in prison and go to see you?' And the King will answer, 'I tell you solemnly, insofar as you did this to the least of these brothers of mine, you did it to me.'

The virtuous seem quite surprised to be saved, or to be saved for *this* reason, doing good in an unselfish but pragmatic and essentially this-worldly sort of way. It's as if Jesus left this essentially humanist message knowing that one day all the supernatural mythology in which it was wrapped would have to be discarded."

Bernard caught the eye of one of the nuns, and essayed an impromptu joke: "It's almost as if someone tipped him off." The nun reddened, and dropped her eyes.

"I think that's enough for today," he said. "I'd like you to look at that chapter of Matthew for next week, and at the commentaries listed on the handout, beginning with Augustine. Mr Barrington," he said, picking on a reliable-looking RE teacher on

283

part-time in-service training. "Do you think you could introduce the discussion with a short paper?"

Barrington grinned nervously and nodded. He came up to Bernard to ask for some advice about further reading, as the other students drifted out of the room. When he had gone, Bernard picked up his papers and made for the Senior Common Room, feeling he'd earned a coffee break. On the way, he called in at the College Office to check his mailbox. Giles Franklin, specialist in Mission Studies, and one of the most senior members of the academic staff, was standing in front of the pigeonholes, thrusting into them stencilled sheets of yellow paper. He greeted Bernard cheerfully – Bernard had never known him to be uncheerful. He was a big, boisterous man designed to be a monk in some earlier age, with cheeks like two rosy, wrinkled apples and a head of naturally tonsured white hair. "Here," he said, thrusting a sheet into Bernard's hand. "The programme for this term's staff seminars. I've put you down for the 15th of November. By the way . . ." He dropped his voice. "I'm delighted to hear that your appointment is going to be made full-time."

"Thankyou. So am I," said Bernard. He took a sheaf of envelopes and papers from his pigeonhole – there was always a lot of internal mail at the beginning of the academic year – and leafed through it. "For one thing it means I'll be able to get a proper –" He came to a large yellow envelope with an airmail sticker on it, and froze.

"What's up?" Franklin said jocularly. "You look as if you're afraid to open it. Some journal rejected an article?"

"No, no. It's personal," said Bernard.

Instead of going to the SCR, he took the letter outside into the College grounds. It was a glorious October day. The sun was warm on his shoulders, but there was a touch of autumnal crispness in the air, which had a limpidity unusual for Rummidge. High pressure and a breeze blowing straight from the Malverns had dispersed the customary haze. Shapes and colours were almost unnaturally vivid and sharply defined, like the Pre-Raphaelite landscapes in the municipal Art Gallery. Small, woolly white clouds drifted like grazing sheep across a brilliantly blue sky. On the far side of the lawn, where a coarse form of croquet was played in summer, a copper beech blazed, like a tree on fire yet unconsumed. There was a wooden seat under it, dedicated to some previous College Principal, that was Bernard's favourite spot for reading poetry. He sat down and weighed the bulky envelope in his hands, scrutinizing Yolande's slanting handwriting as if it might give him some clue to the contents of the letter. Franklin had not been far wide of the mark: he was nervous of opening it. Why had she written to him? She had never written before – it was the first time he had ever seen her handwriting, and he only knew the letter was from her because she had put her name and address in the top left-hand corner of the envelope. She phoned him once a week, early on Sunday morning, British time, when he hung around beside the student payphone in the deserted lobby at the appointed hour, and had only deviated from this arrangement once, ten days previously, when she called him in the middle of the night to say that Ursula had died peacefully in her sleep. She had phoned the following Sunday to report on the funeral, and he was expecting another call this weekend. When she phoned, they spoke only about Ursula or each other's trivial news. The question of their relationship was still, by tacit agreement, "on hold." So why had she written? There was, he seemed to remember, something called a "Dear John" letter. He put his nail under the flap and ripped open the envelope.

Dearest Bernard,

I'm writing to tell you about Ursula's last days, and her funeral, even though I've just put the phone down after talking to you, because it's an unsatisfactory instrument for talking about anything that matters, especially with the echo you sometimes get on the satellite link. And I don't feel relaxed, knowing that you are standing in a public booth in the middle of a student dormitory – now that they've given you a proper job, I hope you'll get a phone of your own!

Ursula, she was a sweetie. I really got to like her in

285

the few weeks we had to get acquainted. We talked a lot about you. She was so grateful that you made the effort to come out here, bringing your father with you – well, you know that already, but it bears repeating, because she made me promise not to bring you out here again when it was obvious that she was sinking fast. She knew you would be just starting your teaching, and even if you could have gotten away, she said it wasn't worth dragging you back all that way – "by the time he gets here, I won't be worth talking to." I'm afraid it was a shock for you when I called to say she had died, but that was the way she wanted it. In her last week she was feeling very poorly, unable to swallow the painkilling pills, so they had to give her injections. She couldn't talk much, but she liked me to go and sit by her and hold her hand. Once she whispered, "Why don't they just let me go?" and that night she died peacefully in her sleep. Enid da Silva called me early the next morning.

We spent quite a lot of time in the preceding weeks discussing the arrangements for her funeral. There wasn't anything morbid or depressing about it, just a concern to get everything in proper shape before she died. At first, she wanted to have her ashes scattered from a place on the coast road near Diamond Head where she stopped with you one time. But there turned out to be a public health regulation against it, and in any case the prevailing wind at this time of year is from the sea, which would have made it a tricky operation. As she said herself (she had a great sense of humour, didn't she?) "I wouldn't want to get in my friends' hair and all over their best clothes." So she settled for having her ashes scattered on the sea off Waikiki.

Father McPhee held a short funeral service in the crematorium. Sophie Knoepflmacher was there, and some other friends of Ursula's, ten or so, mostly old ladies. Sophie used to visit her at Makai Manor on the days when I couldn't make it, and Ursula appreciated it, though she liked to pretend Sophie was just a busybody. Father McPhee said some nice things about Ursula, and what a comfort it had been to her that members of her family were with her in her last illness. After the service, he said he was going to take the ashes down to Fort DeRussy Beach to scatter them, and any of us that liked could come. Sophie and I drove down with him. It was a Saturday afternoon, and he had chosen the time to coincide with a Hawaiian Folk Mass that the Army Chaplains Department have (have? hold? put on? – I don't know the right verb) down on Fort DeRussy beach every Saturday evening in the summer months. There are Army Headquarters right by the beach. Ursula had told Father McPhee that she used to go to the Mass sometimes, and he knew the chaplain who was doing it.

Needless to say, I didn't know about this Mass before I met Ursula. As you know, I'm no churchgoer. The first thing I did on reaching the age of independence was to opt out of Sunday worship at the Presbyterian church my folks used to patronize, and I've never been back inside a church since then except for weddings and funerals and christenings. In fact I think the only time I've attended a Catholic Mass was for the wedding of a college friend of mine. It was in an Italian church in Providence, Rhode Island, stuffed with hideous statuary. The whole thing seemed to me like a TV spectacular, with the altar-boys in their red robes, and the priest in his brocade get-up, parading in and out, and the candles and bells, and the choir belting out *Ave Maria*. But this was quite different, just a simple table set up on the beach, and the congregation sitting or standing around in a loose circle on the sand. People who obviously weren't Catholic, tourists and service people, who just happened to be on the beach, on their way home, stopped to stare, and some of them joined the congregation out of curiosity. There were young local people handing out little booklets with the service printed in it. I'm enclosing a copy in case you're interested. As you see, most of the service was in English, but the sung parts were in Hawaiian, accompanied by some kids on guitars, and during the hymns some local girls in traditional grass skirts danced a hula. Well I knew of course that the hula was originally a religious dance, but it's been so debased by tourism and Hollywood that it's hard to see that way any longer. Even the authentic demonstrations they put on at the Bishop Museum are essentially theatrical, while the hula you see in Waikiki is halfway between belly-dancing and burlesque. So it was quite a shock to see hula dancing at a Mass. But it worked. I think it worked because the girls weren't particularly good at it, and not particularly good-looking. I mean, they were OK, on both counts, but they were nothing special. It was a little like an end-of-semester concert in high school, disarmingly amateurish. And of course they didn't have that fixed, gooey smile that you associate with pro hula girls. They looked serious and reverent. Sophie observed it all with keen interest, and said to me afterwards that it was very charming, but she couldn't see it catching on at Temple.

It was a lovely evening. The heat of the day had gone, a balmy breeze blew off the sea, the shadow of the priest's movements as he lifted the wafer and the cup lengthened on the sand as the sun sank lower in the sky. He said a prayer "for the repose of Ursula's soul," and that struck me as an interesting word, "repose," – almost a pagan idea, as if the soul of the dead person wouldn't be able to rest peacefully unless the proper rites were carried out. Then I thought of that famous quote (is it Shakespeare? You would know) "Our little life is rounded by a sleep."

When the mass was over, and the people were dispersing, Father McPhee and Sophie and I got into a little Army boat, a rubber dinghy with a small outboard motor on the back, and we putt-putted out to sea for maybe a quarter of a mile. Fortunately it was a calm evening, and in any case there isn't a lot of surf at

288

DeRussy, so it was not too bumpy a ride, though Sophie looked alarmed once or twice when we hit a biggish wave, and held on to her hair as if afraid it would blow away. When we were through the breakers, the soldier who was steering the boat switched off the engine and we drifted for a while. Father McPhee opened the casket with Ursula's ashes in it and trailed it in the wake of the boat, letting the sea take the ashes. They stained the water for a moment, then disappeared. He said a short prayer, I can't remember the words exactly, about committing her remains to the deep, and then suggested that we had a couple of minutes silence.

It's funny, this dying business, when you're close to it. I always thought of myself as an atheist, a materialist, that this life is all we have and we had better make the most of it; but that evening it seemed hard to believe that Ursula was totally extinct, gone for ever. I suppose everybody has these moments of doubt – or should I say, faith? Apropos of which, I came across an interesting quotation the other day – in the *Reader's Digest*, of all places. I was reading it in the dentist's and got the receptionist to photocopy it for me. I'm enclosing it. Perhaps you know it already. I never heard of the author, he's Spanish, I guess.

Sophie and Father McPhee had their eyes closed during the silence, but I was looking back at the shore, and I must say Oahu was doing its stuff that evening. Even Waikiki was a thing of beauty. The tall buildings were catching the light of the setting sun as if floodlit, thrown into relief against the hills in the background, which were dark with raincloud. There was a rainbow over one of the hills, behind the tower block in the Hilton Hawaiian Village with the rainbow mural – you must have seen it as you drive into Waikiki along the Ala Moana Boulevard, they say it's the biggest ceramic mural in the world. I suppose that just about sums up Hawaii: the real rainbow cosying up to the artificial one.

289

Nevertheless it did look rather wonderful. Then Father McPhee nodded to the soldier, he started the engine again, and we putt-putted back to the shore. I felt we had secured repose for Ursula's soul.

I think I told you the basic facts about her will, but I ought to come clean and tell you that she asked my advice about it before she consulted Bellucci, and I didn't hesitate to give it. Bellucci, by the way, turned out to be quite smart – the fake Harvard & Yale Club decor of his office is misleading. He was the one who figured out that the best way to help Patrick was to set up a charitable trust in England. That way the UK Government will never be able to claw back any of the money, and if anything should happen to Patrick (I don't know what his life expectancy is) the money would continue to go to kids in need like him. So $150,000 went to set up the Trust (of which you're one of the trustees, of course) and another advantage is that no US inheritance tax is payable on that. The balance of the estate after deduction of tax is going to be about $139,000. $35,000 goes to your father, with the recommendation that he should spend it for his own greater comfort, not save it. It should help him to entertain Sophie Knoepflmacher – I suppose you know she's threatening to visit him next summer? In fact she claims he invited her – I don't suppose he dreamed she'd take him up on it. Ursula, by the way, left Sophie her collection of ornaments, and a gold necklace to me, which I accepted for friendship's sake. She has also left a small legacy to Tess, more than enough to cover her fare to Hawaii, and the rest of her jewellery.

That leaves about $100,000 for you, Bernard. I hope you won't have any scruples about accepting it. Ursula and I spent a lot of time discussing the problem, trying to settle on a sum that would be big enough to be useful and not so big that you'd feel obliged to give it away. From what you told me about property prices in Rummidge, you should be able to afford to buy yourself an apartment with it, or maybe a little house. Speaking as a potential houseguest, I would ask only that it should have central heating and a shower (Ursula told me some disturbing stories about British domestic arrangements, but maybe she was out of date).

From which you will infer that I'm coming to visit you at Christmas, that is, if you still want me to. You've been very patient, dearest Bernard, both during our last week together on Oahu (actually I enjoyed that week very much, the old-fashioned gallantry, the chaste companionship of it, the picnics and the body-surfing and the long leisurely drives around the island) – both then, and when I called you in the following weeks, never pressuring me about Lewis, though I could always hear the unstated question in your voice when we said goodbye.

As you reported, Ellie had gotten tired of him this summer, or maybe she had met someone nearer her own age. Anyway, she walked out on him about three weeks ago, and he wrote me a letter saying he'd been a fool, and couldn't we get together again. He asked me out to dinner, and I agreed (strangely enough he chose that Thai restaurant where I met with you and Tess). He said he didn't want to talk about Ellie or our possible reconciliation that evening, but just to break the ice, get back on terms again, just chat about the kids and so on. Lewis can be very charming, when he puts himself out, and we had a very civilized evening, helped along by a bottle of wine. We talked about safe subjects like the controversy going on over in Maui about planning permission for a new resort development on an ancient Hawaiian burial site. I said vehemently that I didn't think the repose of Hawaiian souls should be disturbed by tourists driving golf carts over their graves. Lewis looked rather startled at that, though he is on the same side, for

291

good, liberal reasons. He had picked me up in his car so he brought me home afterwards and asked himself in for a nightcap. It was still quite early and Roxy wasn't home – I think he'd fixed that with her, because he soon tried to get me to go to bed with him. I refused. He asked me if there was anybody else, and I said, not in Hawaii, and he said, is it this British guy Roxy told me about? and I said, yes, I'm going to spend Christmas with him. I didn't know until that moment that that was what I'd decided, and I've let a couple of weeks go by before telling you, just so I'm sure. But I am. Lewis is all right, but he's not an honest man. Now that I've met one, I can't be content with anything less.

I said I didn't want any more hassle over the divorce, and offered him a straight 50/50 split of our joint property, and shared custody of Roxy. I don't doubt that he'll agree, when he's got over the shock of being turned down.

I don't know yet whether I want to marry you, dearest Bernard, but I intend to find out, by getting to know you better, and that strange-sounding place where you live. I suppose if I married you, I'd have to live there, wouldn't I? Well, I'm ready for a change from Hawaii, and Rummidge would certainly be a change. But I have to stay here at least another year, and maybe two, until Roxy is through high school, and depending on whether or not she decides to go and live with her father next year. Nothing is fixed, nothing is definite – except that I've booked a seat on a charter flight to London Heathrow, December 22nd – can you meet me at the airport? (Don't bother with a *lei*.) Whatever happens, ours is going to be a relationship of long chaste separations and short passionate cohabitations for some time, my dear, but better that than the other way round.

All my love,
Yolande

Inside the envelope was a small, stencilled booklet with the liturgy of the Hawaiian Folk Mass, and a sheet of paper with a photocopied page from the *Reader's Digest*. A quotation from Miguel de Unamuno's *The Tragic Sense of Life* had been marked with green highlighter:

> In the most secret recess of the spirit of the man who believes that death will put an end to his personal consciousness and even to his memory forever, in that inner recess, even without his knowing it perhaps, a shadow hovers, a vague shadow lurks, a shadow of a shadow of uncertainty, and while he tells himself: "There is nothing for it but to live this passing life, for there is no other!" at the same time he hears, in this most secret recess, his own doubt murmur: "Who knows? . . ." He is not sure he hears aright, but he hears. Likewise, in some recess of the soul of the true believer who has faith in the future life, a muffled voice, the voice of uncertainty, murmurs in his spirit's ear: "Who knows? . . . ." Perhaps these voices are no louder than the buzzing of mosquitoes when the wind roars through the trees in the woods; we scarcely make out the humming, and yet, mingled with the roar of the storm, it can be heard. How, without this uncertainty, could we ever live?

Bernard folded up the flimsy sheets of writing paper and put them back in the yellow envelope, with the booklet and the photocopy. He smiled up through the shimmering flamy leaves of the copper beech at the blue sky. The leaves rustled in the breeze, and one or two fluttered down like tiny tongues of fire. He stayed in this posture, head thrown back, arms stretched out along the back of the bench, for some minutes, in a happy reverie. Then he got to his feet and walked briskly back to the College building, suddenly consumed with an intense desire for coffee. Pushing through the swing doors into the Senior Common Room, he nearly collided with Giles Franklin on his way out.

"Hallo again!" said Franklin, holding open the door for

Bernard to pass. He added jocularly, with a glance at the envelope in Bernard's hand, "Good news or bad?"

"Oh, good," said Bernard. "Very good news."